RUINS OF CAMELOT

G. Norman Lippert

ISBN: 1467966193
ISBN-13: 978-1467966191
Cover model: Kayla Marie Cromer
Photographed by Khiem Hoang

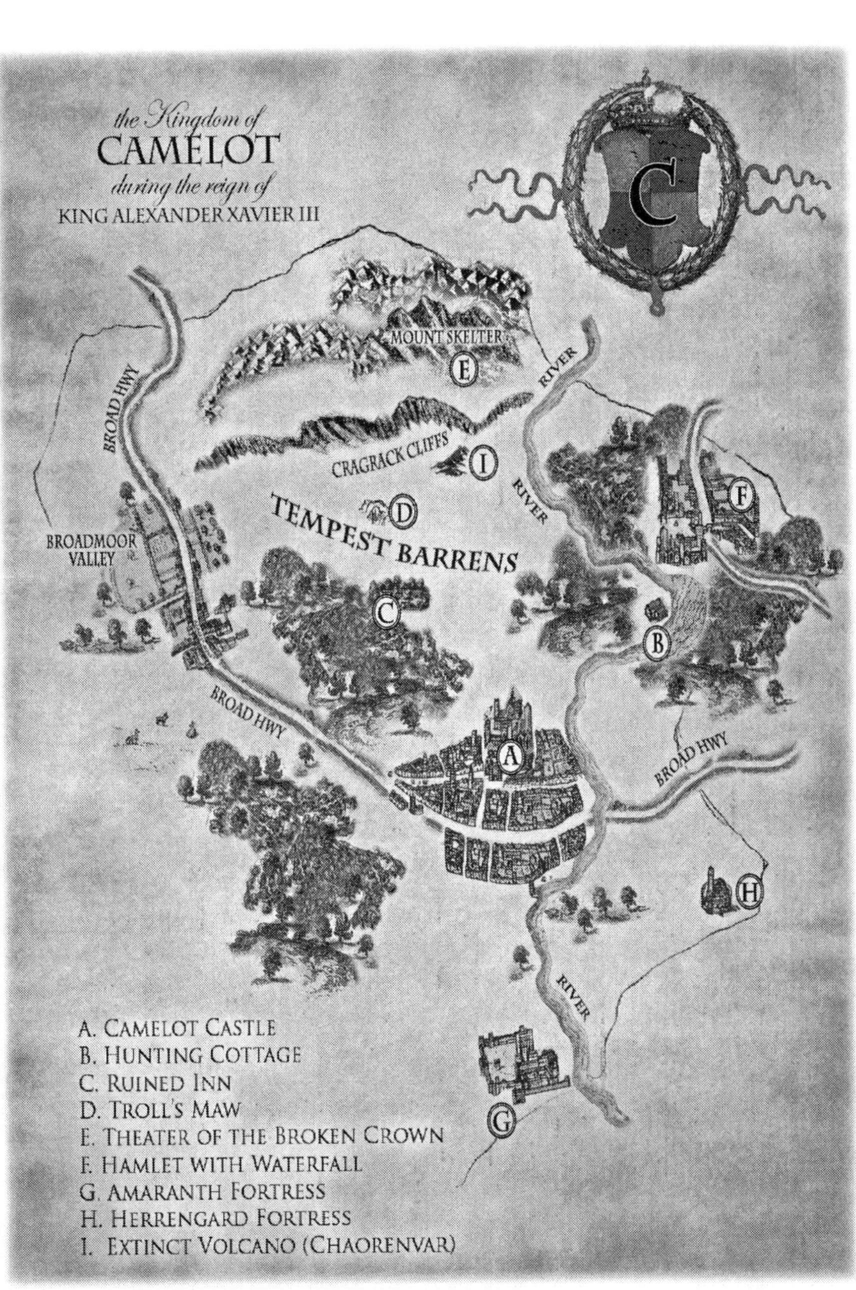
the Kingdom of
CAMELOT
during the reign of
KING ALEXANDER XAVIER III
C
MOUNT SKELTER
E
RIVER
BROAD HWY
CRAGRACK CLIFFS
I
RIVER
F
D
TEMPEST BARRENS
BROADMOOR
VALLEY
C
B
BROAD HWY
A
BROAD HWY
H
RIVER
G
A. CAMELOT CASTLE
B. HUNTING COTTAGE
C. RUINED INN
D. TROLL'S MAW
E. THEATER OF THE BROKEN CROWN
F. HAMLET WITH WATERFALL
G. AMARANTH FORTRESS
H. HERRENGARD FORTRESS
I. EXTINCT VOLCANO (CHAORENVAR)

CONTENTS

For everybody who has ever asked that most essential of all questions:
"Do I have what it takes?"

Gabriella hit the stairs at a full run and took them two at a time. Darkness met her as she followed the curving steps upwards towards a second landing. Here, nooks lined the hallway, each illuminated with a band of moonlight from an arrow slit. Merodach's footsteps clattered behind her, approaching quickly. Gabriella pelted along the landing and ducked into the furthest nook. She threw herself up against the shallow stone wall, gasping for breath

Behind her, unseen, Merodach's footsteps knocked onto the landing, where he seemed to stop.

"This is good sport, Princess," he panted, and giggled lightly. "But I fear it cannot end well for you. Come out and give yourself up. It is the best you can hope for."

He began to pace slowly forwards. She heard him, knew that he had his sword raised, ready to cut her down the moment he discovered her. She pressed back against the wall of the arrow nook, trying not to breathe.

"Do you know?" the villain mused thoughtfully as he approached. "It just occurs to me. With your father dead, you are no longer a mere princess. Do you feel special, my dear? It is official. You are the last Queen of Camelot. Congratulations," he said silkily, "Your Highness."

With a dark shock, Gabriella realised that Merodach was right. If Herrengard had indeed been breached—and she had no doubt that it had—then her father was dead. She was the last of the line. Whatever remained of the Kingdom, it was hers. The realisation did not hearten her.

"Your child is dead," Merodach breathed, relishing the words. "Those that were meant to protect him are destroyed. Everything that you fight for, Queen, all of it... is in ruins. Why continue to resist? There is nothing left for you. Come out. You are the last ruler of Camelot, and as such, you must die. But I can make it quick. Soon, you can join those whom you have failed. Come out and face me. Die like a queen, and I will not even turn your body over to the appetites of my troops. It is only fitting. And admit it. You *desire* this..."

Gabriella's eyes were glassy in the dimness. Her enemy was nearly upon her now. She nodded to herself once. Slowly but resolutely, she stepped forwards, turned past the iron candelabra, and faced her nemesis.

"There," he said, and smiled sympathetically. "That is better, is it not?"

He raised his sword, positioned its tip just above her breastplate, inches from her throat, and began to thrust.

CHAPTER 1

Two men on horseback emerged from the trees, blinking in the low, copper sunlight. The man in the lead was tall, dark-skinned, and bare-armed. He halted his horse, and it immediately dipped its head, nodding wearily.

The second man reined his own horse and raked his fingers through the tangle of his short red beard. "Where are we now?" he asked, pushing his helmet back from his brow and squinting in the sudden brightness.

The taller man dismounted and led his horse into the shushing field grass. His eyes darted around with keen interest. The clearing angled sharply upwards to a rocky plateau, which cut across the blinding glare of the sunset. The man touched the hilt of a short sword on his belt but did not grip it.

"Step lightly, Thomas," he commented. "These uncharted lands are ripe for bandits."

Behind him, his companion slid off his horse and stood next to it warily. After a moment, the two began to work their way carefully up the slope of the clearing.

They found the plateau reinforced with a low wall of brick and stone. The wall ran in both directions, fortifying the hilltop and turning it into a long rampart, an ancient road, choked with field grass and brush. The first man led his horse through a breach, onto the surface of the road, where he stopped and shaded his eyes from the sunset's glare. Thomas joined him there and pulled his leather helmet from his head with an impatient sigh.

"Where are we now, Yazim?" he asked again.

The taller man, Yazim, nodded slowly towards the northern length of the forgotten highway. Thomas followed his companion's gaze, opening his mouth to speak and then closing it again. He raised his head slowly as his eyes widened.

Beyond and above the nearby trees, hazy with distance, rose the spires of an ancient castle. Its conical roofs were broken, revealing the bones of their rafters. Vines clothed the crumbled walls, creeping into the windows and twining the flag staffs.

Yazim dropped his hand from the hilt of his sword. "The ruins of Camelot," he finally answered, gazing up at the silent, ruined castle.

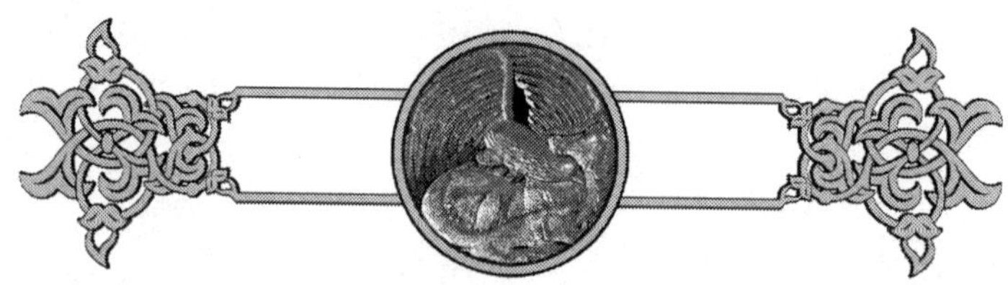

The two camped in the middle of the ancient road. Yazim built a fire whilst Thomas went in search of food. Two hours later, with the bones of a rabbit lying strewn around the crackling fire, the two sat on their packs and stared at the dark hulk of the castle. Moonlight lit half of it, painting it in cold, blue tones. The other half raked the sky, black as pitch against the stars. No lights burnt from within.

"How can you be sure?" Thomas asked quietly.

Yazim shook his head. "What else could it be? Would we not have known of another kingdom worthy of such a headstone?"

Thomas nodded doubtfully. "But Camelot... it's been centuries since the end of the great kingdom. Its history has been lost forever. Some scholars say that such a place never even existed."

Yazim sighed. "Your greatest error, Thomas, is in trusting the accounts of men who speak knowledgeably about things they have never seen. It is the one thing I have never understood about your people."

"You speak as if you aren't one of us yourself, Yazim," Thomas replied, glancing aside. "And yet I myself have known you almost from birth. We grew up in each other's sight."

Yazim nodded and smiled. "True, but my family comes from far outside the walls of the Kingdom of Aachen. We are Moors. My mother and father have not forgotten the histories passed to them through generations, from the very ones who witnessed them. You may trust your scholars, who divine their knowledge from broken pots and dead bones, but I will trust the words of those who saw with their own living eyes."

Thomas shuddered against a hard breeze. The fire buffeted before him, its embers hissing bright red. "So," he commented, drawing his cloak around him, "you knew this castle would be here?"

Yazim shrugged. "I did not know it, but I am not surprised to find it."

"Tell me, what else do your old stories say about this place? How many of the legends are true? And what happened to end such a great empire?"

Yazim turned to Thomas and grinned, showing all of his teeth in the ruddy glow of the flames. "You would not believe the tales even if I told you, my friend. Our world is too far removed from that of the elder King Arthur and his dwindling descendants. It is not our purview to explore such things anyway. There are none alive in yonder castle to tax, save the bats and spiders that now call it home; thus, our lord will have no interest in it. Neither should we."

Thomas narrowed his eyes and studied his companion. "You do not believe that. I can see it in your eyes. Come. Tell me what you know. We have time before sleep. Amuse me."

Yazim's grin faded, but not completely. He sighed and peered up at the dark hulk of the castle. "It is incredible, is it not, that such an edifice was never claimed by another kingdom? What would you make of that?"

Thomas frowned. "It is too remote. It would serve no purpose as either a fortification or a seat of power."

"Not now perhaps," Yazim agreed thoughtfully, "but in ages past, things were different."

Thomas leant back on his elbows, looking out over the ancient highway. A few paces away, the horses stood huddled in the dark, mere outlines against the starry sky. "How different?" he prodded.

Yazim slowly shook his head. "This was Camelot," he said simply, "the kingdom of the mighty and noble King Arthur. In those days, this was the very centre of the world. In those days, kings cared less about such things as commerce and politics, seaports and trade treaties. Back then, there was such a thing as honour."

"We have honour now," Thomas commented, glancing back at his friend with a wry smile.

"We have respect," Yazim countered, turning serious. "King Julius and his sons command the tribute of many nations, yes. But respect is not the same as honour. Nor are tributes and taxes the same as loyal service." He paused, and his eyes narrowed in the darkness. Thomas remembered that his friend's family were not citizens of Aachen by choice, but by conquest. The grass sang restlessly as both men stared into the fire. Finally, Yazim shook himself faintly and went on. "The histories tell us that Camelot was very different. Those who served Arthur and his line did not do so out of fear, but privilege. Back then, the King's men fought in the name of good, not profit. Wars hinged on nobility and right, not the mere expansion of power."

"Be wary," Thomas warned, half-smiling. "Some would call such talk treasonous."

"Inside the walls of the city, yes. Out here, I expect that older rules apply."

Thomas nodded agreeably. The wind gusted along the ancient road, carrying leaves into the air and shushing in the grass. The moon stared down on the distant castle. Far off, a wolf barked and then howled.

"So what else?" Thomas asked after a long silence. "What else do your stories say about that time? How else was it different?"

Yazim didn't answer right away. Finally, with a sigh, he said, "In the days of Camelot, battle was not fought with the sword alone. It is considered foolishness now, but the time of Arthur the King was also the time of Merlinus the Sorcerer. There were wizards in those days. Back then, there was such a thing as magic."

Thomas hunched his shoulders as the wind gusted again, turning cold. He peered up at the castle. Its dark windows glared back down at him, empty but somehow watchful. "Do you believe that, Yazim?" he asked quietly.

Yazim turned to his friend and smiled. "Look at yonder castle," he said, "and tell me that you do not."

Thomas shuddered. The night had grown dank and restless around them. He sat up and prodded the fire with his boot. Orange sparks swirled into the wind like flocks of startled birds.

"Tell me how it all ended."

"I cannot," Yazim answered soberly, "for no one knows."

"Some amusement you are," Thomas replied.

Yazim was quiet again. Finally, he said, "I can tell you the beginning of the end if you wish."

Thomas hunched closer to the fire. He glanced back at his friend. "Is it true?"

Yazim shrugged. "It is a story. Many believe it is true. I admit, I once doubted it myself. Now… I am not so sure."

Thomas nodded. "Tell me."

Yazim drew a deep breath. "It begins long after the golden age of King Arthur," he said sombrely. "Much had changed since the days of the noble Round Table. With no empires large enough or bold enough to rival it, the Kingdom had grown complacent and indulgent. Ancient traditions were traded for whims, so that the integrity of rule was weakened with every succeeding generation. Few who had lived among the Kingdom of Arthur would have recognized it by the time the last King ascended his throne. And yet there was still nobility there, scattered along the line of Arthur like golden threads dispersed in an increasingly dull tapestry. One of those golden threads was a girl, the daughter of the last King of Camelot. Her name... was Gabriella."

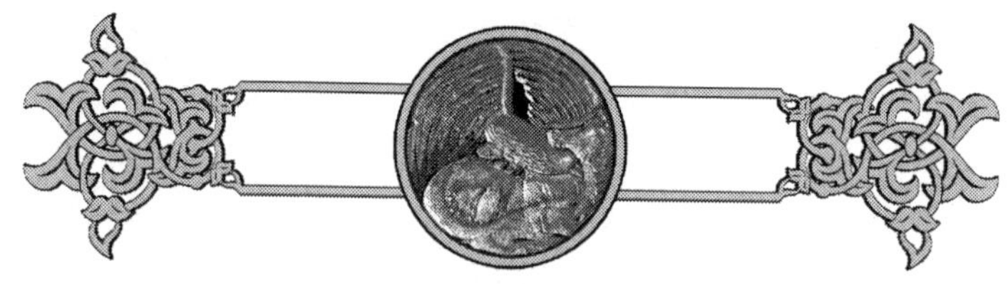

The girls giggled. At nine years old, it seemed to Gabriella that her friends were always giggling, and it annoyed her. She turned and glared at them in the shadow of the bushes, her own face almost comically grave. She did not shush them. Her father had taught her that the noise of shushing carried even further than whispering. Rhyss and Constance bit their lips and grinned. Gabriella turned back towards the bushes and peered through the leaves.

The others stood near the brook, in the shadow of the castle bridge, tossing stones or sitting in pools of sunlight. There were four of them, two boys and two girls. Gabriella knew their names for they were her schoolmates. Their clothes were better than the rags worn by the peasants, but not quite as grand as her own gowns. The oldest of the boys, the only one not born of nobility, wore a plain linen tunic and belt. He would have looked like one of her father's court fools if his colours weren't so drab. He skipped a stone across the surface of the brook and pointed at it, grinning back at the others.

"Wait," Gabriella whispered, holding up a hand to her friends.

"Let us do it now," Rhyss rasped excitedly, fingering a small leather pouch. Gabriella shook her head, and none of the girls moved.

Behind them, the school bell began to toll. It rang pristinely over the hilltop, echoing down into the narrow valley. The children around the brook didn't look up, but they began to move disconsolately, straightening and brushing themselves off.

"Now?" Constance whispered urgently. "Class is starting. We must get back!"

"Hush," Gabriella said quietly, her hand still raised, palm out. They were nervous and impatient, as always. Gabriella, however, had a sense about these things. "Wait..."

The boys were on the opposite side of the brook. They began to cross, hopping idly on the stepping stones. Their female playmates waited, hands on hips, parodies of their mothers. When the boys reached the near bank, Gabriella dropped her hand.

"Now!" she rasped.

As one, Rhyss, Constance, and Gabriella leapt from their hiding place. Rhyss flung open her leather pouch, releasing a small cloud of dust. All three girls blew into the dust as fiercely as they could, and the dust transformed into a sudden, hard wind. It rushed through the bushes, riffled the grass that bordered the brook, and pushed all four of their classmates backwards. Three of them fell into the brook, splashing in the cold, shallow water. The oldest boy, the one in the linen tunic, stumbled but managed to keep his feet in the sparkling brook. He looked around sharply and spied the three girls in the bushes.

Rhyss and Constance exploded into fits of giggles, covering their mouths with their hands. Instantly, they spun and began to bolt up the hill towards the tolling school bell. Gabriella lingered for a moment. The three children that had fallen into the brook were clambering noisily to their feet, the girls squealing and making themselves even wetter as they scrambled, the boy red-faced and grim. The fourth boy looked up at Gabriella and unexpectedly smiled.

Gabriella turned and began to run. She threaded nimbly through the bushes and pushed into the sunlight of the hill. She was halfway up the slope when someone tackled her from behind, driving her down into the tall grass and pinning her. She bucked, rolled over, and found herself looking up into the face of the boy in the linen tunic. His hair hung down in his face, and he was still grinning.

"Let me go, Darrick! Get off me!"

"That was Whisperwind powder," Darrick replied amiably. "Where'd you get it? You thieve it from the Magic Master's supply cupboard? Or do you have your own cache of such things up at the castle?"

"Get off me! How dare you?! I'm the King's daughter!"

"I won't tattle on you if you get me some," Darrick said, growing serious. "Just a little. One pouch."

"I'll call my guard!"

Darrick smiled confidently. "Go ahead then."

The school bell stopped tolling. Its last peal echoed into silence. Gabriella was furious, but they both knew she would not call to her guard. Treynor would surely whip Darrick soundly for daring to touch the Princess, but he would also report to her father that she had slipped away from his watchful eye again and sneaked off to play a prank on her schoolmates. She fumed up at Darrick in the green shadow of the field grass. His smile grew thoughtful.

"Let me go—" she hissed, squirming, but then, suddenly and for no apparent reason, he dipped his head towards her. His lips pressed against the corner of her mouth, firmly and clumsily but quick as a snake. The next moment, he was gone. She heard his footsteps thumping away towards the school.

Gabriella pressed her palm to her cheek, covering the memory of his lips, her mouth open in a small O of angry surprise.

"Gabriella!" a voice called sharply. It was Treynor, irritated and worried, of course. Gabriella scrambled to her feet in the grass and ran towards the rear entrance of the stone building atop the hill. Beyond it, the castle loomed over the trees, poking its spires at the sky. Treynor spied Gabriella and scowled. His dark eyes spoke volumes as she pretended not to notice him.

Darrick was already inside of course.

"What does it mean to be a princess?" Gabriella asked that evening, leaning on the side of the tub.

"Chin up," her nurse, Sigrid, instructed, hefting a small bucket of foaming water. Gabriella lifted her chin dutifully, and Sigrid poured the water down the back of Gabriella's head. It was warm, pasting her hair to her neck and shoulders in dark blond ribbons.

"It means being the daughter of the King," Sigrid answered, clunking the bucket to the floor and retreating to the vanity.

"That's a boring answer," Gabriella said, leaning back against the slope of the tub and flicking her finger at a raft of suds. "That's not what I mean."

"Pity it's the truth," Sigrid commented, selecting a tall bottle of perfumed oil. Gabriella grimaced at it and stuck out her tongue.

"Everyone thinks it's so grand to be the Princess, but what's so special about it? Father says that in the old days, princesses didn't even get to go to school with the noble children or anyone else. They learned everything from tutors and barely even left the castle. Even now, I'm lucky if I am allowed to walk to the school with Treynor, rather than ride in a carriage with four guards. All the ceremony and pomp, it's all just like a mask I wear. It doesn't have anything to do with me. I could just as easily have been born to the potter or the miller. I could have been born a peasant."

Sigrid returned to the tub and settled her considerable bulk onto a stool. She tugged the stopper from the oil, dabbed some onto her palm, and began to rub her hands together briskly.

"Do you wish you'd been born a peasant?"

Gabriella turned in the tub so that she faced the tall, mullioned window. It glowed dusky purple, almost the same colour as the oil in Sigrid's bottle. She didn't answer. After a moment, Sigrid began to stroke the oil onto Gabriella's hair and comb it in. There would be one more washing after that, removing most of the oil but leaving the scent of it. It was nice to be taken care of this way, but it was also strange. Gabriella knew that none of her schoolmates had such luxuries. It should have pleased her, but instead, it gave her a vague unease.

Sigrid spoke as she combed Gabriella's hair. "Being a princess is not all baths and perfume, darling," she said in a mildly chiding voice. "You are afforded such luxuries because you are expected to bear great burdens. You will carry weights and responsibilities that your friends will never know."

"What responsibilities?" Gabriella asked.

"You do not need to know such things now, dearheart," Sigrid said, and Gabriella could tell by the sound of her voice that her nurse was smiling. "Your concern, I think, is much simpler."

Gabriella frowned. "Ow," she said as the nurse tugged at a tangle in her hair. "Tell me then. What is my real concern, Sigrid?" she asked doubtfully.

Sigrid hummed to herself for a moment. Finally, she said, "Your true concern is not what the burdens of a princess will be. Your true concern is... will you be worthy of them? Will you rise to the challenges presented to you?"

Gabriella thought about this. She turned in the tub again and peered gravely back at her nurse, the woman who had known her and cared for her since birth, the woman that she knew better than she knew either of her own parents.

"Will I?" she asked seriously, studying the older woman's face. "Will I be able to do what a princess must do?"

Sigrid lowered the comb in her hand and met the girl's solemn eyes. She nodded, and then shook her head faintly. "You may," she said with a shallow sigh, "if you choose to."

Gabriella nodded to herself and turned around again. "I will. I will choose to."

Sigrid did not reply. Instead, she hummed some more and resumed combing the Princess's long hair.

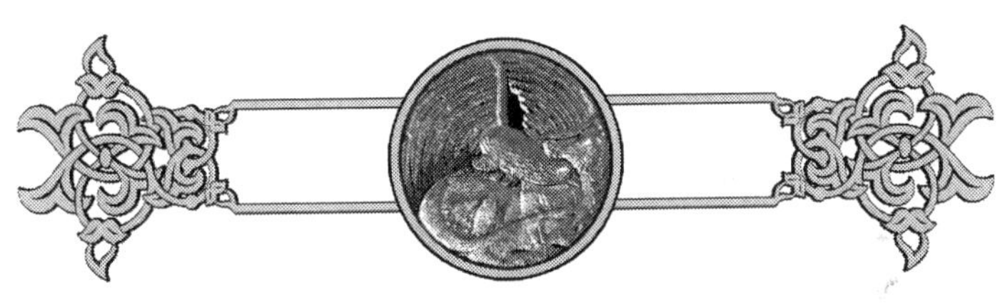

Gabriella's bedroom was on the third floor of the castle. It was large, still filled with the toys she'd played with when she was a baby. She considered herself too old to play much with them anymore, but not too old to still keep them nearby, comforting her with their familiarity. Her rocking horse stood by the hearth, casting its long shadow in the glow of the coals. Her dolls dozed atop the cupboards. A tiny table beneath the window was set with a miniature silver tea set, complete with doilies and lace napkins.

Gabriella rolled over and stared at the tall window. Beyond it, the moon hung like a sickle, thin and sharp. She blinked slowly, not sleepy in the least. After a minute, she flung the covers off and slid over the side of the bed. The floor was smooth and cold to her bare feet. She crept to the door, listened for a moment, and then eased it open.

Her father was in his library, as always. She heard his voice echoing dimly along the outer corridor as she crept down the stairs. He would not be angry if she slipped in to see him, even if he was in the middle of an important meeting. He would beckon her to him, chide her dutifully, and allow her to climb onto his lap for a moment. But then he would send her back to her bed of course. He was the King, and he had weighty matters to attend to.

"You would not be interested, Princess," he would tell her with a weary smile. "Fill your head with pleasant things. I will handle the rest."

And he was right. She was not interested in the matters of state. But she was interested in her father. She liked to hear the deep rumble of his voice. It lulled her and soothed her on nights like this, when sleep seemed far away and her toys no longer beckoned her.

The corridor was empty and dark, lit only with a sliver of firelight from the mostly closed library doors. Her father was meeting with his council, although not all of them were present. They rarely were nowadays. They were important men themselves, with their own affairs to attend to. In truth, it seemed to Gabriella as if the Kingdom ran itself. Her father and his council simply oversaw it. It did not seem like a fun task exactly, but neither did it seem difficult, despite what Sigrid had said.

Gabriella crept along the corridor, dragging one of her blankets behind her. There was a tall cabinet next to the library doors, meant for the coats of her father's visitors. In wintertime, the cabinet was often full of heavy furs, dripping with melted snow and smelling of night air and reindeer. Tonight the cabinet was dry and mostly empty. Gabriella slipped inside and lay down, tucking her blanket around her and resting her head on an old, folded cape. There, she lay blinking in the darkness, staring at nothing and listening to the timbre of the voices beyond the nearby door.

She couldn't remember the first time she had hidden there, drifting to sleep to the drone of voices and pacing feet. She only knew that it was one of her favourite places. Her father, the King, sometimes found her there once his councils were through. He was never angry. He would merely lift her into his arms and carry her back to her bed, kissing her once on the cheek as he lay her down. Gabriella always awoke at these times but never allowed her father to notice. She liked the silent comfort of his arms and the kisses that he gave her even when he thought she was asleep. Of all his kisses, those were the ones that meant the most to her.

The voices rumbled from the library, and she listened. She didn't pay attention to the actual words, but they drifted into her thoughts anyway, skipping like stones on the valley brook.

"There are at least forty of them, Your Highness," a high, nasally voice said. That was Percival, the chief of the castle guard. "They do not meet in the same place, nor in such numbers, but keep council in desolate areas and in small groups of six or seven."

"We could arrest them," another voice suggested.

"No," Gabriella's father, the King, said. "No need to overreact. Some fires burn out better on their own. Stomping on them only spreads the coals."

There was a murmur of mingled agreement and dissent.

"They speak against you, Your Highness," a deep voice warned. "They may be few and remote, but treason is still a deadly poison."

Gabriella's father seemed unperturbed. "We have neither the resources nor the patience to stamp out every stray thought or word in a kingdom as far reaching as Camelot. Such groups are a constant. They burn off the fervour of malcontents before such fervour can stew into action. Let them mutter and rabble. They've done so since the time of my fathers in numbers hardly less than these."

"A slow-growing vine sinks the deepest roots, Your Highness," the low voice replied gravely. "Things are different now than they were in the time of your fathers. I do not think it wise to turn a blind eye to these rebels. Their leader may be vile, but he is persuasive. He may find an audience with your enemies."

There was a silence. Finally, the King said, "Watch him then. If he is found to palaver with the barbarian empire of the north, then bring him in. I am doubtful that even the greatest zealot would dare stoop to such treachery."

Gabriella was barely listening. Her eyes drooped heavily, lulled by the droning voices. Dreams circled her, calling to her.

"Tell me his name again," her father's voice said, echoing from the depths of the library.

"We do not know his true name, but only the name he uses to identify himself to his followers," a voice answered gravely, almost secretively. "He calls himself Merodach."

"Merodach…," the King mused.

Merodach, Gabriella thought dreamily, and shuddered. The name echoed in the corridors of her mind, following her down into the canyons of sleep, fluttering as if on bats' wings.

"Merodach?" Thomas repeated, stepping carefully over a strew of stone blocks.

Yazim shouldered his pack and surveyed the broken walls. Vines and heather had overtaken the ancient structure, hiding it, softening its shape. "A mythical name. Merodach was a god of the underworld. But the man who took that name was no god."

Thomas shaded his eyes and peered down a grassy hill. A brook trickled through a grotto of shadows below, disappearing under an ancient stone bridge. "A rebel with delusions of grandeur then?"

"A monster in the guise of a saviour," Yazim replied. "He was the downfall of Camelot and the usher of a long, dark age. According to the legends, he was handsome. Tall. Charming. But so cruel that his friends dreaded his disfavour and his enemies would kill themselves rather than face him."

"Surely, the tales are exaggerated," Thomas commented, picking his way into the deep shadows of the ruin. Rows of stone benches lay buried in the brush, facing the remains of a collapsed tower. Yazim stood there, peering down at a half-buried shape. Morning sunlight glinted off a smooth, tarnished surface. Thomas saw that it was a bell.

Yazim lifted his eyes and gazed up past the remains of rafters and the encroaching trees. The shadow of the nearby castle spread over the rubble. "The tales are actually very detailed," he said. "Merodach surrounded himself with a small band of soulless villains. Bloodthirsty and inhuman, these were his hands and feet, sent off amongst the populace to recruit the desperate, the dregs, and the haters, for every society, no matter how enlightened, cultivates such people. In time, thanks to the complacence of the King, Merodach assembled a small secret army. These, he employed to begin ravaging the distant outposts of Camelot. His tactics were simple and horrible. A small band of marauders would descend upon a village under cover of darkness and dismember every firstborn child where they slept, leaving the horrors for the adults to find upon waking. In the morning, Merodach would enter the village with his force behind him, summoned by the wails of the mourning parents. He would call forth the men of the village and offer them a bargain: join him and fight to overthrow the King of Camelot or die and join their children in the afterlife."

Thomas looked at his friend with revulsion. "Truly, such a beast could not be counted amongst the brotherhood of humankind. Who would join the man who had murdered their children?"

"Some did," Yazim answered stoically, "out of fear for their lives and that of their women. Others submitted to death at the hand of Merodach's brutes or fell upon their own swords. A few fought, but Merodach was a connoisseur of sadism. He knew that those who fought to avenge their dead children would fight recklessly, blind with grief. These, he made examples of, desecrating their bodies in ways more horrible than I wish to recount.

"Soon, rumours of Merodach's elaborate cruelty began to spread over the Kingdom. To many, the stories were indeed too horrific to be believed. Many doubted, only to discover the truth too late.

"Eventually, the reality of the situation became evident even to the King himself. But by then, Merodach's army had already overwhelmed and decimated the outlying regions. He had fortified his forces in key outposts all around the Kingdom. It was a rude awakening for the King, but even then, he could not bring himself to believe that all was lost. Camelot simply could not fall. He sent diplomats and ambassadors, attempting to negotiate with his enemy. He failed to understand that there is no diplomacy with he whose only desire is to destroy. There is no compromise with the one whose only goal is death."

Thomas shook his head sombrely. It was chilly in the shadows of the ruin. Together, the two men made their way out into the sunlight of the hillside. Some distance away, their horses cropped the grass amiably.

Thomas sighed. "So, in the end, cruelty won."

Yazim frowned thoughtfully. "Cruelty never really wins no matter how things might seem to those observing. If there is any truth in the world, my friend, then it is that."

Thomas looked aside at his companion and then shook his head. "I wish I could believe that."

Yazim didn't offer any debate. After a minute, the two walked down the hill and collected their horses.

Once they were astride their mounts again, heading into the shadow of the derelict castle, Thomas asked, "So what became of Princess Gabriella? What did she do whilst the beast Merodach was planning his war against her father's kingdom?"

Yazim urged his horse forwards into the tree-lined grotto. Its hooves splashed across the brook, wetting its smooth flank. "Princess Gabriella did what all little girls do, God willing," Yazim answered simply, "she grew up."

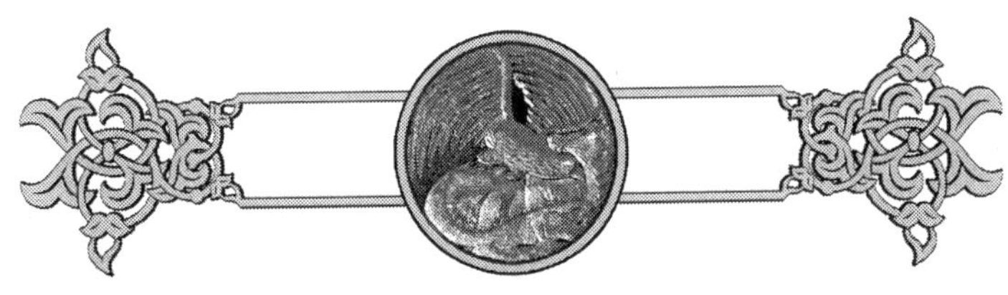

The dueling theatre was very small and dark, located in the cellar of the school cathedral. Gabriella had loved it from the first time she'd ever seen it, eleven years earlier, at the age of eight. Back then, it had seemed huge and regal, like something the gladiators of Rome might have fought in. Now she saw it for what it was: a small, oval floor surrounded by four rows of terraced seating, lit only by a ring of tiny, barred windows. The ceiling was rough beams and planks, covered in soot and decades of cobwebs.

The topmost row of seating, where she herself now sat, was within reach of the nearest rafters, and it showed: the ancient wood was etched with hundreds of names, crude drawings, symbols, and anatomically impossible limericks. Her name was there as well, carved with a dagger point some years past. She remembered doing it, remembered pinching her tongue between her lips with concentration, laboriously shaping each letter: "GABRIELLA G. XAVIER." Since then, some amusing wag had added "DROWNS IN THE RAIN." Gabriella didn't mind. She *had* occasionally been a stuck-up brat in her younger years. If it had not been for the refreshingly brutal honesty of her fellow students, her nose might still be in the air today.

"I'm sweating like a pig under all this armour," Rhyss muttered, tying her red hair back into a ponytail. She clanked faintly whenever she moved, a constant reminder that hers was ill-fitting hand-me-down armour worn by at least two generations of graduates before her. Even so, it gleamed pristinely in the dimness, made of rolled steel and edged with copper. The Feorie family crest shined brightly on the round shield where it leant by Rhyss's feet.

Gabriella sighed. "I cannot wait for this to be over. I'll be happy to live a thousand years and never lift a sword again."

Rhyss shrugged. "It's the price of privilege. The peasants never have to experience the battle floor. How very fortunate we are to be the sons and daughters of nobility. All except for Darrick, of course."

On Gabriella's other side, Darrick buffed his own sword with a thick cloth. "I'll take a blacksmith father over a lazy old duke any day." He said dismissively. At one time, Gabriella had wondered why Darrick was allowed to attend the Royal Academy at all. Now she understood: his family had just enough money, and just enough clout to place him there. More importantly, his father had just enough imagination to hope for a better life for his son. Darrick sheathed his sword and nudged Rhyss. "So who do you face?"

"Vasser," Rhyss replied with a shrug. "I'm not exactly worried about it."

"Vasser's no daisy," Gabriella said. "He is good enough to let you show your skills but not so good that he'll put you down before you draw your own sword." She frowned down at the slip of parchment in her hand and sighed darkly. "Not like *Goethe*."

Darrick and Rhyss murmured sympathetically.

On the floor below, Constance and a taller girl named Destra approached each other warily. Constance's armour was new but sparse, made mostly of hardened leather. Her short sword and shield were the only metal on her. Destra, whose father was Percival, the chief of the palace guard, was clad in a mismatched but intimidating assembly of mail and iron plate. She smiled confidently, hefting a small, evil-looking war hammer.

"One-minute rounds, students," rang the voice of Professor Barth, the Battle Master. "Remember, this is not a contest of strength, nor is it a battle to the death. No one's honour is at stake on this floor today. The goal of this final exam is to prove your grasp of fundamental battle technique. Your only enemy is yourself."

Having spoken, Barth strode to meet Constance and Destra in the centre of the floor. He briefly inspected their weapons, nodded, and returned to his bench near the door. He sat, crossed his huge, bare arms over his chest, and nodded again.

"Begin!" he barked.

Destra lunged first, trying to hook Constance's shield with her war hammer. Constance dodged reflexively, turned, and batted the flat of her sword against Destra's mail-covered shoulder.

"Point," Barth called.

More warily this time, Destra began to circle Constance. Apparently feeling a bit more confident now, Constance lifted her shield and jabbed beneath it. Destra anticipated the maneuver however. She twisted away from Constance's sword and swept her war hammer forwards, low and quick. With a deft jerk, Destra hooked Constance's heel and swept it out from under her. The leather-clad girl went down backwards and dropped her shield.

"Point and fault," Barth shouted, pointing first at Destra, and then at Constance where she lay on the floor. Gabriella felt sorry for her friend as she collected her shield, but it really had been a clumsy maneuver. If only she, Gabriella, had drawn Destra's name from the lot, she'd have felt confident of her chances to defeat the taller girl soundly if magnanimously. She liked Destra after all, even if she was a bit mean-spirited sometimes.

The duel went on for another half minute until Barth struck a small iron bell. When it was over, Constance was awarded three points and one fault, Destra four points and two faults, passing marks for both girls. In reality, except in cases of gross error or injury, every student passed the final battle practical. It wasn't so much graduation that was at stake, but reputation. For many noble families, this duel, even more than the graduation ceremony itself, marked the transition into adulthood. All around the theatre, students watched the proceedings with grim eyes. They might pretend that the outcome didn't matter, but in their hearts, they knew differently. Gabriella saw it on the faces of her classmates, even Rhyss. The only one who seemed completely unfazed by the duel was Darrick.

"She did well," he commented, nodding towards Constance as she exited the battle floor. "Considering."

"Considering she spent more time studying her reflection in her shield than practising with it?" Rhyss said, raising one eyebrow. "I'm sure you're right."

"I wish we could just skip over this part," Gabriella moaned. "I thought I'd be excited about it, but now I feel like I'm going to be sick."

Darrick nudged her gently. "You'll do fine, Bree. There's nothing to worry about."

"Nothing except the fact that Goethe's father is in the castle dungeon for murder," Rhyss nodded. "And that he weighs twice as much as you and practises throwing battle-axes for fun."

"That's very encouraging," Gabriella said, sinking low in her armour. "Thanks, Rhyss."

"I cannot help being truthful," Rhyss replied brightly. "I already told you: if I were in your boots, I'd sneak out through the servants' entrance and hang my armour over the castle hearth once and for all."

Gabriella sighed harshly as the next duel began on the floor below. "Darrick, you've fought Goethe before. What should I do? Does he have any weaknesses?"

Darrick shrugged and sheathed his sword. "He's big."

Gabriella rolled her eyes. "I *know* that much," she muttered. "I have eyes."

"Which means he's slow," Darrick added, glancing aside at her. "It takes a lot of energy to get all that muscle moving around. Watch his shoulders. That's where everything begins. You're small, Bree, so you're quick. He'll squash you if he gets a chance, but you can make sure that chance never comes if you're wary."

Gabriella met his eyes and saw that he was serious. She glanced away, shaking her head. "I don't know..."

Darrick leant closer to her, and she looked back at him. This time, the look in his eyes caught her, and she maintained his gaze.

"You can do this," he said quietly. "If you want to."

She drew a deep breath and let it out shakily. She nodded. "I do want to."

He smiled at her thoughtfully. "I believe you do."

She felt heartened by his confidence, but in some ways, that made it worse. What if she let him down? "I wish I had drawn your name instead."

"It's a *dueling* practical," Rhyss declared with a roll of her eyes. "I've seen the way *you* two wrangle. A lot less blade, a lot more lips. Although it might be instructive for *some* of the people around here."

Soon enough, Gabriella's name was called from the floor. She stood up so quickly that a wave of dizziness rolled over her. Darrick grabbed her hand, supporting her, and she recovered quickly.

"Good luck, Princess," he said, smiling faintly.

Goethe was already on the floor as Gabriella made her way down the worn stone steps. The son of a disgraced army commander, Goethe had hair so short that it was barely a discolouration on his sweaty scalp. His eyes were cold and grey as he surveyed her, fingering his weapon. Gabriella's heart sunk as she saw the battle-axe in his hand. Its haft was easily as tall as she was. The iron head bore a hammer on one side and a curved blade on the other. It looked as if it could hack clean through Gabriella's gleaming gold and steel armour. She drew her own sword as she crossed the floor to meet him. The metallic ring of the blade leaving its scabbard sounded pathetically small on the battle floor.

There was no preamble from Barth this time. He examined both weapons briefly, nodded to himself, and returned to his bench.

"Begin!" he commanded.

Goethe tucked his chin and crouched slightly, flexing his knuckles on the haft of his axe. Gabriella raised her shield and sword, crossing them before her as she had been taught.

Goethe struck first, lunging forwards with the haft of his axe, aiming for Gabriella's exposed left side. She feinted right and angled her shield to deflect the blow. The clank of wood on metal rang out over the theatre. The gathered students cheered and booed variously.

"Your father had my father tortured," Goethe said in a hoarse whisper. His face was completely impassive, almost bored.

"My father has good reason for whatever he does," Gabriella replied under her breath. "Your father is protecting villains worse than himself." She was already panting heavily, more out of nervousness than effort. She darted forwards and raised her shield, meaning to deflect Goethe's axe and strike his thigh with the flat of her sword. The blow that fell upon her shield felt more like a millstone however, and her sword swung short, striking the floor and spitting sparks.

"Point and fault," Barth called.

"Your whole family will pay the price when Merodach comes to power," Goethe growled.

Gabriella was so shocked that she nearly lowered her sword. "Your father never admitted...!"

Goethe spun to strike, drawing his axe around in a sweeping arc, hammer first. Gabriella saw it coming and reacted instinctively, dropping to a crouch and angling her shield over her. The blunt nose of the axe rang off her shield and nearly drove her to the floor. Angrily, she jabbed with her sword, but Goethe parried her blow easily with the haft of his axe.

"Point and fault," Barth barked again.

Gabriella's face felt hot with mingled embarrassment and rage. She leapt to her feet and angled her sword before her.

"Once my father hears that you've mentioned that name..."

"I will deny it, and you will look a fool," Goethe rasped, his eyes boring into hers as he circled. "After all, Merodach is just a bogeyman for frightening children, is he not?"

Gabriella realised that no one else could hear her opponent's whispered words over the sound of their scuffling feet and the occasional cheers and jeers of the observers. She tried to attack again, but Goethe sidestepped and pummeled her with his shield.

"Soon, all of Camelot will know the truth about Merodach and his army," the bigger boy breathed. He grinned, showing filthy, yellow teeth. "You and your father will learn it first."

Gabriella had heard enough. She narrowed her eyes over her shield and spun around. Goethe saw what she was doing and leant to meet her sword as it came around, but Gabriella's shield came up first, catching the boy beneath the arm and slamming into his ribcage. Deftly, she ducked under her shield and came up behind Goethe. Her sword finished its long arc against the middle of his back, thumping smartly on his leather armour. A surprised cheer arose from the gathered students.

"Two points," Barth called with an appreciative nod.

Goethe barely paused. His elbow shot out behind him, knocking Gabriella's sword away. A moment later, he pivoted to meet her, raising the haft of his axe in a blur. Gabriella caught it against her wrist gauntlet, but the force pushed her backwards. Goethe pivoted again, reversing the axe's direction and bringing the blunt end down over her shield, aiming for her helmet. Gabriella ducked to the side and brought her sword down on the lowering axe, driving it to the floor. The heavy axe head clanged to the stone. An instant later, Gabriella's shield rammed upwards into Goethe's chest. The bigger boy grunted with rage and lashed out, using all of his weight. Gabriella stumbled but transformed the momentum into a backwards roll. Deftly, she kicked up with both feet, connected with Goethe's midsection just below his breastplate, and flipped him over her. He crashed to the floor behind her, and his axe clattered away.

Gabriella was back on her feet in seconds. She planted a foot on Goethe's shield, pinning it to the floor with his arm beneath it, and leveled her sword at his heart. Panting and triumphant, she turned to glance back at the Battle Master.

Barth's fingers were steepled beneath his chin, his eyebrows raised patiently. What was he waiting for?

Suddenly, Gabriella was thrown aside. Amazingly, Goethe had lifted his shield despite the weight she exerted on it and used it to fling her to the ground. He scrambled upright, threw himself upon her, and unsheathed a dagger from his wrist gauntlet. In an instant, it was pressed firmly under the shelf of her jaw. She felt the cold metal against her skin. Goethe panted down at her, grinning and sweating, his face only inches from hers. He was going to kill her, right there in the centre of the dueling theatre floor. Gabriella saw it in his eyes.

And then, amazingly, he was gone, pulled away so swiftly that the dagger fell from his hand. Gabriella blinked, gasped, and scrambled backwards, dropping her sword and shield, her armour scraping and clattering on the stone floor.

"Did you *not hear* the Battle Master?" a voice seethed furiously. "NO daggers! NO blood! I will KILL you if you touch her again."

A heavy figure ran past Gabriella. She looked up and saw Barth struggling to get between Goethe and another boy—Darrick of course. Darrick's fists were buried in the fabric of Goethe's tunic, pulling the bigger boy to his feet. Treynor leapt over the low wall, sword drawn, running to join the fracas on the battle floor.

"Let him go!" Barth commanded, shoving Darrick back. "I am the master here! Do as I say!"

Darrick didn't obey at first. He stared balefully into Goethe's eyes. Finally, with a fierce shove, he released his grip on the boy's tunic. Goethe straightened slowly and brushed himself off, his face set with stony triumph despite Barth's obvious fury. Treynor eyed the three severely, his sword still raised.

"Fault!" Barth called furiously at Darrick, pushing him backwards with one meaty hand. He turned to Goethe. "And *double* fault! You know daggers are not permitted in the theatre!"

Goethe shrugged lazily and peered aside towards Gabriella. She had gotten herself to her feet again, but she was shaking. She could still feel the place on her throat where the blade had pressed. She touched it and shuddered.

"I forgot I had the dagger," Goethe said dully, not taking his eyes from hers. He winked, and a beastly smile tugged at the corners of his mouth.

"You forgot," Barth scoffed. "Get out of my theatre. But *leave* the damn dagger."

Darrick stood at the entrance to the dueling floor. He glared at Goethe. Then, as the bigger boy handed his dagger to Treynor and turned to gather his things, Darrick shifted his gaze to Gabriella. He nodded slowly once. Gabriella understood. Goethe had only resorted to the dagger because she had beaten him. It may be that no one else would see it that way, but it was the truth.

No matter what the final score revealed, she had won.

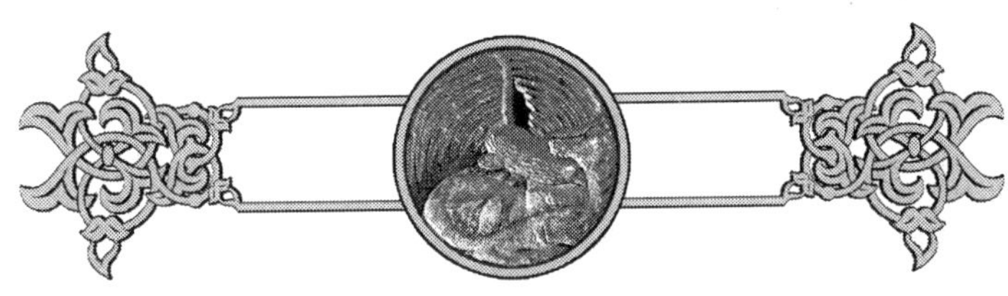

The candle ceremony always took place at sunset. The school cathedral was packed to overflowing, stuffy with the heat of jostling bodies, most wearing their finest and least comfortable clothing. The air was filled with murmuring voices, candle smoke, and wafting threads of incense. Gabriella watched the incense as it streamed lazily from the altar urns, combining and making silent magical shapes in the air. Professor Toph, the Magic Master, tended the urns, teasing the ribbons of smoke with his wand and occasionally sprinkling coloured powders onto the flames, which spurted and flared.

The gathering of students stood on the dais, forming a semicircle around the altar. In their black robes and hoods, it was hard to tell the girls from the boys. Indeed, the throng of students seemed to blend into a seamless, black snake dotted with nervous faces.

"What is that one?" Constance whispered, nudging Rhyss and nodding out over the gathered families.

"Battle of the Wragnaroth," Rhyss replied quietly. "There's King Arthur in the lead, see? His horse is that swirly bit floating in the vault of the apse."

"I don't see it," Darrick breathed, shaking his head.

"That's because you don't have any imagination, dearheart," Rhyss sang under her breath.

Gabriella let her gaze fall from the swirling smoky shapes to the hundreds of people jostling into place on the dim floor below. She saw Darrick's family near the back. His father's prodigious, black beard had been combed and oiled so that it glistened in the torch light. Next to him, Darrick's mother smiled, red-cheeked, and occasionally glanced around in an effort to keep track of Darrick's two younger brothers. Gabriella saw their tousled heads bobbing and darting through the crowd, oblivious of the solemn nature of the evening's ceremony.

She lowered her eyes further to the front row of the cathedral. Most of the attendees were standing of course, packed onto the open cathedral floor, but two rows of stone chairs lined the front of the space immediately before the altar. Here, the royal court reclined in their formal attire. Gabriella saw Percival, Destra's father, and the rest of the men in her father's council. In the centre front, two heavy, wooden thrones dominated the floor, much higher and more ornate than the stone seats on either side. Gabriella's father, King Xavier, sat in the throne on the right. The other throne was empty save for a small alabaster vase, carefully sealed with a crystal stopper.

Gabriella felt a twinge of sadness looking at her mother's ashes, but it was old sadness now. It had been many years since the attack and the midnight flight, many years since those frightening weeks when Gabriella had not known if her parents were living or dead or even if she would ever return to them. Now it was all just dusty memories: a small, snowbound cottage, a red-hooded cloak, long nights of lonely fear. Now Gabriella's mother was barely a wistful dream, a whiff of perfume, an echo of a singing voice. Gabriella missed her, but she did so with her buried child's heart. The young woman that had grown around that heart looked on with only a vague sadness, a pang at the lack of something that she could never know.

Rhyss leant close to Gabriella's ear. "I hope this does not bore you overmuch," she whispered. "It may be that you and Darrick will be back here again soon, only then you'll be wearing white instead of black."

Gabriella blushed and poked Rhyss with her elbow. "You are incorrigible!" she rasped. “You know that tradition insists I marry royalty. Darrick is as royal as a scullery mop.”

"Tradition be damned,” Rhyss suggested with a small shrug. “All the eligible foreign princes are in their sixth decades. You father wouldn’t do that to you. Besides,” she smirked, “I'm graduating at the top of my class in Divination, you know. I'm never wrong."

Gabriella shook her head, still feeling the heat burning from her cheeks. She glanced furtively aside. Darrick hadn't heard, or if he had, he wasn't letting on.

There was a rustling of anticipation in the crowd below. Gabriella looked and saw the school chancellor moving down the centre aisle, parting the crowd. The cathedral fell silent so that the only sound was the echoing tap of the Chancellor's staff on the floor. His steely hair was parted neatly, framing a stony face and accenting the stiff grandeur of his formal gowns. When he reached the altar, he stopped and allowed his gaze to move over the students, resting for a moment on each face. His rugged features were stern but somehow affectionate. His pale blue eyes met Gabriella's for a moment, paused, and then moved onwards. Finally, he turned back to the gathered families.

"This night," he said, his clear voice ringing in the stillness, "your children—these faces you see before you—are no more. They entered this cathedral as your charges, but they leave as men and women, responsible only to themselves and their king. Here, you may say farewell to your babies and meet the new faces of your fellow citizens. From this night forwards, they, like you, are become the Kingdom of Camelot. Tonight our duty to them ends. Tonight their duty to God, the King, and themselves... begins."

A rumble arose from the crowd. Heads bowed and nodded. Handkerchiefs were dabbed at eyes. In the front rows, the lords and ladies beamed with stern goodwill. Gabriella's father met her eyes, and he smiled faintly, proudly.

"And now," the Chancellor said, turning back to the line of students, "you may accept your flame. You have been preparing for this event since your first day in these halls. You know what to do. Come forwards as I call your name."

Then, solemnly and methodically, the Chancellor began to recite the names of Gabriella's fellow students. One by one, the graduates broke away from the line and approached the altar. There, the Magic Master, Professor Toph, met them, smiling in his bedraggled peaked hat and flowing burgundy robes. For each student, he lit a stick of incense from the urn and handed it over to them. Flame in hand, each student turned and climbed the dais, passing by their fellows, heading into the glow of the transept candle gallery.

Darrick went first. Gabriella watched him with a nearly absurd sense of pride. He bowed his head to Professor Toph and took his flame solemnly. In the rear of the cathedral, a pair of young voices hooted triumphantly, and a ripple of laughter moved over the crowd. Gabriella saw Darrick's mother scolding her sons in hushed tones, trying to hide the grin of happiness on her own face. A minute later, Constance was called forwards, and then Rhyss.

Finally, Gabriella heard her own name. The Chancellor peered at her sternly over his spectacles as she approached the altar.

"Welcome and congratulations, Your Highness," Professor Toph said softly, handing her her stick of burning incense. Gabriella smiled up at him, pleased and slightly giddy, and then glanced aside. Her father sat less than ten feet away. His crown glinted as he nodded towards her, his face beaming with pride. Gabriella smiled back at him. She turned, climbed the stairs to the dais, and passed the remaining students.

The glow of the candle gallery was like a constellation, twinkling and flickering with hundreds of yellow flames. Small, white candles were collected in rows and levels, embraced in complicated iron sconces all along the angled transept walls. Darrick stood in front of his family alcove, his face solemn, the incense stick in his hand extinguished but still trailing a thread of smoke. His hood had been pushed back, revealing his unruly dark hair. Even when he was trying to look sombre, Gabriella noticed, a smile seemed to play on the corners of his mouth. His eyes met hers, and the hidden smile deepened a little.

Rhyss stood further on, next to Constance, her second cousin. Gabriella passed them and approached the very centre of the transept. The royal candle alcove stood above the others, immediately below the enormous stained-glass window. Gabriella stopped there and looked at the rows of candles. Most were lit, but a few were dark, their wicks blackened and cold. In the very front row, one candle was unlit but clean, its wick white and straight. This was her candle. She gazed at it for a long moment, wondering about it, wondering what the candle of her life held for her.

Finally, she raised the incense stick. She touched its smouldering tip to the unburnt wick, watched it flare to life, and then stood back. Her candle burnt brightly, its flame tall and straight. It was good. Gabriella nodded at it, and then snuffed out the incense stick between her gloved fingers. She pushed her hood back with her right hand, a sign that her schooling was officially complete. Finally, she turned to face the crowded cathedral, keeping her back straight and her face sober despite the excitement she felt in her breast, glowing much like the flame on the candle behind her.

There were very few students left. Most now stood gathered around their family alcoves, their own candles lit, their incense sticks extinguished in their hands. Dimly, Gabriella realised that Goethe was not present. She wondered about it, but only for a moment. Perhaps he had been expelled for his treachery in the dueling theatre. Perhaps he did not care about the graduation ceremony, especially with his father unable to attend, still locked in the castle dungeons.

Perhaps he simply had better things to do.

For the moment, Gabriella had the luxury not to care. Already, the incident with the hidden dagger on the battle floor seemed small and unimportant. She was of age now. Her whole life was stretched out before her, humming with anticipation, bursting with the promise of good things yet to come.

Outside, the sunset burnt deep red over the mountains, fading upwards to purple and deepest blue. The twilight stars twinkled.

It was the first day of the last glorious spring of the age of Camelot.

CHAPTER 2

As it turned out, the wedding ceremony was to take place in the castle.

Gabriella awoke at dawn and found herself completely unable to get back to sleep. She rolled over and blinked slowly at the linen curtains that surrounded her bed, glowing pink with the day's first light.

This is my last night in the bed I grew up in, she thought to herself. It seemed ridiculous and absurd, and yet she knew it was the truth. She imagined Darrick lying awake in his parents' cottage on the other side of the village, imagined him thinking of her, and felt a tremor of nervous exhilaration.

Gabriella was a sensible girl. She knew that marriage did not usually mean happily ever after, regardless of what the fairy books said. She'd been around enough married people to know that even the best relationships were often fraught with challenges, disagreements, and even that most poisonous of all marital realities, boredom. She was not like Constance, who had grown up to be rather vain and silly, convinced that matrimony was the cure for all ills. She, Gabriella, knew that after the thrill of the honeymoon wore off, the work of marriage would occasionally be difficult.

And yet she also knew that, for reasons she did not fully comprehend, she had been granted a luxury not afforded to many princesses: she had been allowed to marry for love and not politics. After all, Darrick was the son of a common blacksmith, himself from a long line of pot-makers. There was no royalty in her fiancé's blood whatsoever. For this reason, Gabriella had spent years refusing to acknowledge what everyone else had known immediately: that they were meant for each other. As a girl, she had merely seen a dirty common boy, only permitted into the royal school because his parents had made a hefty tithe toward his education. Despite the sacrificial gesture of his parents, the boy had been insolent and brash, completely unimpressed by Her Royal Highness, Princess Gabriella. This had infuriated her, of course, and launched a rivalry that burnt (on her part) until they'd been sixteen years old.

It had all changed on the day that Darrick had defeated Gabriella in a practice duel. This had left her speechless with fury, since none of the other boys had ever bested her before. She had stormed outside, her face brick red with embarrassed indignation, and thrown her wooden practice sword into the grass. When Constance had tried to soothe her, Gabriella had nearly pushed her down the brook hill. Finally, unable to control herself, she had cornered Darrick between the bell tower and the castle wall and demanded that he show her the proper respect.

"I am the Princess of Camelot!" she had rasped hoarsely, leaning into his face. "Bow to me! Show me the respect that I deserve!"

She had known even then that it was a pathetic, stupid thing to say. No true princess ever had to command her subjects to bow to her. Darrick didn't bow, but he didn't mock her either.

"You want me to let you win the duels every time like all the other blokes just because you're the Princess?" he'd asked, squinting seriously at her. "Because if I were you, I'd want a better kind of respect than that. I'd want to be honoured for who I am, not just for my last name."

"How dare you?!" Gabriella had seethed. "You're just a blacksmith's son!"

"I'm the son of the best blacksmith in Camelot," Darrick had replied, lifting his chin. "That's no small feat. There's pride in that, you should know. If my father hadn't worked so hard to get me into the Royal Academy, I'd have been content to become a blacksmith like him and earn the same honour for my skills. What about you, Princess? You wish for me to respect you like all the rest, bowing to you in class but laughing at you behind your back? Or do you want me to honour you for true, for the girl you are and the woman you're becoming?"

Gabriella had not known what to say to that. It had never even occurred to her that the others had let her win duels simply because she was the Princess, or that their respect for her was anything but genuine. She'd wanted to argue with Darrick, but suddenly, horribly, she saw that he was right. As far as the rest of her classmates were concerned, there was nothing to her but a title. She'd simply stared at him, first with affronted anger, and then with shocked dismay. Finally, shamefully, she had turned and stalked away from him.

Before she had reached the corner of the bell tower, however, Darrick had spoken again.

"I like you, Gabriella," he'd said, his voice cool and thoughtful. "Not because you are the Princess, but because you are... special. There's something about you that I can't forget. There's more to you than anyone else sees."

Gabriella had stopped at his words. "You should not say such things," she had said without turning around.

"You feel the same way about me, I would wager," he'd commented in a lower voice.

Gabriella had turned quickly and looked back at him. She'd expected him to be grinning at her, mocking her, but he wasn't. He'd merely looked at her calmly and then gone on.

"If you did not feel the same for me, you would not care so much, I think. You'd just ignore me. Do you know what I think, Gabriella? I think we are made for one another. Perhaps that only happens in stories, but I don't think so. I think we're like those two magnets in Professor Toph's laboratory. We're either going to come smack together like two pieces of hot iron, red from the forge, or push apart like God and the devil. It's all just a matter of which direction you're facing. You've been so busy raging against the truth that I daresay you've never even really seen it."

Gabriella had felt strangely terrified. It was as if he could see through her armour and clothing, even through her skin, right into her deepest being. Suddenly, for the first time in years, she'd remembered the kiss that he had given her, back when they'd both been children, quarreling over a pilfered bag of Whisperwind powder.

"You should not say such things," she'd said again, nearly whispering.

"Perhaps I shouldn't," Darrick had replied with a half shrug. "But that's never stopped me before."

In her bed, Gabriella smiled, remembering it all. She had walked away from him that day feeling the strangest mixture of emotions: shame and embarrassment, yes, but also an unexpected, giddy excitement. She had grown so used to impressing people as the Princess that it had never even occurred to her that she could impress anyone as Gabriella. Suddenly, the thing that she had most detested about Darrick—that he never called her by her title, but by her given name—became the thing she was most intrigued by. Was he right? Were they like magnets, destined either to repel or attract? Even if it were true, how could it ever possibly be? She was the King's daughter after all, and kings' daughters simply did not marry the sons of blacksmiths. Of course, even then, some small part of her had known that such things didn't really matter. Gabriella was a sensible girl, but she was still a girl. Even for her, no amount of imperial politics could win out over the possibility of true love.

She did not love Darrick from that day forwards, of course. But she did begin to turn around, to not defy and resist him at every opportunity. And just like the magnets in Professor Toph's laboratory, the turning around made all the difference. Soon enough, repulsion turned to irresistible attraction. Once she gave in to it, the force of it was so strong, so pervasive, that it was rather frightening. It pushed all of her practicality aside, made all of her sensibility and reasonableness seem insipid, like paper castles on a child's windowsill. She still attempted to goad him sometimes, to command his respect or cow him into submission, but it never worked, and deep down, she was glad. He loved her because she was Gabriella and not because she was the Princess. Over the past three years, this fact had stricken her as simultaneously incredible and sublime.

Now, on the morning of their wedding, it still did.

The door of the bedroom burst open, wafting the curtains that surrounded her bed and admitting a staccato of bare feet on the wooden floor. A moment later, the curtains were thrust aside, and a figure jumped up onto the bed.

"Sun's up, Bree! Who's ready to be the royal blushing bride?" It was Rhyss, of course, who had spent the night in the adjacent bedroom. She knelt on the bed and bounced with excitement. "Because if it isn't you, I'll be happy to take your place. What are friends for, hmm?"

Gabriella smiled. "You had your chance already. You ended it with him, remember?"

Rhyss shrugged languidly. "I was a child then, but I do end it with all of them eventually. I'm born to be a breaker of hearts. It's my lot in life. Come, let's sneak down to the kitchens before Sigrid knows we're awake. It's our last chance to breakfast with the cooks like old times!"

Gabriella looked at her friend affectionately, knowing this really was the last chance they would ever have to simply be girls together. "Race you," she said, throwing off her covers and pushing Rhyss backwards on the bed. Both girls scrambled up. Laughing and shushing each other, they bolted out the door and down the hall.

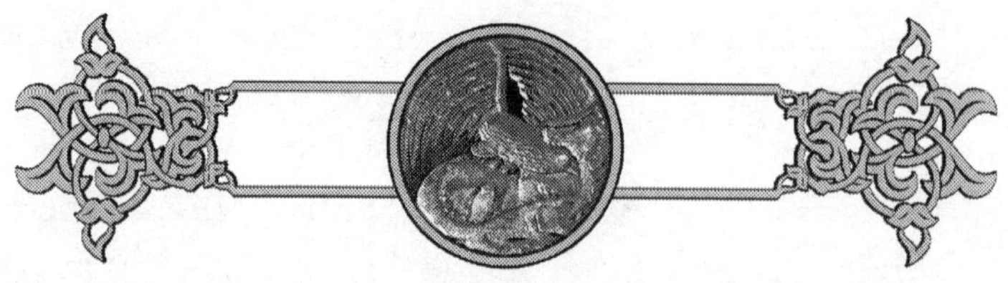

"It's bad luck for you to see me before the wedding," Gabriella scolded Darrick when she met him in the King's reception room four hours later.

"I was summoned, same as you," he smiled, reaching for her as she joined him near the room's only window. The window was tall stained glass, decorated with the stern visage of King Arthur in his armour, his sword gleaming steely blue and his beard streaming regally down his chest. Gathered behind the glassy King was a line of handsome knights resplendent in their own armours, shields bearing the red dragon and holy cross of their order.

Gabriella laced her fingers through Darrick's and stood in front of him. They kissed briefly, and she said, "Father did not tell me you would be here. I hope all is well."

"All is well," Darrick nodded, touching his forehead to hers. "I have spoken to the King already this morning."

Gabriella frowned quizzically up at him. "You have?"

He nodded again. "We're not even married yet, and already I am going over the Princess's head for councils with the King," he smiled, teasing her. "Truth be told, he sought me out. His messenger arrived just after breakfast, bearing the details of my summons."

"Then tell me," Gabriella said with a sigh, plopping onto the bench that ran beneath the window. "I don't like surprises. Especially on a day like today."

"It is your father's news to tell," Darrick replied. "I won't steal his thunder except to say that it seems to involve a story and a mysterious box."

Gabriella glanced up at him from beneath her eyebrows. "It means a bit more than that by the look on your face. What did you discuss?"

Darrick laughed and lowered himself to the bench next to her. He put an arm around her shoulders and squeezed her. "If you must know, we discussed my position in the Kingdom."

This made Gabriella sit up ramrod straight. She looked aside at him seriously. "Your position? But we've already arranged that. When you asked for my hand..."

Darrick nodded. "Of course, and nothing is changed. I no more wish to be King than you wish to be a herring. When you become Queen, I will be the royal consort, Viceroy of Camelot. I will assist you and represent you on those few occasions when a beard may carry more weight than a bustle, but you will be Queen Sovereign, ruler of the Kingdom."

Gabriella studied his face for a moment and then shook her head and slouched. "I'd rather be a herring than Queen. I wish you *could* become ruler someday rather than just Viceroy. But if that arrangement still stands, then what did you discuss?"

Darrick was silent for a long moment. Gabriella glanced aside at him again. He met her eyes, pressed his lips together, and then looked away, out over the dimness of the room.

Gabriella narrowed her eyes. "You're going to be knighted," she said.

"More than that," he answered, returning his gaze to her. "I have been promoted to commissioned officer in the Imperial Army."

"Commissioned officer!" Gabriella gasped, jumping to her feet and rounding on him. "You've barely graduated the academy!"

"I received best marks in our class for Strategy and Battle Skills if you recall," Darrick reminded her. "Besides, it isn't as if I will be High Constable or any such thing. That post is still occupied by Sir Ulric. I shall be his field marshal. The post will provide invaluable experience for when you are Queen and I am your viceroy."

"Those are my father's words, not yours," Gabriella interjected derisively. "Why should you require such experience? As Viceroy, you will have your own men to advise you on military issues."

"The Kingdom does not need another *administrator* right now, Bree," Darrick said in a low voice. "Your father fills that role quite nicely. People are fearful. News from the outposts gets more worrying every day. There are rumours of bands of villains raiding towns, recruiting new members by the point of the sword. Worse, there are tales of wanton bloodshed, of whole villages being wiped out."

"But surely, if these tales were true, father would have received reports..."

Darrick shook his head slowly. "Not if the messengers were killed before they could deliver them," he said meaningfully. "Five of the fourteen provinces have not been heard from in almost half a year. Their tax manifests are overdue. Most troubling of all, there is evidence that two of the manifests from the reporting provinces have been falsified."

"Falsified?" Gabriella repeated, lowering her own voice. "But how can that be? The chamberlains are all loyal to my father. They would not cheat him."

Darrick's eyes had grown hard. "They would not unless they were forced to."

"Forced to... but by whom? And why?"

"The question of why is the simple one. Your father's advisers believe that there is a brute army on the march. The unreported taxes are being used to support and pay them. The tributes of the Kingdom are being used to fund an insurrection force against it."

Gabriella was shocked. Why had her father not told her about these things? Had he believed that he was protecting her? How could she be expected to be Queen someday if she was not welcomed into the council of the King on such matters now? For the first time, she wondered if perhaps her own father did not believe she was capable of the task. Did he himself doubt her ability solely because she was a woman? Her face reddened at the thought.

"I hate that I must learn of these things from you, beloved," she said rather more stiffly than she had intended. "But who does my father believe is responsible for this treason?"

Darrick shook his head. "No one knows for certain, but there are rumours as you well know."

"Merodach," Gabriella breathed, drifting slowly to her seat again. "Goethe told me. On the battle floor. I thought he was just trying to frighten me."

"Again, dearheart, no one knows for certain. The name does not matter. The point is the people are worried. As I said, the Kingdom does not need another administrator."

"What *do* they need?" she asked without looking at him.

Darrick peered back over his shoulder, up at the stained-glass window behind him. "They need heroes," he answered.

Gabriella turned and followed his gaze. Behind them, the glass knights glared down, their faces grave and handsome, their swords and shields at the ready.

"I was taught that it was a good thing that there was no longer a council of the Round Table," she said softly. "Father told me that it meant that we live in a time of peace. There is no need of a coalition of war when there are no wars to be fought."

Darrick nodded. Gabriella continued to frown up at the stained glass. "It always made me sort of sad," she mused. "When I was a girl, I longed for the days when gallant men rode in force against beasts and villains, marauding armies and unstoppable foes."

"Every boy I knew growing up wanted to be brave Sir Lancelot," Darrick added, smiling wistfully. "I was one of them."

"But you *aren't*!" Gabriella hissed suddenly, turning back to him. "You're Darrick. You are to be my husband, not some military officer running into the heat of battle. You belong to me, not the Kingdom."

"We all belong to the Kingdom—" Darrick began, but she interrupted him.

"I won't have it! Let the people have their heroes if they need them, but not you. I need you more than they do."

"Bree," Darrick said, grasping her hand earnestly, "I can be both. It is your father's wish. It is my duty. I do not resist it. What are you afraid of? Surely not some rabble of malcontents hiding in the northern hills? I *long* to rout them out and put an end to their debauchery. Why do you rage against this?"

Gabriella met his gaze, her brow still furrowed in a tense frown. She pressed her lips together and shook her head.

"When you asked my father for my hand," she said quietly, "I was prepared for him to say no. When was the last time a princess was allowed to marry anyone outside of royalty?"

"Even now," Darrick reminded her, "the King's decision is political. He was being pressured to form an alliance with Marche, symbolized by your marriage to that insufferable old Prig, Prince Thurnston. Your choice to marry me sends a clear message, not only to the royal family of Marche, but to the people of Camelot."

"I know all of this," Gabriella said impatiently. "But it is all too easy, somehow."

Darrick raised an eyebrow. "Do you wish your father had said no?"

"Of course not. There's just something about it all that seems wrong." She paused and looked up again, at the stern knights in their glassy frame. "It's as if… my father is hardly even *trying* anymore."

Behind Darrick, the doors to the King's inner chambers swept open. Gabriella let out a pent breath and closed her eyes. Darrick held her hand for a moment longer and then stood.

"Your Highness," he said.

"Sir Darrick," the King said, and Gabriella cringed. She opened her eyes and stood as well. Her father looked at her consideringly. "My daughter, love of my life," he sighed, "I see by your face that you have already learnt the news that I summoned you here for."

"I am sorry, Your Highness," Darrick said, glancing aside at Gabriella. "I could not keep it from her. She asked me directly."

The King accepted this with a nod. "I am glad that the husband of my daughter prizes honesty. Nevertheless, do come into my chambers. There are other less weighty matters for us to attend."

Gabriella was feeling neither jovial nor compliant. "What matters, Father?" she asked, not moving.

The King had begun to turn, but he stopped and looked back at her. His eyes were black and inscrutable, but he smiled. In that smile, she saw that he understood her response completely and did not hold it against her.

"Serious days are upon us, daughter," he said. "There will be plenty of time for congress and debates, and you shall attend them all. Indeed, you have grown so that I daresay I could not keep you from them even if I wished. You will no longer be satisfied to listen from the wardrobe outside my door, will you?"

Gabriella couldn't help smiling at the memory. She shook her head and then moved to join him in the door to his chambers.

"I will welcome you into my council," the King said, placing his arm around her. "But I will miss the little girl in the wardrobe. I hope you won't begrudge me that."

"How could I?" she answered, letting him embrace her. When she stood back from him again, she was somewhat surprised to see the Magic Master, Professor Toph, standing within the King's chambers nearby, smiling somewhat mistily.

"So what is it you wish to discuss, Father?" Gabriella asked, taking Darrick's hand and following the King into his rooms.

"You do not think," the King replied, glancing back with a strange smile, "that I would allow my only child to wed without giving her and her beau a royal gift?"

With that, the King led them through the depths of his chambers, followed quietly by Professor Toph, who smiled and nodded inscrutably when Gabriella glanced at him. She had an idea that the Magic Master was much shyer by nature than his public status allowed him to be. His gold, tasseled robes, ruffed collar, and white peaked hat would have seemed impressively mysterious on anyone else. On him, the ensemble appeared to be worn by a kindly, old, bachelor uncle on his way to a costume ball.

The King's chambers were cluttered, as usual. Books, quills, and sheaves of parchment littered nearly every surface. A white bearskin rug stretched between a collection of low, richly upholstered chairs, all arranged somewhat haphazardly before an enormous hearth. A tea set, now cold, sat on the corner of the rug, awaiting the steward. The curtains were closed, reducing the space to a chilly cave-like gloom even at mid-morning.

Gabriella had dim memories of what these rooms had been like when her mother had still been alive. There had been less disorder then of course. The tables had been regularly cleared, dusted, and made resplendent with fresh flowers arranged in huge, colourful vases. The curtains had always been pulled back to let in the sunlight. Gabriella treasured faint images of her mother sitting in one of the upholstered chairs by the fire, writing letters or reading correspondence as flecks of dust danced like fireflies in the sunbeams all around her. It was a beautiful memory, albeit a little sad.

Fortunately, the King led them past his cluttered den and out into the sunny warmth of the private balcony. A desk had been set up there, with three chairs arranged around it. In the centre of the desk, its polished lid glinting mellowly in the sun, was a small, wooden box.

"Let us be seated," the King said, easing himself into the largest of the chairs. "Professor Toph has a story to tell us before we open this very interesting box."

Gabriella was curious despite herself. She settled into one of the chairs and smoothed her gown over her knees. Darrick sat next to her, placing her between him and her father.

"The first bit of the story really is not mine to tell, Your Majesty," Toph said, drifting slowly behind the desk and resting his thin hands upon the wooden box.

"Indeed," the King answered, "but you tell it so much better than I. Go on. Regale us."

Toph nodded and closed his eyes for a moment. When he opened them again, he was looking at Gabriella.

"Forgive me, Princess. Some of this will provoke unpleasant memories. Bear with me, for it will end well."

Gabriella nodded, smiling and frowning slightly at the same time. Toph began to speak.

"Many years ago, as you will certainly recall, upon a winter's midnight, there came an attack upon this very castle led by a well-organised band of assassins. Barbarian men from the north had infiltrated the city, trickling in by ones and twos as part of a coordinated plan to murder your parents and capture Camelot in the name of Emperor Aurengzia. But for the quick action of the palace guard, these men might have succeeded. Sir Percival roused your father, who immediately ordered that you and your grandmother be evacuated from the castle under the protection of three royal guards. These men helped you escape via the servants' entry but were waylaid at the city gates. There, your guards gave their lives fighting off the murderers whilst you and your grandmother fled, riding in a common hay cart.

"By evening of the next day, the marauders were finally captured and dispatched. Unfortunately, as you well know, the villains were not stopped soon enough to prevent them from partially succeeding in their vicious plot. Your mother, the Queen, was murdered in these very halls, cornered by a lone, rogue barbarian who had managed to slip past the guards."

Toph paused for a moment in his retelling. Gabriella felt Darrick's eyes on her. She glanced at him and gave a small smile. *It is sad,* her smile seemed to say, *but it was a long time ago, and I'm all right now.* Darrick didn't look convinced.

"When it was finished," Toph continued, "your father, the King, was stricken with grief, and yet his worries were far from over. He sent men to retrieve you from your hiding place, a tower keep on the southern border, but they found the tower empty with no sign of your occupation. Further, he learnt that the guards that had been assigned to protect you had been killed. He feared the worst but did not abandon hope. A search was launched, scouring the snowbound Kingdom for word of your whereabouts.

"Finally, after twelve days, your father remembered a small lakefront hunting cottage in the eastern hills that his own father, King William Xavier the Second, had sometimes taken him to as a child. It was remote, virtually forgotten by all save for himself and his mother. Perhaps, he surmised, this was where she had escaped with you. Desperate but hopeful, he himself led the search party, crossing the snowy wilderness and finally reaching the lake and the small cottage that stood by it. He recognised the old building by the broken vane upon its roof, and sure enough, to the surprise and delight of all, he found you inside, both you and your grandmother, safe and sound."

"I remember it as if it were happening this very moment," the King said soberly, reaching to cover Gabriella's hand with his own. "My mother was weakened with hunger and the exertion of the journey, but she told me how you had cared for her even though you were barely seven years old. She told how you had gone out each evening, dressed in your red hood and cloak, in search of winter berries and firewood. She explained how you melted snow to make drinking water, warming it on the stove. You cared for her even when it was she who was meant to protect you."

"And she told of something else as well," Toph added seriously, "something that has been a secret for many years, known only to her, myself, and your father."

He paused again, his brow low and thoughtful. Gabriella waited for her father to urge the professor on, but he did not. Finally, she spoke up herself.

"That's a fine secret if you do not intend to share it even now."

Toph blinked at her and then smiled slightly. Gabriella noticed that, for the moment, the professor seemed neither shy nor silly. His robes and tassels gleamed in the sunlight. Finally, he lowered his eyes, dipped a hand into his inner pocket, and produced his black walnut wand.

"You know the truth, I think, that I am not an actual wizard," he said, holding the wand up and turning it slowly between his fingers. "I can perform some small magic with this wand of course, but the magic is not my own. The power belongs solely to this wand as the symbol of my post. Its enchantments can be performed by anyone with the patience and the dexterity to learn its use. It was carried by Magic Master Gaunt before me and Leofrick before him. In fact, the use of this wand goes all the way back to the time of Arthur the King himself, to the great Merlinus Ambrosius, who crafted it. It was he who gave this wand its magic, and do you know why?"

Toph looked from face to face, and Gabriella saw that he was not expecting a response. He drew a deep breath and soberly answered his own question.

"Because Merlin was no mere man like myself and the others before me. Merlin was a true magical creature, a sorcerer. Back then, there was living magic, practised by a society of witches and wizards that dwelt amongst us and beside us. They had their own king, a noble wizard named Kreagle, and their own councils, courts, and colleges. The world of men called upon the society of wizards in times of need. Kings sought their wise counsel and magical assistance. This led, of course, to the establishment of the official post of Royal Magic Master, and to Merlin himself, who walked these walls, the first and last true wizard to hold the title.

"But jealousies bred between the kingdoms of men and their wizarding counterparts. Magic began to be misused, even by the great Merlin, who was rumoured to hire out his services to any kingdom with enough coin to pay for them. Finally, there came a breach. Wizardkind broke ties with the world of men. The kingdom of the wizards hid itself away from us, for our own good as well as theirs. Their cities were clouded from our eyes so that we could not see them or even remember where they had been."

"But they are not hidden completely," Darrick interjected as Toph paused. "We all know of distant corners of the Kingdom where witches and wizards mingle amongst us. They sell us magical tools, enchanted powders, and potions, though carefully and in very small amounts. We have a store of such things in the academy as you know, Professor, and even in this very castle."

"You speak true," Toph nodded, smiling. "Wizardkind does move amongst us, though in small numbers. Most are hidden away, forgotten, conducting their affairs in secret. Even today, there are tales that a society of wizardry has settled itself in Lord Hayden's abandoned castle, near the rim of Direwood Forest. It was rumoured to be haunted after his untimely death so that none dared claim it. Wizardkind fears no ghosts however; thus, the property was theirs for the taking. I have even heard tell that a small non-magical peasant community lives within sight of the castle, working around and even within it, though forbidden from observing any of the mysterious acts wrought by those within its walls."

"Poppycock and codswallop," Gabriella's father proclaimed jovially. "I sent scouts to inspect Lord Hayden's properties in the years since his death. They reported nothing more than a hulking ruin surrounded by a band of deluded wanderers. It may be haunted, but it is certainly not the site of any magical society."

"Pardon me for saying so, Your Highness," Toph commented, "but I suspect that is exactly what any magical denizens would wish your scouts to see. And I have no doubt that their enchantments would be extremely convincing."

"As you say, Professor," the King allowed, waving a hand and smiling.

"I fail to see what this has to do with Grandmother and me hiding out in the old cottage," Gabriella said, growing impatient.

"Quite right, Your Highness," Toph agreed. "It is easy to become distracted by tales of the magical folk. The point is simply this: whilst wizardkind once lived amongst us and greatly influenced our world with their enchantments, they now abide in secret, leaving only the slightest magical footprint upon the affairs of men. Like the dragons and ancient beasts known to roam the northernmost barrens, we sense their presence mostly by the size of the legends they leave behind, echoing through the veil of history."

"But," the King said, peering aside at his daughter meaningfully, "unlike the dragons of the northern barrens, the magical folk do still make the very rare appearance in the Kingdom. In the most unexpected and mysterious ways, when we least expect it, they intervene in our affairs."

"I don't understand," Gabriella said, glancing from her father to Professor Toph. "As you just said, no witches or wizards have set foot within the castle walls for well over a century."

The King nodded. He drew a deep breath and resumed the story, taking it over from Professor Toph. "When we discovered you and your grandmother in the hunting cabin, we immediately bundled you into blankets and hid you away in the warmth of a covered sledge. Before we embarked upon the return trip to the castle, however, a group of soldiers searched the cottage, collecting any remaining provisions and possessions. It was then that something strange was discovered, something curious enough to call myself and the Magic Master forth."

Toph spoke again then. "There was sign of a struggle in the snow behind the cottage," he said gravely. "The fresh drifts had been disturbed at the rear entrance, as if someone or something had been thrown down there and had scrambled away. Large footprints led off into the wood. Whether the prints belonged to a mannish beast or a very large human, there was no way to tell. What was apparent, however, was that whatever struggle had occurred in the snow behind the cottage, it had ended with one party fleeing into the wood and the other departing via a sleigh of some kind, pulled by reindeer."

"Surely, Grandmother or I would have recalled such an event," Gabriella commented, smiling crookedly, as if this were a sort of elaborate joke. "There were no visitors during our stay there. Of that I am certain."

"Indeed," the King agreed, "my own mother offered the same assurances, and unlike you, she did not once leave the cottage during your occupation there."

There was a tense pause as Gabriella and Darrick considered this. Finally, Darrick said, "That defies common sense, does it not? Surely, one of them would have seen or heard if a struggle had occurred so nearby."

"This is what we thought as well," Toph agreed. "Once the princess' grandmother was made warm and given some hot mead, we invited her to witness the markings in the snow behind the cottage.

When she looked at the evidence with her own eyes, she fainted dead away, only to be revived sometime later, during the return trip to the castle."

"What does it mean?" Gabriella frowned. "Surely, Grandmother would not have lied about such a thing."

"My mother may have been many things," the King smiled, "but a liar she was not."

"We wondered about these things ourselves," Toph said. "It was quite an odd circumstance. That was before we discovered the emblem however."

"Emblem?" Darrick said, leaning forwards in his seat.

The King nodded. "I commanded a full search of the cottage, seeking any clue to what might have happened there. Only then did we find the strange object lost in the shadows beneath the cottage's bed."

"A sigil pin of some kind," Toph explained, "perhaps meant to secure a cloak. It was black, made of some unknown alloy, surprisingly heavy. In the cold of the room, it was strangely warm to the touch. It was round as the moon, with an asp curled on its front. Two emeralds marked its eyes, glittering rather more than could be accounted for by the dim light of the room.

"It had been dropped there recently, for none of the dust from beneath the bed had accumulated on its surface. To be sure, we knew that such a thing did not belong to either you, Princess, or the Queen Mother. We asked the guards who had accompanied us if any of them had ever seen the object or the symbol it bore, but of course, none of them had.

"The truth is," Toph said in a confidential tone, "that even in that moment, I recognised that the sigil was of magical origin. We made deductions and concluded that, for reasons completely unknown, some witch or wizard had, in fact, visited the cottage during your stay and had used their arts to cloud your grandmother's mind and assure their secrecy."

"But why?" Darrick asked, shaking his head in wonder. "How would they even have known anyone was there?"

Professor Toph smiled slowly and shook his head. "We can only guess. Suffice it to say, the magical folk have ways of knowing things that we cannot imagine."

Gabriella frowned at the box, now beginning to guess what might be inside it. "Whoever it was," she said, "did they mean us harm... or good?"

The King considered this. "After my mother's response to the sight of the snowy footprints, I did not wish to show her the mysterious sigil. Eventually, however, my curiosity got the best of me. I invited her to my chamber and produced the pin. When she gazed upon the black shape and those glittering emerald eyes, it was as if she fell into a sort of trance. Only when I placed the sigil back in its box, out of her sight, did she regain herself."

"I was present on this occasion," Toph added. "I asked the Queen Mother if she had ever seen the sigil before. She nodded yes. When asked if she could tell us where she had seen it, upon whom, and what had transpired on that occasion, she was silent. She either did not fully remember or was prevented from answering by the power of some enchantment. In the years that followed, I occasionally questioned her again, gently but methodically, in the hopes that the spell might lift. Alas, it did not. There was only one thing that the Queen Mother assured us of, certainly and with great emphasis."

"What?" Gabriella asked impatiently. Darrick shushed her.

"That it had been a male wizard," the King answered gravely, "and that if he had not come, both you and my mother would not have lived to see another day. For reasons completely unknown to us, and by means we cannot guess, this mysterious magical visitor somehow saved your lives."

The group considered this revelation in silence for a long moment. Finally, Professor Toph cleared his throat and touched the small box again.

"For this reason, the mysterious snake sigil was kept and treasured, as much for its providential significance as its magical origin. We knew not what to do with it but could not justify its disposal. Finally, however, your father had an idea."

The King smiled and nodded for Toph to open the box. Gabriella watched intently, curious to see what the object actually looked like. Carefully, Toph dipped his hand into the box's velvet-lined interior. What he withdrew, however, was *two* small, black sigils, each dangling from a length of fine silver chain. Carrying them, he came around the desk, approaching Gabriella and Darrick.

"I determined," the King explained, "that if the mysterious talisman had been there to save your life as a child, then perhaps it should go with you as you begin your life as a woman."

"I broke its power," Toph said, holding the pendants out, one each, towards Darrick and Gabriella. "Divided, it is still magical, but only as a shadow of its former self. Now, reforged into matching halves, it is become anew. It represents you both, for like you, it is separate but of one heart."

Gabriella was slightly afraid to touch the dangling pendant, but when Darrick reached for his, easily and with obvious interest, she gingerly accepted her own. It was black, heavy in her hand, and still slightly warm to the touch. Hers was fashioned into the shape of a falcon in profile, its wings half-furled. Darrick's was in the form of a dragon, its tail curled around its flank. It was evident that both pendants, if placed together, would fit like puzzle pieces. One green emerald eye glittered from each half.

"Wear them from this day forth," Toph said solemnly. "Let them be a symbol of the love you bear for one another. They will be a bond between you: a beacon of help in time of need, a talisman of fortune as long as you both shall live, filling in the space between them with your living love."

Gabriella looked at the black pendant in her hand and then up at the eyes of Professor Toph where he stood before her. Despite his confident words, she thought she detected a note of nervousness in his smile. *This was my father's idea,* she thought to herself. *Professor Toph is not comfortable with it. Only he knows the powers such a sigil might bear even in its broken state.*

Next to her, Darrick bowed his head and slipped the silver chain around his neck. Gabriella looked aside at him, saw the black dragon shape where it lay on his chest. She blinked at it and then smiled. It looked very handsome there. In fact, it looked exactly right. He saw her looking and met her gaze, giving her that crooked, irreverent grin that had once so infuriated her and since commanded her deepest affection.

"Put it on, daughter," the King said gently, proudly. "It is my gift to you. Wear it all the days of your life, both of you. And may those days be very long and filled with happiness."

Gabriella turned to her father. Slowly, she lowered her chin and raised the pendant's chain over her head. She felt the warm weight of the sigil settle beneath her throat.

Darrick took her hand and squeezed it.

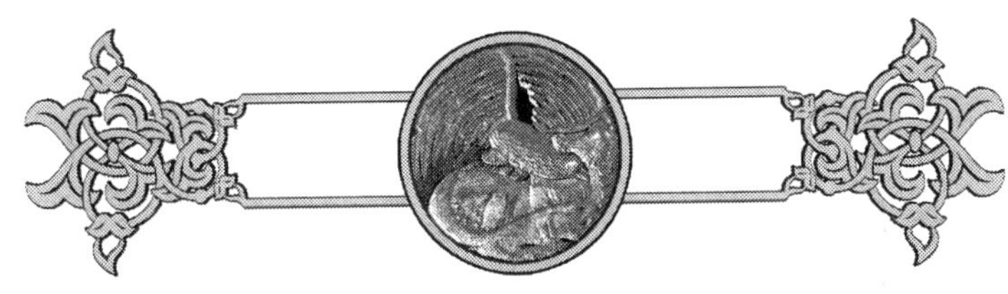

The story of Darrick and Gabriella—the blacksmith's son and the Princess—had spread amongst the people of Camelot, becoming necessarily embellished and romanticised, so that by the evening of the wedding, the castle courtyard had become a scene of spontaneous celebration. Those returning tired from the fields met their wives and children in the square, establishing little family camps along the walls and in hay-filled corners. Street vendors had set up their carts to feed and profit from the crowd. Those who could not afford their wares satisfied themselves with baskets of home-made bread and cheese. Children danced and chased each other through the jovial throng. Musicians fluted and drummed noisily, competing with each other from opposite corners of the courtyard.

Gabriella observed this with bemusement from her balcony. She knew that most of the people below had gathered as much for the festival atmosphere as to celebrate her marriage to Darrick, but this did not bother her in the least.

"It is very nearly time," Sigrid announced, stopping in the open balcony doors. "We should make our way down to the ballroom. You're as ready as you will ever be, methinks."

Gabriella nodded but did not move. "They look so happy," she said, smiling wistfully.

"Of course they do," Sigrid answered. "It's not every day that a princess marries a commoner."

Gabriella looked down at the noisome throng in the twilight. "Darrick isn't common," she said with quiet confidence.

Sigrid waited impatiently for a moment and then sighed and moved to join her charge at the balcony railing. "Do you wish to learn a truth on this day, dear one?" she asked, peering down into the square.

"You've taught me nearly every day of my life whether I liked it or not," Gabriella replied. "Why should today be any different?"

Sigrid shrugged. "Today that will end. I am no longer your nurse, but your lady-in-waiting. From now on, if you wish me to advise you, you will ask me for it."

"I will always ask you for it," Gabriella said, suddenly feeling very sad. Tears came to her eyes, surprising her, and she swiped at them with annoyance.

"This is how it always is," Sigrid nodded, softening her expression. "Every great beginning means something else must end. It is the way of all good things. Sadness and joy are the twins of every momentous event."

"I don't think that's the lesson you meant to teach me," Gabriella chided, swallowing thickly and producing a handkerchief. "Don't remind me of what is ending. Teach me a happy truth for once, woman."

Sigrid nodded agreeably and crossed her large forearms on the balcony railing. "You say that your Darrick is not common, and you are right," she said, peering down into the torchlight of the courtyard. "Today's happy truth, Princess, is that neither are any of them."

Gabriella followed the older woman's gaze, allowing it to drift over the faces of those gathered below. Some were smiling, laughing, singing. Others looked on with stern solemnity or argued amiably amongst themselves. Mothers watched their children, fathers cuffed them lightly as they ran past or held them on their shoulders, pointing up at the castle, perhaps even at Gabriella herself where she watched from high above.

"What does it mean to be a princess?" Gabriella wondered aloud, repeating her old question.

Sigrid turned and regarded her for a long moment. "From now on, whatever you do, that's what it means. For good or for ill, you are the Princess. What that means to me and Darrick and all of those below is up to you."

Gabriella accepted this with a deep sigh. She felt a strange reluctance to leave the balcony railing even though her moment was soon coming, the moment she had been waiting for much of her life. She was going to be married. In every way that mattered, she was no longer a child. She had yearned ardently for this day, had rushed impatiently through her schooling, anxious to throw off the rules and boundaries of childhood. Only now, looking over the precipice of adulthood, did she realise how secretly reassuring those boundaries had been.

Sigrid seemed to understand these things without Gabriella explaining them. They waited together under the darkening sky. Finally, Sigrid stood back and touched Gabriella's elbow. Gabriella nodded down at the celebrating crowd below her and then drew herself up and smoothed her gown. It was, of course, an extremely impressive gown, embroidered with pearls and white ribbons, shimmering with what felt like acres of heavy silk. It was beautiful, and yet, like so many other adult things, it almost seemed to be wearing her rather than the other way around. She sighed once more. Silently, she turned and followed Sigrid back into the yellow warmth of her rooms.

They passed through, out into the upper castle corridor and the main stairway. Hundreds of candles lit the way, their flames lining the walls and hanging from iron chandeliers. As the two women descended the staircase, Gabriella saw that a small, waiting crowd had gathered on the floor below. Unlike the crowd outside, however, these were nobles and ladies, resplendent in their colourful, formal best. They smiled and looked up at her, and Gabriella saw that, above their ruffed collars and tasseled shoulders, their faces were exactly the same as the ones in the square outside. Here, like there, were the regal and the rogue, valiants and villains, all mingling together and looking up at her expectantly.

Near the back of the hall, flanking the entrance to the grand ballroom, stood her father and his entourage. He wore his crown, but for once, this did not make him the centre of attention. He seemed pleased by this. Near him, looking less comfortable in his formal attire, stood Rufus Barth, the academy Battle Master, in his role as chief of security for the castle wedding. His black eyes roved endlessly over the crowd, flicking from face to face with nearly mechanical precision.

Gabriella was halfway down the curving staircase when someone called the traditional question.

"Has the young lady chosen a groom from the men of the world?" The speaker was a young man, Jakar, a former classmate and a friend of Darrick. He smiled up at her from where he stood next to his father, an archduke with a very impressive, grey moustache.

"The young lady has," Sigrid replied loudly.

Half a dozen voices picked up the traditional response. "Is he amongst us this night?"

Sigrid stopped and turned expectantly back to Gabriella, smiling and raising one eyebrow.

"He is," Gabriella answered. "He shall meet me in the ballroom, and there, we shall be wed."

A small cheer went up from the gathering of nobles and ladies, mingled with laughter and jostling as everyone turned towards the doors at the far end of the hall. The King preceded them through, and Barth moved aside, taking up his post next to the doors and making room for the throng. Gabriella could see that the grand ballroom was already quite full. Brightly coloured coats and gowns filled the space, competing with the frescoes that covered the walls and ceiling. Fire roared in the monstrous hearth that fronted the room, illuminating the small dais and altar that had been erected there. Bishop Tremaine stood before the altar in his vestments, glowing white and gold in the candlelight. Next to him, turned to face the crowd, was Darrick. Gabriella saw him, but he did not see her. He nodded and smiled as the room filled up with faces, some familiar, most not. Even now, he seemed completely at ease. It was remarkable, Gabriella thought, and not for the first time, how perfectly suited he was for the role of Viceroy and husband of the future Queen. It was as if he were made for the Kingdom, and the Kingdom did indeed seem to need him. But he belonged to her first, and this pleased her immensely.

The entrance hall's marble floor slowly emptied, and Gabriella was joined there by Rhyss and Constance, her attendants. They wore yellow silk gowns, Rhyss with understated confidence and Constance with overt delight, examining herself obsessively in the mirrors that lined the paneled walls.

"Are you ready?" Rhyss asked seriously.

Gabriella nodded. "I am. I just can't quite take it all in. Perhaps we should have gotten married in the church after all. This feels so...," she shrugged, "so *royal.*"

Constance grinned at her as if she were very silly. "You're the Princess," she whispered harshly. "Royalty is something you'd better get used to."

"It's time, girls," Sigrid ordered, joining them near the doors of the ballroom. "Constance, you first now. Stop across from Jakar. He will attend you afterwards."

Constance rolled her eyes. "Honestly, Sigrid, I've been preparing for this day longer than Bree, methinks. I know what to do." She turned back briefly and touched Gabriella's shoulder. "Bree," she said solemnly, "this is it. Your big day." She shook her head and sighed.

"Don't bollix it all up by tripping over your skirts on the way to the altar."

"Thank you, Constance," Gabriella nodded ruefully, and then embraced her friend.

"Go!" Sigrid rasped, virtually pushing Constance through the ballroom doors.

Gabriella watched as Constance entered the ballroom and started towards the altar. The throng of observers were parted to form a long aisle flanked by brass braziers and lined with a long, burgundy rug. Constance walked with great deliberation, her chin held high, the scroll of the scriptures held reverently before her. When she reached the altar, she bowed her head and handed the scroll to Bishop Tremaine, then took her place to the right. When she turned back, her face was flush with pleasure.

Rhyss leant close to Gabriella's ear. "I love you, Bree," she said in a small voice. "Remember this day forever. Long life to both of you." She gripped Gabriella's arm for a moment, nodded curtly, and then turned towards the ballroom doors. Gabriella watched nervously as her best friend began to make her way down the aisle, bearing the golden rings in a satin pouch.

Sigrid watched as well, and then a terrible expression came over her face. She turned to Gabriella and looked her quickly up and down.

"Where's your bouquet?" she demanded in a harsh whisper.

"My—" Gabriella began, and then stopped. They both knew where it was. It was lying on the bureau in her bedroom, next to the basin where she had left it.

"You didn't," Sigrid breathed.

"You should've reminded me!" Gabriella rasped, her eyes widening.

Sigrid smacked her own forehead in annoyance. "I'm not your nursemaid any more, Princess."

"I'll run back for it," Gabriella whispered, hiking up her skirts and turning back to the stairs, but Sigrid caught her by the elbow.

"You will do no such thing," she ordered. "Stay here!"

With that, the older woman rushed back towards the stairs and took them two at a time. Gabriella watched this, bemused at Sigrid's surprising speed. A moment later, she turned back to the ballroom doors. Rhyss was nearly halfway to the altar, walking slowly, her long, red hair hanging in waves down her back. Most of the crowd watched her with bright interest, but a few eyes were turned back towards the doorway, awaiting Gabriella's entrance.

It's just a bouquet, she thought to herself. *Just a bunch of silly flowers. Who needs them?* She imagined walking down the aisle empty-handed, however, and realised that it would feel extremely awkward. Frowning, she glanced back towards the stairs. Sigrid was nowhere in sight. Gabriella cast her eyes helplessly about the room, and suddenly, an idea struck her. Gathering up her skirts, she turned and dashed back across the room, heading for the main entry. Turning a corner, she entered the vestibule and saw what she was looking for. A credenza sat against the wall, dominated by a large vase of pink and yellow tulips. Gabriella lunged for the vase, jerked the bundle of flowers out of it, and violently shook the water from their stems.

She was about to return to the ballroom doors, pleased with her ingenuity, when a low sound caught her attention. There were voices muttering nearby. Gabriella heard them echoing from a corridor, and the tone of the speaker caught her interest even before the words did. She stopped and listened despite her hurry.

"It is foolish of you to be here!" the voice was saying, so low and harsh that it was almost a growl. "If you were to be seen by Percival's royal guards you would be thrown into the dungeons before you knew what hit you! Are you completely daft?"

Another voice spoke in response, low and truculent. "The guards won't matter if you do your job. Soon, the dungeons will belong to someone else, and we'll see who gets thrown into them."

Gabriella's eyes widened, and she covered her mouth with one hand. She recognised the second speaker. It was Goethe, her nemesis from the battle floor. But how could he have gained entrance to the castle? He was not on the wedding guest list of course, and all the entrances were well guarded.

"Damn you for your rash pride, boy!" Barth hissed. "You risked everything with that idiotic stunt during the battle practical, and now you dare to show your face before the wedding has even begun! Begone before I report you to the royal guard myself!"

"You would not dare," Goethe muttered darkly, but Gabriella could tell by the way he spoke that he would comply. Barth exhaled sharply.

"The guests are all gathered in the ballroom," he commanded quietly. "Go through the vestibule now, whilst the entrance hall is empty."

A dart of panic shot through Gabriella. She spun on her heels and bolted out of the vestibule, clutching the makeshift bouquet to her chest. When she got within sight of the ballroom doors, she saw that the entire crowd inside was turned back, waiting expectantly for her entrance. The eyes of some of the nearer observers widened when they saw the Princess running across the hall floor. With a force of will, Gabriella slowed, composed herself, and straightened her back. She passed through the ballroom doors with practised poise and began her journey down the long aisle.

Seeing this, the band of minstrels at the front of the room finally struck up a fanfare. Near them, the King visibly exhaled and shook his head, smiling crookedly at his approaching daughter. As usual, Darrick merely watched, his face quietly confident as she came to meet him. Rhyss's expression was mildly amused. Next to her, Constance dabbed at her eyes with a lace-fringed handkerchief.

Firelight flickered hypnotically up onto the frescoed ceiling, bringing the painted faces of long gone royalty to life. Gabriella drew a deep breath and let it out shakily, both happy and nervous in equal measures. Finally, she met Darrick in front of the altar. He looked at her appreciatively, taking in the sight of her grand dress and her unusual bouquet but resting his gaze finally on her face. His eyes sparkled in the candlelight, and she remembered that day behind the bell tower, when he had first revealed his feelings for her.

There's something about you that I cannot forget, he had said. *There's more to you than anyone else sees.* But of course, the very same had been true in reverse. She had known it almost from the first time she had met him. The reality of their relationship had confused and riled her until she had finally understood it for what it was.

I think we are made for one another. Perhaps that only happens in stories, but I don't think so...

Darrick took Gabriella's hand, and together, they turned towards Bishop Tremaine. For the moment, gratefully, she forgot all about the troubling mystery of the uninvited Goethe.

She would have plenty of time to remember it later.

CHAPTER 3

It was very late when she awoke. A thrill of fear came over her as she looked around in the darkness, momentarily forgetting where she was.

An arm, not her own, curled around her. She gasped.

"What is it?" Darrick asked sleepily.

At the sound of his voice, everything rushed back. This was the first night of her honeymoon. Darrick lay next to her, his warm body pressed against hers beneath the blankets. Gabriella felt a pang of belated anxiety about being naked with him, but it was small and perfunctory. Beneath it, she felt a deep sense of belonging and was quite certain that this was a feeling she could become very accustomed to.

"It's nothing," she said, pressing against him. "Something woke me up."

Mentally, she replayed the beginning of their first night together. To be sure, it had been somewhat awkward, and at first, she had been quite sure that he had been just as nervous as she. But then, gradually, she had ceased speaking, ceased thinking about what was happening, and given herself over to it, to him. Darrick had done the same, and in that wonderful bliss between the words, she had tasted the depths of what was to be their life together. In the end, of course, they had slept, at least until now.

"It's so hot," he said, squirming away and pushing off the covers. He plucked a robe from a nearby hook and shrugged into it. The black dragon sigil hung around his neck, catching the dim light with its glittering green eye. "The steward stoked the fire as if it was the dead of winter," he laughed, and reached for the window. "What woke you up? Do you remember?"

"It was a noise," Gabriella answered, staring into the fire. "I don't remember what—"

A knock came at their door. It was so hard and so sudden that Gabriella jumped.

Darrick still had his hand on the window knob. "What is it?" he asked loudly. Both of them knew that no one would knock on this night if it was not important.

"Sire," the muffled voice came, "there is trouble in the dungeons. A prisoner has escaped into the castle proper."

Darrick absorbed this, and his face hardened slightly. He glanced at Gabriella and said, "I will return, Bree. There must be a mistake."

With that, he strode to the chamber door, opened it just enough to frame his body, and stood there, half in and half out.

"What is the meaning of this?" he asked quietly. "Surely, you know this is the Princess's bridal chamber and our very wedding night."

"I do, sire," the guard's voice replied in a hushed tone. "But you are the ranking officer in the castle this night, save the King, and I dare not wake him on such a matter without the order of such as yourself."

Gabriella could see Darrick's face, lit in profile by the brighter light of the corridor. He looked pensive for a moment and then said, "You say there is trouble in the dungeons. How is this possible?"

"The night watch was killed, sire," the guard said, nearly whispering. "His throat was cut. By the time he was found, the prisoner had already been released. The perimeter guards report no one leaving the castle during the past three hours. We must assume that the prisoner and his rescuer are still inside. This is an immediate threat, sire. Shall I wake the King?"

Darrick did not answer immediately. He leant back and peered aside, meeting Gabriella's eyes, which were wide in the darkness.

"Yes," Darrick nodded, and then turned back to the doorway. "But allow me to do it. You gather the palace guard, those not watching the perimeter, and begin a thorough search of the castle. Begin at the top and work down. We wish to flush them away from the royal chambers, not towards them."

"Yes, sire," the guard replied quickly.

"You," Darrick said, apparently speaking to another guard in the corridor, "stay here and watch this door with your life. Do you understand?"

"No," Gabriella interrupted, throwing off the blankets and reaching for her own robe. "I'm not staying here! I'm coming with you to my father's chambers."

Darrick closed the door and came to meet her. "You know you cannot do that, Bree. Until we find the intruder and the escaped prisoner, the castle must be considered breached. The Princess and the King cannot be in the same place, lest they both be cut down by the same assassin."

"I know the protocol," she said, pulling on her robe. "But these aren't assassins. They're trapped mice who can't find an open door. I won't wait here."

Darrick put his hands on her shoulders. "You must. We cannot take the chance. The protocol is there for your safety."

"The *protocol*," Gabriella replied with low emphasis, "is why my mother died alone in her rooms."

Darrick shook his head. "If your father had been with her, he might have been killed as well."

"If my father had been *with* her," Gabriella answered, taking his hands from her shoulders and gripping them firmly, "he might have saved her *life*!"

Darrick studied her face for a long moment. Finally, he drew a deep breath and nodded once. "All right. Come with me, but remember, this is a military action, and I am commissioned officer. Until this is over, I outrank you."

"Only until I'm Queen," Gabriella answered, unable to prevent a small smile from curling her lip.

Darrick nodded again. Together, they robed. Darrick took the time to put on his sandals and strap on his sword. Gabriella tied her hair back with a length of ribbon, just to keep it out of her face. A minute later, they both left the room.

"Join your fellows," Darrick said to the older guard outside the door. "Find the intruder and the prisoner and report to me."

"Aye, sire," the guard agreed gruffly, apparently happy to join the hunt. He trotted off, his hand on the hilt of his sword.

"Stay near me," Darrick said, turning and striding swiftly down the narrow corridor. Lanterns lit the way, but the castle was still very dark at this hour. Shadowy alcoves and nooks lined the halls.

"Should we wake Rhyss and the rest of the bridal party?" Gabriella asked, keeping her voice low.

Darrick shook his head. "They are safer in their rooms. In all truth, this will probably be over in a matter of minutes. This is the best-guarded structure in all of Camelot. No one can hide within these halls for long."

"Darrick," Gabriella said suddenly, "I think I know who did this!"

Darrick stopped and looked back at her. "Who?"

"Goethe," she answered firmly. "He was here earlier. I heard him and Professor Barth in the halls right before the wedding. Barth was preparing to throw him out."

"Goethe's father," Darrick nodded in understanding. "That lying dog. Goethe took the opportunity of the wedding to sneak in with the intention of releasing his father. Why did you not tell someone?"

"Barth insisted that he leave," Gabriella said as they resumed their walk. "He was chief of security for the wedding after all. That was his job. Besides, I've been a bit busy if you had not noticed."

He glanced back at her over his shoulder, and she saw that he was smiling crookedly. "I did notice."

"That's not what I meant," she said, her cheeks reddening.

"We're here," Darrick announced as they reached the entrance to the King's chambers. "Stay here outside the door. I will wake him."

Gabriella grabbed his wrist. "I'm not waiting out here. I already told you—"

"And I told you," Darrick interrupted calmly, "that for now, I outrank you. The King will not remain in his quarters once he is roused, as you well know. It is dark inside, and unlikely as it is, there may be someone lying there in wait. Here."

He unsheathed his sword and handed it to her, hilt first.

"I can't take this," she said, shaking her head. "What if you're right and someone is hiding inside?"

"It'd be too dark for swords to be of use anyway," he answered quietly. He drew his dagger from his belt and smiled darkly. "This will do nicely. Don't worry."

She accepted his sword then and gripped the hilt expertly. "Hurry, Darrick."

"I shall, Princess," he said, and gave her a small kiss. A moment later, he opened the door of the King's outer chamber and was gone.

Gabriella listened. The castle seemed deceptively quiet at this hour. From where she stood, there was no sign whatsoever of the search that must be going on. She fiddled with the sword, certain that there was no chance she would need to use it but comforted by it nonetheless. It was too long for her, and the hilt felt unnaturally bulky. Slowly, she pressed her back against the stone wall and slid down it, crouching with the sword held upright between her knees.

A tense minute crept past, then Gabriella jumped as something tickled her neck. She scrabbled at it, nearly dropping the sword, and felt the scuttle of a spider on her hand. Fortunately, she was not afraid of spiders. The tiny arachnid crawled over her fingers and rested on the back of her hand, regarding her with its strange, alien eyes. A filament of web hung before her, nearly invisible in the darkness. She followed it and found that it seemed to connect with the falcon sigil that hung at her throat. She frowned curiously.

From some distance away, a voice spoke.

Gabriella's eyes darted around, looking for the speaker even though she could tell by the sound that they were too far away to see. It was a woman's voice, echoing indistinctly. There was a brief exclamation and then silence.

Gabriella strained her ears. After a tense moment, she shook the spider from her hand and pushed herself upright.

"Who goes there?" she asked in a hoarse whisper. There was no reply. Clutching Darrick's sword, she crept towards the nearest cross-corridor. Firelight flickered on the walls, making dancing shadows. Grim faces peered down from tapestries, watching the young woman with the gleaming, oversized sword.

Gabriella reached the intervening corridor and peered down its length. Doors lined the left wall, all of them apparently closed. On the right, deep alcoves led to recessed windows. Moonlight lay across the floor in pale stripes. Nothing moved. Slowly, Gabriella made her way down the hall, letting her gaze roam from side to side, peering into the window alcoves and doorways.

She stopped. One of the doors was not completely closed. Gabriella could see a dim bar of light from the fireplace inside. Was it Constance's room?

"Constance," Gabriella rasped, "are you all right?"

There was a scuffling sound. Gabriella startled, realising that the sound was not coming from the partially open door. It came from further down the corridor, from one of the deep window alcoves. She raised her sword and stepped forwards.

A flicker of colour appeared from inside the alcove, a flash of golden fabric. Then someone backed partially into view. It was Rhyss, still wearing her yellow bridesmaid dress.

"Rhyss!" Gabriella called, lowering her sword as relief flooded over her. "You nearly frightened me to—"

Rhyss turned her head, peering around the edge of the alcove, and the look on her face stopped Gabriella cold.

"Bree," Rhyss said faintly. "Run."

Slowly, Rhyss began to fall backwards, coming fully into view. As she did, Gabriella saw the long blade protruding from her chest, drawing out even as she fell away from it. Her blood smeared it brightly.

"*Rhyyyss!*" Gabriella screamed, lunging forwards. Darrick's sword clattered to the stone floor, dropped unthinkingly as Gabriella scrambled towards her friend, falling upon her.

"Rhyss! This can't be! What…?!" She collected the other girl in her arms, mad with shock and disbelief.

"I told you," Rhyss whispered with her dying breath, "to run."

A shadow fell over both of them, cast in the blue moonlight. Gabriella spun, thrashing about for Darrick's sword, forgetting that she had dropped it five paces away. Goethe stood behind her, his face red and strained, sweat running down his forehead in streaks. He raised the bloody sword in his hands.

"Do not scream," he said in a low growl. "Die like a princess."

Gabriella didn't hesitate. As he raised his sword to run her through, she launched herself beneath it, slamming against him. He stumbled backwards, still clinging to his sword, and struck the window. It cracked into a hundred pieces, but the iron framework miraculously held his weight. Realising the precariousness of his position, Goethe dropped his sword and scrambled for something to hold onto. Gabriella heard the sword clatter to the ground and immediately kicked it backwards. She lunged away from him then, revolted and horrified.

"How could you…," she said, her voice unnaturally high. "Rhyss…"

His eyes darted towards the sword where it lay behind her. He coiled to lunge for it, but she realised his intention. Being smaller and quicker, she leapt forwards once more, connecting with his chest and driving him backwards yet again. This time, the iron framework buckled, snapped, and exploded outwards with a ringing screech. Glass shattered away into the night, and Goethe followed it, clawing desperately at Gabriella in an attempt to take her with him. His fingers nearly captured her ponytail as it flopped over her shoulder. There was a tug, and then he was gone, dropping away into darkness.

Gabriella tottered and nearly fell after him. Her hands scrambled and clutched onto the stonework of the alcove, arresting her fall.

Weakly, she pushed back from the broken window and stumbled to the floor. She panted, staring into the gaping eye of night, shocked at the suddenness of what had transpired. Then, remembering, she turned and crawled back to her friend's body.

Rhyss lay with her feet tangled, one arm across her chest, hiding the bloody wound. Her eyes stared calmly up at the ceiling, as if lost in the deepest of thoughts.

"Oh, Rhyss," Gabriella sobbed, laying her cheek on the girl's breast. "Oh my dear Rhyss, no... no..."

She was still sobbing, cradling the girl's dead body, when, minutes later, Darrick and the palace guard found her.

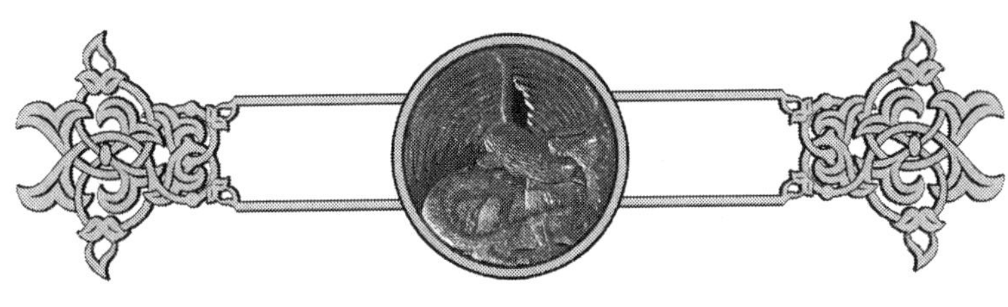

"It was the Battle Master," Thomas said, examining a broken vase with the toe of his boot. "He let the murderer in. He was in league with the villains. Wasn't he?"

Yazim nodded as he walked into the gloom of the castle ruin. Sunlight speared through the shattered remains, making hard beams in the darkness. "They say that he held a grudge against the King for the loss of his wife and child years earlier. A plague had spread through the city, and Barth had been refused succour within the walls of the castle. The King's guard had declared that the woman and boy were already infected and would compromise the castle quarantine. They died of course, although the stories say that Barth swore that they had not been sick when he came to the castle. Perhaps he was even right."

Together, the two men picked their way into a grand room. Its ceilings and walls were mostly intact, although a large section had caved in over the hearth, burying its once impressive façade. The ghosts of ancient frescoes showed on the walls and ceilings, faded and cracked nearly to obscurity. Rubble and grit covered what remained of the marble floor. Many of the blocks had been pried up and carted away, probably decades earlier.

Thomas reached the centre of the ballroom and turned on the spot, trying to imagine the space as it might once have looked. "The prisoner, the father of the boy Gabriella killed, what became of him?"

"Escaped," Yazim replied, hunkering down near the rubble of the collapsed ceiling. "His intention was to murder the King in his bed whilst his son guarded their escape. With the death of the boy, however, the plan was ruined. The father fled, taking the life of another guard whilst gaining his exit. The Princess's new husband led the search for him that night, canvassing the sleeping city, but to no avail."

"And all of this," Thomas said, rejoining his friend in the decrepit darkness, "at the order and command of the brute, Merodach himself. Yes?"

"This was the spearhead of his final plan," Yazim nodded. "Merodach did not expect the prisoner to succeed in killing the King or even to escape. The farce was meant only to make a point, and the point was very simple: 'I can get to you, O King. Trust no one. My people are everywhere.'"

Thomas asked, "Did the King understand this?"

Yazim remained hunkered near the pile of rubble. He reached and plucked an object from the debris. It was a bit of broken plaster, still coloured with the remains of its ancient fresco. The image showed part of a face, with one stern blue eye peering out, patient and grim. "Yes, the King understood Merodach's point very clearly. They hanged the man, Barth, and he went to his demise willingly. The King intended to send his own message, that traitors would be dealt with severely, but by then, it was too late. The flames of doubt and fear had already been lit and were spreading swiftly."

Thomas shook his head. "Surely, he did not merely sit idly by and allow the villain to wrest control of Camelot from him?"

"No, he did not," Yazim admitted. "King Xavier launched an attack, intending to finally rout out the beast and his rogue armies. It was a daunting task, and one that many said was doomed to fail. It was, as they say, too little and too late. But the King refused to believe all was lost. The attempt on his life had been thwarted after all. He was still the ruler of the grandest kingdom on the earth. He believed, to his great shame, that no force mounted against Camelot could ever succeed."

Slowly, Yazim stood again. He dropped the bit of painted plaster, and it broke at his feet. "If he had only acted sooner," he said quietly, "that might even have been true."

It took nearly four months for the King's forces to amass and prepare the rout of Merodach's rogue armies. By the time Darrick and High Constable Ulric were ready to disembark, summer was in high bloom. Outside the city gates, heat shimmers arose from the grand thoroughfare as the Army assembled, camping on the grassy hills and beneath the trees that lined the great road's walls. To Gabriella, the line of tents seemed to stretch off towards the horizon in nearly infinite numbers, and yet she knew that the sight was deceiving. It was a relatively small militia disguised as a larger one, embellished with full armour, archers, trebuchets, and even a pair of enormous ballistas—monstrous crossbows mounted on carts, bristling with twelve-foot, iron-tipped spears.

Gabriella walked along the thoroughfare with her father and Sir Ulric as they inspected the troops.

"Are the trebuchets and siege engines truly necessary?" the King asked, shading his eyes with the flat of his hand. "After all, they will be Camelot's own fortresses upon which you will be descending."

"Camelot's fortresses which have fallen into the hand of your enemies, sire," Ulric replied gruffly. He was a barrel of a man with a shock of red hair, pork-chop sideburns, and a matching pointed goatee. His short leather cape flapped in the hot breeze. "The war machines are a show of force if nothing else. It is essential to let the brutes see the might of the Army they have chosen to oppose. Our magical arsenal includes Whisperwind bellows, Scattershot flares, and twelve score lightning arrows. I expect that many of them will turn and flee, tails between their legs, the moment they witness our approach."

Gabriella asked, "How many trebuchets does this leave to defend the city walls?"

"Four, Your Highness," Ulric answered stiffly, not meeting her eyes. "But it is of no consequence. These six will be returned under my command before the first snow of winter."

"What if Merodach and his forces attack us before your return?" Gabriella pressed evenly.

"I assure you, Princess," Ulric said, changing his tone to one of indulgent condescension. "*Whoever* is in charge of this rogue band of villains, they will be far too busy fleeing the Royal Army to mount any attack here at the city walls."

"I appreciate your confidence, Sir Ulric," Gabriella commented, meeting the large man's eyes, "but what if you are wrong?"

There was a short, awkward silence, and then the King spoke, "Sir Ulric is High Constable and our chief strategic adviser, my dear. He has our complete trust in such matters. Tell me, Constable: how long will it take you and your men to reach the rogue encampments?"

Ulric nodded and resumed his walk along the thoroughfare. "Two months, sire. We have mapped a route that takes us around the western edge of the Tempest Barrens, meeting the enemy before they can force their way into the more populated villages at Broadmoor Valley. There, we shall descend upon the hills and rout the villains into the open, camp by camp if necessary."

"And what if Broadmoor Valley is not in fact the destination of this 'rogue band', Constable?" Gabriella asked pointedly. "What if their intention is to cut straight across the Tempest Barrens, driving directly into the heart of Camelot?"

Ulric glanced back at Gabriella, his face tense with annoyance. Quickly, however, he covered this with a show of patient amusement. "My dear Princess, what a delightful imagination you do have."

"The Barrens are not a place through which any sane general would lead his troops, Gabriella," the King explained pedantically. "They are, as the name suggests, a desolate wilderness, treacherous, haunted by horrors and divided by the Cragrack Cliffs. Surely, you have heard the history of the Tempest Barrens from Professor Toph. Centuries ago, wizarding armies warred there, decimating the land with their black magic for miles in every direction. For that reason, the Barrens form a protection against any attack from the north."

Gabriella had heard the histories. She nodded, tight-lipped, unconvinced but disinclined to argue with her father.

"I assure you, Your Highnesses," Ulric went on confidently, "upon our return, not six months hence, we will declare the complete victory of your sovereign forces over the scourge of this rabble of malcontents. Fear not, either of you."

Satisfied, both the King and Sir Ulric turned and began to walk back towards the open city gates. After a minute, still frowning dourly, Gabriella followed them.

"I do not trust Ulric's plans," she said later that evening, speaking to Darrick under the shelter of his father's blacksmith shop. Outside, the sky was a bruised purple, full of switching wind and heat lightning, hinting at a midnight storm. "And frankly, I do not trust *him*. He's arrogant. He does not take the threat seriously."

Darrick sighed harshly, leant his hammer against the anvil, and ran a bare arm across his forehead. His features were lit by the orange light of the forge. "Everyone knows what we are facing," he said wearily. "Ulric's plans are solid. For the Lord's sake, Bree, they're my plans as well. I helped draw them up."

Gabriella heard him but only shook her head, staring into the glare of the furnace. "I do not like it. I sense that this is a grave error."

"I understand your worries," Darrick said, hefting the hammer again and laying a fresh sword across the anvil. With careful precision, he struck the glowing red metal, shaping it and sending up bursts of sparks. He didn't need to smith his own swords, of course, but insisted upon it, claiming that there was no better or more loyal weapon than one forged with one's own hands. Gabriella, of course, found this habit both silly and endearing. Darrick examined the line of the sword critically and then turned and dipped it into a barrel of water. It hissed as steam poured into the air. "It's natural to feel nervous before a campaign," he soothed, swiping an arm across his brow. "But I will be there, Bree. I will fight to keep Camelot safe."

"That's what I mean, Darrick," Gabriella said, slipping off the worktable and approaching him. "It feels all wrong *because* you are going to be there. You should not go. I need you here." She glanced out the front of the shop towards the guards that waited in the gathering dark and then lowered her voice. "*We* need you here," she whispered, taking his hand and pressing it to her belly. "I fear for you not only as my husband, but as the father of your baby. What if something goes wrong?"

"It won't go wrong," Darrick began, reaching to embrace her, but she pushed him away.

"What if it does?" she demanded hoarsely, peering up into his face. "You cannot *know*! How can you be so certain?"

Darrick looked at her, his face sweaty and tense in the furnace's red glow but his eyes softening. He smiled at her. "I know because of this, Bree," he said, moving his hand from her belly to the swell of her breast, covering her heart. The confidence in his voice both relieved and maddened her. "I know because of what we have right here, dear one. You feel it, do you not? Death has no power over that which we share. Wars are fought with brute instruments," he nodded towards the sword that still steamed in the water barrel. "Metal and blade, shields and armour, none of those things can stand against the world-changing weight of true love. What we have, wife, no sword can pierce."

Gabriella shook her head again slowly. "Poppycock and codswallop," she whispered.

His smile broadened, and his eyes twinkled. "That's your father talking," he chided. "Not you. You know the truth of my words."

She studied his face intently for a long moment and then broke away from his gaze. "No," she declared quietly. "No. I do not know what you know. I only know that I do love you. I do need you. And that if you go on this journey and some villain puts a sword between your ribs—"

"Rhyss was unarmed," Darrick interrupted, raising his chin. The mention of Rhyss's name was like a dark shiver in the air. "The beast struck her down in cold blood. She was defenceless. *I* shall not be. I shall be prepared to meet the enemy on my terms. And when I do, I shall visit my vengeance upon him. For both of us."

"Goethe is dead!" Gabriella cried, turning on her husband. "Whatever vengeance there was to be had, it is already satisfied! Rhyss is still *gone*! And so might *you* be!" Her voice splintered on the last words. Darrick moved to her and caught her into his arms. She resisted, but only for a moment. He held her in the hot darkness of the shop, one hand clutched to the back of her head, pressing her to him. Finally, she shuddered and relaxed against him, annoyed to feel tears wetting her cheeks and soaking into his tunic.

"Gabriella," he said softly, "I *must* go on this journey. I must do my part, not only for the Kingdom, but for myself. You know this. I cannot allow Rhyss's death to go unpunished. The powers that caused it must pay, blood for blood."

He released her but gripped her shoulders gently. She looked up at him so that their noses touched. He drew a breath and went on. "Tomorrow morning, I shall take my leave and go to perform this duty of high honour. But Bree, I promise you this with all that I am… *this* is where my heart is. With you and with the baby in your womb. No matter what, I *will* return to you."

Gabriella looked up at him, her brow still knitted with worry. As she looked, however, her brow smoothed. The future was inevitable. He would go. And then, if his promise was true, he would return to her. There was nothing more she could do.

Nothing more except believe him.

The army marched at dawn. It was a pearly grey morning, mostly obscured by a caul of low clouds. There was rain, but it was misty and sparse, beading greasily on the soldiers' helmets. Sir Ulric led the march on his black horse. Darrick followed in the rear, riding his own mount. He turned back to Gabriella as the last of the soldiers rounded the bend of the thoroughfare, some half mile distant. Darrick was barely a silhouette against the fog, but she could easily recognise him by his stance in the saddle and the lift of his chin. He raised his arm once, palm out, bidding a silent farewell. She did the same in response, hoping he could see her where she stood by the city gates under the gloom of a canvas awning.

He lowered his arm slowly and seemed to watch her through the misty distance. Finally, as the tips of the armies' pikes and the dull gleam of their helmets disappeared around the bend and over the hill, Darrick turned. He urged his mount forwards. A moment later, he was gone as well.

Gabriella stood under the awning and watched the empty thoroughfare. Puddles made dull mirrors of the sky. All around was the drab patter of rain dripping from the trees. Eventually, Sigrid stepped forwards and peered up at the sky, squinting.

"You'll catch your death out here, Princess," she said stoically. "Your guards will stand here with you all the day long, but I for one suggest we head back to the warmth of the castle. I expect some hot tea is in order, would you not agree?"

Gabriella didn't move. She stared at the distant place where the thoroughfare bent around a thick stand of trees. It was hard to imagine that the Army had ever been there at all.

"*Come*, love," Sigrid said, putting an arm around Gabriella's waist. "They are gone now, but they will return. For now, your baby needs you to eat. Come."

Gabriella drew a deep breath and nodded. She turned away from the thoroughfare.

As she climbed into the waiting carriage with Sigrid right behind her, she unconsciously reached up and wrapped her hand around the falcon sigil where it hung beneath her cloak. It was warm.

Please, she prayed, silently and solemnly, not even sure who she was praying to anymore, *watch over him. Let him be all right.*

The carriage jerked as it began its return to the castle. Gabriella stared unseeingly through the rain-streaked windows. *Let him keep his promise to me,* she prayed fiercely, challengingly. *Don't you dare… don't you* dare… *make him a liar.*

The summer months crept past with infuriating slowness. It was an unbearably hot year, reducing the valley brook to a mere muddy trickle and leaving the air still and dense even at midnight. Gabriella busied herself as well as she could with learning the intricacies of imperial government as well as managing the constant business of being pregnant. She found herself unaccountably weary by most afternoons, but retiring to her chambers was rarely any help. The upper rooms of the castle were the hottest of all, with barely a breath of breeze to disturb the bed curtains. Most days, she lay awake during these respites, stripped to her dressing gown and lying with one hand on the increasing swell of her belly, the other behind her head. She would stare through the linens at the afternoon sunlight and think of Darrick.

Sometimes, she would pray for him. Other times, she was afraid to, as if the very act of mentioning him might remind God of him with fearful results. After all, awful things happened to people every day, apparently with divine permission. According to the scriptures, God had seen fit to sacrifice His own perfect son for the good of fallen mankind, had He not? What would one small soldier mean to Him for the sake of Camelot? She knew her fear was not precisely pious—Bishop Tremaine would surely rebuke her for doubting God the Father's will—but this realisation did not change her fears. Battle Master Barth had been as stout a believer as anyone, and he had still seen his wife and child taken from him, sacrificed to the plague some years earlier. If anything or anyone could be blamed for the death of Rhyss, it might as well be the deadly plague that eventually led Barth to his traitorous enmity. Or even the God that allowed such plagues to happen.

"Do not make him a liar," she would pray on those hot afternoons, muttering quietly on her bed. It was as much a threat as a request. "He's mine. You gave him to me. He promised he would return to me. And I believed him… I believed…"

There was never any answer on those quiet, hot afternoons, but that was all right. In the stillness of her own heart, she feared any answer that might come. Silence was better. She stroked the bulge of her belly, felt the baby growing there. Darrick's baby.

"A boy, methinks," Sigrid said one evening in the castle rose gardens as Gabriella and she walked. The roses were small and listless.

Drifts of wilted petals lined the path. "You should choose a name from the royal lineage."

"I shall upon Darrick's returning."

"The baby will be born before the Army's scheduled return, Princess," Sigrid insisted mildly. "Do you wish for the poor boy to go nameless during the intervening days?"

"I will not name him without Darrick," Gabriella repeated stubbornly. "The baby may even wait until his father's return. Sometimes, births are later than what the doctors say."

Sigrid nodded equably. "It is possible, love. If it were me, I would not count on such things."

"It is not you, Sigrid," Gabriella stated flatly. "Your childbearing days are past you. This one is mine, and I will choose to wait."

She instantly regretted her words. She was worried and angry, tired and uncomfortable, but that did not give her permission to speak harshly to the woman who had practically raised her.

"I'm sorry, Sigrid," she said, stopping and turning to the older woman. "That was callous of me. Please forgive me."

Sigrid merely nodded. After a moment, she smiled, and Gabriella thought that there was a hint of sadness in it. Sigrid had no children of her own, after all. They resumed their walk.

There were no more words on the subject that evening.

As the summer months unwound and began their descent into fall, the swell of Gabriella's belly became hard and pronounced. The baby inside moved sometimes, both delighting and endearing himself to his mother. She read stories to him when he was most active, stroked the shape of him beneath her skin when he was still. She was not surprised that she had come to think of him as a boy based solely on Sigrid's assurance. Sigrid was rarely wrong about such things. Gabriella had long wondered if there was some faint witchiness hidden in the woman's blood. Such things happened of course. Witches and wizards were sometimes born spontaneously in the non-magical kingdoms. Toph had said so himself. Often, such people spent their whole lives ignorant of their abilities, experiencing only the vaguest magical expressions—an ability to divine the tea leaves, or to find water under barren land, or to predict sudden storms and spring floods. It was exceedingly rare, of course, and even more mysteriously subjective, but if anyone had the hint of witchiness in her, it was Sigrid.

Thus, Gabriella believed her when she proclaimed the unborn baby a boy. She had even, despite her stubborn refusal to do so, begun to consider names for him. She was helpless not to. There were plenty of royal names to choose from, and she systematically tried them on her baby, testing them to see how they might fit him. None of them felt precisely right, not even in her mind, but she knew that she would find the perfect one when the time came.

Darrick would help her.

As autumn began to creep over the land and the time of the Army's scheduled return grew nearer, Gabriella tried to stay away from the academy cathedral. It was difficult. She allowed herself one visit per week, and she always pretended to herself that she was there on some unrelated errand—carrying a message to Professor Toph or inspecting the new students—but no one doubted her real reasons for visiting.

The candle gallery was eternally quiet, filled with the busy flicker of the thousands of tiny flames. Her own candle burnt brightly, its fire leaping up nearly twice as high as those around it. It was the baby inside her of course, adding his own heat to the flame of her candle. Soon enough, he would be born, and his glow would separate from hers, awaiting the day when he would light his own candle. It was a solemn thrill to see her own flame burning with that strange double light, but this was not the real reason she visited the candle gallery. After observing her own flame and that of her family (including the cold, dark candle of her long dead mother), she would walk along the aisle until she came to Darrick's family vault.

His candle was there, flickering brightly every time, and each time she saw it, she exhaled a pent breath, flush with relief. *Of course, Bree,* his voice would seem to say in her head, full of smiling confidence. *Like I told you, this is where my heart is. With you and with the baby in your womb…*

A week before her baby was born, as the heat of summer finally broke over the land and leaves dropped from the trees, as if exhausted, Gabriella left the academy cathedral via the rear entrance and found herself drawn to the cemetery.

Rhyss's grave was bright with sunlight, carpeted with leaves so that the fresh dirt was gratefully hidden. Her headstone was a simple obelisk, carved only with her name and a single short phrase: "aged eighteen years".

"I wish you were here, Rhyss," Gabriella said quietly. The wind gusted, rattling the dead leaves and batting her words away. She sighed. "I'm lonely. I rarely see Constance any more now that school is done and I've married. Besides, it was always you who… who…"

She stopped, unsure how to finish the statement. The words eluded her. Rhyss would have known somehow, even without any explanation. Perhaps that was what Gabriella missed the most, that bosom friendship that seemed to go beyond words and reason. She remembered the night of Rhyss's death, remembered first thinking that it had been Constance who had arisen from her bedchamber and discovered the lurking Goethe. Sometimes (though she hated herself for it), she wished she had been right.

"Rhyss," she said, looking up at the hard autumn sky. "Rhyss, it all seems so empty without you, especially with Darrick away. No matter what was happening, you were always so funny. So amused. It was almost as if you were immune to it all. I need some of that now. I hate that you had to go away. I hate… I hate that they took you…"

Tears welled in her eyes, blurring the sky and the cemetery all around. As always, Gabriella resented the tears. She swiped at them and felt that familiar blend of misery and anger spreading inside her. She glanced around the graveyard, her face settling into a hard frown, and spied something leaning against a nearby tree: a rusty spade, its wooden handle worn smooth with use. She set off towards it, first at a stroll, shaking her head, and then falling into a resolute stride. She snatched up the spade as she passed the tree and quickened her pace, heading towards the rear of the cemetery, the part beyond the hallowed earth of the cathedral.

"You bastard," she seethed through gritted teeth, tears still trembling in her eyes. "Why? How could you do such a thing?"

She reached the nearest of the apostate graves. It was still fresh, partly covered with its own scatter of dead leaves. There was no headstone, no way to know if it was the grave of Barth or Goethe. It made no difference. She hefted the spade over her head like an axe and brought it down as hard as she could, pounding the fresh dirt hard enough to make the handle vibrate painfully in her fists.

"You hideous *bastard*!" she shouted, giving vent to her rage. Tears ran down her face, hot in the cooling breeze. "You horrible, hateful blot of human rubbish! I hate you! Death is too good for you! Come back so I can kill you all over again! You took her from me! She was a hundred times better than you, a thousand times more beautiful than any cur like you could ever know, and you took her *away*! You murdered her, you beast! *You murdered her!*"

She beat the dirt of the grave over and over again as she shouted. The carpet of dead leaves scattered beneath the onslaught. The spade scarred and tore at the earth as Gabriella swung it. Finally, exhausted and sweating, she dropped the spade and fell to her hands and knees, panting, her face wet with tears. The baby fluttered inside her, as if alarmed at the rush of emotion and activity.

"You took her from me," she breathed harshly. The strength fled her, and she fell back onto her haunches, cradling her face in her hands. She sobbed, suddenly and deeply, because she realised that she was not, in fact, talking about Rhyss. The death of her best friend was merely the catalyst, opening a much older, much more deeply buried lament of loss.

The tears racked her body, and this time, she let them come. She wailed to herself helplessly, like a baby. Finally, after several minutes, she pushed herself upright. Feeling hollow and washed out, she looked back over the cemetery, towards the larger gravestones that lined the front.

"She was my mother...," she said weakly, speaking no longer to the unmarked graves and rustling dead leaves, speaking in a voice that only she and God could hear. "She was my mother... and You took her from me."

CHAPTER 4

Gabriella had fully expected the baby to wait until his father's return. There was no rationale for it apart from a deep hope and a sense of the way things ought to be. Unfortunately, as she was quickly learning, life rarely corresponded to what was expected from it.

She began feeling the unmistakable signs of labour at breakfast a week before the Army's predicted return. The pangs were faint but regular. When Sigrid suggested she retire to the chamber designated as the lying-in room, located conveniently on the main floor, Gabriella declined.

"It's nothing," she announced, pushing herself out of her chair. "The midwife predicted there might be false signs that the baby was ready. Come, let us take our walk as usual."

Sigrid agreed but kept a sharp eye on Gabriella. They had barely entered the covered bridge that led into the rose garden when the first hard spasm struck. Gabriella bent forwards and clutched the bridge railing, pressing a hand to her belly.

"Princess," Sigrid said, grabbing her elbow, "it is time."

"It's not," Gabriella insisted faintly, still bent over. "It cannot be."

"It certainly can. Guard! Help Her Highness back to the castle. Quickly."

Gabriella felt practically carried along, supported on one side by Sigrid, on the other by Treynor, the guard who had been accompanying her since she'd been a child. His short beard bristled as he frowned, full of solemn purpose.

"One would think, Treynor," Gabriella commented between spasms, "that it was your own daughter preparing to give birth."

Treynor glanced at her as they whisked her into the castle, his face etched with concern and surprise. "You are the Princess, Your Highness," he answered seriously. "You are the Kingdom's daughter."

The lying-in room was a spacious bed chamber near the entrance hall. A fire burnt in the hearth despite the morning's warmth. The midwife, a woman named Alianor, was already there, her forearms bare and scrubbed in preparation. She met Gabriella at the door, apparently already aware of her state.

"Leave her," she said to Treynor. "Have Daphne bring us a pot of water from the kitchens. Sigrid, place it on the fire when it arrives."

Gently, Alianor led Gabriella to the bed, which was luxuriously made with the best linens and a carefully arranged stack of down pillows.

"Up you go," she instructed Gabriella, helping her onto the wooden steps next to the bed as if she were a young child. "You just settle yourself right there on the bed, that's a lass. How much time between birth pains?" This last, she addressed to Sigrid.

"Twenty breaths. Perhaps a bit more," Sigrid replied, rolling up her own sleeves. "Coming quicker each time."

The two women moved busily about the bed, adjusting the coverlet and pillows and arranging Gabriella into the proper position.

"It's too early," Gabriella said, shaking her head. "He cannot come so soon."

"That decision is between God and your baby, dear," Alianor replied. "All we can do is play along. Ready?"

Gabriella frowned. Her face was already glistening with the heat of the room and the exertion of the spasms. "Ready for what?"

"Why, to push, my dear. Your time of breeding is nearly done. The baby will soon enter the world."

Gabriella shook her head again and opened her mouth to protest, but another birth pain struck, tensing her belly and drawing her chin towards her knees.

"Unngh!" she groaned helplessly. "It hurts!"

"Of course it does, Princess," Sigrid smiled, suddenly beside her and taking her hand. "Nothing good comes without pain. But you can withstand it. It is what mothers do."

Gabriella nodded, realising there was no way to stop what was happening. The spasms came quicker, harder.

"Push, Princess! Push!" Alianor commanded, preparing to receive the baby when it came.

Gabriella pushed. Sweat sprang out on her brow and trickled into her eyes. The pain was monumental, dampened only by the knowledge that it would all be over soon, in the next few minutes, one way or another.

"Something is wrong," Sigrid said softly, almost to herself. She let go of Gabriella's hand as the young woman flopped back against her pillows, panting in the respite between birth pains. Sigrid moved next to Alianor.

"What is it?" she asked in a low voice.

Alianor touched Gabriella's belly, felt it with her palms. "Breech perhaps," she answered quickly. "More likely the cord is wrapped around the child."

"What's wrong?" Gabriella breathed, barely hearing. "What's happening with my baby?"

"Hush, child," Alianor instructed. "Don't you worry."

With that, she pushed on the side of Gabriella's distended belly, using both hands, as if attempting to shift the baby inside by brute force. Gabriella let out a cry of alarm.

"He's moving!" she exclaimed fearfully. "You're making him move! What's wrong?"

Alianor shook her head. She, too, was sweating. Curls of hair had come loose from her bonnet and stuck to her forehead.

Gabriella lunged forwards again as another spasm took hold of her.

"Push now, daughter," Alianor said hoarsely. "Push as hard as you can."

The world went grey around Gabriella as she tensed every muscle in her body. She clenched both her eyes and her teeth. The tension gripped her belly for what seemed an eternity, and then, finally, it faded.

"The baby wants to come," Alianor said, arming sweat from her brow. "Something is keeping it. There's nothing we can do now but pray and hope."

"You hope," Sigrid answered, moving to the window. In one swift motion, she stripped the curtains back, letting in the breeze and the morning sunlight. "Daphne, open those cupboards by the door. And the drawers of the wardrobe."

Daphne moved quickly, apparently glad of something to do. "What are we looking for, Miss?"

"We're not looking for anything," Sigrid answered evenly. "Just open them. Open everything you can find. Treynor!"

The door cracked ajar immediately. "Yes, Sigrid?" the man answered from without.

"Send a guard out to the courtyard. Instruct him to fire a single red-feathered arrow into the air."

To his credit, Treynor did not question this order. "One arrow only?"

"Yes. Just make sure he does not accidentally kill any of the stable boys. We do not wish to end one life in the hopes of beginning another."

The door clunked shut. An instant later, Treynor's muffled voice could be heard relaying the order.

"Now," Sigrid said, returning to Gabriella's side, "we have done everything we can do. The symbols are in order. The prayers have been said. The rest, Princess, is up to you. Bear your boy child so that his face may greet your husband upon his returning."

Gabriella nodded weakly. A minute of calm passed. Then the next birth pain began to coil within her, spreading its tentacles around her belly and grabbing hold of her spine. It struck. She pushed.

"He comes!" Sigrid cried out, squeezing Gabriella's hand. "Do not stop now! Your baby comes!"

Gabriella felt it. She let out a low wail of exertion and pain. Alianor moved industriously. Finally, after what seemed to be hours, there came a flood of blissful relief, a relaxation that was nearly heaven. And then, out of the hot silence, a tiny voice cried out.

"Your child is indeed a boy," Alianor announced, her own face flush with relief. She cleaned him quickly and gently with Daphne's help and wrapped him in fresh linen.

Gabriella held her hands out, weak and exhausted, shaking with spent energy. "Give him to me," she said.

Alianor laid the child in his mother's arms. He cried for a moment, blinking in awe at the suddenly huge world that surrounded him. Gabriella smiled helplessly at him as she cradled him.

"He's beautiful," Sigrid announced, laying her hand gently over the boy's brow. "Well done, Gabriella. Well done to both of you."

Alianor mopped her forehead with a cloth and sighed happily. "What is his name, Your Highness?"

Gabriella glanced up at the midwife thoughtfully and then looked down at her son. He stopped crying as his cheek pressed against her chest, as if he was listening. Of course he was. He'd been hearing her heart beating for the past nine months. It was the most comforting sound in the world to him.

"I don't know," she said, and laughed wearily. "I had not decided. It is not a mother's decision alone. His father will help."

Sigrid accepted this patiently. "What shall we call him until then?"

Gabriella smiled at her baby. "Call him what he is," she answered. "Call him... the Little Prince."

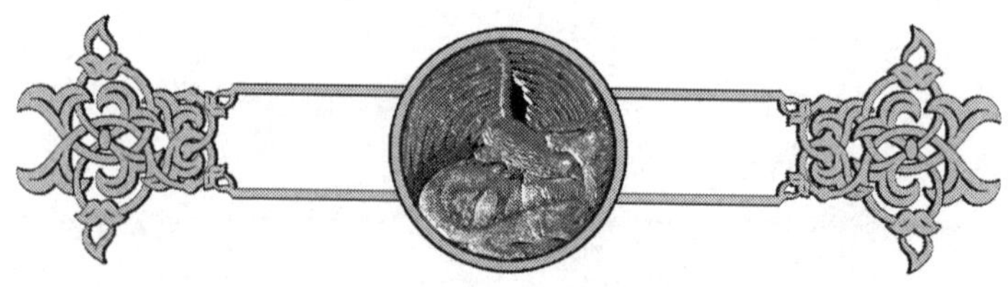

"And so," Bishop Tremaine said later that night, his voice echoing in the expanse of the academy cathedral, "we thank You, our Heavenly Father, for the gift of this new life. Even in the midst of our earthly travails, You provide us the proof of Your everlasting promise through rebirth."

Gabriella cradled the baby in her arms where she stood before the bishop. The Little Prince was asleep, his lips pressed together in a solemn, little bow. She turned back and smiled at her father, who sat on his throne in the front row. He nodded at her, his eyes twinkling, obviously anxious to hold his grandchild again as soon as the ceremony was over. Behind him, a rather surprising amount of people had gathered, forming a reassuring mix of nobles and peasants. They smiled in the dimness, lit only by the rosy light of the sunset, tinted by the stained-glass windows.

"I am somewhat challenged by this christening ceremony," Tremaine commented wryly, changing his tone of voice, "since a christening ceremony usually requires a name to christen with."

There was a murmur of congenial laughter. Tremaine beamed indulgently at Gabriella and then touched her baby lightly on the foot.

"But God our Father does not need us to tell Him the name of this young Prince. As the scriptures proclaim, our Lord has knitted this child even whilst he was still in his mother's womb. His name is already well-known to the hosts of heaven, as are the number of his days and the course of his entire life."

Gabriella hugged her baby gently, thrilled with the warmth of his small weight and the slow, metronomic rise and fall of his chest. Someone sniffed behind her. She wasn't certain, but she thought it was Professor Toph.

"And thus, we christen this young Prince with the name his parents will soon choose for him," Tremaine went on. "The name that God Almighty has already writ upon his tiny beating heart. May he live long, bear much fruit, and surpass us all in wisdom, stature, and nobility. Amen."

The crowd responded in unison, echoing the bishop's final word.

The front doors of the cathedral were thrown open, letting in the evening breeze and the burnished light of the sunset. Outside, the bells of the tower began to toll, ringing stridently in the clear air. The noise woke the baby, who stirred, stretched out his little fists, and began to cry.

"Allow me, daughter," the King said, approaching her as the crowd broke apart. "It seems only yesterday that I was calming your infant cries. Let us see if I still know the way."

Gabriella reluctantly turned her son over to her father and then smiled at the sight of the two of them. All around was the sound of chattering voices, laughter, and shuffling feet as the throng milled towards the wide open doors. Over it all, the bells continued to toll, operated enthusiastically by a pair of young altar boys at the bell pulls.

"The Little Prince," the King said, tickling the boy beneath his chin. The baby glared up at him solemnly and blew a bubble between his lips. "Name him soon, Gabriella, lest the moniker stick to him for life."

"We will, Father," she promised, accompanying him into the twilight near the doors. A thought struck her, and she touched his elbow. "Wait for me outside. I've left my cloak at the altar."

The King nodded, barely listening as he peered happily into the face of his grandson.

Lightly (much lighter than she could have earlier that morning), Gabriella strode through the emptying cathedral, approaching the altar. Her cloak, looking red as blood in the dimness, lay over the altar, exactly where she had left it. She scooped it up, turned back towards the entrance, and then stopped.

The last bell tolled, leaving only its echo to roll across the valley into silence. With it, the thrum of voices finally drained out of the cathedral. Near the entrance, standing just outside, were Sigrid and Treynor, talking quietly in the coppery light. Gabriella drew a deep breath and let it out slowly, enjoying, for the moment, the unusual sense of being alone.

She turned around again and rested her hands upon the altar. The light of the central stained-glass window coloured her features as she stared up at it. On it, King Arthur knelt nobly at the feet of Jesus, who stood in radiant glory with his hands spread, showing the ruby red of his nail wounds.

"Thank You, Lord, for my boy," she prayed, merely mouthing the words. Her relationship with God, as evidenced by her tantrum in the graveyard only a few days earlier, was far from perfect. He still frightened her nearly as much as He comforted her. But for now, she was grateful, and she felt she should express it. "Thank You... thank You for my Little Prince."

The cathedral was thick with silence, alive only with the subtle flicker of the candles in the gallery of vaults.

Gabriella looked at them for a long moment. Slowly, a thoughtful frown deepened her features.

She left her cloak, rounded the altar carefully without taking her eyes from the candle gallery, and climbed onto the dais. Her movement was slow and deliberate, diminishing, so that she stopped some feet away from one of the alcoves. She stared into its gently glimmering light, her frown deepening, her brow furrowing in silent disbelief.

Finally, she crept closer, almost as if she were in a dream. She placed her hands on the railing that lined the vault.

"No." She said the word calmly, just above a whisper.

Before her, surrounded by the dancing lights of all the other candles, Darrick's candle stood cold, its wick burnt black but utterly, finally, dark.

"The candles are only symbols, Gabriella," Sigrid assured her that night. "An errant breath of wind might blow one out, or a drop of water from a leak in the cathedral roof might accidentally extinguish it."

"I sensed it even before he left, Sigrid," Gabriella whispered, laying her son in his crib. "This mission was doomed. Darrick's involvement was a terrible mistake. I should have ordered him to stay."

"You couldn't have even if you'd tried," Sigrid admonished, leading Gabriella out of the dark nursery and easing the door shut. "You are not yet Queen. The King's commission supersedes all." She turned to Gabriella and softened her expression. "You cannot give up hope, Princess. Your husband will return along with the Army and Sir Ulric. For all we know, they are nearly here, even this very night. How foolish will you feel when he greets you again, you who were convinced that his soul had already departed?"

The older woman made to touch Gabriella's shoulder, but Gabriella turned away. She crossed the room to the window. Deep blue night pressed against the glass.

"I fear you are wrong, Sigrid, and that you yourself know it. His candle was burnt out. Just like my mother's."

"They are *symbols*, Gabriella," Sigrid insisted, still standing near the nursery door. "We light them upon our graduation into adulthood. We extinguish them when those that we love die. They are not any more magical than we are, despite what Professor Toph might say."

Gabriella stared through her own reflection on the window glass. Her eyes were swollen and tinged with red. She shifted her gaze to the reflection of Sigrid behind her.

"On the night my mother died," she said softly, "my father sent you to extinguish her candle. He told me so himself. You have spoken of it as well."

Sigrid nodded. "Yes. It was my duty, not only to the dead Queen, but to the Kingdom. It was the first announcement of her murder to the people."

Gabriella turned and met Sigrid's eyes. Sigrid looked back at her, her expression tense and waiting, almost wary.

"Tell me, Sigrid," Gabriella asked quietly, studying her nurse's face, "*did* you extinguish the candle? Or was it already cold when you arrived there that night?"

There was a long pause. Sigrid's expression did not change. Finally, she drew a breath and answered slowly, "I extinguished it. I pinched the flame with my own two fingers. I still remember the heat of it. I wept, Princess, as the smoke arose from your mother's candle for the last and faded away."

Gabriella continued to stare at Sigrid's face, seeking any sign of falsehood. After a moment, she turned back to the window. She drew a deep breath, and it hitched in her chest.

"Dear one," Sigrid said, approaching her now and taking her by the shoulders. Gabriella submitted this time and allowed her old nurse to gather her into a matronly embrace. "Don't fret. Don't fear. Pray.

If God wills it, our loved ones will return to us. We shall soon see. Darrick will relight his own candle. After all, only he can, yes? He will indeed return to us. If the Lord wills it..."

Gabriella allowed Sigrid to embrace her, but there was no comfort in it, and she did not close her eyes. She stared towards the indigo glass of the window, her eyes red but dry now. *If the Lord wills it: that's what I am afraid of,* she thought but did not say. *That's exactly what I am afraid of...*

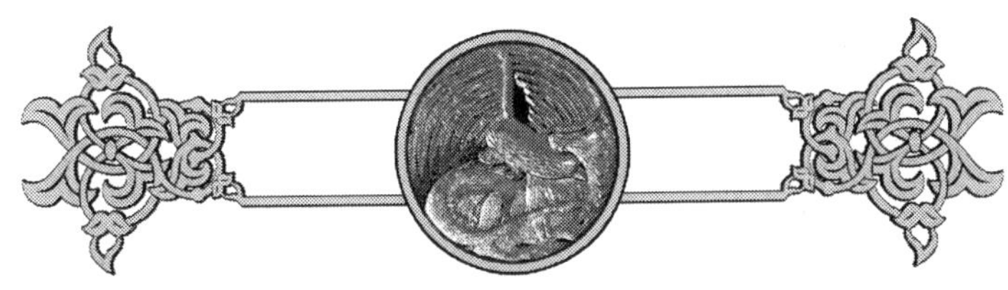

Thomas and Yazim camped that night in the shadow of the dead castle. Its broken turrets and spires made a black hulk against the sky, blocking out the moon. The wind gusted capriciously, buffeting their fire and throwing its light beyond the clearing, up onto the brambly wilds of an ancient rose garden. The thorny vines embraced a nearby bridge, nearly burying it, whilst lush blooms filled the air with an almost sickly sweet perfume.

"Do you believe in haunts?" Thomas asked, peering up at the dark ruin.

Yazim shrugged. "Perhaps."

They sat in silence, letting the night unwind, listening to the rush of the wind in the rosy wilds. Finally, Thomas spoke again.

"Was the lady-in-waiting right? Did the Princess's husband return?"

Yazim looked aside at his companion. "What do you think?"

"I do not wish to say."

Yazim nodded slowly. "The young Field Marshal, along with the High Constable Sir Ulric, did reach the encampments of the enemy. They took their time setting up divisions and drawing their plan of attack. Such things were hardly subtle, and they consumed many weeks. The Army spread across the valley in tents, arranged their siege machines and trebuchets in such a way as to inspire fear and awe. Spies were sent to study the strongholds of the enemy. There was much careful deliberation and planning. Eventually, the Princess's husband, Darrick, grew impatient with Ulric's approach. He sensed something wrong, just as the Princess had warned him."

"But surely, the King's forces greatly outnumbered that of the enemy," Thomas interjected. "They were a mere collection of brutes and peasants, many of the latter conscripted against their will. What could they do against an organised royal militia?"

"Such were surely the thoughts of High Constable Ulric," Yazim agreed. "But Field Marshal Darrick was in charge of the spies, and what he heard in their reports made him wary. None today know the details of those reports. It may be that Merodach had stricken alliances with foreign powers, securing a much larger secret force to help overthrow Camelot. If so, nothing was ever proven. Regardless, Darrick advised Ulric to strike covertly, to flank the enemy camps by night rather than confront them head-on by daylight, as was the High Constable's plan."

"But Ulric refused, I should guess," Thomas commented. "After all, stealth and trickery are hardly the tactics of a noble army. Why resort to cunning by dark when one can rely on the might of numbers and the courage of conviction?"

"You would make an excellent High Constable yourself, my friend," Yazim smiled grimly.

"Alas, I would not, for I do not labour under such convictions myself. I am far too interested in the solidarity of my own skin to risk it for that of the Kingdom. But we are speaking of Camelot. Men were indeed willing to die on its behalf. They considered it a high honour."

"To die, yes," Yazim nodded, turning his face to the fire, "but not to be slaughtered."

Thomas shook his head slowly. "But how could such a thing happen?"

"It is a mystery that has vexed the tellers of histories for many decades," Yazim admitted. "All that is known for sure is that Merodach simply waited. He appeared to mount no preparation against the camps of the King's army. When the Army attacked, Merodach's forces merely fought back, but with strange, deadly ferocity. There was no contest. The King's ranks fell before the sword of the enemy like wheat before a scythe. It is said that a freak storm fell upon the melee, driving the Army back from the foothills and allowing the enemy to descend upon them in the open, surrounding them like a noose. When it was over, the valley floor was beaten to mud and stained red with the blood of the King's soldiers, most of whom died horribly and viciously."

"Thus, Darrick did die on that day," Thomas nodded gravely.

"No," Yazim countered, looking up at his friend. "Sir Ulric and the Princess's husband were captured. His tale was told by his personal page, who managed to escape from the enemy camp that night along with a few others. By the time they straggled back to the castle, the day after the birth of the young Prince, there were barely a hundred left to tell the tale."

Thomas frowned as the wind gusted again, carrying dead rose petals into the air. "To what end? Did the brute Merodach intend to use them as bartering tokens?"

Yazim let out a small, derisive laugh. "To barter for what? There was nothing the King had that Merodach wanted, save for the throne itself. Merodach's only aim was destruction and mayhem."

"Then what did he want with the Princess's man, Darrick?"

Yazim glanced at Thomas again and then up at the silhouette of the ruined castle. "It is quite simple, I suppose," he answered speculatively. "He wanted to interview him."

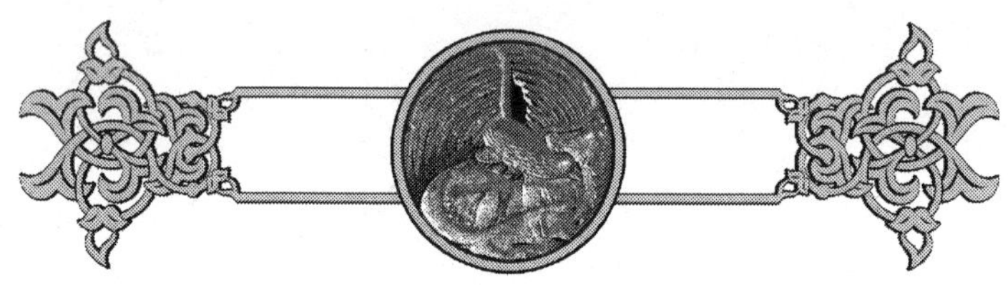

Merodach's stronghold was at the top of a short tower keep that had been captured many months earlier. It had been barely guarded at the time, being mostly forgotten and overgrown, but Merodach had transformed it into a thriving hub, fortified by no less than thirty watchmen and guards.

Darrick sat on a bench next to High Constable Ulric near the centre of the round room, surrounded by six of the hardest, most inhuman-looking men he had ever seen. Two other prisoners, Darrick's and Ulric's pages, were chained to the wall by manacles. Their captors stood against the curved walls, arms crossed or hands on the hilts of their swords, their faces nearly expressionless in the evening gloom. Rain fell beyond the narrow windows, filling the room with its steady roar and cool mist. In the middle of the room was a heavy table, close enough that Darrick could see parchments scattered over it. A large scroll had been sketched neatly, showing a detailed outline of the King's army encampments. Behind the table sat an ornate chair, still impressive despite its age and wear.

"They mean to interrogate us," Ulric muttered to Darrick, his voice gravelly. He'd been injured, but not mortally. The left side of his face was covered with a mask of dried blood, staining his red sideburns and goatee dark maroon. "We must withstand whatever torture they inflict upon us for the sake of the Kingdom. If we survive the night, I have devised a plan—"

"Be still your tongue," one of the guards growled with slow emphasis, "or we'll take it away from you."

"Do what you must," Ulric replied, lifting his chin. "We will not obey your orders."

The guard's eyes narrowed, and his fingers tightened on the hilt of his sword. A moment later, however, a shadow moved as light bloomed in the room. A man climbed the stairs, carrying a torch.

"Forgive me for making you wait, good sirs," the man said, smiling at Darrick and Ulric and notching the torch into an iron stand. He was thin but muscular, with slightly receding dark hair, cut short and swept forwards so that it accentuated his square, regular features. He looked more like a pleasant school professor than a warlord. "Battle is a very time-consuming business, as you surely know," he went on, forgoing the chair and leaning against the corner of the table nearest the captives. "Fortunately, it seems that this particular skirmish is, for the most part, behind us now. Even you must be relieved by that fact, despite your predicament."

Merodach glanced over the table, spied a wad of cloth on its ledge, and reached for it. Drawing his sword with a flourish, he held it before him, showing the streaks of dark blood that stained it. He raised the cloth to wipe off the blade and then paused, glancing up at Darrick and Ulric.

"Now, there's no reason that this needs to be at all unpleasant," he said glancing from one to the other. "I presume that you already know why I have brought you here, yes?"

"Do your *worst*, you cur," Ulric spat, drawing himself upright and making to stand. "We will never bow to you, never give you the satisfaction of—"

Merodach moved almost lazily. He swung his sword around in a short, sweeping arc, slashing it diagonally across Ulric's throat. Darrick ducked as blood spurted forth in a curtain. Ulric gagged, choking on his own blood, and clutched uselessly at his neck. When Darrick looked up at him, he saw that Ulric's head was very nearly severed. A moment later, the High Constable keeled back over the bench and hit the floor, dead. He lay there crumpled, one heel still hooked over the bench, his eyes staring up with blank shock.

"There," Merodach said, leaning back against the table and looking at his sword. "As I said, there is no reason for unpleasantness. *You* won't be unpleasant," he asked, glancing up at Darrick, "will you, my good sir?"

Darrick was too stunned to speak. He looked at Merodach and willed himself to stay calm. *The amazing thing,* he thought, *is that if I were pitted against him on the battle floor, I think I could defeat him. What is it about him that makes him so confident?*

"That's better," Merodach replied, as if Darrick had answered him. "I only have a few simple questions. Nothing I could not learn via other sources if it became necessary, so you must not feel you are doing your king a disservice by answering them."

"And why," Darrick began in a dry rasp, then cleared his throat, firming his voice, "and why should I answer you? You'll just kill me when you are through."

Merodach frowned slightly. "Why would I do something like that? You think I enjoy killing people? You are but a young man with a full life ahead of you. I'd sooner destroy a priceless work of art than end your noble life. Answer me my questions, and surely, you will live to see another day."

Darrick considered this and then shook his head slowly. "You're lying," he said, narrowing his eyes. "You've murdered hundreds of people. We all know the stories of your cruelty. Your name is a tale of horror throughout the Kingdom."

At this, Merodach grimaced. He lowered his sword across one knee and began to clean it with the cloth in his left hand. "Regrettable but necessary propaganda," he announced with a sigh. "Alas, I have been forced to take some rather unfortunate actions in the name of my quest, but that does not make me into some sort of monster. Still, I respect that you doubt my word. The truth is," he said, raising his eyes again, "I need you alive. You are the King's son-in-law, are you not? You have his very ear. He will listen to you. I need you alive... to take him a message for me."

Darrick studied Merodach's face, looked into the man's eyes. "What message?"

"In good time," Merodach replied, waving the rag in his hand as if the issue was unimportant. "First, let us get a few niggling questions out of the way. Tell me, good Sir Field Marshal, how many trebuchets are left to guard the city walls of Camelot proper?"

Darrick paused. He lowered his chin thoughtfully and then raised it again. "Fifteen," he answered, looking directly into Merodach's eyes.

Merodach smiled at Darrick and then chuckled. The chuckle turned into a light laugh, and he lowered his sword so that its tip touched the floor. None of the guards, Darrick noticed, joined their leader in his mirth.

"Good sir," Merodach laughed, shaking his head. "That, I believe, is the worst lie I have ever heard. Come now, be reasonable. I *want* to let you live, if only so you can perform my little errand. Don't make me kill you for such pathetically feeble attempts at deception. Answer me truthfully. How many trebuchets defend the city walls?"

Darrick sighed deeply. He looked away towards the narrow windows and the falling rain beyond. "Six," he answered, and then shook his head. "Perhaps less. I don't recall."

"I think you recall very well, sir," Merodach said with a knowing smirk, "but good enough. Thank you. Now, what number is the King's retinue, and what is his daily schedule?"

Darrick met Merodach's gaze again and frowned. "I do not know what you mean. I only moved into the castle upon my wedding, and I left very shortly thereafter. I am not aware—"

"*The King's daily schedule!*" Merodach shouted suddenly, leaping to his feet and flashing his sword. "When does he leave the castle?! Who accompanies him? How many?!" Spittle flew from Merodach's lips as he screamed, leaning close to Darrick's face. "Lie to me one more time and you may return to the castle lacking your hands and feet! *Tell me now!*"

"He does not keep a regular schedule!" Darrick answered loudly, leaning back and hating himself for the waver in his voice. "He does as he pleases! He is the King!"

"*How many are in his retinue?!*" Merodach demanded, his eyes bulging.

"Three!" Darrick cried. "He keeps three guards with him when he leaves the castle!"

"Only three?" Merodach said in his normal voice, standing up straight and cocking his head quizzically at Darrick. "Why, I recall past Kings who took an entourage of no less than six armed escorts with them whenever they toured the countryside. King Xavier has become rather complacent, would you not say?"

Darrick shuddered. Sweat trickled down his temples. He struggled to control his breathing, to not show his fear.

"Three it is," Merodach commented jovially. "A manageable number, I must say. Thank you, my friend. Please, do you mind if I call you Darrick? I hate to stand on formality, especially given the circumstances."

Darrick merely stared at him, keeping his lips pressed firmly together. Outside, lightning flashed silently.

"Excellent, Darrick," Merodach said, half sitting on the table and turning his sword over on his knee. He resumed cleaning it with the cloth. "How many passages are there into the castle? Besides the portcullis entrance of course."

Darrick was silent. He firmed his jaw and looked away, out of the dark windows again. The rain fell steadily into the gathering darkness.

"You really do not seem to know how this works, Darrick," Merodach commented, pausing his cleaning. "I really am trying to be patient with you. Do you wish me to ask Brom here to break some of your fingers? I don't want to do it, but—"

"Four," Darrick answered, glaring up at his captor. "And I am only answering that because it is common knowledge to anyone who lives within sight of the castle."

Merodach smiled disarmingly. "Thank you for sparing us that ugly drudgery, Darrick. It is nice to deal with someone who exhibits such striking common sense. I know of the four main entrances of course. There are no secret passageways then? Are you quite certain?"

Darrick's face was pale but bravely stolid. "I am certain."

"Good," Merodach nodded. "Because if I discovered that you had lied to me... well, I have already illustrated the necessity of maintaining a rather fearsome image, yes? You would place me in the unfortunate position of having to teach you a lesson. I am sure I do not need to explain what that would entail."

"I am not lying," Darrick said, deflating a little on the bench.

"Excellent. Then we are very nearly through. Brom, if you would please fetch the message I have prepared for King Xavier. It is in the lock-box in my quarters. Here is the key."

Brom, the guard who had first threatened Ulric to stay silent, stepped forwards. He had ragged, black hair and pocked skin. His eyes were strangely dead as he took Merodach's key. A moment later, he disappeared down the tower stairs.

"You see," Merodach said, examining the glint of his sword and putting down the cloth, "I can be a reasonable man. The stories about me are not *entirely* true."

Darrick did not respond. He watched his captor finger his sword thoughtfully. The stench of Ulric's blood filled the room now, mingling with the mist of the storm.

"There *is* one more thing, if you please," Merodach said, as if the idea had just stricken him. "A trifle. An afterthought. Tell me, Darrick: if King Xavier determines that flight is his only hope of salvation, to where would he retreat? I understand that there are many fortresses at his disposal. Which would he choose for his stronghold?"

Darrick's brow lowered. Mustering all of his courage, he straightened his back and looked Merodach in the eye. "I'm through helping you," he answered in a low voice. "I will not be held responsible for your success in attacking the castle and routing out the King. My life is not worth the curse of such guilt or the deaths that would result."

Merodach frowned consideringly and then nodded. "I understand your predicament, my friend. If you answer my question, you may see your people destroyed. If you resist me, perhaps only you will be destroyed. Yes? But surely, you see the flaw in this, do you not?"

"I do not," Darrick replied, firming his resolve. "I am a soldier of Camelot. I am proud to offer myself for its preservation."

Merodach drew a deep sigh and shook his head slowly, almost regretfully. "I hate to disillusion you, Darrick, but I *will* succeed in my quest, regardless of what you deign to say or whether you choose to live or die. By remaining silent, you will neither save Camelot nor yourself. But by telling me the truth..." He raised his eyebrows and tilted his head in a conciliatory gesture.

"There is nothing you can offer me that will make such treason worthwhile," Darrick said stiffly, turning away.

"Do you suppose," Merodach asked lightly, "that the Princess, your wife, would agree?"

Darrick froze. He stared unseeingly into the shadows, feeling the blood drain from his face.

"I understand that she is with child," Merodach added, sighing. "It may be that the babe, your son or daughter, is even now born. Is this not so?"

Darrick drew his eyes back to Merodach, his expression cold. "If you touch them..."

"Please," Merodach interrupted, rolling his eyes. "Idle threats are such an interminable waste of time. As I said, Darrick, I am a reasonable man. I am offering you a bargain. Answer me what I require, and when the time comes, I will see that your wife and child are spared. Refuse me, and... well, I really cannot be held responsible for what happens, can I? It is your choice."

Darrick glared at the hateful man before him. A long silence spread out between them, filled only with the shush of the rain and the faint crackle of the torch. Finally, Brom reappeared from below. He approached Merodach and handed him a small package, sealed with red wax. Merodach took it without breaking eye contact with Darrick.

Finally, in a rough voice, Darrick asked, "How do I know you will keep your word?"

Merodach grimaced again and lifted his right hand, gesturing vaguely with his sword. "You cannot, I am afraid. It is the nature of this type of bargain. But I will tell you this: it is the King that I want, and his throne. Once he is deposed, the Princess will pose no threat. There is no point in my harming her or the child she has borne you."

Darrick shook his head very slightly, his face contorted in a rictus of agonised indecision.

"I'll tell you what," Merodach said, taking a step forwards. "You don't have to answer aloud for all to hear. You may whisper your answer into my ear. It is that simple. Let me ask again: where, in the event of flight, will the King and his people retreat to? Answer me this, and your wife and child may live."

Merodach took another step forwards, cautiously, as if Darrick were a deer that might flee at the slightest provocation. Then, almost comically, he leant forwards and placed his ear next to Darrick's lips.

Darrick was silent for a long, horrible moment. And then, almost soundlessly, his lips moved. He spoke one word, and the expression on Merodach's face changed. His smile hardened, and his eyes grew dark. He stood up and straightened his cape and breastplate.

"I owe you my deepest gratitude, good Sir Darrick," Merodach announced, turning back to the table. "You have been of great help to me. I shall not forget it." He sheathed his sword with a ring of metal on metal. Behind him, Darrick hung his head. His sweaty hair fell over his face.

"What is the message?" he muttered.

Merodach glanced back, frowning slightly. "Excuse me?"

"The *message*," Darrick repeated, an edge of ragged anger creeping into his voice. He lifted his head defiantly. "What is the message you mean for me to deliver to the King?"

"Ah, yes," Merodach replied, holding up the package in his hand and looking at it. The red seal looked like a blot of blood in the dimness. "You know, Darrick, you have been such a great help to me, such an *excellent* help," he said, drawing a short dagger from his belt, "that I think I may be able to deliver this message... *without* your help."

"And then," the page said, trembling, unable to meet either the King's or the Princess's eyes, "and then the beast... *launched* himself upon the Field Marshal. He bared his teeth like a sort of wild animal and struck with his dagger, not once, just to kill, but over and over, even after—" He choked a little and then raised his eyes imploringly. "Even after the poor man was dead. It was...," he admitted faintly, "the worst thing I have ever seen in my life. When it was over, Merodach stood over the body, panting, and—"

"Stop!" Gabriella said suddenly, her voice getting away from her so that it came out as a half scream of anguish. "Stop! I can hear no more! It is too much!"

Her father reached towards her throne and covered her hand with his own. Helplessly, Gabriella buried her face in her other hand. She squeezed her eyes shut, trying to stem the flood of emotion that was threatening to overwhelm her. She couldn't bear to share her grief with the court, with these seemingly random people, none of whom had known Darrick like she had, most of whom would see his death as merely another casualty, one more in a long line of deaths at the hand of the unholy brute Merodach.

"How did you escape?" the King asked the page gravely.

"Sir Ulric," the page answered, swallowing past a lump in his throat. "He had already arranged it. He had entrusted his personal retinue to be prepared to rescue us in the event of our capture. He knew of a hidden rear entrance to the tower, long buried in vines and most likely unknown to Merodach and his men. This door was unguarded, allowing Sir Ulric's remaining men to steal in by dark and release us. They killed the dungeon guard, and we were gone before anyone else came looking."

"Tell me, Master Brice," Toph said from where he stood on the other side of the King's throne, "I know this is not your purview, but in the absence of Sirs Ulric and Darrick, what is the final tally of those who returned with you?"

"Seventy-seven men at last count," the page answered, shaking his head slowly.

The King sighed deeply. "And what of the trebuchets and siege engines?"

"Captured or destroyed, Your Highness. None return with us."

There was a long, dreadful silence as everyone in the King's ready room considered this, realising the enormity of the threat they now faced.

"Your Highness," Percival, the chief of the palace guard, said carefully, stepping forwards, "we are left in a very unfortunate position indeed. There is no assurance whatsoever that Merodach will take time to gloat over his victory. Even now, we must assume that he is preparing to march upon the city."

King Xavier looked up at Percival as if the idea had not yet occurred to him. His expression conveyed nothing but grim uncertainty. Gabriella saw this with both pity and dismay.

Finally, the King looked away, frowning worriedly. "What do you suggest, Percival?"

"I see no other options, Your Highness," Percival announced hesitantly. "We must remove ourselves from the castle."

The King startled on his throne, his frown deepening. "Flee, you say? But surely, that will not be necessary—"

"With all due respect, sire," Toph interjected softly, "we are left with barely enough men to stand watch over the city walls, unless we begin conscripting school children and the elderly. We cannot mount a thwart of any meaningful force nor withstand any determined siege of the city. Flight is, in fact, our only true option."

"But," the King said, his brow furrowing in consternation, "what of the people? Without us here to protect them, to watch over them…"

"In fact, Your Highness," Percival countered carefully, "it may serve them best if you are *not* here. We must assume that it is you the villain wants, not the castle or the city. With you absent, ruling in secret, if only for a time, Merodach may in fact spare the city."

"This is madness!" Gabriella suddenly exclaimed, unable to contain herself any longer. "He will destroy everything and everyone within the city walls! This man does not spare cities because they are unguarded and pose no threat! You heard what he did to Darrick! It is the same thing he has done to every village and town he has encountered in his bloodthirsty path! He burns and destroys as much for his own mirth as for any strategic benefit! He is a raving madman!"

"Highness," Toph began gently, "there are few other options left to us. We simply do not have the manpower to mount a serious resistance."

"There are more than *men* in this city," Gabriella seethed, rising suddenly to her feet. "If given the opportunity to flee, cower, or fight, I daresay that every man, *woman*, and *child* within these city walls would choose the latter!"

"But we cannot *win*, Princess," Percival protested sternly.

"Then we die with honour!" Gabriella cried, overriding him. "Better that than to live in cowardice!"

"Daughter," the King said, raising his eyes to where she stood. His voice was soft, but the authority had come back into it. She stopped herself, fuming, and then looked back at him.

"Daughter, tell me, can you go stand amongst the people and tell a mother that she will soon watch her child die for the sake of honour?"

"I am a mother myself now, you may remember," Gabriella replied, trembling with anger and misery.

"I remember it well, dear one. But you were the Princess first, and as such, you are well-acquainted with loss and sacrifice. The others below may not be. Are you willing to make this choice for all? Are you prepared to order them all to their deaths and the deaths of their children? Some may indeed choose to stay and fight, but many more may come with us if we leave the city. The fortresses can hold hundreds, if necessary, for however long the siege may last. Still others will hide away in the surrounding fiefs and villages with distant family, safe from whatever may befall this city. Will you take that option away from them? Can you?"

Gabriella felt the weight of her father's words settling on her like sand. She tried to resist, but slowly, sadly, she realised he was right. Her knees weakened, and she drifted back into her seat.

"Sometimes, daughter," the King said quietly, "being Princess and King and Queen means more than sacrificing one's life. Sometimes, for the sake of all, it means sacrificing one's nobility."

Gabriella's face hardened at these words, but she did not reply. She gripped the arms of her throne tightly so that her knuckles whitened.

"How soon can we mount the journey?" the King asked, addressing Percival.

"If we post the edict today, Your Highness, we can rally the castle population within two, perhaps three, days. We shall conduct a lottery to determine who amongst the citizenry may accompany us based on those who express such a desire. The rest shall retreat to the country or stay in the city as they so deem. I would recommend leaving a small detachment to guard the castle entries, however, to protect against the rare looter."

"That soon," the King replied solemnly. "Is it necessary to go so quickly?"

"We cannot take chances, Your Highness," Toph pressed. "If Merodach and his men are on their way now, as we are forced to assume, then they will be here in a matter of weeks. We must not only be shut of the castle by then, but firmly established in whichever stronghold you choose."

"Which does bring us to the question," Percival nodded, peering closely at the King, "considering the tale of the unfortunate Sir Darrick's page, what stronghold shall we consider?"

"It is sadly clear, is it not?" the King said, glancing regretfully at Gabriella. "We must fly southwest, to the border fortress at Herrengard."

Gabriella sat up in her throne and turned on her father. "Herrengard? It is in no wise the best choice! It is smaller and far less defensible than the eastern stronghold at Amaranth!"

"Princess," Percival said in an attempt at a reasonable voice, "you heard the tale of the page. The Field Marshal revealed the primary choice of retreat for the King. Amaranth will be useless to us if Merodach knows that it is our destination. He will likely have men there lying in wait or even prepared to ambush us en route."

"His name," Gabriella said lividly, "was Darrick. Call him that if you mean to denounce him as traitor."

"Daughter," the King began again, but Gabriella spoke first, turning to him.

"Father, Darrick would *not* betray us. The page did not hear the answer Darrick gave when Merodach asked about a royal retreat. He would never have revealed our primary plan. He would have lied, sending Merodach and his men off on a useless chase!"

Toph shook his head. "We cannot *know* that, Princess—"

"*I* know it," she interrupted fiercely. "He was my husband! You have to trust me! He lied to the villain, gave him a false location! I assure you, he deceived them into believing that the primary retreat would in fact be *Herrengard* and *not* Amaranth! We will be fleeing straight into the arms of a trap, nullifying Darrick's attempt to save us all!"

"We cannot take such a chance, Princess!" Percival insisted, becoming impatient.

"It is *no* chance!" Gabriella cried, standing again. "No other southern or eastern fortress is near enough or defensible enough as Amaranth stronghold!"

"*No* fortress is solid enough to save us if the villain is *already within it*!"

"*If you refuse to believe me,*" Gabriella shouted, tears of anger welling in her eyes, "then we will all die, and Darrick's sacrifice will have been for nothing!"

"Silence!" the King commanded, striking the arm of his throne with his fist. The echo of his voice rang through the room as the others fell quiet. Gabriella remained standing, her eyes firmly on Percival, breathing harshly through her nose. Percival dropped his own gaze and pressed his lips into a thin line.

"I will not have any member of my council speak to my daughter in that manner," the King said with quiet emphasis. "Percival, you forget yourself."

"Yes, Your Highness," Percival answered immediately, his eyes still on the floor. "I apologise profusely. Please accept my humblest regret."

The King lowered his head and closed his eyes. Gabriella looked back at him. Her father seemed to be deep in thought, his brow pinched in a tight frown. Finally, after a long silence, he lifted his head again.

"Post the edict," he said sombrely. "The royal family of Camelot will disembark from the castle and the city proper in two days and two nights. Those who wish to accompany the journey will apply to the chief of the palace guard, who will give preference to those with children, the women, and the elderly, in that order. Those who remain may evacuate to surrounding fiefs or villages or stay within the city walls at their own discretion."

He paused, ruminating, and then went on. "Should any of those who remain choose to mount a defence of the city or the castle itself, they will be duly honoured, even in the event of death, by His Highness, King Xavier, and his daughter, Princess Gabriella. Until our return, let it be known that even in absence, the royal family still rules seamlessly and properly over the Kingdom of Camelot until the day of our triumphant return."

Percival nodded, making mental notes of every point. Finally, he raised his head and looked directly at the King once more. "Very good, Your Highness. And to which destination shall we prepare to journey?"

The King drew a deep breath and looked at Gabriella. "Have the remaining soldiers prepare an escort march to Herrengard," he said. "But do not reveal the location to anyone else."

Gabriella felt her stomach drop within her. She met her father's gaze, speechless.

"Herrengard it is, Your Highness," Percival nodded again. "We shall begin preparations immediately."

The King ignored him. "I'm sorry, Gabriella," he said, but she turned away from him. She was too furious to reply. She was still standing, uselessly now that the council was finished. The room was full of subtle motion as the council members gathered themselves and prepared to leave.

"Daughter," the King said, raising his voice slightly.

"I have packing to see to," Gabriella replied evenly, her voice a low monotone. With that, she gathered her skirts and turned towards the side door, leaving before he could speak again.

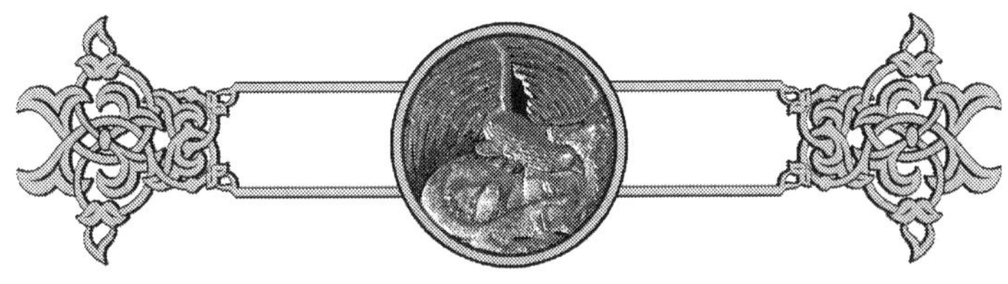

She did not pack that day, however. She returned to her quarters just as the Little Prince was waking up. Sigrid approached the crib, but Gabriella called her back, meaning to greet her baby herself. She scooped him carefully from his bedding and laid him over her shoulder. He was still sleepy, but his cries stopped as he rested his head against her shoulder. He sighed, shuddering, and relaxed in her arms.

She thought of Darrick.

"Can I get you anything, Princess?" Sigrid asked softly.

Slowly, without looking at her, Gabriella shook her head.

There was a breath of air and a soft click as the older woman left the room.

Tears filled Gabriella's eyes again. As always, she resented them. She blinked, squeezed her eyes shut, and moved towards the window. It was open, admitting a fresh autumn breeze. The air was blissfully cool, filled with the scent of crisp leaves and distant storms. The curtains belled softly. The baby shifted, coming fully to wakefulness.

Gabriella used her hip to push the rocking chair closer to the window. Then she sat, cradled her baby, and began to nurse him.

Again, she thought of Darrick.

He'll never see this, she mused helplessly, testing the waters of her grief. *He'll never watch his wife feed his child. Never hold the boy in his own arms, never feel this tiny fist wrapped tightly around his finger.*

The tears came now despite her resistance. They rolled silently down her cheeks even as the Little Prince suckled, oblivious of his own loss. Gabriella felt as if her sorrow was an ocean, frozen over, and she was walking on it. She knew the ice would crack soon, and she would fall into it. It would overwhelm her. She was afraid of it, afraid that once her grief swallowed her up, it would never let her go no matter how long she lived.

Her chest hitched, disturbing the baby, but he was intent. He continued hungrily.

Tears hung from her chin and dropped onto her lap, onto the Little Prince's arm, where he snuggled against her.

He will never know his father, she thought, and her grief began to harden, to develop an edge. *He will barely even know what he has lost, except for the emptiness, the void where his father should have been.*

The tears still came, but her face grew still. Anyone who saw her would have seen a woman of eerie, almost preternatural calm. Her chin was raised to the window so that its light fell fully across her cheeks, the line of her nose, and lit the dark glimmer of her eyes. For several minutes, she did not move.

Finally, the Little Prince finished. He stirred, stretched languidly, and yawned, making a soft O with his perfect, little lips. Gabriella looked down at him and smiled despite the tears that were still drying on her cheeks. He blinked up at her. He had Darrick's eyes, she saw.

"Sweet Little Prince," she soothed, still smiling. "Mama's sweet Little Prince."

Outside, wafting up from the courtyard, Gabriella could hear the rising clamour of voices. The edict had already been posted. Confusion and alarm were spreading out into the city like tentacles. Merodach was coming. Even without his name on the edict, no one doubted the truth of that fact.

"Don't you worry," Gabriella said, her smile fading only slightly. "Don't you worry, my Little Prince. Mama will keep you safe. Somehow..."

CHAPTER 5

The next day, Gabriella began to pack. The sky was stormy, low and sullen, and the wet wind brought a hard chill with it. Sigrid closed the windows and stoked the fire.

"Have the servants pack only a few gowns, Princess," the older woman instructed busily. "There will be no luxury for months' worth of clothing. We shall have to suffice with wearing the same things week to week."

Gabriella nodded silently, sombrely.

The rest of the castle was a hive of nervous energy. Meals were hushed, filled with low voices as plans were refined, routes considered, revised, rejected. Gabriella stayed out of it. The only time she smiled was when she held the Little Prince, fed him, soothed him to sleep. His cries, shrill as they sometimes were, were like music to her. Sigrid watched her with the baby, always prepared to help, but never intervening. Sigrid loved the Little Prince nearly as much as she, his mother, did. Gabriella recognised it in the way the older woman looked at the boy, held him, cooed to him even as she worked.

By the end of the second day of preparation, the city already seemed half-empty. Gabriella stood on her balcony in the blowing chill, hugging herself. There was less light in the streets below despite the windy darkness. Many chimneys issued no smoke. Most of those that were left in the city, she knew, were preparing to leave their homes the next morning, to join the escort to Herrengard. She couldn't help feeling, despite her father's confident words, that this sight, and the journey that was to follow, signaled the creeping end of Camelot.

"The city needed you," she whispered, speaking to the memory of her husband. "They needed a hero, just as you said. You were right. Perhaps Camelot did need you even more than I did. But you promised me..." She shook her head slowly. "You promised me. And I believed."

Somewhere out there, the beast that had forced Darrick to break his promise was alive and well. And he was coming, coming to do to the rest of them what he had already done to her husband. If he found them, he would spare no one. Not even her child.

"We are packed, Princess," Sigrid announced, opening the balcony door just enough to speak through it. "The Little Prince sleeps. You should as well. The morning will come quickly."

Gabriella did not move for a long moment. Finally, she turned back to the light of her quarters.

"Thank you, Sigrid. Goodnight."

The older woman frowned slightly and blinked, as if sensing something on the Princess's face. She remained hunched in the doorway, studying her.

Gabriella spoke again, calmly. "*Goodnight*, Sigrid."

Sigrid straightened herself. Still frowning, she nodded. A moment later, the balcony door closed, and she left.

Gabriella waited a few minutes longer. When she went back inside, she closed and locked the balcony doors behind her. The Little Prince snored softly from his crib. Gabriella checked on him, brushing her hair away from her cheek as she leant to gaze in at him. Then she turned and looked thoughtfully at the trunks stacked near the door. She frowned slowly.

As quietly as she could, she let herself out of the main bedroom, leaving the door partly open, and crossed into the common hall at the top of the stairs. The fire in the huge stone hearth was stoked for the night, providing the room's only illumination. Across from it, glinting mellowly on its display stand, was her battle armour. She moved to it, still frowning, and laid her hand on the breastplate. The metal was cold to the touch. There was hardly a scratch on the gold and steel. After all, such extravagant pieces were meant for display more than actual battle. Everyone knew that.

Behind her, footsteps sounded lightly on the stairs and then stopped.

"Your Highness," a man's voice said softly, carefully. She recognised her visitor even without turning. It was Darrick's page, Brice.

"Yes," she replied, still touching the metal of her armour.

"I'm sorry, Princess," Brice apologised, apparently struggling with himself. "I know you did not wish to hear all of my tale. I understand completely. But..."

She turned now, looking over her shoulder at the man. He was only a year or two older than she. She remembered him from the academy. "What is it, Brice?" she prodded cautiously.

He pressed his lips together, still standing on the top riser of the staircase, and then sighed quickly, resolutely. "I thought you should know, Your Highness," he went on, raising his eyes to meet hers, "your husband, Sir Darrick, he... he died well. He was brave. He never faltered or begged, even after Sir Ulric was killed right in front of him."

Gabriella had known this of course, but hearing the fact of it from the man who had witnessed it struck her unexpectedly. A deep pang sank into her heart.

"Thank you, Brice," she said, trying to keep her voice even. She began to turn away again.

"There's something else, Your Highness," Brice said in a different voice.

Gabriella stopped but did not turn back. She waited.

"When Merodach killed him...," Brice went on, struggling with the words, "when... when Darrick was dead, the brute saw something on him. He took it."

Gabriella felt a wave of sudden coldness descend over her, filling her and hardening in her eyes. "Tell me," she said calmly.

"It was… a pendant," Brice replied in a quiet voice. "A sigil of some kind. Dark but with a green stone embedded in it. Merodach seemed extremely curious about it, almost as if he knew what it was, or that it was… important somehow."

Gabriella still did not turn back to the page. Her face was a mask of cold anger. Softly, she said, "Thank you, Brice. Goodnight."

Brice watched her for a moment. She sensed it. Then his footsteps sounded again, receding back the way he had come.

She reached up, covered the sigil at her own throat. As always, it was warm, its metal rough and heavy.

She let go of the sigil and began to collect her armour.

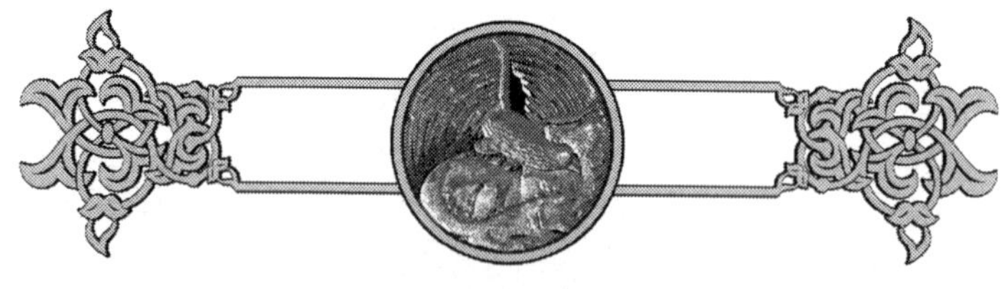

"Sigrid," Gabriella whispered urgently, shaking the woman in her bed. The room was adjacent to her own quarters, with only the light of the open doorway laying a golden band across the floor. "Sigrid, please wake. I need you to do something."

Sigrid muttered sleepily and then startled, coming fully awake in a matter of seconds. She sat up in her bed, eyes wide. "What is it? Are they here?"

Gabriella shook her head. "No. But you must leave. This night."

Sigrid blinked quickly, shaking her head in confusion. "But the journey to Herrengard does not set out until morning. I do not—"

"You cannot go to Herrengard," Gabriella interrupted, clutching Sigrid's shoulder firmly. "It is a trap. Merodach's men will already be there, or if not, they will fall upon the caravan even as it travels."

Sigrid frowned in consternation. "But the King..."

"My father refuses to listen. He has been warned, but he will not change his plan."

"I don't understand... who warned him? Why—"

"*I* warned him, Sigrid," Gabriella hissed urgently. "Darrick died trying to save us all, and my father refuses to trust that. His council is as stubborn and arrogant as was the idiot Ulric!"

"Do not speak thus of the dead!" Sigrid admonished quickly, growing alarmed. "Gabriella, you are scaring me. What is... are you..." Her eyes widened. "Are you wearing your...!"

Gabriella drew her cloak tighter around her shoulders. Her breastplate glinted in the dim light. "I am sorry, Sigrid," she said, shaking her head sadly. "I do not have time to explain further. You must go this night. Take Treynor with you and tell him it is by my order. Flee to Amaranth. You will be safe there. And Sigrid..." She stopped, swallowed hard, and went on in a lower voice. "You must take the baby with you."

Sigrid's frown deepened as the weight of the Princess's request settled over her. "You believe that those in the caravan will die," she breathed. "The King and all who accompany him. But... you cannot..."

"Please, Sigrid," Gabriella begged. "There is no time. You must leave tonight!"

"But this is madness!" Sigrid whispered, throwing off her covers and lowering her feet to the floor. "What are you planning to do? If I did not know better, I would fear that you were setting off on an errand of doomed vengeance! You cannot possibly..."

Gabriella's face darkened. She rose up to her full height and took a step back.

Sigrid's face paled, even in the darkness. "This is insanity!" she rasped. "Princess, I refuse to… I… I forbid this!"

Gabriella couldn't help it. She smiled in spite of everything. "Oh, dear Sigrid, I do so love you."

"Stop this," Sigrid said firmly, standing and approaching the Princess. "Please, Gabriella! Your baby needs you!"

"It is for his sake that I take my leave, Sigrid," Gabriella insisted gravely, meeting the older woman's eyes in the darkness. "His and everyone else's. But you *must* go tonight. Take the Little Prince and Treynor. You will need to find a wet nurse as well, but you must hurry. Fly to Amaranth and hide. I will find you there when I am through, if I can."

"And if you cannot?" Sigrid demanded hoarsely. "What then?"

"Then you must raise him," Gabriella answered. "*You* must be his mother, just as you were mine when all was said and done. Keep his lineage a secret. Let no one know that he is the last of the line of the royalty of Camelot. For his own safety. Promise me, Sigrid."

Sigrid chewed her own lips miserably. She shook her head. "I cannot, Princess," she replied miserably, reaching for her. "It is too much. It is not mine—"

"*Promise me!*" Gabriella hissed, grabbing the woman's hands. "You are the only person I can trust!"

Sigrid shook her head, lowering her eyes. Then, with an apparent force of will, she drew a deep breath. Without raising her head, she nodded. "I will do what I can, Princess. For your sake and that of the Prince."

"Thank you," Gabriella breathed, letting go of Sigrid's hands. "Thank you."

"Where are you going?" Sigrid asked in a low voice. "Tell me that much."

Gabriella stopped as she turned towards the door. "Before he left, my husband told me," she answered faintly, "that the people needed a hero."

The gravity of her words hung in the air like the toll of a bell. Finally, she moved. She approached the door. Without looking back, she slipped out.

She made it halfway down the stairs, clanking faintly in her gold and steel armour, carrying only a thin rucksack of supplies and clothing, before she heard the door open above her. She stopped, one hand on the banister, and looked up.

Sigrid peered down at her, her face set into a grim line of resolve. Slowly, she drew a deep breath and opened her mouth.

"*Guaaarrds!*" she shouted, putting everything she could behind it, so that her voice cracked with the effort. "Guards! The Princess is in danger! Come now! *NOW!*"

Gabriella paused for barely a second. In the next, she was bolting down the stairs, cursing urgently under her breath. Sigrid continued to shout her alarm. Behind her, echoing distantly, the Little Prince's wakened cries joined the fracas.

Gabriella darted beneath the stairs, through the vestibule, and down a narrow hall. There were no guards in the kitchen, and the servants' doors were propped wide open, surrounded by trunks of food, prepared for the journey. Cold air pushed in, filled with the whisper of night.

"Who goes there?" someone shouted suddenly, unseen, as Gabriella bolted out into the rear courtyard. "Who is it, I say? Guards!"

Behind her, lights began to glow in the castle windows. Gabriella tried not to look back. The stables loomed before her, smelling of hay and horse dung. She ran in through the main door and stopped, panting. No lanterns were lit inside.

"The Princess is missing!" someone shouted nearby, their voice echoing in the courtyard.

"Here!" another voice cried. "I just saw someone run past, leaving the castle! An intruder!"

"This way!"

"Search the stables but beware ambush! It may be that the villains are already amongst us!"

Two soldiers ran towards the stable doors, taking up position on either side. They drew their swords cautiously.

"On my mark," the one on the left growled, nodding towards the entrance. "One... two..."

A horse exploded through the open door, already in full gallop. Its rider crouched low on the mount, riding expertly if desperately, visible as nothing more than a dark shape and a snapping cloak. In a matter of seconds, the horse and its rider sped towards the courtyard gates, left open in preparation for tomorrow's journey, and vanished into the dark streets.

"Follow!" the first guard commanded loudly. "Search the city! The Princess's very life may be at stake!"

But it was too late, and the remaining guards knew it. By the time they mounted their own horses, the intruder—whoever it had been—would be long gone.

Careening through the silent mist of the city streets, Gabriella clung desperately to the reins. Her armour clanked and lurched on her body as her horse galloped on, baring its teeth, its eyes rolling wildly at the moon.

Within less than a minute, she was out of the city, onto the thoroughfare, and descending into the dark chill of the night, not looking back.

CHAPTER 6

Gabriella rode through the remainder of the night, turning west, away from the thoroughfare, and navigating by the great northern star. After her initial, thunderous rush, she was soon reduced to a careful cantor along wandering paths, deer trails, and even through unmarked forest. The night air was cold, drying her sweat and reducing her to shivers as she rode onwards, still unsure exactly where she was going or how she would get there. She only knew for certain that she had to maintain a westerly course—the direction from which the Army remnant had returned.

Eventually, as the sky began to grow faint, rimmed with pearly pink light beyond the trees, Gabriella stopped. She was exhausted, both from lack of sleep and her lengthy ride. She slid from her mount, patting his flank wearily, and tossed the reins over a branch. Her legs trembled beneath her, and her middle ached abominably from the abuse of the ride so soon after the rigours of childbirth.

After tending to her horse, she opened her light pack, unrolled a blanket onto the dewy ground, and fell upon it as dead. After a minute, she rolled over onto her back and stared up at the pinking sky, seen through a lace of branches and dwindling leaves.

A little sleep, she promised herself. *Just a few hours. That's all I can afford. I have to hurry if I am to get there in time...*

But even as she thought these things, despite the lumpy coldness of the ground and the dew that dripped all around, her eyes drifted shut.

The pink rim of the horizon brightened, spread, and then grew brilliant with the revelation of the rising sun. The dew sparkled on the weeds and dripping dead leaves. Soon, the air began to warm, and the dew turned to mist. In the trees, the birds began to chorus, first as a twitter, and then a chattering cacophony.

A scuffling sound arose from the weeds near Gabriella. A drift of dead leaves fell apart as a nose emerged, sleek and red, whiskers twitching, followed by the black eyes of a female fox. The vixen spied the sleeping human some distance away and whined to herself. After some secret inner struggle, she leapt nimbly out of the pile of leaves, her black-gloved feet making no noise on the grass, and circled cautiously closer, alternately growling and whining softly. She raised her head, spied a tiny glitter of green, and became silent. The glitter came from the shadows near the throat of the sleeping human.

More confidently now, the vixen approached. She stopped near Gabriella's head, sniffed her hair and cheek. Apparently satisfied, she perked up her ears and looked around, her bright eyes scanning the misty valley. Finally, neatly, she lay down, curling herself around Gabriella's head and tucking her tail under the young woman's chin, where it met the fox's black nose. The vixen drew a deep breath and snuffled as she let out it, relaxing in the climbing sun.

The day began. Beneath it, helplessly and fitfully, accompanied by her strange companion, Gabriella slept.

When she awoke, the sun was a huge, golden ball, halfway between the horizon and the sapphire dome of the sky.

She was sore and stiff but instantly roused herself, forcing herself upright and rolling up her blanket. Strange dreams still clouded her thoughts, weird visions of Darrick and the Little Prince, Sigrid screaming for the guards, herself being caught by them and dragged along to Herrengard, where death awaited them all. Even stranger, she recalled dreams of being watched in her sleep, as if all sorts of creatures, from scuttling spiders to great forest beasts, had crept past her, dipping their own wild thoughts into her sleeping mind. Impatiently, she shook herself, clearing her head and preparing for the day.

She was ravenously hungry, and she ached for a hot bath, and more than anything, she felt a deep, urgent fear that it was already too late, that her journey was already doomed.

"Stop it," she admonished herself under her breath, stuffing her blanket into her pack and digging out a hunk of bread. "Just keep moving. Nothing else matters."

Her pack was exceedingly light, filled only a small gather of stores from the castle kitchen, a flint, a flask, and a few coins. She dug near the bottom, seeking a bit of leather strap for her hair, and saw a heavy lump, wrapped in cloth. It touched her hand, and she withdrew the object, sighing.

This, of course, had not come from the castle kitchen. It had come from the academy cathedral. She had gone there to retrieve it the night before, after packing the rest of her meagre provisions but before donning her armour and going to wake Sigrid. It was, of course, Darrick's candle, taken from his family's vault in the transept gallery. She felt its small, dense weight, considered unwrapping it for just a moment, and then rejected the idea. She was in a hurry after all. It was good enough just to know that it was there, accompanying her, even if it really was just a symbol. She replaced the wrapped candle in her pack and cinched the knot tight.

And yet that sense of creeping unease only grew. Finally, as she stood and shouldered her pack, cocking her head to listen for the sound of the stream that she knew was nearby, she realised what it was.

The angle of the sun did not indicate late morning, but early evening. She had slept almost an entire day away.

A moan of panicked frustration came from deep in her throat. She turned on the spot and then realised something even worse. Her eyes widened beneath the tangled thicket of her hair.

"No!" she half whispered, shaking her head in denial. "No! How could I have been so stupid?"

She ran several paces this way and that, glancing feverishly through the trees. After a minute, her feet splashed in the stream she had originally been looking for. It was small comfort now.

Her horse was gone.

She clapped a hand to her forehead, clawed her fingers into her hair, and let out a guttural cry of mingled anger and despair. She hadn't properly secured the reins when she had stopped for the morning. Chances were that the horse had already retraced his steps all the way back to the castle stables.

She would have to travel the rest of the way on foot.

After several minutes of useless raging, Gabriella forcibly calmed herself. Still fuming, she knelt by the stream, splashed her hands and face, pulled her hair back in a tangled but economical ponytail, and re-shouldered her pack. After a moment's inspection of the angle of the shadows and the height of the sun, she set off.

She was young, she reminded herself. She could travel much further in a day than could any Army division with its supplies and arsenals. Besides, she wasn't traveling the same path that the Army had gone. They had been forced to take the thoroughfares and highways. More important, they had not approached Merodach via the most direct route. They had skirted through the Shambles, and Godramgate Hills, and Broadmoor Valley, finally approaching Merodach's camps in the rocky foothills of Mount Skelter.

Now, however, Merodach and his armies would be on the move. Gabriella had no time to take the long route, especially if she was reduced to traveling on foot. She had no choice but to get to the man as quickly as possible. To do so, she would take the only short cut she knew—the best and worst short cut imaginable.

She would head straight through the cursed steppe of the Tempest Barrens.

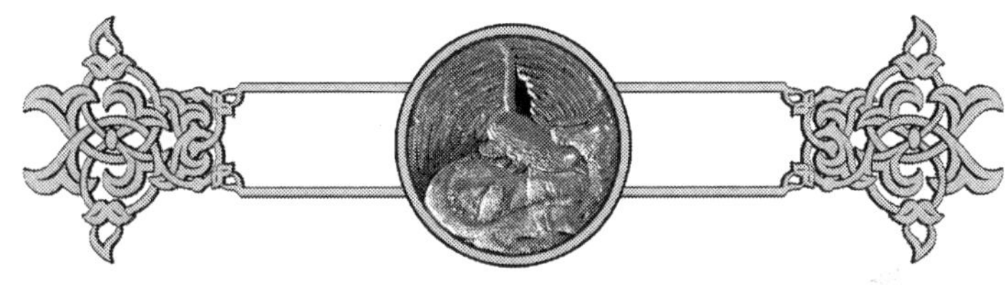

The sun crept downwards as she plodded on, making decent progress even without her horse. For now, her journey was taking her through such dense forest that she would not have made much better time even on horseback. The gloom of the trees blotted out the daylight, hearkening a very early evening, and Gabriella determined that she would continue into the night, traveling by starlight in order to make up for lost time. As she walked, she nibbled more of the bread and dried venison from her pack, careful only to eat enough to keep up her strength. Fortunately, she encountered numerous streams along the way, allowing her to replenish and preserve the water in her flask. These were often bordered by wild blackberry bushes, which she harvested and ate even as she walked.

Slowly, night began to settle firmly across the sky, and the distance between the trees began to increase. The huge, ancient oaks, their trunks carpeted with moss and as thick as pillars, began to give way to fresh birches and spruces. The air cooled and grew busy, gusting noisily. Colourful dead leaves crunched and swished before Gabriella's persistent footsteps, occasionally catching in the wind and swirling away like startled birds.

She began to see signs of human occupation. Clearings appeared, pocked with stumps and often centred with small cabins or cottages, candles lit within their windows and thin streams of smoke issuing from their fieldstone chimneys. These, she skirted around, all the while deeply longing to approach, to knock at the heavy doors and seek shelter, even just a simple straw bed and a cup of hot broth. But she resisted. She had to keep moving. On some level, despite the gravity of her mission, she feared that if she stopped once, even for a small comfort, she might find it doubly difficult ever to begin again.

For the Little Prince, she thought, forcing herself onwards. *And for Sigrid, and my father, and all the rest.* Then, more darkly: *And for Darrick. And Rhyss. For their memory, and vengeance…*

She pressed onwards as the moon arced high over the trees, casting its cold light down and creating its own spindly shadows on the forest floor.

Scars of grey bedrock began to show through the undergrowth, protruding in occasional humps and spines. Gabriella walked over these with growing trepidation, knowing she was nearing the outermost reaches of the dreaded Tempest Barrens. The further she traveled, the fewer human outposts she would discover. This, along with the gusting wind and the silent eye of the moon, filled her with quiet dread. Still, she did not stop or slow her pace. She was committed to the path regardless of her unspoken fears.

There were many stories about the Barrens. Most of them, she reminded herself, were pure fantasy, invented for sport, to be told around midnight hearths in the safe confines of taverns and castles. Perhaps only a small percentage of the tales were true.

But, she couldn't help wondering, *which* percentage?

Unbidden, her mind dredged up the old legends, things she had collected in her memory since she had been a very young girl. The barren steppe was cursed with ancient black magic, the histories claimed, leftover from the days when wizardkind warred there, scorching the earth with their worst and most inventive battle spells. The magic had tainted the very rocks and plains, never dissipating, but sinking into the earth like acid. It pooled invisibly in caves and depressions, growing in the very grass, poisoning the creatures that fed there and turning them horrible and mutant.

Worse, the legends declared that the magical armies had employed mystical creatures in their forces—dragons and centaurs, elves and goblins, giants and cyclopses, even monstrous spiders, walking trees, and rock trolls with boulders for fists. Many of these creatures had been left behind, wandering the Barrens for centuries, mad and vicious, stalking the unwary traveler.

Most awful of all, however, the myths whispered of dead armies that still roamed the plains, cursed ghosts rejected even by hell, forever marching in search of an enemy to destroy and devour, to claim unto themselves.

Surely, the worst of the stories could not be true. As with most legends, the reality was surely far less horrible than the tales that had grown up around it. Even today, brave adventurers occasionally trekked off into the Barrens in search of artifacts and treasures, magical remnants that could be exploited for gain. Many of these adventurers returned full of wild tales, eager to impress their meeker listeners. Surely, exaggerations were to be expected. Probably, the worst the steppe had to offer was a dearth of drinkable water and the occasional cursed burial mound or rogue wildcat.

She told herself these things as the night deepened around her and the trees thinned, became scraggly and bare. She walked on, and the ground seemed to terrace vaguely downwards, descending and growing barren, marked by increasingly larger patches of dead rock and scree.

She encountered ancient campsites, reduced to little more than black scorch marks where fires had once burnt, surrounded by litters of small bones. Once, she came upon an abandoned cottage, mostly buried in vines, pulled apart by a crooked oak tree that had grown through its roof. Symbols had long ago been painted across the open doorway, but now they were faded to worrying obscurity. Gabriella walked around this, keeping her distance, and tried not to think that the leaning structure was watching her as she passed on.

Tall, yellow grass became the dominant feature of the landscape, dotted only occasionally with stunted trees and scrubby bushes. The grass tossed busily as the wind threaded through it, making thousands of whispering voices, hinting at words.

The moon climbed the sky, became a lantern high overhead. Gabriella's shadow moved alongside her now, short but distinct, like an inky ghost.

She was weary and hungry. The chill of the deepest watch of the night weighed heavily upon her. She stopped finally in the centre of an ocean of shushing grass and considered lying down for a few hours. She must be very near the border of the Barrens now, and she did not wish to close her eyes within that cursed landscape even one more night than she had to.

She ate just a little more, unrolled her blanket, and then, achingly, removed some of her armour and lay down.

She longed for a fire but was too exhausted to search for kindling and work the flint. Even in the cold, however, she felt the subtle warmth of the sigil around her neck. Perhaps it was her imagination, but the falcon emblem almost seemed to radiate heat in waves, soothing her and calming her shivers. It was impossible of course, but she did not reject its comfort, even if it was only a figment of her exhausted mind. Nearby, bobbing jovially in the breeze, a spider hung in a web between two stalks. It seemed to regard her, and she was reminded of the spider in the castle halls, the one that had visited her briefly on the night Rhyss had been killed.

"Watch over me, friend," she whispered, turning away. "Be my guardian this night."

She lay in the tall grass, blinking slowly, feeling a dismaying sense of déjà vu. It seemed to her that she could hear the bell of the academy tolling faintly under the rush of the wind, could feel the slope of the hill beneath her, leading down towards the valley brook and the castle bridge. She closed her eyes and remembered the shadow of Darrick as a young boy, his dirty face and wild hair silhouetted against the sun.

That was Whisperwind powder... I won't tattle on you if you get me some.

She was always very good with the magical tools and potions. That was why she was always the one to blow the Whisperwind, or pluck the strings of the enchanted harp, or speak the words to conjure the smoke visions. Toph had always told her she was talented in the magical arts.

She closed her eyes. Fleetingly, she felt the memory of Darrick's first, impetuous kiss pressed onto the corner of her mouth like a promise of good things yet to come. In her memory, she covered that kiss with her hand even as he ran towards the academy, grinning mischievously.

In reality, lying amongst the dead grass and pale moonlight of the borderland, she slept. The spider watched, unmoving, bobbing in the constant wind.

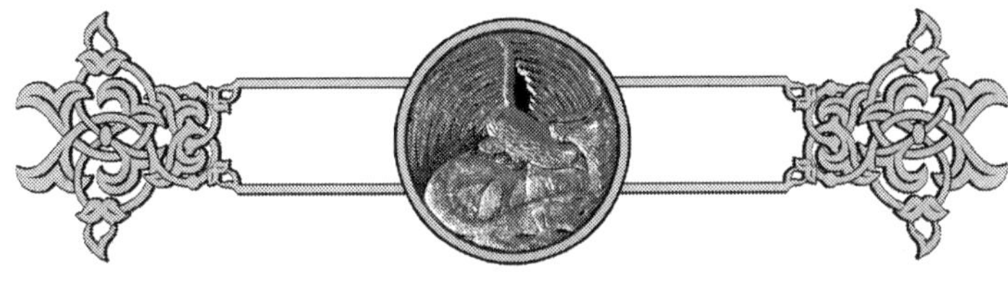

The next morning dawned bright and clear, waking her with its blazing orange light. She sat up, chilled to the bone and once again ravenously hungry. Blinking and rubbing her eyes, she looked around.

A small pile of berries sat nearby her at the very edge of the mashed stalks of her erstwhile bed. She frowned down at it. The berries were tiny but bright, tumbled into a neat pile of red and deep purple. Wild elderberries and raspberries, she thought. There were even a few acorns scattered into the mix, as if whoever or whatever had left the pile had been slightly unsure of what, exactly, a creature like Gabriella might best breakfast on.

She raised her eyes and looked about her, scanning over the waving stalks of grass. There was nothing else in sight save for a few distant trees and thin bushes.

Carefully, she reached for the berries, plucked one up. She popped it into her mouth and chewed it thoughtfully. Wherever it had come from, it was extremely welcome. Her stomach rumbled eagerly at the burst of flavour, and she quickly scooped up the rest of the pile. The berries were methodically consumed, leaving only the acorns. She considered trying one, even tested the nut of it between her teeth. In the end, however, she decided to save them just in case she was less fortunate as the journey continued. She slipped the acorns into her pack, stood up, and stretched in the morning sunlight.

Whoever her mysterious benefactor had been—and strange as it certainly seemed—it was a much different awakening than she had expected. Perhaps the magic of this bizarre place so close to the Tempest Barrens was not entirely dark after all.

Unless, of course, the berries were poison.

Considering this a bit worriedly, she set off again.

The grassy valley continued on for some time, becoming golden in the morning light. She encountered one more stream, trickling thinly through a highway of round, purplish stones, and stopped to refresh herself. Filling her flask once more, she felt cautiously confident that water would not be an issue as she crossed the steppe. Food, however, could soon become a scarcity, assuming that her strange night-time benefactor did not show up again. She puzzled over the mystery as she continued onwards.

Shortly after noon, Gabriella spied a structure on the horizon. It jutted up irregularly, forming the unmistakable shape of a ruin. It was too small to be a castle but too large to be a cottage. As she neared it, squinting in the hard noon sunlight, it began to take on the shape of a long forgotten inn. The main building stood devoid of any roof. Its brick and stone walls looked as barren as bones in the grass. Behind this, a stable was almost entirely lost in vines, bent crookedly in the constant wind. Finally, approaching the ancient structure's shadow, Gabriella spied the remains of a well, its bucket long gone and its stones collapsed sadly inwards.

She slowed as she neared the main building. Part of her wanted to enter it, if only to search for any supplies or tools that might be of use. Another part of her, much deeper and less articulate, insisted she stay far away from it.

It is cursed, she thought suddenly, as if the idea had come to her from the very air around her, whistling and moaning through the bones of the old inn. *Something awful happened here. And I think I know why. This is the boundary. This was the last outpost of humanity, right at the edge of the Barrens, catering to the adventurers and magical treasure hunters. It lasted awhile, maybe even decades, but eventually, the Tempest claimed it, completely and irreversibly.*

Gabriella took a step backwards. Normally, she prided herself on not being a superstitious person. This, however, was more than idle nervousness, like she had felt whilst skirting the abandoned cottage the day before. This was like a smell in the air or a dull throb, just outside the range of hearing but sensed nonetheless. *Stay away,* it warned unmistakably. She determined that that was good advice.

She began to pace a wide circle around the property, watching it constantly. The skeleton of a large horse lay in the weeds alongside the inn. Grass swished and whined through the cage of its ribs. Its skull seemed to have three eye sockets. Of course, that had to be an illusion.

She looked again, felt her blood chill at the sight of it, and then looked away.

The inn was perfectly still and silent as she rounded it, and yet it did not feel dead. She shuddered, unable to shake the feeling that the stillness was a façade, that the inn was watching her with its empty black windows and doorways, measuring her, debating whether or not to allow her to pass.

Finally, thankfully, it was behind her. She walked on, throwing looks back over her shoulder at it, unwilling to let its watchful emptiness out of her sight until she was well away from it. As it dwindled into distance, she felt the intensity of its gaze seem to lighten. She drew a deep breath, turned away from it for the last time, and continued on her way.

She had passed into the Barrens. The desolate steppe stretched out before her now like a stone ocean, unbroken by trees, shimmering with the waves of its yellow grass. A pall of loneliness filled the space, expanding all the way to the flat horizon.

Gabriella walked on.

She sang to herself, just to fill the void of silence. She recalled every bard's tale she could remember and recited the bits that she liked best. Her voice rang out pristinely, with no echo yet clear as silver bells in the whispering emptiness. Eventually, however, even the sound of her own voice began to spook her. She fell quiet and plodded onwards, her boots leaving a wake of bent stalks behind her.

Sometimes, the grasses gave way to expanses of smooth, cracked rock, some of them larger than the courtyard of the castle she had grown up in. Here, nothing grew, and yet, occasionally, strange cairns of stones would stand erect in the sun, casting hard shadows. Some of these cairns were nearly as tall as she, balanced so precariously that it seemed that the slightest breath of wind should knock them tumbling. Other times, the rocky shelves would be carved with ancient symbols, some so large that she could not make them out even whilst standing in the middle of them. It was as if they had been meant to be viewed from high up, by the very birds of the air. None of the symbols made any sense to her, even the ones that were small enough to be seen in their entirety, and all of them left her feeling strange and feverish, shivering even in the warmth of the autumn sunlight.

Eventually, the sun began to descend behind her, casting her shadow out before her. She followed it, watching it stretch longer and longer. The yellow grass became coppery in the descending light. A few trees dotted the landscape now, looking gnarled and dead. Odd, gigantic boulders arose from the grass, as if cast from enormous trebuchets eons ago, forgotten like playing pieces on a monstrous game board.

Gabriella stopped near one of these and leant against it, her back to the sun where it blazed on the western horizon, its red light melting into the dark line of the earth.

She withdrew her flask from her pack and drunk from it sparingly, careful not to let even a drop dribble down her chin. She considered stopping to sleep. It had been a long, wearying day, and as much as she dreaded the lost time, she knew that she would only waste her supplies by traveling tired, when she was less efficient.

She lowered her pack and knelt down next to it. Before she could unroll her blanket, however, a subtle sensation drifted over her. She frowned slightly and then lowered her hand, touching the rocky ground before her.

There was a dull rumble. It was very faint, and she couldn't tell if she was feeling it or hearing it. Leaving her pack, she stood up again and scanned the steppe all around her. Rounding the boulder, she peered toward the northern horizon. At first glance, she saw nothing. Then, faintly, she spied a cloud rising, drifting off into the wind. She watched it, squinting in the dying light, and felt her heart begin to quicken.

The rumble became more pronounced, and dark specks began to take shape beneath the cloud. They were too low to be horses and riders, yet too few to be a stampede of some native steppe animal. The size of them made it difficult to judge distance. Before she knew what was happening, the shapes were nearly upon her. She watched, grimly transfixed, as the nearest of the creatures came fully into view. It was a large, brutish beast with a blunt, shaggy head, tossing and huffing, its wide-spaced eyes glinting yellowly in the sunset. Twisted horns grew from the sides of its head, curving down and out. Its feet were hooves, churning the ground like pistons, sending up gouts of torn earth and grass in its wake. Gabriella recognized the creature from the magical histories. They were called chortha, the beastly, feral offspring of the ancient minotaur. Something was riding on the chortha's back, clinging grimly and hunkered low, as if prodding the beast onwards with maddening whispers in its ears.

Gabriella realised the chortha were nearly upon her. She began to back away towards the nearby boulder, and then turned and bolted, fearing the beasts might overrun her, trampling her in their haste.

She lunged behind the boulder just as the first of the chortha thundered past, shaking the ground and pulling a cloud of gritty dust. Gabriella pressed her back up against the rock and hugged her knees, boggling as the creature pounded onwards, bearing its strange burden. The rider appeared to be human but was dressed only in rags, so that streams and tatters of cloth trailed behind it. Pale skin was stretched over prominent ribs, and the hunched spine was picked out in a row of ugly bumps. A shock of wild, black hair tossed between the rider's knobby shoulders.

More of the chortha appeared now, buffeting Gabriella with the noise and rumble of their passage. Each of the beasts bore a rider, and Gabriella saw that they were armed. Swords were strapped to belts on the riders' wasted hips or worn slung across their backs, but there were no shields or helmets.

An icicle of suspicion suddenly pressed into Gabriella's chest, chilling her. What if these horrid men were in the employ of Merodach? What if this was his advance force, rushing toward Herrengard to waylay the royal caravan? Without thinking, she jumped up and drew her own sword with a ring of metal.

She spun, peered around the boulder, and saw three more of the chortha thundering towards her, their mouths gnashing and their riders glaring forwards, lying low on the backs of their mounts. Gabriella steeled her nerve, spun her sword so that the blade protruded down rather than up, and then scrambled up onto the boulder, climbing into full sight of the oncoming riders.

"Stop in the name of the Princess of Camelot!" she shouted, raising both of her hands, her sword still jutting from the bottom of her right fist.

The beasts neither slowed nor showed any deviation in their course. The blank faces of the riders did not so much as flinch. The nearer riders passed the boulder upon which Gabriella stood, first on the right, and then the left. The third chortha galloped straight towards her, as if it meant to ram head first into the sloped face of the boulder. Gabriella watched, eyes widening, resisting the urge to jump out of the way. She crouched and spun her sword upright again, clutching the hilt with both hands.

At the last moment, the rider twitched the mane of its beast, and the great creature lunged upwards, scissoring its forelegs into the air and, incredibly, launching onto the slope of the boulder. Its hot breath chugged into Gabriella's face, its hooves clawed and scrabbled at the rock, carrying it up and over.

Gabriella leapt sideways, throwing herself clear and swinging her sword downwards in a steely blur. It connected with the rider, hacking into it, and then both the beast and Gabriella fell away from each other.

She struck the ground and rolled, dropping her sword. A split second later, the chortha landed, shaking the ground, momentum forcing it into a shuddering stumble. It tripped over itself, scrambled, dug in its hooves, and then launched forwards again, pushing onwards in the wake of its fellows.

The rider, however, had fallen off. The horrid figure rolled awkwardly on the ground, its scabbard flapping like a fin, and then it began to struggle upright.

Gabriella's shoulder throbbed where she had landed on it, but she leapt to her feet, scooped up her sword, and gave chase. Ahead of her, the figure began to lope after its beast, huffing raggedly.

"Stop!" Gabriella cried out, panting. "I command you! What is your business? Where are you going? *Tell me!* I don't want to have to hurt you!"

But, as she could clearly see, she already had. The figure's gait was clumsy despite its speed, because it was missing its left arm. It had been severed raggedly just above the elbow. Black blood dribbled from the wound, staining the remains of the figure's tunic.

Gabriella's stomach turned, but she did not slow. She was gaining on the figure. It was tall and gangly like a young man, albeit with an old woman's ragged, grey hair. Its remaining arm was rippled with muscle, pumping awkwardly as it ran.

"*Stop*, damn you!" Gabriella commanded, lunging and hooking a handful of the figure's tattered clothes. She yanked, and it stumbled. Suddenly, it spun around, raised its remaining hand into a claw, and lunged back towards her. The creature's face was slack and wasted around a gaping mouth, out of which came a rough exhale of bestial loathing. Its eyes were cloudy, white marbles, rolling grotesquely.

Gabriella let go of the figure's torn tunic and scrambled backwards, repulsed. Her feet slipped, and she fell back, raising her sword instinctively, if wildly, against the horror. It was not a man. At least, not anymore.

The creature stopped immediately. Without a second look, it spun around and ran on again, following its fellows. They rumbled onwards, already merely a drifting cloud against the last rays of the sun.

Gabriella still held up her sword, trembling. She looked at it, saw the swipe of black blood smeared across its middle, and then dropped it in horror. She scuttled backwards, her breath coming in harsh gasps.

The awful figure dwindled into a distant silhouette, still running, blood still dripping from the stump of its left arm.

She had thought that the riders might be an advance force sent out by Merodach, meaning to head off the caravan on its way to Herrengard. Whatever they were, however, they were not human soldiers. They were monsters. Such things simply could not be in the employ of Merodach.

Could they?

Slowly, still trembling, Gabriella got to her feet and retrieved her sword. She retraced her steps back towards the boulder. The tracks of the chortha were a scarred highway of torn earth and trampled grass.

Lying in the sunset at the base of the boulder was the severed arm. Blood leaked thinly from the stump, the colour of plum in the dying sunlight. The white fingers flexed and relaxed slowly, rhythmically, like the legs of a dead spider.

Seeing this, Gabriella nearly vomited. She felt her gorge rise, then clapped the back of her hand over her mouth, desperate to hold it in.

She ran, stumbling around the boulder. Her pack was still lying in the shadow on the other side. She scooped it up, not slowing, and pelted onwards, weary but intent, meaning only to put as much distance between that awful severed arm and herself as possible.

The riders had neither been living nor dead. The severed arm, its fingers flexing and spasming, proved it. Perhaps it would crawl after its master, just as its master had run off after the others, following whatever grim duty it was that propelled them. Worse, what if the severed arm crawled after her instead, making its way slowly but doggedly through the whispering grass, leaking that awful black blood in its wake?

She ran on, gasping and stumbling on the rocky earth as the sun finally slipped over the horizon. She simply could not sleep within sight of the horrid dismembered thing.

Dimly, she wondered if she would ever be able to sleep again.

Exhaustion eventually overtook her.

It caught up to her as she crossed a large plate of rock, scoured of grass and cracked like an enormous platter. She stumbled to one knee, panting, and simply could not get up again. She remained there, one hand and one knee pressed to the cold stone. After a minute, she sank fully to the ground, hugged her pack like a pillow, and huddled there against the wind.

She slept. And dreamt.

Warmth covered her slowly. It buzzed in her joints, soothing her soreness. For what seemed like a long time, she simply lay there and soaked in that pleasant, calming warmth. It was a familiar sensation. It was, in fact, sunlight.

Gabriella opened her eyes slowly without getting up. The rocky shelf was awash with golden sunbeams. The rays stroked her cheek. A soft breeze combed the nearby grass and lifted her hair. It smelled like heather. Gabriella pushed herself upright and looked around. The steppe was transformed by the cheery sunlight. What had earlier seemed desolate and barren now seemed merely quiet and strangely expectant.

The change was very welcome, as was the accompanying shift in her attitude. The creeping dread was replaced by a solemn tranquillity. Everything, she felt with calm certainty, was going to be all right. Her mission, whatever it had been, suddenly didn't seem to matter any more. Of course it didn't. The disaster (whatever it was) had been averted. The horrors had been made right. The Little Prince would be fine, as would Sigrid, and Father, and even—

Darrick.

He was still alive. And so was Rhyss. They were coming to meet her.

Elation filled Gabriella, and she leapt to her feet. Her face was flush with overwhelmed delight as she looked all around, shading her eyes with her hand, breathlessly hoping that she might see them already. The sun-washed Barrens shushed all around, empty for miles in every direction. Neither Darrick nor Rhyss were anywhere in sight.

That was all right too. Gabriella dropped her hand and sighed deeply, happily. The suspense of Darrick and Rhyss's coming was a joy in itself. She would savour it and wait for them there on her expanse of cracked, white rock. Funny how she had come to think of it as *her* rock, and yet it made sense. This was where her greatest loves would find her. They would seek her here, and here only, for it was a magical beacon to them. Until they came, it would be her home. She would wait patiently, expectantly.

Someone else was coming as well, someone whose voice she had almost, but not quite, forgotten, someone whom she had missed far longer than the others. Someone who would hug her, and cradle her, and sing her songs. Her mother. She would be there soon. The mere thought of it brought tears of joy.

There was a noise, a rustling behind Gabriella. Darrick was there! He had arrived! He was coming out of the grass behind her, smiling with love, holding out his arms to embrace her. She spun around to greet him, launching herself in his direction. And then she frowned, because he wasn't there after all. It had been the wind.

No, not the wind. It was Rhyss, not Darrick. She was hiding in the bushes near the other end of the clearing, playing her old games.

"Rhyss!" Gabriella called, turning around and laughing. "Please, don't tease me! Come and let me see your face! Laugh with me, Rhyss!"

She heard her but didn't see her. Rhyss's laughter was like a ribbon in the wind. She was not behind the bushes, but still far off, her voice carrying on the breeze through the lonely distance. Gabriella lowered her hands and shook her head, smiling crookedly. Her friend would be here soon. Darrick would be with her. And then, not long after them, her mother would come. They would all be there together, and they would never have to be apart again. Until then, Gabriella would wait.

She would wait.

She sat down on the warm rock and hugged her knees to her chest. The wind whispered and shushed, making undulating patterns on the grass beyond the stony shelf. She watched it, listening for those that she loved.

Something screeched behind her. It was a sudden, jarring sound, and Gabriella couldn't help jumping. She spun onto her knees, looking back.

A large bird stood in the sunlight, its beady eye cocked at her severely. It had a hooked, grey beak and tawny feathers on its chest. Its wings were darker, each feather rimmed with tan. As she watched, it ruffled its feathers, nearly doubling in size, and unfurled its wings. It squawked at her piercingly.

Go away, she thought at it, frowning. The noise of the bird was horrible. It would keep the others away. She knew it instinctively. *Be quiet and go away!*

The bird—she recognised it as a falcon—took a flapping, hopping step towards her and screeched again. It darted its head forwards, as if it meant to tear at her face. She flinched backwards, instinctively raising a hand to her cheek.

"Go!" she rasped at it, keeping her voice hushed like the whispering breeze all around. "Leave me alone, you filthy thing!"

The bird did not go. It tilted its head, staring at her in that odd sidelong way that birds do. It spread its wings fully and hopped towards her again, flapping into the air and raising its talons. The talons, Gabriella saw, were black and needle-sharp, hooked like thorns. She scrambled away from the bird, struggling to get her feet beneath her and shield her face at the same time.

When she looked up, the bird was still there, still flapping and screeching, nearly upon her. Its gold-ringed eyes seemed as large as saucers.

Gabriella threw herself backwards, kicking with both feet. She landed in the grass at the ledge of the stone clearing and rolled, covering her head with her hands.

The grass around her was shockingly cold. She opened her eyes and lifted her head. Darkness blanketed the ground, full of hissing, icy wind.

"No!" she barked hoarsely, scrambling to her feet in dismay. "No! Darrick! Rhyss! I didn't mean it! I didn't mean to get off the—"

But even as she stumbled to her feet, the reality of the dream faded to tatters. It blew away into the darkness and was replaced with only aching loneliness. Darrick and Rhyss were dead. They were never coming back. If she did not hurry on her journey, the Little Prince might soon be dead as well, along with Sigrid, Treynor, her father, and the whole of Camelot.

"No," she moaned, sinking back into the grass, letting her hands fall limp into her lap. It had been such a lovely dream, unlike anything she had ever known before. It had been so real. She had felt the beams of the sun, smelled the heather, heard the distant voices of those she loved, laughing as they returned to her.

She looked aside at the rocky shelf upon which she had slept. To her great surprise, the falcon was still there, looking surprisingly small in the blue darkness. It had furled its wings again and now merely stood there, regarding her with one golden eye. Its feathers fluttered faintly in the wind.

"It's a trap, isn't it?" she said faintly. "A place to lure people to their dooms. They'd stop there, camp there, and dream. And once they had started dreaming, they'd never wish to stop. They would stay there forever, no matter what, even if they knew that it was a trap. Because sometimes...," she sighed wistfully, "sometimes the dream is better, and more real, than any reality."

The bird cocked its head, not seeming to listen. After a moment, it turned around, ruffled its wings, and hopped away. Gabriella thought it was leaving, and then she saw where it was actually heading. The falcon stopped near her pack, dipped its beak, and caught the loop of rope that closed it. Then, flapping its wings for balance, it began to pull the pack across the face of the cracked rock. When it was nearly to the grassy edge, it stumbled and dropped the rope, letting out a frustrated screech.

"Thank you," Gabriella said, reaching over the boundary to grab her pack. The falcon immediately darted its head forwards and nipped the back of her wrist, drawing a line of blood. Gabriella hissed and yanked her arm back, clapping her other hand over the scratch.

"Curse you, you damn bird!" she cried angrily. The falcon merely stared, tilting its head up at her, as if measuring her. Finally, it turned back once more, caught the rope into its beak, and pulled her pack the rest of the way out of the stony clearing.

This done, the falcon immediately clapped its wings, launched into the air, and flapped away.

Gabriella watched, frowning miserably, and then drew a deep sigh. She uncovered the scratch on her wrist, saw that it was quite shallow, and washed it with a few drops of water from her flask.

There were no mysterious piles of berries for her to breakfast on that morning. Instead, she ate some more of her dwindling bread and dried venison, sipped a few swallows of water, and then climbed to her feet.

She stopped. Slowly, almost helplessly, she turned back to the bare clearing of rock behind her. It called to her, promising its happy lies. She realised, with deep dismay, that she desired those lies. She could, if she so chose, step right back onto that plate of stone, lie down, and be swallowed up again in the delicious hope of the dream. So what if the hope was only a mirage? Why should an imagined delight be worse than a real horror?

She almost did it. The only thing that prevented her, of course, was her remembrance of the Little Prince. Darrick, Rhyss, and her mother were dead, but the Little Prince was alive, and he needed her. She was his only hope.

She sighed deeply, shuddering as she looked down at the cold, grey stone. Finally, reluctantly, she turned away from it.

The sky was low and steely, moving swiftly overhead. Thunder made a dull rumble far off, so that the sound seemed to go on for minutes. Distant foggy shapes clung to the horizon, and Gabriella turned towards them, knowing what they were. The Cragrack Cliffs were her last, and perhaps greatest, obstacle, and they were finally in sight.

Gabriella walked on into the cold, pale light of dawn.

CHAPTER 7

It began to snow.

Tiny, white flakes skirled through the air and stuck to the grass as well as Gabriella's hair and eyelashes. Close up, the snow looked like white sand. Further away, it was a drifting pale fog, closing off the world around her and hiding the jagged line of the distant Cliffs.

They were the most prominent and storied feature of the Tempest Barrens. The Cragrack Cliffs formed a hundred-mile-long rift, crossing the Barrens in a jagged line and forming a nearly impossible obstruction. No one knew the origin of the Cliffs, except that they were not a natural phenomenon. It was as if a cosmic hammer had fallen onto the Barrens, breaking them in half and crushing one of those halves lower than the other, forming a ragged, impossible stair step hundreds of feet tall.

There were ways over it, Gabriella knew. Adventurers and wanderers had mapped switchback paths up the Cliffs, marking them however possible. The paths might be very difficult to find, and they would probably be extremely treacherous, but she knew that they must exist. Whole wizarding armies were known to have crossed the Cliffs. If the chortha riders of the previous day had indeed come from Merodach, then they had to have crossed the Cragrack Cliffs themselves along with their mounts. If she could find the route they had taken, perhaps she could go up the way they had come down.

It was a thin chance, she knew. She would confront that challenge when she reached it.

The more difficult challenge was still further ahead of her, and it was not a physical one. She needed to find Merodach and his forces in order to head them off even as they marched towards Camelot. She had no idea how she would locate them. If they were skirting the Barrens, as her father's army had done, then she would eventually have to veer west and meet them head on. But where? How far might they have traveled already? Not far, she assumed, because of their numbers and the weight of their armaments and supplies, but she knew that her guess was uninformed and vague at best.

Worse, what precisely would she do when she did find them? At this concern, however, her thoughts ceased, became a blur of red mist behind her eyes. That challenge would be confronted when the time came as well. She was certain of it. She only knew that she had to find the rogue army. Then destiny would have its way.

Gabriella was hungry. Her store of food was running very low; thus, she preserved what little she had left, trying not to think about it in her pack. Soon enough, however, cold began to overtake hunger as her chief concern. She hugged herself as she continued onwards, squinting against the gritty, blowing white.

The ground began to descend beneath her, dipping into a hidden depression. The wind lessened, broken by a scatter of surrounding boulders. Gabriella followed the slope of the ground until the grass became broken earth, hard and grey as ash. Warm air pressed gently up towards her, as if exhaled from a massive throat. As it did, it pushed away a raft of drifting snowflakes, revealing a low crevice, a secret cavern. Sharp boulders surrounded the entrance like teeth.

Gabriella had heard of this place, although (she admitted with a shiver) she had assumed it to be one of the myths. It was called the Troll's Maw. The legends were that a massive rock troll had been killed in battle and subsequently buried, leaving only its gaping stony mouth visible. True or not, the Troll's Maw was purported to actually lead to a chain of tunnels and caverns that webbed beneath the Tempest Barrens. These had been used by the magical armies of eons past, serving as hidden shelters, hideouts, even fortresses. There were stories of buried riches in the forgotten depths of the caverns, enchanted throne rooms, magical kings entombed with all of their treasure.

More importantly, Gabriella remembered, the more lucid myths claimed that the caverns formed safe highways beneath the wasted land of the Barrens, coming up on the other side of the Cragrack Cliffs.

She hovered near the entrance, feeling the warm air of the earth's bowels pushing out at her, melting the snowflakes even as they fell. It would certainly be a warmer route, but what if she could not find her way? The thought of becoming lost in the endless tunnels and caverns was deeply unsettling. She began to turn away, and then another thought struck her. What if the chortha riders had come via this route? What if there were not, in fact, paths up the Cragrack Cliffs? She might walk all the way to the base of the Cliffs only to have to turn back, hoping against hope to find the entrance of the Troll's Maw again.

And by then, it would surely be too late anyway.

Indecision froze her in place. Finally, cautiously, she approached the Troll's Maw again. The ashy ground sloped towards it, falling into darkness beneath the shelf of rock that formed the cavern's roof. She had no light. It would be hopeless to attempt such a passage without a torch or lantern.

But then, as she neared the cavern entrance and peered into its depths, she saw that it was not completely dark inside. A dull, milky glow emanated from deep within, teasing her eyes. Gabriella crept closer and then, after only a short pause, ducked beneath the roof of the cavern, moving carefully into its shadow.

The ground continued to slope away into the throat of the cave, becoming loose scree that slipped and scrabbled beneath her boots. The roof of the cavern rose as she descended, feeling her way blindly. The glow ahead of her was faint but unmistakable. It didn't seem to illuminate anything, but rather hung as a faint cloud in the air, slightly brighter at its base. Gabriella inched towards it. After a minute, her eyes adjusted to the gloom, and she saw that the glow was very near her now. It emanated from a long crack in the cavern floor. The crack itself glowed like a faint bolt of lightning, spreading off into the depths.

Gabriella followed the crack, careful not to step on it, fearing that she might fall through into some hidden chamber beneath. Eventually, as her eyes fully adjusted to the dimness, she could see her surroundings. She was in a narrow corridor, apparently worn naturally into the rock. The crack laced along the descending floor, forming a glowing beacon for many hundreds of feet. Finally, as Gabriella followed it into a wider, higher fissure, the crack opened completely. Stairs led down into the bluish glow, carved by hand but worn smooth with the centuries. Gabriella descended the steps carefully. The stone was wet and slick, shiny in the increasing light. Still, she could not see the source of the strange glow.

Finally, the stairs turned, emptying into a large subterranean chamber. Gabriella peered into the depths and gasped, nearly falling backwards onto the stairs.

The chamber was lit with unearthly lanterns, each one filled like a jar with a sort of cloudy, blue liquid, glowing like swamp fire. There were dozens of them, bolted along the walls and marching into dimness. These, however, were not what had surprised Gabriella. It was the ranks of shapes that stood in their faint glow, filling the space in perfect rows and columns.

It was an army, still as stone, their faces as calm and inscrutable as statues. Gabriella stared at them, her heart pounding, and slowly realised that this, in fact, was exactly what they were. She recovered herself and crept forwards, raising her right hand. Her shadow fell over the nearest of the soldiers, and she willed herself to touch it. It was stone, utterly dead and cold to the touch.

Gabriella exhaled, shuddering, and looked around at the others. Each statue was distinct, dressed in full (if ancient) battle armour and armed with carefully sculpted swords, bows, axes, and daggers. Some wore high helmets on their brows. Others bore shields nearly as tall as themselves. Morbidly curious, Gabriella began to walk through them, threading carefully between their ranks. Eerily, some of the statues had been overtaken by growths of stalagmites, their smooth cones reaching up towards the cavern ceiling, stretching to reach their dripping counterparts above. Further in, some of the statues had fallen over like dominoes, perhaps toppled by a long-ago earthquake. Some of the fallen figures were still intact, lying awkwardly on their faces. More, however, had broken and even shattered. Arms, legs, and heads lay scattered like broken toys. Gabriella shivered at the sight and hurried onwards.

She was deep amongst the statue army now and realised that she was unsure from which direction she had come. She fought a panicked urge to try to retrace her steps. Instead, she approached the nearest of the cavern walls, heading towards one of the strange lanterns. She looked up at it and saw that it was indeed rather like a glass jar, although quite thick and as round as a pumpkin. It was embraced in a brass frame, which itself was hung on an iron hook bolted directly into the cavern wall. Below it, lying in the shadows where it had apparently fallen, was an iron pole with a hooked loop on its end. Gabriella understood its purpose immediately and breathed a shallow sigh of relief. Retrieving the pole, she used it to reach upwards, hooking the lantern from its place and lowering it.

The globe of glass was small and relatively light, stoppered with a ceramic plug. The liquid inside was thick as syrup, shimmering with blue light that intensified as it moved. She shook the globe gently, and the light bloomed, cold but bright, casting her shadow up onto the stone wall. She left the globe hanging on the pole's hook and simply leant the pole against her shoulder. The lamp bobbed, casting its light all around her.

She had a lantern now. She could move onwards.

A sudden breath of air pushed past her, sighing harshly. It lifted her hair, swirled around her, and then coursed off into the ranks of stone statues. Gabriella sucked in a breath and spun on her heels, crouching instinctively.

Silence pressed upon her ears again, punctuated only by the distant drips of the stalactites. She waited, her eyes bulging at the dimness. Nothing moved.

Cautiously, still looking about her, she began to move. She followed the line of the cavern wall, hoping it would lead her into the tunnels and eventually to her passage beyond the Cragrack Cliffs. Gradually, she picked up her pace, passing rank after rank of the statue army.

Behind her, a stir of whispers arose, and then a low howl. It rushed through the soldiers, seeming to come from many directions at once, approaching.

Gabriella spun around, her eyes going wide and her free hand dropping to her sword. Even in the midst of her fear, she reminded herself not to drop the glass lantern, not to shatter it and spill its mysterious contents.

The rushing howl increased, splitting into several sources and snaking through the statue army. Gabriella cast around, looking, but could see nothing. Her heart pounded now, pulsing in the corners of her vision.

Suddenly, there was movement between the ranks of statues. A ribbon of dust lifted into the air and rushed towards her, swirling through the petrified soldiers. As it came, it emitted a low, harsh roar.

Gabriella turned, gripped the lantern pole with both hands, and ran. She dashed along the wall, her feet slipping on the loose shale, and bumped one of the stone soldiers with her elbow. The statue began to totter, but Gabriella did not look back to watch. There was a loud clack of stone on stone as the statue keeled over, knocking its closest counterpart. More cracks rang into the air as a chain reaction ensued. The howling tendrils of wind seemed to grow enraged by this. Their voices rose to furious shrieks, and their numbers seemed to increase, even into the hundreds, all swirling closer to her.

The tottering statues caught up to Gabriella as she ran. She sensed the movement of them next to her as they keeled over, breaking against their mates. Heads cracked off and rolled into the aisle before her. A cacophony of crashes filled the air, competing with the screams of her hidden pursuers.

Then, horribly, a rank of the stone soldiers leant ponderously across the aisle ahead of her, almost as if they had come alive. Their calm faces leered at her as they toppled over, striking the cavern wall and shattering. Her path was suddenly blocked, filled with crumbling statues and choked with dust.

Gabriella turned, dropping the lantern pole and grabbing for her sword. The lantern globe struck the ground and shattered, sending up a burst of blinding, blue light and then falling dark. Gabriella boggled in the sudden dimness. Shadows loomed over her, faint in the light of the distant lanterns. The howling winds surrounded her now, collapsing upon her, becoming visible as snakes of dust and grit. They had faces, each one a mask of gaping rage. Gabriella raised her sword to them, knowing it was useless, ridiculous.

A burst of air suddenly swarmed over her shoulder, beaten by a fury of wings. There was a screech, a flurry of motion, and Gabriella realised that the dark shape was a bird flapping wildly against the howling tendrils and forcing them back. It screeched again, switching its tail feathers in the air like a rudder. The snaking winds recoiled slightly from the bird, pushed by its wings, but did not retreat. They strained closer, their incessant howls merging into a ululating roar.

"Fall back!" a voice called out, so loudly and suddenly that Gabriella cringed in terror. It was a woman's voice, clear and strong in the rushing dark. "Fall back, armies of Orudhor! This is not your enemy! Your day of vengeance still awaits! Fall back now and return to your slumber!"

A burst of pristine, white light exploded before Gabriella. Before it, the swirling tendrils shrank away, diminished and fading. The light remained, glimmering, and Gabriella saw that it came from the end of a wand. The wand was held in a woman's hand, but she herself was not visible through the light.

Gabriella collapsed to her knees, still gripping her sword, weak with relief and confusion. The bird landed before her, and she saw that it was a falcon, the very same one that had visited her early that morning and chased her out of the cursed stone clearing. It cocked its head at her, showing her one gold-ringed eye, seeming pleased with itself.

The white light finally faded but did not completely vanish. It moved now, lowering, revealing a tall woman with red braids framing a pale, narrow face. She was dressed in robes the colour of sunflowers with a black cloak pulled over her shoulders.

"That," she said gravely, inclining her head to meet Gabriella's eyes, "was far too close for comfort."

Gabriella's voice came out as a hoarse rasp. "What was that?" she asked breathlessly. "Who are you?"

"Alas, the spectral army of Orudhor," the woman replied, glancing back out over the ranks of stone soldiers, "They are cursed to remain with their frozen bodies until their time of reckoning. They were once quite noble, before being turned to stone by a certain mercenary sorcerer. Now, being dead, they are no longer… exactly sane."

Gabriella looked around at the frozen army, many of them now toppled and broken. Stone dust still arose from the shattered ranks. She chilled with the realisation that these were not in fact statues, but petrified men, lost to the ages. She gulped thickly.

"And to answer your other question," the woman answered, switching her wand to her other hand and reaching to help Gabriella to her feet, "we are Featherbolt and Helena. I presume you can guess who is who."

The woman, Helena, led Gabriella out of the chamber of the frozen army, following a jagged rift that descended even deeper into the earth. Featherbolt flew ahead, occasionally circling back and landing on the woman's shoulder. Shortly, another cavern opened before them, lit with a strangely glowing subterranean river.

"It is I," Helena called out, her voice echoing into the depths of the chamber. "And I bring a guest."

A point of light arose in the dim distance, and Gabriella saw that it was another wand, held upright in the fist of a tall man.

"That is good news," the figure called back. "Featherbolt found his quarry then, I assume."

"It would appear yes," Helena answered, glancing aside at Gabriella. At the mention of his name, Featherbolt launched from the woman's shoulder and spiraled up into the murky heights of the cavern. Clusters of brown shapes hung there, chittering faintly.

Helena watched after the bird and shook her head. "He fancies himself kindred with the bats," she commented. "Why he should wish to consort with winged rodents, I cannot guess, but it does occasionally serve a purpose."

The man approached, lowering his wand as he came. To Gabriella, he looked like a taller, less fussy version of the late High Constable Ulric. His red goatee made a neat point on his chin below a rugged face and rather severe eyes. He was dressed similarly to the woman, although his robes were mostly deep crimson, offset with a fur-lined cape. He smiled a bit grimly as he reached the two women.

"This is an unexpected meeting," he said, turning to Gabriella. "You may call me Goodrik. You have already met my traveling companions, I see. Would you be so kind as to join us in a palaver? We do not often meet human travelers this deep in the Tempest Barrens. And you, for reasons as yet unknown, have attracted the rather insistent attention of our falcon friend."

Gabriella agreed to this, feeling that she owed as much to her benefactors in spite of knowing nearly nothing about them. The three approached the shore of the subterranean river, and Gabriella saw that its glow came from thousands of tiny, incandescent fish that swam in its depths, remaining nearly motionless against the swift current.

The man, Goodrik, produced his wand and pointed it at an arbitrary spot on the rocky cavern floor. He spoke a short phrase, and a burst of fire appeared on the rocks, burning merrily on nothing. Turning slightly, he flicked his wand three more times, and then, after a short consideration, a fourth. Three small but ornate chairs appeared around the fire, carved of wood and looking appropriately rustic. The fourth flick produced a camp table with a tidy silver serving tray upon it.

"There," Goodrik announced, pocketing his wand. "That should provide us some much welcome atmosphere. Tea?"

"Why," Gabriella replied, impressed almost speechless, "yes. I think."

"It is merely transfigured river water," Helena commented as she sat down. "Just as these chairs are bits of driftwood. Nonetheless, they will both comfort and warm us whilst we discuss. Do sit. There is nothing to be afraid of."

"I am not afraid," Gabriella said, smiling as she drifted onto her chair. "I am just... I have never been in the presence of..."

"You can say it, my dear," Goodrik interjected, leaning to hand her a cup and saucer. "We are witch and wizard. I am glad we need not explain ourselves."

Gabriella took the tea and examined it. The cup and saucer were bone china, smooth and delicate as seashells. She raised the cup to her face, felt the steam on her cheeks, and smelled the fragrant richness. It was black tea, piping hot. "Who are you?" she asked, not yet daring to sip. "Why are you here?"

"We are administrators at a certain society for our arts," Helena answered carefully. "There once were four of us, but now there are only three. That, in short, is why we are here in the Barrens."

"We are seeking someone," Goodrik added, sensing Gabriella's curiosity. "A member of our society who has... gone missing. The fourth of our council has remained behind to manage our affairs. We were about to abandon our search when Featherbolt became interested in you and drew us here to find you."

"I see," Gabriella nodded, frowning. "You are just as secretive as Professor Toph said you would be."

Goodrik smiled a bit stiffly at this, but Helena laughed. "Our notoriety knows no ends, it seems. Even after these many years of secrecy."

"Just because the magical folk have hidden their kingdoms away," Gabriella said, turning to Helena, "does not mean that we have been allowed to forget about you. Some of your people still move amongst us, peddling their enchantments. I have used some of their wares myself."

Goodrik raised his eyebrows. "Have you? Perhaps this is what drew Featherbolt's attention."

Gabriella shook her head. "I did not bring any magic with me on my journey. I have touched neither powder nor potion since the academy."

"Then what," Helena asked evenly, "do you think it was that drew our falcon friend to assist you, and so ardently that we were forced to follow him here in pursuit of you?"

Gabriella shrugged, settling her cup back onto its saucer. "I could not guess," she answered, and then stopped thoughtfully. "Unless it was this." She reached beneath the clasp of her cloak and produced the falcon sigil on its length of chain.

The witch and wizard peered at it. Goodrik's face grew slowly tense. He looked meaningfully aside at Helena.

"What, pray tell," the taller woman asked, not taking her eyes from the falcon sigil, "is your name, daughter?"

Gabriella suddenly felt very wary. She considered lying, but no suitable falsehood came to her mind. "Gabriella Xavier," she answered guardedly.

"Gabriella," Goodrik repeated, nodding enigmatically. "Well then, perhaps you might tell us what it is *you* are doing here, my dear, so very far from your home?"

Again, for reasons she did not quite understand, she considered lying to the witch and wizard. Perhaps they were not as pleasant as they seemed. As before, however, she could think of nothing to say other than the truth. Gabriella was not much in the habit of deception.

"I am on a mission to confront a murderer and a madman," she finally said in a low voice. "To protect my loved ones who are yet alive, and to avenge my loved ones who are no more."

Helena nodded very slowly, considering. "And this murderer and madman," she clarified, "are they two distinct people or one and the same?"

"Do not mock me," Gabriella replied, raising her voice slightly in the echoing cavern. "It is a man called Merodach that I am after. My mission is to seek him... and to kill him."

Goodrik settled his teacup back onto the silver tray. "You must pardon us, Gabriella," he said carefully, "we do not keep up with the affairs of the kingdoms of men as closely as we used to. Please, if you would be so kind... tell us your story."

And Gabriella did. As briefly as she could, she told them of the history of Merodach, of his brutal tactics and his murderous rampages. She told them about Darrick and Rhyss, and the slaughter of her father's army at the hand of Merodach's forces. Goodrik and Helena did not raise an eyebrow at the idea that Gabriella was the daughter of the King of Camelot, nor did they flinch at the atrocities of Merodach or the possibility that he might, if unchecked, destroy all those that she loved and assume control of the Kingdom. More than once, however, their eyes left hers and drifted towards the falcon sigil at her throat. This worried Gabriella far more than she allowed herself to let on.

"Thus," she concluded, "I must attempt to stop him. For my baby and for Camelot."

Helena tilted her head slightly. "But you warned your lady-in-waiting to escape with your son," she commented smoothly. "He will be safe in any event, yes?"

"I did warn Sigrid," Gabriella sighed. "But she did not believe me. She attempted to alert the guards of my leaving. I was nearly caught. I fear that, in the end, she may have rejected my orders and accompanied the caravan to Herrengard."

Goodrik seemed to consider this very seriously. Then he shook his head. "I do hope you are wrong about that," he said. "If you had her trust, then she would have obeyed you even if she did not believe your tale. You must assume that this is the case. Still, perhaps you are better served by returning to them and spiriting the child away yourself."

Gabriella sighed again, deeply. "Perhaps," she agreed. "But it is too late now. I have warred with myself at nearly every step. I must go on now. It is the only hope."

"If you will pardon me, Princess," Helena said, bowing her head slightly, "this seems rather a hopeless endeavour. This man, you say, wiped out the better of your kingdom's army, and you mean to take him alone?"

Gabriella's face hardened. She refused to look at the witch or the wizard. "I do not care to hear your discouragements. I had my fill of such talk in my father's own council. Sometimes, it only takes one person to stand up. Sometimes… that is enough to turn the tide."

"In stories perhaps," Helena said, shaking her head. "But Princess, surely, you must know that a beast of such hate will only—" She stopped as Goodrik raised a hand, commanding her gaze. His face was stern.

"Gabriella," he said, and the gravity of his tone made her look at him. "I respect your courage. Truth be known, I am heartened by it. If there were a hundred of you—nay, a dozen of you—I would see you forth with my blessing and a hearty war cry. But Helena is right. On your own, one young woman against a rogue army, such courage is not valorous. It is foolhardy." It seemed to pain him to say it, but his eyes did not flinch from hers.

Softly, Helena added, "There may be another way, Princess. If God wills your kingdom to be saved, then—"

"Do *not*," Gabriella interrupted, her voice low and fierce, "speak to me of God."

There was an awkward, ringing silence. The river babbled quietly nearby. The magical fire burnt brightly, sending up drifts of sparks, making almost no noise. Finally, Helena spoke again, softly.

"Do you happen to know," she asked, seeming to change the topic, "where your sigil came from, Princess?"

Reflexively, Gabriella reached up and wrapped her hand around the falcon sigil. As always, it was warm. She swallowed and said, "It was a wedding gift. From my father."

Helena tightened her lips. "It is more than that, and I daresay you are well-aware of it."

"Tell me what you know about it," Gabriella asked, almost whispering.

There was a long pause. Goodrik looked at Helena, his face inscrutable.

"It belonged to one of our council," he said carefully. "I sensed the memory of his touch on it the moment you showed it to us, even though it has been altered from its original shape and quite wisely broken. The glitter of that green stone is unmistakable."

Gabriella felt as if the world was sinking away beneath her slowly, dizzyingly. "Who was he?" she implored.

"Ironically," Helena answered, "he is the very one that we traveled to the Barrens in search of."

Goodrik went on. "He was with us on a certain night over a decade ago when we visited a small, snowbound cottage. We had been summoned there to protect a certain little girl—you, I must assume—from a dangerously misguided creature. A werewolf in fact."

"By—" Gabriella began, but her voice failed her. She sipped a gulp of her tea, swallowed audibly, and tried again. "By whom? Who could have known to send you? What happened that night?"

Helena was already shaking her head. "A certain sorcerer, Merlinus Ambrosius, came to us with a premonition of your demise.

He had learned of it by his arts, and divined by the same means that such a thing could not be allowed to happen. With his help, we searched for your lakefront cottage and discovered the werewolf there, lying in wait for your return, for you had apparently gone in search of sustenance. The monster had already subdued your grandmother, and being, in its human form, a man of a certain dramatic bent, had donned the old woman's clothing in an attempt to fool you. One of our council managed to rescue your grandmother, dispatch the werewolf, and chase it into the nearby wood."

Gabriella's mind was spinning. "Merlinus?" she repeated faintly. "But surely you do not mean... but he is long dead! Unless..." Her eyes widened. "Unless time means less to those such as he...?"

"We cannot reveal more, my dear," Helena smiled tightly. "Not just because they are secrets, which they are, but because each answer would only lead to more questions. The days of magical and non-magical coexistence are regrettably over. We cannot tell you any more without risking the secrecy of our world."

"We have only revealed to you what we have," Goodrik added sombrely, leaning forwards in his chair, "because the sigil that you wear about your neck is infused with some very deep magic. Surely, this is indeed what drew the attention of Featherbolt, and I would wager that it was not the first time the emblem exerted such influence over the lesser beasts. Its magic is untethered and directionless, but it has apparently adhered itself to you and taken on a reflection of your being, your motives."

Gabriella's eyes widened as she remembered the pile of berries left mysteriously for her by some midnight visitor. And before that, there had been the dream of the forest beasts all passing her, as if circling her in the darkness, watching over her. And even before that, the spider in the halls of the castle, which had alit directly on the sigil at her throat.

"Yes," she said softly. "Toph always said that… I had an affinity for magic. Does this mean that I am a… a…?"

"No, my daughter," Helena shook her head, smiling slightly. "You are not a witch. Although I daresay that there might be a touch of magic in your blood, buried deep. Perhaps, someday, your line might manifest it fully, but not yet. And not, I am afraid, in you. You are, in all your gloriously stubborn nobility, fully human."

Gabriella deflated slightly, her hand still wrapped protectively around the falcon sigil.

"And yet," Goodrik commented, "you do have magic at your disposal. You cannot control it, and its influence may be exceedingly capricious, but for now, it reflects you, just as the moon reflects the sun. Whilst you wear it—you and whoever bears the emblem's other half—its magic may choose to assist you. Or it may not. You must be careful and vigilant, Gabriella of Camelot: such magic can be a blessing, but it can also be a curse."

Gabriella absorbed this sombrely. Finally, she let go of the sigil and tucked it back beneath her cloak.

"I must be off," she announced, looking from Helena to Goodrik. "But perhaps you may assist me if you would be so willing."

Helena merely pressed her lips together, apparently reluctant to assist the young woman on what she believed to be a doomed errand. Goodrik, however, studied Gabriella's face.

"What might you require that we could provide?" he asked.

Gabriella set her teacup on the ground next to her and gave the witch and wizard the full weight of her attention. "It is said that your people moved through these caverns as if they were highways. The legends say that one could pass right beneath the Cragrack Cliffs and come up on the other side. If this is true, show me the way."

"How will you find him?" Helena asked suddenly, apparently ignoring Gabriella's request.

Gabriella looked at her. "Merodach?" she replied. "I... I do not yet know."

"So hell-bent on seeking him are you," the tall woman said, almost reproachfully, "and you have no plan even to find him?"

"I have a plan," Gabriella answered defensively. "I am just managing one thing at a time. I will veer west to meet him as he skirts the Barrens. He and his army cannot have gotten far."

"Helena," Goodrik began, but she turned towards him and glared at him.

"If the young lady is intent," she said firmly, "then let her know exactly what she is getting herself into."

Goodrik narrowed his eyes. "What are you suggesting?"

"Let her visit Coalroot. He will tell her everything she needs to know."

Goodrik shook his head. "That is unnecessary and dangerous—"

"More dangerous than confronting a madman and his army?" Helena insisted archly. "The rule is simple. If she follows it, then she has nothing to fear."

Impatiently, Gabriella asked, "Who is Coalroot? Why should I seek him?"

"Not a he," Helena corrected, "an it. Coalroot is very, very old, and as such, it knows a great deal. Very little escapes its notice. If this Merodach is camped anywhere within reach of the Tempest Barrens, Coalroot will know exactly where. It will tell you *everything* that you need to know."

"Helena," Goodrik said in a low voice, "this is a mistake. Let the girl go as she wishes. We can tell her how to find her way beneath the cliffs."

Helena looked at him and sighed. "*If* this is indeed her destiny, Goodrik," she insisted sombrely, "then let her walk into it with her eyes wide open."

Goodrik considered this for a long moment. Then he turned to Gabriella. "It is your choice, Princess. Shall you pass directly beneath the Cliffs at our direction, or shall you go to meet Coalroot and seek its counsel?"

Gabriella looked back and forth between the witch and wizard. She could tell that something complicated was happening between them, but she could not quite understand what it was. Finally, she stood up and nodded resolutely.

"Let me go to this Coalroot," she said stoutly. "If its counsel will lead me to the villain, then I must seek it."

Goodrik nodded slowly, resignedly. "Then we will prepare you for your journey. You may embark as soon as you desire."

Gabriella looked aside at Helena, but the woman was still seated, not seeming to pay attention. She had retrieved Gabriella's empty teacup from the floor and was peering into it, studying the dreg of tea leaves scattered on its bottom.

"Yes," the woman answered slowly. "Go to Coalroot. Speak to it. But if you are pursuing this mission in the hopes of saving your child, you may wish to reconsider."

Gabriella frowned worriedly. "Why do you say such a thing?"

"Because," Helena said, looking up from the teacup and smiling tightly, "your son is not at Herrengard. Neither is the woman Sigrid. It would seem that they heeded your advice after all."

It was on the tip of Gabriella's tongue to ask how the witch could know such a thing, but the answer was obvious. She had divined it simply by peering into the strew of leaves at the bottom of Gabriella's cup.

Helplessly, gratefully, Gabriella smiled. She drew a great, shuddering sigh.

How very nice it must be, she thought in the midst of her relief, *to be a witch.*

CHAPTER 8

It had been a short visit, and not entirely pleasant, and yet Gabriella felt far lonelier setting off on her own again after her encounter with the strange witch and wizard. Even over the short course of her journey, such mundane comforts as a chair, hot tea, and friendly voices had become seemingly distant memories. Experiencing them in the unexpected dimness of the cavern had only succeeded in making her feel acutely homesick.

This was only worsened by the knowledge that, for now at least, there was no home to return to. Her castle would now be virtually empty, as would be the streets and cottages around it. Perhaps they would soon fill again, and life would go on as always, but Gabriella did not expect this. In the deepest, unspoken part of her heart, she feared that things had changed irrevocably and forever.

She walked on, her footsteps now making the only noise in the cavernous dark.

Goodrik and Helena had given her a few things to assist her on her journey. The first one had been the fire that Goodrik had conjured. Goblinfire, he called it, attaching it to a club of driftwood to form a torch. The flame, he explained, would burn magically, consuming nothing so long as she did not wet it. Even magical fire, it seemed, could not withstand a dousing. The torch was exceedingly light in her hand as she walked on, casting its flickering brilliance in a pool around her. The only odd thing about the goblinfire, she noticed, was that its flames moved rather slower than normal fire, like something glimpsed in a dream. Its sparks drifted up and skirled away ahead of her. She followed them.

"The sparks will lead you to Coalroot," Helena had explained. "After all, every fire seeks its own. Follow the sparks, and you will find what you are looking for."

A flutter of wings buffeted Gabriella as she walked. Featherbolt soared ahead of her, arcing from side to side in the still air. He had chosen to come with her, apparently of his own free will. The goblinfire and Featherbolt, however, were not the only things that Gabriella had gained from her meeting with the magical folk.

"Take this," Goodrik had said as she'd turned to leave. When she had looked back, he had been holding a thin shaft of wood. It was a wand, though not his own.

"But I am not a witch," Gabriella had replied, meeting his eyes. "I am only a human."

"You are not *only* anything," Goodrik had countered. "Take it. The magic of the sigil that accompanies you is unfocused. This old wand may serve as a sort of focussing point for it if ever the need arises. I expect it will only work once, but if at any point you require a certain...," he shrugged vaguely, "*magical flux*, you may attempt to use this."

Gabriella had taken the wand and then merely held it curiously. It felt like nothing more than a cast-off stick. "How?" she had asked, looking up at the wizard.

He had merely shaken his head and smiled cryptically. "I cannot say. I wish you good fortune on your quest, Princess. I am tempted to join you myself, but alas..." Here, he sighed deeply and looked back at Helena, who watched the proceedings with sombre eyes. "We have vowed not to meddle in the affairs of men. It is work enough, I am afraid, to manage the realm of witches and wizards."

Gabriella had thanked them sincerely, if dolefully. Then, without another word, she had set off.

It was a long trek through the subterranean world of the Barrens. Gabriella quickly realised that had she not encountered the witch and wizard and received their direction, she would indeed have become hopelessly lost in the interconnected maze of caverns and tunnels. The light of her torch soothed her eyes, making a dome of golden warmth around her, and the ever-present flutter of Featherbolt was a far greater comfort than she could have expected.

The first time he alit on her shoulder, clicking his talons on her armour, she had been so startled that she had nearly dropped her torch. Shortly, however, she came to appreciate his subtle weight and the warmth of his feathers as they brushed her cheek.

She began to talk to him.

"I don't even know what watch of the day it is," she commented darkly. "Or even if it is morning or night outside. At this rate, it would be easy to walk on and on, not even realising one was tired until one dropped from exhaustion."

Featherbolt ruffled his chest feathers and then polished his beak on his wing, not seeming to care.

For a long time, Gabriella did not feel hungry. She wondered if the constant darkness was having some strange effect on her appetite but chose not to worry about it. Her store of food was nearly gone. She welcomed anything that helped her preserve what little she had left.

Then, for the first time, she wondered about the falcon. Would she have to feed him as well? Shortly, however, this was answered by the bird himself. He launched from her shoulder violently, darting forwards and soaring low over the ground. With a flick of his tail, he seemed to pluck something from the stony floor. Circling back, Gabriella saw the wriggling grey body of a rat clutched in the bird's talons. She shuddered as he landed on a nearby boulder, dipped his beak, and happily eviscerated the creature. She stopped whilst he ate but refused to watch. She had always detested rats.

"Ugh," she said, shuddering. "I can hear you. It's still squeaking, isn't it?"

Featherbolt clicked his beak and then tore at the rat again, apparently enjoying his meal.

The journey progressed, passing through wildly different areas of the Barrens underground.

Sometimes, Gabriella and Featherbolt followed the course of the underground river, even as it crashed through rocky rapids and waterfalls or widened into eerily calm doldrums. The water always glowed with its freight of illuminated fish. At one point, the river widened into a massive lake so broad that its distant shores were invisible in the darkness. Here, ephemeral, blue shapes plowed the abyss slowly and rhythmically, like silk scarves caught in a spring breeze. The stillness of the lake was like glass so that Gabriella could see the creatures clearly, despite their obvious depths. Streamers of deep purple followed behind the shapes, forming whip-like tentacles. There seemed to be hundreds of them fading away into the unimaginable deep.

At other times, however, Gabriella and Featherbolt angled away from the river, following the ever-present sparks of the goblinfire torch. They would find themselves in narrow shafts so close that Gabriella could easily touch both walls, and so low that she had to duck. These would progress for hundreds of feet only to open up onto great cathedrals of stalactites and stalagmites standing as regal as pillars and soaring into lofty darkness.

Once, the sparks led them into a sort of avenue with an unnaturally flat floor and complicated shapes looming on the walls. Raising her torch, Gabriella saw that the walls were in fact carved into rows of doorways and windows, steps and entries, forming a silent tableau of forgotten civilisation. She wondered how old the strange underground city was. There were words engraved over many of the entrances, but they were strange and completely indecipherable. Near the end of the avenue, a mass of stalactites formed an eerie growth against the building façade. Hidden within it, nearly buried inside the ancient formation, was a strew of bones. With a shudder, Gabriella saw that there were several skeletons, none of them exactly human. The heads were too big, the bodies far too small. Dwarfs, she thought, or gnomes. There was no way to tell for sure.

She hurried on.

Eventually, she stopped. She had finally become hungry. Featherbolt landed on a nearby ledge as Gabriella opened her pack. She was down to her last crust of stale bread and strip of venison. Feeling eerily calm, she ate most of the remaining food. The last few bites, she wrapped in a cloth and replaced in her pack.

"That's it," she told Featherbolt, sighing as she stared into the goblinfire. "Only one more little meal left."

There did not seem to be anything further to say on the subject.

Weariness stole over her. She had not planned to sleep yet, but now it seemed inevitable.

Without getting up, she merely rolled onto her side, tucked her pack beneath her head, and closed her eyes. A minute passed, and then two. Her breathing slowed.

In the darkness, spiders scuttled out from beneath the rocks and trickled down from the dim ceilings, using the stalactites like highways. They approached Gabriella, many as pale as bones, some as large as a man's hand, and surrounded her. Featherbolt watched this warily, his golden eyes flicking over the scuttling assembly, prepared to strike.

Finally, having collected in their dozens, the spiders turned away from Gabriella. They formed a ring around her, their alien eyes turned outwards, watching the cavern darkness.

Featherbolt saw this. After a moment, he relaxed.

Eventually, even he slept.

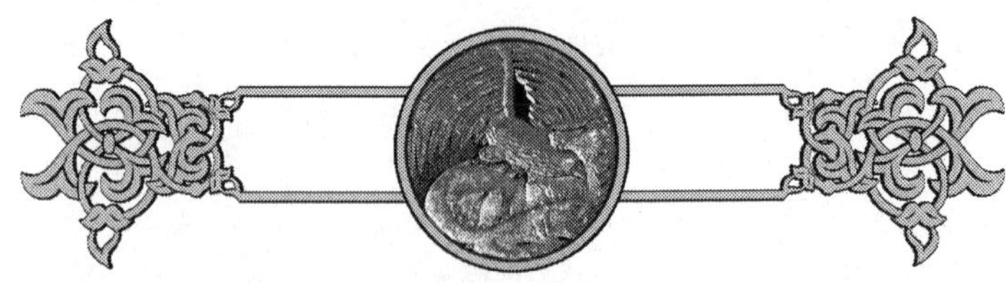

The next day, Gabriella finally found Coalroot.

She had spent the morning (not that she could tell if it truly was morning or not) descending a long, straight shaft ever deeper into the earth. The walls of the tunnel had grown increasingly taller and narrower as she walked, so that she felt like a mouse crawling within the walls of a cottage. The air had become warmer as she progressed and was now quite hot. Sweat trickled into her eyes, and she swiped it away with the inside of her wrist.

There was light as well. Unlike every other glow that she had encountered in the caverns, however, this light was neither blue nor cold. It was a burnished red, growing gradually brighter as she progressed. The sparks of her torch streaked ahead, following the course of the tunnel as if in the teeth of a hard wind despite the perfect stillness of the air.

"Whatever you do," Gabriella repeated under her breath, "do not talk about treasure. That's the only rule. Do not so much as say the word. Can we do that, Featherbolt?"

Featherbolt stood on her shoulder, his feathers fluffed out in an effort to cool himself. His wing felt hot against her cheek.

"Get off," she whispered, flapping a hand at him. "You're making me even hotter."

The bird launched into the air and squawked in irritation. He circled her, apparently unwilling to get too far ahead.

A vertical bar of deep red became visible between the walls of the tunnel some unknown distance away. There was subtle motion within its depths, as though from a slowly shifting cloud.

"I think we are very nearly there," Gabriella said, swallowing. "According to Helena and Goodrik, Coalroot will tell us what we need to know. So long as we do not say the wrong thing."

The air had developed a whiff of sulphur. The goblinfire rippled and flared, leaping towards the reddish light ahead. The rift grew as they neared it.

There was a noise. Gabriella heard it and realised that it had been going on for some time just below the level of audibility. It was a dull rumble, a sort of groan, as if the earth itself were shifting very subtly around her.

Featherbolt landed upon her shoulder again. He clicked his beak and shivered his head violently, raising the tiny feathers of his forehead into hackles.

"I know," Gabriella replied nervously.

Finally, after what seemed like far too long a time, they reached the end of the tunnel. Beyond its high walls, red depths stirred massively, like storm clouds at sunset. The stench of sulphur was overwhelming. Gabriella stopped and drew a deep breath through her mouth. Then, steeling her nerve, she stepped out into the red light.

The cavern was monumental. Its floor was a shattered valley, broken and jagged, strewn with boulders. Smoke poured from the cracks, dimming the air, and yet red light filled the space, reaching even to the ragged cone of the ceiling hundreds of feet up.

In the centre of the space, dominating it, was a shape that Gabriella simply could not comprehend. It was something like a twisted tree, so enormous that it would have dwarfed the entire castle of Camelot. It was black as coal, wrinkled with deep crags, cracks, and fissures. Its branches jutted up and out in all directions, thick as highways and driven deep into the cavern's ceiling. Far below this, the tree's roots spread like rocky tentacles, laced with cracks. The cracks glowed orange, as if the core of each root was pure fire. Worst of all, the centre of the tree's trunk bore a gaping maw, burning bright red, as if lined with live coals. This was the source of the ruddy light that filled the cavern.

Featherbolt clung to Gabriella's shoulder, his talons scratching tightly on the edge of her armour. Slowly, staring wide-eyed up at the incredible shape, Gabriella walked out onto the broken plane of the floor.

GABRIELLA XAVIER.

The voice that spoke her name was not human. It was hardly even a voice. It seemed to be formed of the guttural rumblings of the earth itself, vibrating deep into her ears and thrumming in her bowels. It was simultaneously almost silent and massively deafening.

"Yes," she replied. Her own voice came out as a dry croak, but she could not seem to bring herself to speak any louder.

Gabriella Xavier... Xavier... Gabriella... avier... ella...

The voice rumbled onwards, breaking into echoes, dozens and hundreds of them. The echoes seemed to fade into great distance, and Gabriella had the eerie sense that they were being broadcast throughout every dark depth of the Barrens underground.

"Heh hee!" a much smaller voice suddenly called out. Coming on the heels of the diminishing monstrous echoes, this new voice was tiny and merry, like a jingle bell in the disastrous expanse of the cavern. Gabriella glanced around, seeking its source.

A small man was seated amongst the snaking roots of the tree shape. His back was bowed with age, and his bald head bobbled as he waved at her. Against all probability, he seemed to be sitting in an old rocking chair. He worked it gleefully, bobbing back and forth on its curved rails. Even through the distance, Gabriella could see that he was grinning at her merrily, beckoning her forwards.

"*What* in *hell...*," Gabriella muttered, her eyes still wide.

Carefully and warily, she began to move towards the wizened figure. It was slow work due to the disastrously broken floor and the rafts of noxious smoke that poured through the cracks. As she skirted these, Gabriella saw that the crevices glowed faintly in their depths, some as wide and deep as canyons. The rumble of the earth was still audible. She could feel it through the soles of her boots. Before her, the awful tree shape loomed ever larger. Waves of heat baked from its jagged surface, beating down on her. Featherbolt switched his head back and forth restlessly, still clinging to the lip of her breastplate.

"Hee hee! Come forth, Princess!" the tiny, old man called thinly, still waving. "Come and greet me. Let us speak! Oh my, yes." He cackled wheezily, gaily.

The floor around the snaking roots was shattered into sharp, uneven terraces, each one higher than the one before it. Gabriella climbed these cautiously as she neared the man. The enormous, black roots of the tree shape spread around her now, each one as charred and deeply cracked as embers. Where they sank into the ground, the rocks rippled with heat shimmers. The twisted trunk rose above her, scorched black and ribbed with deep, sharp crags.

"That's a girl," the old man laughed. His voice was nearly as cracked as the rocks around him. He smiled at her gummily, chewing his lips, but his eyes were brilliantly sharp, blue like the ice of a winter millpond. "Come closer. Have a rest and visit awhile. Ask me your questions, Princess, and tell me your tales."

Gabriella was close enough to the old man now that he didn't have to raise his voice to speak. She neared him warily, and he simply looked up at her, his head bobbing on the stubbly stalk of his neck. He wore a rough, nondescript cowl, its hood pushed back between the knobs of his shoulders. Between his clasped hands was the head of a black cane apparently made of stone. Its tip was notched into the cracks before his bare feet. He rocked energetically, watching his visitor, apparently waiting for her to speak.

Gabriella studied him, frowning with consternation. Finally, she asked, "Are you… Coalroot?"

The old man grinned suddenly, stretching his wrinkled lips and showing his toothlessness. He rocked slightly faster. This, Gabriella figured, was answer enough.

"What was that voice I heard earlier? The one that sounded like the earth itself and spoke my name?"

"Hm-*hmm*!" the old man laughed secretively, his eyes dancing. He raised one hand and touched a finger to the side of his nose. He nodded and giggled.

Gabriella's frown deepened. "I was sent here," she announced. "I was told that you could help me in my quest. Is this true?"

"Perhaps!" the old man replied, nodding. "It all depends, does it not?"

"On what does it depend?" Gabriella pressed evenly.

The old man's eyes cleared for a moment. "On whether you ask the right questions."

Gabriella drew a sigh. She didn't have time for riddles from demented, old men. She looked around the ruddy depths of the cavern.

"What is this place?" she asked, curiosity getting the better of her. "And who are you?"

"Ah-hah!" the old man brightened. "A question that I can answer! This is the restless grave of Chaorenvar, also known as Lord Vulcan, the undisputed ruler of the molten deep. These," the old man raised an arm, gesturing at the charred tree-shape overhead, "are his frozen bones!"

"Chaorenvar," Gabriella repeated slowly. "The ancient fire mountain?"

"Aye," the man rasped passionately, "ancient but never at rest. This cavern is the negative of the mountain peak that once framed him! Alas, the broken slopes of his mighty shoulders have fallen away, leaving only its shadow in this tomb of earth, but the bones of Chaorenvar's fiery core remain. Do not let his tree-like appearance fool you! His branches are the shafts that broke to the surface above, spilling rivers of rock. His roots are the conduits to the molten oceans of the earth's heart. And his trunk is the hellish throat of his wrath, what once belched liquid fire high into the clouds, raining ashy death onto the lands above for miles in every direction."

Gabriella was dumbstruck. She looked up at the petrified bones of the mythic volcano. Its molten heart still glowed, proving that it was not dead, but only dormant. The old man rocked and muttered to himself happily. He giggled. After a minute, Gabriella lowered her eyes to his again.

"Then that must make you the spirit of the volcano," she ventured, "I have read of such things in the myths. You are not as you may appear, but change your form for whomever you meet. Is this so?"

The old man grinned up at her and shrugged his bony shoulders, not as if he didn't know the answer, but as if he had no intention of giving it. The blue of his eyes seemed to flash in the baleful dimness. He leant towards her. "You may indeed call me Coalroot," he whispered harshly, as if sharing a delicious secret.

Gabriella went on, "What do you know of me besides my name?"

Coalroot tilted his head back and forth thoughtfully. "I know your past and future but not your present. It is the nature of my being. Time is to us exactly the reverse of what it is to you, for you know the present but never the future and barely the past. Oh yes. Heh hee! Many have come to me over the eons, and I always sense their approach. I know as well the nature of their leaving. If, of course," here, his eyes switched towards her and grew sharp, "they are *allowed* to leave. Heh hee!"

He sighed with amusement and then became more subdued. "But alas, I never know what anyone might do or say during the moments that they are with me. Perhaps they come to seek their futures. Or perhaps, instead, they come to steal from my hoard! *Many* come with that very intent, you know, for I have collected much treasure from the forgotten depths of the earth! More than most can imagine. It amuses me!" He cackled again, wheezing almost silently, and then asked with a conspiratorial leer, "Do *you* know of my hoard, Gabriella Xavier?"

Gabriella shook her head carefully. "I have come for knowledge," she answered. "That is all."

Coalroot chewed his lips as he considered this, nodding his head speculatively. His fingers squeezed and gripped the head of his cane, making balls of knuckles. "I have very *much* treasure," he acknowledged, winking one eye up at her. "It is right behind me, buried in a vast hollow. The gold shines like the sun in the light of my fires. You wish to see it, do you not?"

"No," Gabriella replied warily, fear uncoiling in her belly like a snake. "I am here to ask questions. The only thing I seek is knowledge."

Coalroot's eyes narrowed, and his smile snapped shut like a trap. He stopped rocking and glared at her. After a very long pause, he began to rock again, more slowly now.

"I remember why it is that you have come to me," he admitted.

Gabriella exhaled with relief. "You know what I seek? And what is my mission?"

Coalroot shrugged slowly, his eyes still narrowed. She was going to have to ask of course. Creatures such as this never gave willingly. She straightened her back and drew a deep breath.

"I seek the one called Merodach," she stated clearly. "I must find him and confront him. I am given to understand that you know where he is."

Coalroot's lips stretched into a sly smile. "I know where he was yesterday, and I know where he shall be on the morrow; thus, I can offer a satisfactory guess of where he is at this moment. But you must know, Gabriella Xavier, that such knowledge does not come without a price."

Gabriella looked at him. The heat of the cavern baked over her, drying the sweat on her brow even as it appeared. "I have little to offer," she replied. "What do you require of me?"

"Oh, it is not that sort of price," Coalroot grinned, his rocking speeding up again. "The cost of knowledge, Princess, is *more* knowledge. You cannot leave here learning only that which you *wish* to know. You must take with you the burden of full clarity. It is the only way."

Gabriella's brow furrowed uncertainly. "You mean," she said, "that you will tell me more than I ask for? That is all?"

Coalroot's cackle filled the hot air, rising like bats into the darkness. On Gabriella's shoulder, Featherbolt ruffled his feathers violently and clicked his beak.

"Yes!" Coalroot wheezed gleefully. "Yes, that is all! But beware, Princess! It is indeed a price that many do not wish to pay! Full clarity can destroy a human as surely as any sword! Many have chosen to lie down and die beneath the weight of knowledge! Heh hee! Their bones are scattered amongst the rocks below, along with the skeletons of those who came in search of my treasure! Indeed, many more have come to see me than have left again!" He laughed shrilly, delighted.

Gabriella stood stoically in the face of the old man's mad glee. She tried to imagine what sort of knowledge could possibly lead to her mortal despair but could think of nothing. When Coalroot's cackles finally subsided, she faced him stolidly.

"Tell me what I wish to know," she declared, "and I will accept the burden of whatever else you give me."

Coalroot still tittered to himself, even as his eyes locked on hers, narrowing. "As you wish, Princess," he agreed. "The man Merodach is not himself on the march as you have supposed. He shall be in the same place tomorrow as he was yesterday. He awaits at the Theatre of the Broken Crown, just beyond the northernmost edge of the Tempest Barrens. There, your man died, and there Merodach has established his fortress."

Gabriella absorbed this with growing confusion. "He awaits...?" she asked faintly, worriedly. "For what?"

The old man giggled through closed lips, leaning forwards in his chair even as he continued rocking. "For something," he allowed, "but not for you."

Gabriella frowned in disbelief. "Then he is not on the march?"

"*He* is not," Coalroot winked cagily. "But his armies are, and they are many! Oh my yes! Many indeed! They are further than you have guessed, very nearly upon their prey! Heh hee!"

Gabriella's heart grew heavy as lead inside her. She nodded slowly, clenching her jaw. "I will go to him nonetheless. The beast must die. Vengeance will visit him, and his armies will scatter."

Coalroot did not laugh at this. Instead, he ceased rocking in his chair and leant even further forwards, his eyes turning icy as he commanded her gaze. "*Will* you?" he asked meaningfully. "And *shall* they?"

Gabriella stared into his cold eyes. A shiver coursed over her despite the heat of the cavern. She began to sense just how steep the price of her information might be. She took a step back from the old man's piercing stare.

"Yes," he breathed. "You begin to see, do you not? Your Darrick understood at the very last, even with his dying breath. Even your mother, *she* knew the truth as she lay on her chamber floor bleeding out her last, her eyes glazing over, feeling the life force ebb slowly from her body. You have been granted a great gift, Gabriella Xavier. You will know that which others only learn when it is too late to matter. You will know the cords of fate, and see just how small you are in comparison to them..."

Gabriella wished to shrink back, but her feet remained locked to the stone. In the face of that mad glare, she regretted her choice. She wished she could take back her questions. Suddenly, the knowledge she had gained felt small and paltry compared to what might be about to come. Coalroot's eyes seemed to grow larger, expanding to icy pits, deep as the cavern lake she had encountered on her journey. The rumbling earth spoke his words along with him, forming a cataclysmic unison.

"You will go to the man Merodach in his fortress, and you will face him. It is your destiny," the voices rang, filling the cavern, their words falling like weights. "But... you shall fail in your quest. Your father's kingdom is already in ruins. Camelot will be no more. Its name shall be swallowed into oblivion, reduced to myth, dismissed as legend. All those that you love... shall die. They will pass unto Sheol. And soon, Gabriella Xavier, *you shall join them.*"

The echo of Coalroot's words rang through the darkness, no longer wheezing and shrill but clanging like iron, shaking the very cavern walls. He continued to stare at her, to glare straight into her, measuring the collapse of her will and seeming to delight in it. His smile was razor thin, sharp as flint.

Finally, after what seemed like several minutes, the echoes of his proclamation faded away, diminishing into the hidden depths of the Barrens underground. Gabriella stood there in the heat, the ruddy light glinting from her armour.

Slowly, she nodded.

"*So be it,*" she whispered to herself.

Coalroot stared up at the young woman, his smile fading, and did something that he had not done for centuries, perhaps even millennia.

He blinked.

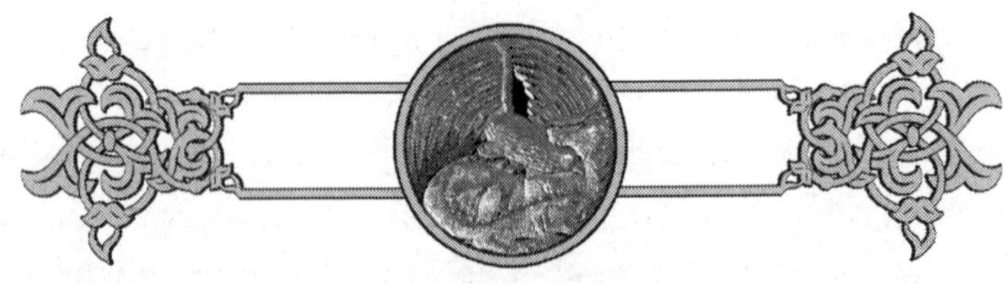

The remainder of the underground journey was mostly uphill.

The heat of the cavern of Chaorenvar gradually fell away as Gabriella and Featherbolt ascended long subterranean slopes roofed with plates of stone and still as crypts. Here, there were no buried rivers or lakes and very few stalactites and stalagmites. The cave stone was as dry as bone, so that puffs of dust arose beneath Gabriella's boots. The air itself seemed dead, as if it had been baked sterile by some unimaginable heat in eons past.

As they progressed, Gabriella began to get a sense of the underground geography of the Barrens. The cavern of Chaorenvar was the deepest point and was probably in the very centre, directly beneath the Cragrack Cliffs. Perhaps, she surmised, the volcano had been responsible for the cliffs. Perhaps, in some remote past, it had erupted so violently, so suddenly, that it had broken the very bones of the earth, splitting the land in two and shifting the masses apart.

Further, what if the eruption had not been a purely natural event? There were legends that the most powerful wizarding armies had employed devastating spells to summon such forces as earthquakes, wind storms, lightning, and floods. Even the great Merlinus himself was rumoured to have had a hand in such things.

In the cave of the petrified army, the witch Helena had referred to a certain "mercenary sorcerer" by whose hand the entire army had been turned to stone. What if the same sorcerer had summoned the wrath of the volcano Chaorenvar and provoked its deadly forces to unnatural strength? Was it possible that the great sorcerer himself, Merlinus Ambrosius, was indeed still alive somewhere? Was the passage of time different for such beings as he? And if so, could it possibly be true that the great sorcerer, whose counsels had benefited the Elder King Arthur himself, had known of Gabriella, and had a hand in her fate? Could Helena's tale of the werewolf and the midnight rescue in the snowbound lake cottage be true?

Every time she doubted it, she remembered the sigil at her throat. It was still warm.

Darrick had worn the other half, until Merodach had taken it.

Gabriella mused on these things darkly, occupying her mind as she traversed the tunnels' perpetual night.

She and Featherbolt slept twice during this segment of the journey. Her food was gone now, and her flask was finally empty. The last few swallows she poured into a hollow on the stone floor for Featherbolt. He drank methodically, dipping and then tossing back his head, letting the water run down his throat. When it was gone, he launched lightly into the air and landed on her shoulder.

"That's all," Gabriella sighed, trying not to feel hopeless. "Let us hope we are near the end of our underground trek."

Hungrily, parched from the arid environment, the two continued on.

Finally, on the third day of their gradual ascent, Gabriella spied a faint glow of light somewhere ahead. She stopped, her eyes going wide, and stared, half-certain that it was a mirage.

"Do you see that, Featherbolt?" she asked. "Is it really there?"

Featherbolt took off from her shoulder and flapped ahead. After a moment, he vanished from the glow of the goblinfire torch. His screech came back to her, echoing. Then she saw him again, a black shape against the slightly less black background. The light was real enough, although so faint that it was barely a cloud of grey.

Gabriella made towards it, increasing her pace despite her weariness. It had been so long since she had seen daylight that the promise of it was almost too sweet to bear. She began to run. The light of the torch bobbed on the jagged walls, casting wild shadows in every direction. Her own breath sounded harsh and ragged to her, echoing back in the confines of the tunnel.

Featherbolt screeched again from some distance ahead, leading her onwards.

Slowly but gloriously, the light grew. What was once only a milky cloud was now a persistent glow, picking out the roughness of the walls and floor in stark contrast. As Gabriella moved into the light, she relished the breadth of its reach. For days, she had been living in a world no larger than her dome of torch light. Here, finally, the tunnel opened up ahead of her, becoming wider, taller, and framed with a deadfall of rocks and boulders. The light came from a point around the next bend. A shaft of dusty brilliance pierced the tunnel from left to right, falling at an angle across a tumble of broken rock. Framed against this, perched on one of the larger boulders, Featherbolt watched and waited for her, switching his head anxiously from side to side.

"We are almost there," Gabriella proclaimed, catching up to Featherbolt. The broken rocks behind him framed a wide rift, apparently opening onto a large cave filled with the white light. Gabriella smiled excitedly as she circumvented the tumble of rock and moved into the beam of light, letting it wash over her.

It was indeed daylight. A huge, ragged opening bloomed ahead some hundred or so paces away. The world beyond the cave entrance was seamlessly, blindingly white. Cold air pushed through the rift, making a low moan amongst the rocks. The floor of the final cave was carpeted with broken rock and gravel, criss-crossed with great scraped areas, as if something extremely large had been repeatedly dragged around the cavern.

And there was a smell.

"Ugh," Gabriella said, wrinkling her nose as she moved into the light of the space. "What is that? It's like the time Professor Toph's potions laboratory got flooded. But worse, somehow..."

It was worse because it wasn't just the smell of scorched chemicals and rot. It was the smell of fresh death. The purple stench of blood was rich in the cold air. Featherbolt flapped ahead, arcing towards the nearer wall on the left. He alit on what at first appeared to be a tangle of uprooted trees. With a sinking dread, Gabriella realised that it was a pile of very large bones, black with rotted gristle. Featherbolt alit on a rib and pecked his beak at it. He fluttered his head, apparently with distaste.

"Featherbolt," Gabriella called worriedly, her eyes wide, "I think we had better leave as quickly—"

There was a large noise behind her, a sort of prolonged rattling scrape. It ended with a sound like air in a gigantic bellows, snuffling slightly as it diminished. The chemical smell grew suddenly sharper.

Gabriella froze in place, eyes wide and heart trip-hammering. Then, as the noise faded back to silence, she turned, careful to make no noise on the gravel-strewn floor.

There was a monstrous shape pressed up against the opposite wall of the cave. It appeared to be a sort of lumpy, brown hill, carpeted with scales. A row of jagged plates were planted into the hill like a fence, diminishing in size as they marched down a sort of bony ridge. Where it neared the cave floor, the bony ridge separated from the shape and became a long, tapering tail lined with three rows of serrated spines.

As Gabriella watched, the lumpy hill expanded slightly, and the snuffling bellows sound came again. There was no mistaking the shape, even though Gabriella had never seen such a thing before in her life. She froze to the spot, petrified with fear.

Slowly, massively, the shape began to uncoil. The tail slid backwards in its bed of gravel, making that crunching scrape again. A pair of lumps near the top became shifting shoulder blades beneath scaly skin. There was a thump as a gigantic, muscular leg hove into view, revealed from behind the slithering tail. Sharp extrusions of bone marked the elbow and heel of the appendage. Hooked claws scratched the cave floor.

Slowly, the dragon began to stand, its snuffling breath filling the cave and reeking of chemical.

Gabriella's paralysis finally broke as the snake-like neck began to heave into view. She dropped her torch and scrambled backwards, terrified to turn away from the monster but desperate to find a hiding place. With a frantic lunge, she threw herself behind the pile of rotting carcasses. Featherbolt was still there, fearlessly perched on a massive ribcage. The stench of death was nearly enough to make Gabriella sick, but she hunkered low and covered her mouth, resisting the lurch of her gorge.

She could still see the dragon through the forest of gristly bones. It stood slowly, languidly, and raised its head in a luxurious stretch. The vertebrae of its neck and back popped like pine knots in a fire, and the plates of its spine snapped visibly upright as their joints aligned. The dragon was large enough that its bulk filled nearly a fifth of the cave. Suddenly, with disconcerting litheness, the great beast turned its great, serpentine neck, sweeping its horned head low over the floor, its nostrils trailing ribbons of smoke. It regarded its home suspiciously, its orange eyes flicking busily, as if it smelled something amiss. It stopped, and Gabriella was sure that it had seen her.

A gurgling noise began to sound, and Gabriella realised with dismay that it was the dragon's stomach. The dragon huffed, turning the gurgle into a flaming belch. Gabriella swallowed past a lump in her throat and willed herself not to move. Above her, Featherbolt preened himself on his ribcage perch.

The dragon coiled, narrowed its eyes, and lunged forwards. Great, leathery wings unfurled from its back and caught the air like sails, lifting the beast from the ground as it pounced. The jaws unhinged, and the head cocked sideways, snapping forwards on its long neck to strike. There was no time for Gabriella to react. She squeezed her eyes shut and buried her head in her hands as the shadow of the monstrous beast fell over her.

The dragon's four feet struck the ground with massive thumps, and the jaws snapped shut like a trap. There was a horrible, wet crunch of breaking bone and tearing flesh, mingled with a seething grunt that was half roar, half growl.

Gabriella uncovered her head. She was still in one piece, still lying amidst the pile of rotting carcasses. She peered through the bones, faint with relief.

The dragon was directly in front of the pile of carcasses, violently dismembering the freshest of the lot. The corpse in its jaws appeared to a chortha, like the ones Gabriella had confronted earlier in her journey. Its blunt head and curved horns lolled as the dragon ripped one of its rear legs off, devouring it whole and crunching noisily on the bones. The dragon was an exceptionally messy eater, snarling great, furious gusts around its food, cooking it with its flaming breath. The air was fetid with the reek of burnt fur.

Suddenly, the dragon lunged backwards and violently whipped its head. The carcass, still clamped in the dragon's jaws, ripped grotesquely in two. The front half of the dead beast flew back towards the dragon's nest, trailing ropes of innards. It struck the ground and rolled. The dragon pounced upon it, snarling viciously, as if the pathetic half-corpse had been trying to escape. The dragon's massive claws scraped and dug at the broken floor, spraying rocks in every direction. Its tail rose towards the ceiling and then thumped down, shaking the ground and sending up a great cloud of grit.

Gabriella was terrified. She glanced away from the rampaging dragon, saw the opening of the cave some thirty paces away, and scrambled desperately to her feet. Feeling hopelessly slow and clumsy, she tumbled out of the strew of carcasses, nearly tripped on the loose rock of the cave floor, righted herself, and began to run.

Behind her, the dragon slammed and roared, its breath sending up gouts of blue fire, lighting the cave all around. Rock and gravel kicked back from its scraping claws, pelting Gabriella from behind as she ran on, nearing the light of the cave's entrance. Something heavy flew over her shoulder and landed with a wet thump on the stony floor in front of her. It was the head of the dead chortha. Its blunt muzzle was open and masked with blood. Its eyes boggled in two different directions. The head itself was nearly as big as Gabriella.

Behind her, sounding horribly near, the dragon let out a sustained roar. The heat of its breath blew Gabriella's hair forwards, making it swat wildly around her cheeks.

She hurdled the severed chortha's head, using one of its twisted horns as leverage. As she landed on the other side, she slid on the broken gravel and fell.

A wall of scaly muscle hurtled behind her, taking the chortha head with it. A spray of blood misted over Gabriella. She scrambled forwards, numb with terror, and launched herself towards the cave entrance. Its light fell over her, blinding her, but she ran on, stumbling, sliding, leaping out into the freezing white.

She fell forwards. Her face dashed into a mass of snow, and she found herself rolling head over heels down a steep hill. Brilliant white surrounded her, making no distinction between earth and sky. Finally, she landed on her back, skidded down the remaining slope into a mass of snow-crusted yellow grass, and scraped to a halt.

She scrambled quickly upright and looked back. Behind and above her, the cave mouth was a black crevice surrounded by snow-covered boulders. The dragon still raged from within, its roars echoing dimly, the ground trembling with its wild rampage. Gabriella struggled to her feet, slipping on the cold ground, and retreated some distance further away from the cave. She found a large boulder, ducked into its shadow, and collapsed with fear-induced exhaustion.

She was trembling, and the trembles were quickly turning to shivers in the frosty cold. She hugged herself and tried to calm her thoughts.

After a while, the noise of the dragon diminished and faded away. Silence fell over the snowy landscape. At first, this was a relief. Then Gabriella began to fear that the dragon had smelled her. Perhaps it was stalking her, creeping along the frozen grass behind her.

Carefully, she rolled onto her knees and peered around the side of the boulder, forcing herself to look.

There was no sign of the dragon on the hillside. The snow was broken only by the zigzagging tracks of her own feet. Then she reminded herself that dragons could fly. She peered up into the blinding white of the sky.

Something was indeed flying overhead, but it was far smaller than the dragon. It was Featherbolt, and he seemed to be carrying something, labouring with the added weight. He circled, seemed to spy her, and let out a distant screech. Silently, he began to wheel down towards her, and she saw that he was carrying the driftwood torch in his talons. The goblinfire streaked into the cold air, nearly invisible in the glaring whiteness.

Gabriella reached up and caught the torch as Featherbolt reached her.

"You must think yourself pretty brave," she commented gratefully, her teeth chattering in the cold.

He landed atop the boulder and shook himself, fluffing his feathers. He screeched thinly and looked away out over the cold, white hills. Gabriella followed his gaze.

They had indeed passed beyond the Cragrack Cliffs. Here, the ground was broken into rolling hills, many peaked with black rocks and outcroppings of brush and trees. Further north, standing like pale blue saw teeth against the white sky, was a range of mountains. Largest of these was the centre peak, Mount Skelter. In its shadow, Gabriella knew, she would find the unusual, round valley ringed with jagged foothills known as the Theatre of the Broken Crown. She was only a few days away. Her quest, hopeless as it might be, was near an end.

"Perhaps Coalroot was wrong," she said to herself, staring into the distance at that faint, uneven peak. "Perhaps..."

But she did not believe it. That was why the witch Helena had insisted that she, Gabriella, visit the volcano spirit. "He will tell you *everything* you need to know," she had declared cryptically. Now Gabriella knew exactly what she had intended. Helena had meant to dissuade her, to show her the deadly foolishness of her errand. It hadn't worked, of course.

Because Coalroot had not told her anything that she had not, in her deepest heart, already known.

After a short rest, warmed by the magical fire of her torch, Gabriella began the final leg of her journey.

CHAPTER 9

Three men sat around a rough, wooden table lit by the afternoon light of a small window.

"There," the largest of the men said flatly, plinking a short stack of coins onto the table and pushing it next to two similar stacks. He had a square, sunburnt face and meaty forearms. He crossed them before his leather tack vest. "The takings for one week. Like I have already told you, this is far more than average. It is the peak of the season after all."

Yazim nodded equably and bent to scribble a note on a piece of thick parchment. Thomas frowned and looked around the low room. There were four other tables besides the bar, but only one patron was visible, and Thomas suspected that it was the proprietor's father. The old man leant against the wall in his chair, hands folded over his thin chest, snoring faintly.

Yazim tapped the parchment with his quill. "How many cattle and horses did you say you keep, sir?"

"Three and two," the proprietor answered without blinking. "My best packhorse broke a leg last autumn, and we had to put her down. It has been a true challenge without her, guv'nor, do not doubt it."

"I do not," Yazim replied sincerely. "How long have you operated this establishment then, sir?"

"Four winters. The first two were the hardest. Barely made a copper, what with all the building and repair. The place bore hardly a standing wall when we moved into it. Almost starved, we did."

Yazim nodded. His quill scritched on the parchment. "And this is why you have not yet reported this establishment to the local tax authority?"

The proprietor nodded warily. "I been meaning to, you understand. Fair is fair. Me and the missus, we always mean to do our part, small as it might be."

Thomas sighed and looked around. "It must get dreadfully lonely out here once the peak season ends," he commented, raising an eyebrow, "if this is how it is when business is at its height. Travel and livery must not be a particularly thriving industry this far off the main roads."

"Right you are, guv'nor," the proprietor agreed somewhat suspiciously. "Why, we can go weeks at a stretch with nary a passer-by."

"Makes one wonder," Thomas pressed evenly, meeting the proprietor's eyes, "why one would go to the trouble to operate an inn in such a place."

"Simple human kindness, I expect," Yazim announced, rolling the quill and ink pot up into the parchment and stashing both into his pack. "A quality we see far too little of in the city proper, I am afraid. Thank you, good sir. You may expect a friendly visit from the tax constabulatory of this region within the year. For our part, however, we bid you good day."

With that, Yazim stood, and Thomas moved to join him. The proprietor blinked up at Yazim and then down at the small stacks of coins on the table. A question seemed to form on his face, but it vanished quickly. He began to scoop the coins into the hollow of one huge, callused palm.

"Always a pleasure to host the agents of the King," he said loudly, as if to cover the clink of his coins. "As I say, me and the missus, we just want to do our part. Glad to be of service. Fare thee well then, gentlemen. Safe travels."

Ten minutes later, the two were astride their horses again, cantering away from the stone inn along a barely visible road.

"I've enjoyed better accommodations in barbarian prison camps," Thomas declared, glancing back.

"As a descendent of those 'barbarians' myself," Yazim commented smoothly, "I suggest that that might say more about the differences between our cultures' concepts of hospitality than it does about that specific inn."

Thomas frowned and shook his head. "I shall dismiss the fact that you did not collect any surtax from the proprietor. But you must know he stables more than two horses. There were four stalls, and all of them fresh. Why did you let him account for only the two?"

Yazim smiled a little crookedly and urged his horse onwards. "A taxpayer who believes he is outsmarting his government can be a surprisingly loyal citizen. Revolutions do not grow well amongst such people, for they fear that a new ruler may be less easy to fool. That kind of security is worth a few lost coppers a year."

"Did you learn this from the Archduke himself? Somehow, I failed to perceive that directive when we were assigned our duty," Thomas mused, looking aside at his friend.

Yazim shrugged. "We 'barbarians' are adept at reading between the lines."

Thomas nodded. They rode for a few minutes in silence. The roadway turned, passed into a thicket of new trees. The shadows felt cool after the hard light of the afternoon sun.

Finally, Thomas said, "Speaking of reading between the lines, I have been thinking upon your tale."

"Indeed."

"Indeed. And I am forced to wonder how much of it really is true and how much of it is, well, pure fancy. No disrespect intended, for it is quite a good tale and I am rather enthralled by it, and yet..."

Yazim pursed his lips sympathetically. "It does seem rather fantastic, yes. In truth, I had not thought upon the tale in many years, not since I was a child. Youth is far quicker than adulthood to absorb such things as wizards and werewolves, volcano spirits and dragons."

Thomas seemed mildly disappointed. "Does this mean that you do not believe the story yourself?"

Yazim drew a long breath. The clop of the horses' hooves was loud in the afternoon stillness. "I do not disbelieve it," he answered, "but I do not believe it the same way I once did. Not yet at least."

Thomas glanced at his friend. "What does that mean?"

"It means that it has been a long time since magic tainted the world. Its power is mostly gone from the land. But hints of it remain, giving evidence of a time much different than that which we know."

"You have witnessed this evidence?"

Yazim considered. "I have sensed it," he replied thoughtfully. "We are, after all, on the verge of that land once known, in the time of Camelot, as the Tempest Barrens. Now it is merely an uncharted wilderness, dotted with small forests and populated mostly by nomads. The magic is gone from the land, but the land has not forgotten it. Do you not sense it?"

Thomas shook his head. "I sense you attempting to spook me as the evening descends but nothing more. And I daresay it will not work. With the derelict castle far behind us, your tale has become increasingly that: a tale. But do not let that stop your telling of it. It interests me greatly, even if it is pure fantasy."

"That way station," Yazim said, almost to himself, "it is old. Far older than even the proprietor knows. The stone of its walls speaks of centuries, not decades. It may be that what we saw, the inn in which we stayed this night past, is rebuilt from the very place that the Princess, Gabriella Xavier herself, passed as a ruin, the cursed way station that marked her crossing into the Tempest Barrens." Yazim's gaze sharpened, and he looked askance at his companion. "The curse may be long passed from the land, but there is something bent about that place nonetheless. Tell me that you did not feel it."

Thomas frowned. He glanced at the darker man and then looked away again. "I slept within its walls. I still breathe today with it behind us."

"And yet you are relieved," Yazim commented, narrowing his eyes slightly. "This is why you did not press for any surtax. You, like me, were glad to be shut of the place. You sensed its wrongness, same as me. You need not admit it. I see it on your very face."

"You see only weariness and irritation," Thomas sighed, still not meeting his friend's gaze. "But I admit to being glad that the place is behind us, if only because sleeping under the stars is more comfortable than those damned ratty mattresses."

Yazim accepted this with a slow nod. They rode on.

"The Cragrack Cliffs are still there," he mused aloud. "Even now, they present a daunting pass for man or army. To this day, there are rumours of endless tunnels and caverns, lost cities hidden beneath the scrubby wilderness."

"But Camelot is dead," Thomas declared. "Even if your tale is true, the Princess could not have succeeded in her quest."

Yazim shrugged. "There are many measures of success," he suggested enigmatically. Thomas scoffed but merely shook his head.

"Where are we off to now?" he asked after a minute. "North, into the Barrens itself?"

"No. There is nothing there of interest to the Kingdom of Aachen. We head East now."

"East?" Thomas repeated, glancing aside. "Our mission was to travel north, then follow the feudal highway back south and east, visiting the townships along the way. The East is well accounted for."

"The eastern border, yes," Yazim agreed. "But not the middle lands. There may be something there."

Thomas frowned quizzically. "What are you not telling me, Yazim? You are hiding something."

"Something may indeed be hiding," Yazim smiled in agreement, "but our aim is to reveal it. Fear not. If I am wrong, we will merely extend our journey by a week. If I am right, the Archduke will reward our thoroughness."

"You believe there is a village in the hills?" Thomas prodded, tilting his head. "Is this part of your strange history?"

Yazim merely nudged his horse onwards with a click of his tongue.

Thomas sighed. "Intriguing, I admit. But it hardly seems worth the journey just to discover some forgotten hamlet in the forested foothills. The taxes will likely be a pittance."

"We do not search merely for taxes, Thomas," Yazim said loftily.

"Amuse me then," Thomas replied, shaking his head. "For what do we search?"

Yazim smiled faintly as the two of them passed beneath the trees. "We search for something far more valuable than coin," he answered quietly. "We search for information. We search... for evidence."

Thomas's frown deepened, but he did not protest the change in plans.

The sun began to descend into evening, stretching the trees' shadows across the road. The two travelers made good progress, enjoying the companionable silence. Finally, Thomas spoke up again.

"Tell me, at the very least, that the beast Merodach was destroyed in the end."

Yazim smiled grimly. "Does it matter? As you say, it may be that there never was such person. It is a mere fairy story."

"I did not say that. I expressed a logical skepticism. Tell me the ending and do not tease me."

Yazim's smile faded. "I cannot, I am afraid. There is a bit more of the story to tell, but the final ending is not a part of it."

"Curse you," Thomas fumed impatiently. "How can you say this? Why will you not tell me the ending?"

Yazim sighed deeply. "Because," he admitted reluctantly, "no one alive knows it. The ballad of the Princess Gabriella ends with a mystery. Many have guessed outcomes, but none can recount the truth with certainty."

"Curse you a thousand times," Thomas cried, but he didn't really mean it. "Very well then. Tell me the rest of what you know. I will make up my own damn ending if need be."

Yazim seemed to agree to this. He collected his thoughts as the sun continued to descend towards the horizon. Finally, he drew a breath and said, "The Princess's journey was nearing its completion, and yet the hardest part was yet to come. The most difficult obstacle of all lay before her."

"What shall it be now?" Thomas demanded wearily. "Ghosts? Demons? Giant two-headed billy goats? What fantastic enemy was yet to befall her?"

Yazim laughed drily. "The worst one of all," he replied. "The enemy of all who travel the empty wilderness. Gabriella's final challenge… was starvation."

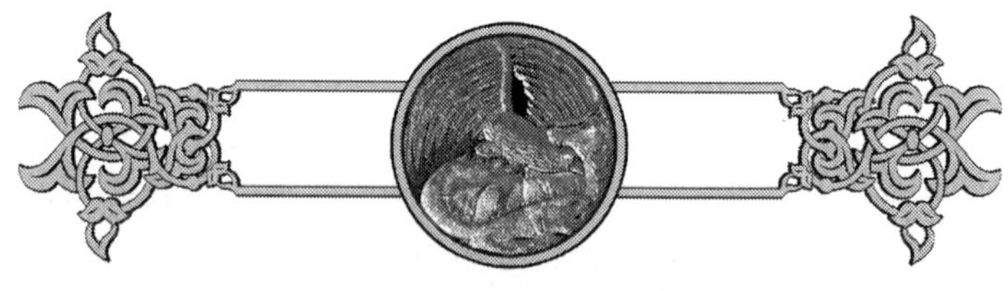

Gabriella melted snow for water, but the lack of food began to wear on her by the time darkness fell on her second day above ground. She made camp in the hollow of a steep hill, planted the goblinfire torch into the earth, and considered eating some of the frozen yellow grass. She knew it would bear no sustenance for her, even if she could manage to keep it down. Perhaps tomorrow she would find another gift pile of berries left by her secret midnight visitors. She did not hope greatly in this however. Since leaving the dragon's cave, she had seen virtually no sign of life save for the very occasional track of a wild hare.

The thought of hare made her mouth water frustratingly. She had no bow, and the trapping techniques she had practised at the academy were woefully forgotten. *Why would a Princess need to learn to catch food?* she had thought to herself at the time. Now, slowly starving in the darkening cold, she remembered this and laughed with bitter irony.

Featherbolt circled the evening sky far above, seeking his own dinner. She watched. Eventually, he tucked his wings and dove towards the ground, transforming himself into a hurtling feathered arrow, proving his name. A few minutes later, he appeared in the shadow of the hollow, the half-devoured remains of a mouse in his talons. He dropped this near the torch, as if offering it to Gabriella.

"Thanks, Featherbolt," she sighed, smiling. "You saved me the best bits, didn't you? The head and the tail."

She could not bring herself to eat his offering, but it was a close thing. If she did not find food tomorrow, she may indeed be happy to consume a mouse head. She shuddered, and yet her stomach growled eagerly at the prospect.

She slept.

Hauntingly vivid dreams visited her that night. She dreamt of Merodach in his stronghold surrounded by the corpses of those she loved. Darrick was there, pale and bloody, as was Rhyss, looking pathetically emaciated in her bridesmaid dress. Gabriella's mother lay in a dried pool of black blood, her eyes open, horribly empty in the darkness.

Worse, her father was there as well, impaled by a rusty sword. Next to him was Sigrid and the Little Prince, laid out on the floor like cordwood, dead but not buried, never buried.

Goethe was there as well. His body was propped upright against a pillar.

Merodach grinned and stalked through this, laughing to himself. He paced over the dead bodies, nearly stepping on them or kicking them aside as he passed, and Gabriella tried to shout out to him, to beg him not to hurt them any more.

They're already dead! she tried to scream through sealed lips. *Please, don't hurt them any more! Let me come to them and take them away and honour them with a decent burial! Please!*

But the madman did not hear her. He paced endlessly, humming thoughtfully and drumming his fingers on his short beard, and every time his shadow passed over those pale faces, Gabriella cringed with helpless misery, unable to look away but horrified to watch.

And then Goethe began to move. He was dead, and yet he pushed himself fully upright, standing independent of the pillar he'd been leant against. His eyes did not look at anything, but they turned towards her blankly. His lips peeled back in a parody of a smile, showing rotten teeth and black gums. His right hand raised jerkily, like the arm of a string marionette, and then dropped clumsily to the sword on his wasted hips. It missed, jerked again, and then gripped the hilt. Slowly, the corpse withdrew the sword from its scabbard. The blade was tacky with dried blood.

Goethe's body began to walk. It was a thoroughly inhuman walk, each step a different length, the feet slapping bonelessly to the ground. The head lolled, still grinning. The sword raised into the air. He was going to dismember the bodies for no other reason than Merodach's black amusement.

Or perhaps that was not his intent at all. Perhaps he had much worse in mind…

Gabriella tried to scream through the layers of sleep. She switched on the frozen ground, kicking off the cloak she had covered herself with. Featherbolt awoke. He withdrew his head from beneath his wing and peered at his sleeping companion. She moaned and tossed by the light of the goblinfire, her hair falling over her face.

"No…," she muttered. "No, Goethe. Get out of the black light. You're just a shadow, a shade. You're dead. Don't…" She shifted plaintively, her moans growing panicked, her voice clearing, turning gradually into shouts. "No, Goethe! It is Merodach! He dabbles and despoils! Don't make them puppets of the black light! No! *NO!!*"

And yet she did not awaken. She rolled fitfully onto her side and let out a long, diminishing moan. Tears wet her cheeks. Shortly, however, her restlessness subsided. Her breathing became even again. The tension leaked out of her sleeping face.

Featherbolt watched this intently. He hopped closer, moving into the light of the fire, and stood near Gabriella's shoulder. The dream had spent itself for now. He clicked his beak and shook his feathers.

He did not sleep for the rest of the night.

In the morning, Gabriella dug in her pack, seeking any crumb of food that might be left. She found the acorns that she had tucked away earlier, the ones that had come in the mysterious pile of berries. She ate them. They were extremely tough and tasted like mouldy parchment, and yet her stomach attacked them eagerly. A small surge of energy fanned out in her veins, making her feel slightly light-headed.

She turned the energy towards walking.

The sun burnt through the clouds as it rose, turning the snowy hills into a sparkling tableau. Gabriella crossed this doggedly, aiming for the distant mountain peaks.

Her mind wandered. Daydreams of her youth preoccupied her for unknown lengths of time. In them, she thought of her mother. Gabriella was a small child sitting on her mother's lap and listening to stories. Her mother turned the pages of the storybooks, and the colourful drawings seemed to come alive. Happy green dragons flew off the paper and carried her away, lifting her into gold-rimmed clouds and warm, blue skies. Her mother's voice followed her, telling the tale, and Gabriella realised that she was remembering the sound of her mother's actual voice, something she believed she had long ago forgotten.

Her feet plowed onwards, drawing troughs through the snow, and Gabriella came back to herself as if from a long distance. There were tears standing in her eyes. Hunger was making her faint, and the faintness was taking the form of delirium. She did not fight this. The visions were better than the constant trudge of her footsteps or the frustrating monotony of the snowy hills.

The mountain peaks remained as far away as ever.

"I have to make it," she panted to Featherbolt as he wheeled overhead. "I have to stop Merodach. If I kill him, it will be over. His armies will stop. Camelot will stand. Everything will be saved. Everything will be saved..."

She repeated the mantra to herself, forcing herself onwards, defying the growing weakness of her body. Time was running out, she knew. Merodach's armies may well have already reached Camelot. If she did not find the warlord and kill him very soon, then all would be lost. Darrick and Rhyss would be unavenged, and those that remained would be hunted down and killed. Camelot would fall, and everyone she loved would die.

Thinking this, using it like a whip on her weary body, Gabriella trudged onwards.

Another night. Another spate of fever dreams. And yet, at dawn, she forced herself to continue on.

"He said that I would make it," she breathed, stumbling forwards through the snow. "Coalroot. Said I would confront Merodach. It was... it was my destiny, he said. I won't starve. I won—"

She fell forwards into the snow, and did not know it.

Sometime later, Featherbolt was nuzzling at her, pecking gently at her ear. The warmth of his feathers was pressed against her cheek. Her other cheek was numb with cold, packed into the snow.

She groaned and pushed herself to her knees. Her eyes felt gummed shut with ice.

"Featherbolt," she whispered, rubbing her face. "What happened...?"

He screeched, and she finally forced her eyes open. She looked around and saw the falcon standing on the pale haft of her driftwood torch. Its blunt end was buried in the snow. The goblinfire had been snuffed out.

"Oh no!" she moaned pathetically, reaching for the pale wood. She picked it up, peered at its end. The wood was completely unmarked, cold as bone. "No... no...," she repeated, scolding herself. "How could I have been so careless?"

Featherbolt jumped into the air and landed on her shoulder. He pressed himself against her cheek, as if urging her onwards, but Gabriella merely stared at the cold torch in her hand. It had become a symbol of her quest. It was hopeless. Regardless of what Coalroot had said, she would die on the steppe, starved and frozen stiff.

She dropped the torch and sat back on her haunches. For several minutes, she merely watched the declining sun, chilled so deeply that she no longer even shivered.

Then, simply because she did not know what else to do, she struggled to her feet. Slowly, haltingly, she began to walk again.

The sun lowered until it kissed the western horizon. Gabriella's shadow stretched beside her like an arrow. Featherbolt launched from her shoulder and soared up into the copper glow of the sunset. He would find his own dinner and bring her back half of it. This time, she knew she would eat it if she could.

She trudged onwards.

There was a flicker of movement in a nearby strand of bushes. Gabriella saw it and stopped abruptly, scanning the shadows. The tawny flank of a large hare could be seen through the frosted grass. Its ears were perked upright, and its beady eyes were turned towards her, watching her brightly.

Gabriella barely allowed herself to breathe. There was no chance she could catch the hare, of course. It would bolt at her slightest movement. Still, her stomach growled audibly, painfully, at the sight of it.

She couldn't help herself. She began to creep towards it, biting her lip with concentration.

The hare watched. When she had approached it enough that her shadow moved over the bushes, it leapt. One bounding jump took it out of the weeds and onto the snow of the receding slope.

"Wait!" Gabriella exclaimed desperately, halting and raising her hands, palms out.

Amazingly, the hare did. It stopped a safe distance away, turned, and stood up on its hind legs, its nose twitching.

Gabriella inched forwards. Her breath came in shallow pants. "Please do not go," she pleaded. "Please, just... just wait..."

The hare watched her intently as she crept closer. She hunkered low, trying to make herself small. With deliberate slowness, she reached up and touched the sigil that hung at her throat. She resisted the urge to sob with desperate frustration.

"Just wait," she breathed faintly. "Do not run..."

The hare's nose twitched. Its eyes tracked the motion of her hand as she touched the sigil, felt its secret warmth. Gabriella was nearly close enough to leap upon the creature. Only two more steps… one…

The hare twitched, spun on the snow, and bounded away.

Gabriella watched this, her expression unchanging, her fingers still touching the falcon sigil. The sound of the hare's movements receded into silence as it crested the next hill, leaving only its tracks in the snow.

Slowly, Gabriella lowered her hand. Her strength left her, and she fell ponderously to her knees, and then forwards onto her face. She tried to crawl, pulled herself nearly to the top of the next slope, and then failed.

The wind blew over her, carrying tendrils of snow. It felt so very good just to lie down. She barely even felt the cold any more. Behind her, the sun finally dipped below the horizon. The world turned deep blue, tinged with bronze.

A ripple of disturbed air buffeted Gabriella, but she didn't look up. Perhaps it was Featherbolt returning with a scrap of rodent. She waited.

Instead of the soft nuzzle of his wing on her cheek, however, the ground shuddered with a series of surprisingly heavy thumps, emanating from the slope directly ahead of her. A gust of warm air blew back over the hillside, riffling the icy grass and lifting the hair from her brow.

Gabriella attempted to raise her head. Something very large loomed before her, making a huge, dark blot against the snow and sky. It was approaching slowly, raising and lowering its great, clawed feet, shuddering the ground with its weight.

He's tracked me all this way, she thought blandly. *He's come to devour me in my weakness. Let him. Let him eat me and be done with it…* Then from another, fevered part of her mind: *Perhaps it is the storybook dragon from my daydream. Perhaps he has come to spirit me away to happy clouds and warm sunlight…*

A low, gurgling growl arose from the depths of the beast's throat. The strength of its exhalation blew over Gabriella's face. It stank of rotten meat and chemical. She felt its shadow move over her, heard the subtle scrape of its leathery skin. Its jaw creaked as it opened wide.

And then, unexpectedly, a large weight dropped to the ground directly in front of Gabriella. She startled despite her weakness and lifted her head. Her eyes widened slightly. Slowly, unblinking, she pushed herself back onto her knees.

The dragon took a massive step backwards. Its orange eyes surveyed her meaningfully, and a grating rumble uncoiled from deep in its throat. In front of the dragon's feet, lying on the snowy ground between it and Gabriella, was an enormous dismembered leg. It had belonged to one of the chortha, although the trickling blood implied that this was a fresh kill.

The fur was almost entirely burnt off of it. Its meat was already cooked.

There was a flicker of dark wings, and suddenly, Featherbolt landed atop the gigantic flank, fearlessly ignoring the great dragon behind him. He pecked at the singed meat, tore off a strip, and gobbled it greedily.

Gabriella stared at the steaming hunk of beast, then over it, to the waiting dragon. The smell of meat, tainted by the dragon's breath as it was, acted like evil magic on her stomach. It growled eagerly. Was it a trap? A trick? A figment of her delirious imagination? She crept forwards almost involuntarily.

The dragon watched, exhaling great, low gusts of heat.

Gabriella touched the flesh of the dismembered leg. Slowly, casting a glance up at the watching dragon, she drew her sword, cut off a strip of the meat, and smelled it. A moment later, she devoured it. A wave of dizziness and warmth washed over her as the sustenance sank into her stomach.

The dragon observed this stoically. Then it coiled low to the ground, snarled a puff of blue fire, unhinged its wings, and threw itself up into the darkening air. Snow swirled as it swooped overhead and wheeled around in a wide arc. It landed again some distance away, dropping to a strangely disgruntled crouch with its head lifted, watching. After a moment, it furled its wings and lay down. Its orange eyes glowed in the dimness.

Still perched atop the steaming hunk of leg, Featherbolt let out a screech. He bent and tore off another chunk of meat.

Feeling like someone in a very strange dream, Gabriella looked from the dismembered leg to the dragon and back again. The bite of meat in her belly called hungrily for another.

She ate.

Heat and strength flowed into her with astonishing quickness. She scooped handfuls of snow and consumed those as well, quenching her thirst.

When she looked up again, stopping her meal before she overwhelmed her stomach, the moon was high overhead. Stars spread across the sky like silver dust.

The dragon had crept closer. It lay full-length on the snowy hill, its head no more than ten paces away. Snow had melted around it, revealing the dead yellow grass of the steppe. Its orange eyes were half-lidded but opened up fully as Gabriella rose to her feet. A puff of blue flame blew from its nostrils.

Deliberately and carefully, Gabriella approached the dragon.

When she was three paces away, the dragon raised its great head and breathed a long, grating growl, lifting its lips to show rows of dagger-like teeth. Gabriella stopped for a moment. She stared into the beast's orange eyes, and then began to move forwards again.

The dragon arose suddenly, keeping its head low, and drew back a step. A deep snarl rumbled in its throat. Ribbons of smoke began to issue from its nostrils.

A shudder of fear shook Gabriella. And yet she continued to move forwards, slowly raising her right hand, palm out, fingers spread. The falcon sigil swung at her throat. She sensed it there, felt its warmth against her skin.

She touched the dragon's great, scaly snout. It was hot and hard, rough to the touch. Slowly, barely breathing, she stroked it.

"It's all right," she whispered, her voice trembling faintly. "I know how difficult this must be for you."

Gradually, the dragon seemed to relax. Together, the young woman and the dragon stood there in the moonlight. Some distance away, Featherbolt perched on the remains of the dismembered leg, watching with interest, his head cocked to one side.

Eventually, Gabriella drew back. She felt more alive and awake than she had in weeks. She turned her back on the dragon and began to scout carefully around the hills, seeking scraps of wood to use for a fire.

When she was through, she piled them into a small, neat stack.

The dragon lit it.

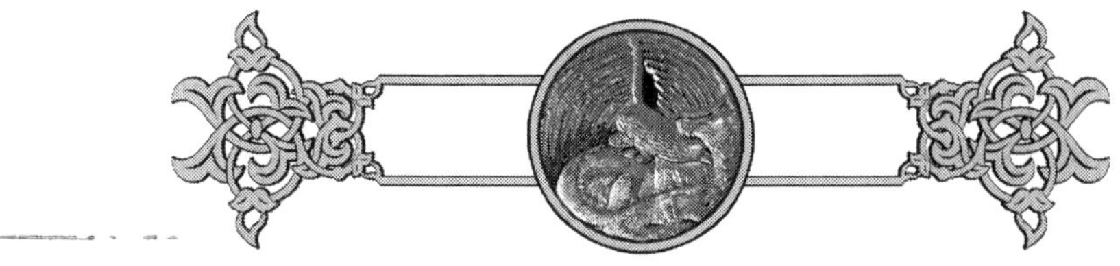

When morning came, she found that the dragon had distanced itself again. It lay several hills away, making a brownish lump against the dawn sky. Its head lifted as she stood up.

The fire had burnt down to embers, but heat still radiated from it, making a dry circle of dead grass on the hill. Gabriella breakfasted on more of the dismembered chortha leg, then carefully cut and wrapped several strips of the now cold meat. These, she placed in her pack. As she slung it onto her back, Featherbolt screeched once and leapt to her shoulder with a flurry of brown wings.

She began to walk again. She had only gotten a few paces when the dragon launched itself into the air with a great clap of its wings. It swooped low over the snow, racing its shadow, and then landed with disconcerting heaviness directly in front of Gabriella. It lowered its head and stared at her, its orange eyes blazing intently. Heat snuffed at her from its flared nostrils.

"What?" she said, willing herself not to step backwards. Perhaps the dragon had rethought the logic of their strange alliance. Perhaps its violent, bestial nature was reasserting itself. Gabriella swallowed hard. "What do you want? You're... er... in my way."

The dragon growled. The noise of it was like gravel in a deep, muddy well. Its breath hissed, hot as a furnace.

With a force of will, Gabriella moved to walk around the dragon. It watched her piercingly. When she moved past its extended head, the great beast reared up. A gust of flame melted the snow where she had been standing moments before, and Gabriella halted, her hand dropping instinctively to the hilt of her sword. Featherbolt startled and took off. The dragon leapt nimbly but heavily backwards, its claws tearing ragged, dark strips in the hilltop. Once again, it blocked her path and lowered its head to face her.

Gabriella stared at it. If its intention was to eat her, she thought darkly, then it would have done so already. She tilted her head at it and frowned.

Overhead, Featherbolt circled against the brightening sky. He screeched impatiently.

"You want me...," Gabriella mused aloud, "to... *ride* you?"

The dragon huffed. It did not understand her words, and yet it regarded her meaningfully, as if trembling on the verge of non-verbal communication. Tentatively, she reached out to the dragon's snout again. Its nostrils flared at the scent of her nearness. She touched it, and it flinched slightly, as if fighting the urge to snap her arm off at the shoulder.

She moved aside the massive head, trailing her hand along the line of its shut mouth. Snaggles of fangs protruded up and down along the lips, forming an interlocking mesh. Gabriella touched one of the teeth.

Its edge was serrated, sharp as broken glass. The dragon did not move but watched her warily. Slowly, Gabriella moved past the head, still drawing her hand along the scaly skin, feeling the bundle of monstrous jaw muscles and the tensed sinews of the long neck. The plates of the dragon's spine jutted up in a line over her, casting her in their shadow. There was a break in them between the beast's shoulder blades. As Gabriella neared this, the dragon hunkered lower, kneeling on the snow and pressing its belly flat to the ground.

Gabriella stopped. She was terrified at what she was about to do, and yet she knew she must attempt it. The dragon was apparently not going to let her pass on foot. If the beast was indeed going to let her ride it, however, she might actually get to Merodach and his citadel in time to stop the attack on Camelot.

Still, she thought fearfully, *that is a very big* if.

She steeled her nerve and reached up, hooking her hand around the rough edge of the nearest of the dragon's spinal plates. The beast did not move. Holding her breath, Gabriella placed her foot on the dragon's bent shin, using it like an enormous step, and pushed herself up. A moment later, with a heave and a turn, she straddled the dragon's neck, fitting herself into the narrow gap of its spine plates. She was positioned above the very base of the neck. The bony humps of the dragon's shoulders were behind her on either side.

The beast inhaled. She felt the expansion of its chest, the subtle lift of its spine. Then, with a whump of air and motion, the wings unfurled. She sensed the shadow of them fall over her and barely had time to embrace the spinal plate ahead of her before the dragon kicked massively upwards, hurling itself into the air. The wings clapped down, catching the air and tossing snow up in swirling clouds. Gabriella hugged the rough plate of the dragon's back and squeezed her eyes shut. Her stomach sank away as the dragon bore her up, up, accelerating into the cold sky. The enormous, leathery wings pounded the air, making a noise like ocean waves, only faster and deeper.

When Gabriella opened her eyes again, she was terrified to see the ground far below, dotted with tiny trees, their shadows stretched out behind them in the dawn light. The hills had become crescents of lavender shadow, dropping gradually behind as the dragon hurtled onwards, still picking up speed. The wind whipped around Gabriella's face and made her eyes water. Slowly, however, her terror began to fade, and a cautious, heady exhilaration began to take its place.

She raised her gaze from the unrolling ground far below and peered ahead, daring to shade her eyes with one hand. The mountains were still far off, but they already seemed closer. There was a screech in the near distance. She turned towards it and saw Featherbolt swooping along next to her, tracking the dragon easily, his wing feathers fluttering in the rush of the wind. For the first time in days, Gabriella felt the subtle resurgence of determination. She was going to make it in time, perhaps even by the end of the day. She would find Merodach's hidden citadel in the Theatre of the Broken Crown. There, finally, she would confront him.

Then whatever was destined to happen would happen. Her thoughts and plans ended there. It was as if the enormity of what she had to do when that time came was simply too big, too monumental, for her mind to grasp.

Despite her determination, she had to admit to herself that she was afraid to confront the madman. She was, in fact, more afraid than she had ever been in her entire life—more than when she had faced the murderous Goethe over the corpse of her best friend, more even than when she had encountered the rampaging dragon in its own den. Her fear was like a poison elixir, rich and potent, but one that she forced herself to drink fully, one drop at a time. There was no turning back now. Her duty was unavoidable. With the help of Featherbolt and the dragon, she would go to her destiny willingly, her eyes wide open.

And when the finale came—*whatever* it held for her—she would welcome it.

She would embrace it.

CHAPTER 10

The broken peak of Mount Skelter became increasingly prominent as the day wore on. The dragon interrupted its flight three times, twice to eat and drink and once to empty its prodigious bowels. This last, it did with surprising delicacy, instinctively hiding itself away in the shadows of a rocky cleft. Gabriella stretched her limbs near the bend of a stream whilst Featherbolt preened on a nearby rock, his glossy feathers glinting in the waning sunlight.

The air had warmed throughout the day, melting the ground snow into a thin, icy crust and sending up great rafts of fog. More often than not, the dragon flew through these purposely, banking its great wings and using the serpentine curl of its tail as a rudder. Each time, Gabriella clung to the dragon's neck plate and squinted her eyes as the shock of grey dampness pulsed over them. The fog banks grew thicker and broader as the day descended into evening so that eventually, they seemed to be flying over a rippling cloudscape, tinged with the light of the low sun. For long stretches, Mount Skelter was the only visible landscape, pushing its craggy slopes and crumbled peak up out of the fog like an island.

Amazingly, the act of riding the dragon became monotonous. The wax and weft of its mighty wings became like the rhythm of a metronome, like the ticking pendulum used by her old harpsichord instructor, a tiny, ancient lord with heavy spectacles and knuckly hands. Gabriella had never been inclined to music despite her teacher's persistent efforts, but he had always been kind to her anyway, patting her dotingly on the shoulder and promising that, with practice, she would be a fine player someday.

"Don't give up, young Princess," he would say, holding back the pendulum with the first two fingers of his right hand and eyeing her gravely. "If your hands stumble on the keys, do not give up. The metronome will not stop, nor should you, lest it conquer you. Are you going to let such a thing best you, Princess? Keep playing even if you stumble a dozen times. The point is not perfection, but perseverance. Make the tempo your slave. Only then will the music come."

The music had not come, unfortunately, but there was a deeper truth in the music teacher's words. Gabriella had not known it at the time, but she had acted upon it in the years since. *The point is not perfection,* she thought to herself, *but perseverance. Don't give up, Princess. Make the tempo your slave...*

The thought of her old harpsichord teacher made her think of Darrick as a young man. He'd never had the luxury of private teachers, never experienced the comforts that were so commonplace to royalty like her. And yet in him had resided a nobility much deeper and truer than could be found in most of the lords she had ever known.

"Every boy I knew wanted to be brave Sir Lancelot," he had once confided in her, "I was one of them."

It seemed like years and decades ago. Even now, she could barely remember the feeling of his touch. He had treated her like a flower, like a delicate treasure, to be protected and cherished, loved in the intimate dark of a lifetime's nights. That had not happened, of course. Now the hands that he had caressed were chapped and rough. The hair he had nuzzled in the quiet embrace of their few nights was now a tangled mat, tamed by a length of dirty leather. Darrick's delicate flower had cast off her beauty and grown thorns.

"I'm sorry, my love," she said aloud, speaking into the rushing wind and fog. "I'm sorry for everything that was taken away from you.

Your life... and the thing that you cared for even more. Me. I probably never really was the girl you believed me to be. But now I fear that you would not even recognise who I have become. I'm sorry." She swallowed hard and frowned, her eyes glistening. "I'm sorry... that you lost me."

The dragon soared on beneath her. Night began to creep over the cloudy sky, turning the light a haunting pearly lavender. The peak of Mount Skelter loomed before them now, huge and sprawling. Beneath it, glimpsed occasionally through the sweeping fog, were the rock-edged foothills. Gabriella sensed that they were very close to their destination. Soon, the dragon would descend and land. From there, she would travel the rest of the way on foot, meaning to enter the enemies' camp secretly, stealthily. At that point, instinct would take over.

The dragon flew over a patchy bank of fog so low that tendrils of it curled up around them, reaching for them like thin fingers. Gabriella watched this as if mesmerised.

Something lofted up out of the fog. It moved with almost balletic grace, turning as it arced over the humps of the clouds. Gabriella was too surprised by it to be afraid. It looked, more than anything, like a large canvas bag stuffed with something dense, its mouth tied in a neat knot. The shape traced a gentle parabola through the air on the dragon's right and then fell back, disappearing again into the fog.

"What was—" she began, but was interrupted by a violent explosion directly beneath her.

The dragon recoiled in mid-air, nearly throwing her from its back. Something had stricken it and erupted into a cloud of thick, yellow powder. Gabriella choked on the dust as it swirled up around her, blinding her. A moment later, the dragon fell out of the yellow cloud, struggling to fly but clawing wildly at the air and writhing its long neck. Gabriella clung to her mount, but the dragon's frantic movements made it very difficult. The wings struggled to grasp the air. Wind rushed up past them, and Gabriella realised with a sick jolt of fear that they were falling.

Another of the strange sacks arced up towards them, spinning lazily and trailing yellow dust. It struck the dragon on the flank and exploded, coating the beast with more of the ugly powder. The dragon lunged away in mid-air, its tail thrashing. An instant later, the fog swept up over them, hiding everything in its seamless depths. Gabriella clung frantically to the dragon, not even knowing which way was up. The beast dropped through the ceiling of the fog, and the earth opened up beneath them, looking huge and close and unforgivably hard.

There were men down there, at least a dozen of them, all looking up, shouting and pointing. They were near enough that Gabriella could see their individual faces.

The dragon writhed violently in mid-air, clapped its wings in a last, desperate attempt to capture the wind, and succeeded. Its fall was arrested, transforming it into a hurtling swoop, but it was too late to pull up. The stone-crested foothills rushed up beneath them, reaching for them, and Gabriella squeezed her eyes shut.

There was a whistling silence followed inexorably by a hard, deafening *whump*. The dragon convulsed dreadfully beneath Gabriella, and she felt herself thrown free. The wings whipped past her, smacked at her armour. A moment later, she struck the ground herself. She was rolling, skipping over the earth like a discus, her hair flying wildly and her armour clanging against the rocks. Finally, she tumbled to a halt, eyes still closed, dazed and face down on the earth.

"This way," a rough voice called gleefully. "It's down! It's down! Bring the nets!"

The rabble grew closer, calling and shouting commands, laughing raucously. Gabriella moaned and tried to push herself upright. A bolt of blinding pain seared up her left arm accompanied by a horrid, grinding sensation. She fell back, crying out involuntarily.

The ground shuddered beneath her. The dragon was getting up. She heard it. It thrashed and growled thickly, but there was something wrong with it. It wheezed, and when it tried to roar, to bury its adversaries in gouts of blue flame, its throat produced only a choked hiss.

"Flame us through that, you great blowhard!" a voice laughed. "Bring another bag of the Damproot powder! Let's have one more dose for good measure!"

"Should we wheel the catapult over and fire it straight into the big lizard's kisser?" another voice suggested, and there was a round of hearty laughter and encouragement.

"It's rearing!" another shouted. "More nets! This is a big'n!"

There was a creak of straining rope and a shuddering thrash. The dragon was fighting. Gabriella struggled up again, using her right arm, and stumbled towards the sound.

"Mind the jaws!" a deep voice bellowed happily. "He may not be able to roast us, but those teeth might still subtract a leg. Stand fast!"

"Stop!" Gabriella cried, but her voice failed her. Her chest ached from her fall, and the pain in her left arm spiked with every step. "Leave him alone, you monsters!" She descended the hill and spotted shapes moving in the fog.

"Wait," a voice called gruffly. "What was that?"

"Someone approaches!"

Swords rang from scabbards as Gabriella stumbled into the shallow valley. "Leave him be!" she shouted angrily.

Before her, the dragon lay imprisoned in a tangle of thick nets, each one edged with heavy iron balls, knotting the mass into an ugly prison. The beast struggled and thrashed, trying desperately to flame but producing only dry, choked gusts. Dozens of men clustered around the dragon, some poking it savagely with pikes, all wearing mismatched collections of armour and ragged beards. Others gathered by a small, wheeled catapult. A wagon loaded with more of the canvas powder bags stood nearby.

"You beasts!" Gabriella raged, forgetting the pain in her arm and dashing forwards.

"Whoever she is," one of the men growled, pointing a thick finger at Gabriella, "take her."

They fell upon her. Acting purely on instinct, Gabriella unsheathed her sword. She swung one-handed and felt the ringing clang of blade on metal. A battle-axe caught her sword in its fork, and the man holding the axe gave it a hard twist. The blade snapped off, leaving only the hilt in her fist. She turned on the man, baring her teeth in blind anger and raising the hilt like a bludgeon. He caught her wrist easily, laughing and showing a mouthful of rotten teeth.

"Look what we have here, men," the man bellowed, twisting Gabriella's wrist and forcing her to drop her broken sword. "First a dragon, and now a she-warrior, armour and all!"

Gabriella struggled, broke away from the man, and swung at him wildly. He caught her left forearm this time, and a jolt of crippling pain rammed up her arm. A second later, the man's other fist struck her on the temple, driving her to her knees and making the world go swimmy before her eyes. Blood immediately began to run down her cheek, hot in the winter air. He still did not release her arm. The broken bone grated excruciatingly, and she cried out with the pain of it.

"She's a feisty one," a nearby voice laughed wickedly. "Can you handle her, Radnic?"

"Where did she come from?" another figure demanded, stepping forwards to peer at her. "Are there others? A girl so young surely would not brave the wilderness alone."

A much taller and darker man pushed past him. He approached Gabriella, his eyes narrowed above a tangled, black beard. When he knelt on one knee before her, she recoiled from him, not out of fear, but revulsion. Even through the red mist of her pain, the man reeked of death. His eyes were as empty as marbles.

"No," he said slowly, "she is the only one."

Gabriella's captor squeezed her forearm again, twisting it upright over her head. "You know her?"

The leader shook his head thoughtfully. "No. But I smell vengeance upon her. She has come alone, of her own volition." And then, with a hint of amusement, he added, "She intends… to fight."

"What do we do with her, Brom?" the man behind him asked warily. "Do we kill her?"

The leader, Brom, smiled evilly. "Not yet," he growled. "That would be a terrible waste. Bring her. She shall be my… guest."

A chorus of hoots and catcalls followed this, building to a raucous crescendo.

Gabriella gritted her teeth and pushed herself upright, fighting a wave of faintness. Her captor still held her broken forearm in a vise-like grip.

"Release me!" she commanded hoarsely. "I am the Princess of Camelot. My father is the King. Obey my command!"

The chorus of laughter died away. Before her, Brom rose up again to his full height. He was more than a foot taller than she and twice as wide. His eyes did not leave hers, nor did his smile falter as he stepped directly in front of her. The stench of death was thick around him. He raised a callused hand and traced his fingers down the angle of her cheek, drawing a dirty line in her own fresh blood. She flinched away but could not escape his presence. The pain in her arm was breathtaking.

Brom drew his hand back from her face, showed her the blood that coated his fingers. Slowly, deliberately, he licked her blood from his fingers. He closed his eyes slightly and moaned with pleasure.

"Out here, Your Highness," he said, breathing down into her face like a lover, "there is a much *different* command. I think you shall learn it well… in the short time you have left."

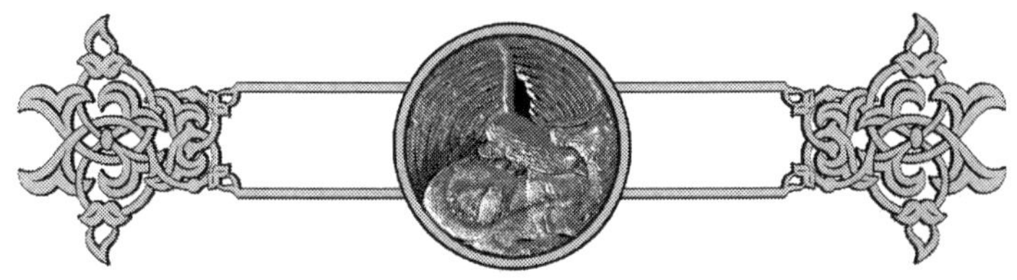

They hauled her behind the catapult, which was itself pulled by a pair of chortha. A length of rope bound her wrists before her, attaching her to the rear of the war machine and yanking her mercilessly forwards. The pain in her forearm had become a deep ache, throbbing so hard that she felt it in the veins of her neck, saw it in the corners of her eyes.

The dragon was dragged along as well. Still imprisoned in nets, thrashing uselessly, it was pulled bodily over the rocky snow by a team of chortha. They snarled and gnashed at their harnesses, struggling with the massive weight. The awful men whipped the beasts with studded chains, ripping hanks of fur out with each strike.

Fortunately, the troop was not far from their camp. They clambered up a jagged rise and over its ledge, and Gabriella saw the small valley below them. It was almost perfectly round, ringed with sharp outcroppings of rock and nestled firmly at the base of Mount Skelter. The Theatre of the Broken Crown was filled with ranks of rough soldiers, makeshift tents, and smoking campfires. On its furthest edge, a small citadel stood. It looked like an overgrown chess rook, made of grey stone and marked only with arrow slits.

The catapult picked up speed as it rocked down the inside slope of the valley. It jerked Gabriella forwards, making her stumble and eliciting a cry of agony for her broken forearm. As the caravan entered the camp, soldiers stopped what they were doing to watch. Gabriella avoided their gaze, but felt their eyes crawling over her unabashedly. The grounds of the enemy camp were mashed to mud and streaked with puddles. Smoke rolled between the tents, pressed to the ground by the strange atmosphere of the natural depression. Large, bloody racks of meat turned slowly on iron spits over greasy fires. Gabriella shuddered as she looked at them.

She had intended, once she caught her breath, to demand to know what the horrible soldiers meant to do with the dragon. Now she suspected the ugly truth. They meant to eat it.

Finally, nearing the centre of the camp, the catapult jerked to a stop. Brom approached, his feet squelching on the mucky ground. He unsheathed his sword with a flourish. Gabriella tried not to flinch as he swung it over her. There was a hard thunk of metal on wood as his blade cut Gabriella's rope free of the catapult. He caught the end of it, turned, and gave it a yank, pulling her forwards.

"Stop!" she gasped, slipping on the mud, but it was no use. He led her down a swampy aisle between two canvas tents. She tripped over one of the tent's long, wooden stakes and stumbled to the mud, but Brom did not break his stride. He yanked her forwards almost effortlessly, and Gabriella screamed for her tortured arm.

She was heaved into a larger tent. As soon as the shadow of it fell over her, the smell of death, fetid throughout the entire camp, became a noxious reek. Gabriella sucked in a lungful of it involuntarily and wretched.

Brom dropped the rope, and Gabriella collapsed to the floor of the tent, gasping.

For a long minute, there was silence, punctuated only by the ragged tide of Gabriella's breathing as she recovered herself. Finally, she pushed herself up onto her knees.

The tent was large but very dark. Complicated shapes loomed—a chair, a table, a rope hung with thick, wet hanks of animal skins and furs, other things that, for the moment, Gabriella could not comprehend.

And Brom. He stood near the entrance, barely a silhouette in the darkness, his arms dangling loosely at his sides, his tangle of beard bristling. He was staring at her motionlessly.

Gabriella mustered her resolve and took a deep breath. "Let me *go*!" she rasped furiously.

Brom did not reply, nor did he move.

Gabriella pulled at the ropes twined about her wrists but immediately collapsed in anguish at her poor broken arm. Tears of anger and frustration welled in her eyes. She pushed herself onto her knees again and glared up at the dark figure.

"Take me to him," she seethed through gritted teeth. "Take me to Merodach. He will wish to see me. I am the Princess. I demand an audience."

Still, Brom did not move. Gabriella's fury boiled over at him. She thrashed to her feet and flung herself at his silhouette.

"I… demand… an *audience*!" she shouted, and kicked at her captor.

His fist moved as if of its own accord, catching her just below the jaw. She tumbled backwards, gasping, sure that the beast had crushed her windpipe. She blinked past a dizzying wave of greyness and rolled onto her side to catch her breath.

Behind her, a shuffle of fabric sounded. There was a flash of firelight and a rabble of voices and then darkness again. Amazingly, without a word, Brom had left.

Gabriella rolled back towards the entrance again, straining her eyes in the dimness. Two shadows could be seen on the flaps of the tent's door. There were guards outside of course, each one nearly as tall and vicious as Brom. There would be no escape that way.

She cast around in the gloom, weak with pain, barely breathing for the thick stench of the place, and her gaze fell upon the mysterious mass she had seen earlier. It looked familiar, although she could not quite place where she had seen anything like it before. She crept towards it in the darkness, hissing through her teeth at the pain of her arm. The stink seemed to be coming from it.

With a wave of horror, Gabriella realised what it reminded her of. It was like the mound of carcasses heaped in the corner of the dragon's cave. Only this mound was rather smaller. And it was not comprised of dead beasts.

Human corpses were piled like rag dolls, most stripped to bare bones streaked black with rotting tissue. The hands, feet, and heads, however, still bore flesh and skin, as if whatever had consumed the bodies had not wished to waste time on such sparse meat. Shoes and sandals adorned some of the feet. Rings glittered on some of the fingers. A shock of bloody red hair was evident near the edge of the pile. Gabriella did not wish to look any further, and yet she could not tear her gaze away. Her eyes widened in the darkness, taking in the hideous sight. Surely, this was what was to become of her. Brom was that most awful of all possible villains. He was an eater of the dead.

But it was worse even than that, and Gabriella knew it. It was as if Brom himself was dead and yet animated, his corpse haunted by something otherworldly, sustained only by the consumption of more death.

Gabriella shuddered violently. It was completely insane of course. It could not be true. But then she remembered the beast riders that she had encountered earlier in her journey, remembered hacking the arm from one of them and it not even slowing down. Its eyes, when it had reared on her, had been milky white, utterly blank. And the severed arm had continued flexing… flexing…

"No wonder Father's army could not defeat them," she said to herself, and her voice was a high tremolo of horror. "How can you kill something… that's already dead?"

And then, like the final, most devastating blow, Gabriella realised what she had been looking at all along. It glittered before her, loose on one wasted, pale hand. It was a gold ring.

It was the mate of the one on her own finger.

"No!" she moaned desperately. She pushed herself forwards, willing it not to be what she knew it was. The hand was slender but strong, the fingers curled gently, palm up, as if offering a gift. The ring was unmistakable.

"Darrick," she sobbed, reaching her bound wrists forwards and touching the cold, pale hand. "No! No, no, no…," she repeated helplessly, shaking her head and closing her eyes. In the darkness, she pressed her hands into his, tried desperately to remember what it had felt like when his fingers were warm and strong.

She could not.

For several minutes, grief swallowed her up. Nothing else mattered. She sobbed into the dirt of the floor, still resting her hand in his dead palm.

And then, finally, the pain of her body merged with the agony of her heart and overwhelmed her. Darkness fell upon her, seamlessly and heavily, and for a long while, she knew no more.

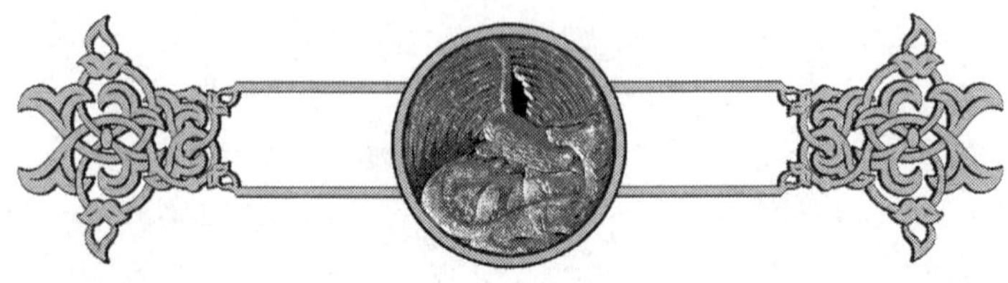

She came back to herself slowly. She was lying on a dirt floor, surrounded by darkness and the stench of death. But more nagging even than that, something was tickling her hands. She moaned and stirred, and a busy squeaking chitter caught her ear. It was very near.

She startled and thrashed to her knees. When she opened her eyes in the dimness, she could just make out the shape of a large rodent in the darkness. It had retreated from her and now stood near the mound of dead bodies. It was, of course, a rat.

Gabriella shuddered violently. She hated rats.

"Go away," she hissed at the thing. It flinched but did not run. Gabriella raised her bound wrists to shoo it and then stopped. The thick ropes were frayed into tufts of loose fibre. They were nearly broken through completely.

The rat had been gnawing her free.

She shuddered again. She really did hate rats. And yet…

She lowered her wrists gently towards the ground. The rat watched this with its beady, black eyes. Then, haltingly, it moved forwards again. After an anxious moment, it darted towards her hands. Gabriella tensed with loathing and clenched her eyes shut. The rat's tiny, cold feet clambered over her fingers and the backs of her hands.

"Ungh...," she shivered as it began to gnaw again. "Just the ropes. Do you understand? I appreciate the help... but I can barely resist the urge to crush your skull with my boot."

Suddenly, she realised that this must have been very close to how the dragon had felt about her.

The ropes loosened gradually. Finally, with a faint pop, the coils fell away. The rat squeaked once, then kicked off from her hands. It scampered towards the tent's wall and vanished beneath it.

Gabriella raised her hands and peered at them in the dimness. Her left forearm was swollen and bruised beneath her wrist gauntlet. The subtle grate of the broken bone had become almost bearable, but the fingers of her left hand were stiff and weak. She flexed them experimentally. It was painful, but not excruciating. Or perhaps excruciating was simply something she was getting used to.

They did this to me.

It was a small thought, like a candle flame in a dark room, but it was very bright. *They killed Darrick, and they mean to kill me. And when they are through, they will seek out and kill everyone else. Father. Sigrid. And the Little Prince.*

The flicker of her anger stoked gradually to a flame. She had felt her anguish, tasted the full draught of her grief. Now, on the other side of that, all that was left inside her was rage. She relished it, allowed it to well up in her chest, to fuel her.

Gingerly, she took off her wrist gauntlet. She would have to move fast, for even her rediscovered determination would not last long in the face of what she was about to do. She patted the flesh of her left forearm with her right hand, probing for the broken bone beneath. The pain was intense, but it was nothing compared to what was yet to come. She found the break. The smaller of her two forearm bones was snapped completely in two.

I cannot scream, she told herself. She looked up, saw the shadows of the guards still evident on the tent's flaps. They were just outside the door. *I cannot let them hear me. If they come to investigate, all will be lost...*

She drew several deep, long breaths. And then, sealing her mouth shut as tightly as possible, she gripped the lean flesh of her left forearm in her right hand. Her fingers embraced the shape of the broken bone beneath, and *squeezed.*

The pain was like a white sheet. It filled her vision, and every muscle in her body strained to hold in the scream of anguish that boiled up in her throat. Then, with an audible snap, the broken lengths of bone aligned. Gabriella exhaled harshly, and tears streamed from her eyes, running down her face and mingling with the dried blood on her cheek. A wave of faintness drifted over her as she held the bones in place. She fought to remain alert. Finally, the pain receded to a ringing ache. Gabriella released her forearm slowly, and the bone remained set.

The rope that had bound her wrists was still lying on the floor in loose coils. She collected this, then got carefully to her feet. Stealthily, she moved towards the table in the rear of the tent. As she had suspected, its surface was cluttered with plotting tools, although the coating of dust implied that they had not been used in a long while. She found a heavy ruler and carefully began to bind it to her left forearm, supporting the broken bone with a rudimentary splint.

Then, finally, she put her wrist gauntlet back on.

Her sword was gone. She had no weapon whatsoever. Still, having regained the nominal use of her left arm, Gabriella felt better, if only slightly. She examined the tent once more, hoping that perhaps she could slip out beneath one of the canvas walls just as the rat had done. The silence of the camp implied the very depths of night; thus, she might actually be capable of stealing her way to the citadel unnoticed if only she could get past the guards at the tent's entrance. The canvas walls were secured tightly to the ground via a series of heavy, wooden stakes, but she thought she could wriggle beneath if she was very careful.

She crept across the dirt floor, approaching the side of the tent opposite the pathetic mound of corpses. Here, the ground dipped slightly. A band of moonlight could be seen beneath the taut canvas. Gabriella lowered to her knees and gripped the hem of the tent's wall.

It was just loose enough, she thought. She began to slip her leg beneath it.

It was then that the guards moved outside. Gabriella heard the subtle clank of their mismatched armour, the creak of their leather belts and vests. They had heard something and were finally moving to investigate.

She glanced up, frozen in place, one leg half pushed beneath the side wall. The shadows of the guards moved over the entry. And then, worst of all, a third shadow heaved into view, even taller than the others. The guards stepped aside without a word.

Brom had returned.

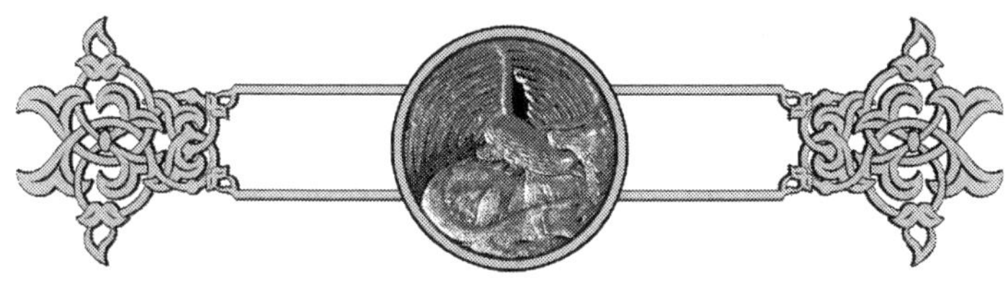

The tent flaps twitched as Brom began to pull them back.

Gabriella scrambled. She clawed at the tent wall, yanking it up as far as she could and shimmying beneath it. Firelight flickered in the dark tent as Brom entered. He scanned the room, saw her, and his eyes flared angrily. Gabriella's lower body was already out of the tent, but Brom moved with incredible speed, crossing the tent floor and letting out a low roar. He did not waste time bending to grasp her but raised his boot instead, intending to stamp down upon her neck. She rolled frantically, ducking her head and twisting beneath the taut canvas. An instant later, Brom's boot slammed down. He missed her neck but stomped down upon a sweep of her hair. It pulled painfully as she rolled into the mud between the tents.

Brom roared again, and she sensed him bending, gripping her hair on the other side of the tent wall. She scrambled to her knees and pushed as hard as she could. Her head snapped back as her hair went taut, pulled hard by the root, but Brom held it firm and began to wrestle her backwards, dragging her back under the tent wall.

There was a ring of metal, then a slash. Brom's sword unzipped a huge tear in the tent wall, barely missing Gabriella's neck. It snagged there, and Brom grunted, trying to pull it back without releasing his fistful of her hair. Gabriella twisted, saw the glimmer of the blade protruding from the tent wall, and lunged upwards towards it. The taut hank of her hair hissed along the blade, which cut it neatly. An instant later, she was free, scrambling forwards between the tents, her boots slipping in the thick mud.

Brom roared, louder this time, and slashed again at the wall of his tent, cutting an exit.

"She escapes!" he bellowed, ripping his way into the open air. "Tell me where she goes! But do not touch her! She is mine!"

Gabriella reached the end of the tent, leapt over one of the support ropes, and struggled into a wider pathway. The fires had mostly burnt low, and there were no torches or lanterns anywhere in the camp. Worse, the fog obscured the moon, rendering the night almost completely black. Gabriella ran, desperate for a weapon but finding nothing.

Voices rabbled behind her.

"She's gone back that way."

"She will not get far."

And then Brom's voice: "I smell her fear. Leave her to me. I will save you each a bite."

Gabriella ducked between another rank of tents. Voices muttered inside, rousing. She leapt over more stakes and guide ropes, cursing them for slowing her down, and ran headlong into a dead end beneath a ragged outcropping of rock. The shadows were thick here, but there was a tree nearby. Gabriella thought she might be able to climb it. Then, inspiration struck her. She ducked back to the nearest tent and gripped the stake embedded at its corner. Inside the tent, a voice growled thickly, and Gabriella froze in fear. After a moment, however, the voice subsided to a mutter and then to slow, rattling breath.

Gabriella began to work the huge stake back and forth in the mud, prying it loose. Soon enough, the stake came free of the earth, and she pulled it up, pushing its loop of rope from the muddy tip. The tent's corner sagged slightly. She leapt to her feet, hefted the stake, and dashed nimbly towards the nearby tree. As quietly as she could, she scrambled up into its branches, panting harshly through her nose, her heart pounding.

There was a minute of silence. Gabriella had begun to think that Brom had lost her trail. Then a shadow moved from between the line of tents. He was stalking her, as quiet as a snake. His nostrils flared as he moved into the open. He did not see her in the tree, but he sensed her nearness. He crept closer, weaving slowly back and forth, homing in on her.

"Princessssss...," he whispered. "I know you are here. Come out, come out, wherever you are..."

Gabriella held her breath in the tree. The branches were bare of leaves and would not conceal her much longer. If he got any closer, he would smell her above him. She gripped the stake. It was long but virtually useless as a weapon. Still, it was better than nothing.

Brom circled closer, coming into the shadows of the rocks. "I smell you, my darling," he sang under his breath. Then he stopped. He swiveled his head, his nostrils flaring.

"I remember him, you know," he said very quietly. "Your man. I recall him well. I watched him die."

In the tree, Gabriella's face hardened. He was trying to provoke her of course. It was working.

"I watched Merodach stab him over and over until the blood sprayed like a pretty fountain. He was so handsome, even in death. Do you miss him, Princess? Is he the reason you are here?"

Gabriella's hand tightened on the stake. He was nearly below her now. He moved like a cat.

"When Merodach was through with him," he whispered delicately, "he gave him to me. I kept him for you. You may have him back if you wish, what is left of him. Come out, Princess. Your Darrick awaits you."

He stopped. Slowly, he looked up.

Gabriella dropped on him, bringing the stake down point first and driving it home with all of her weight. The stake punched into the slope of his shoulder, boring deep between his collarbone and shoulder blade. It sank in almost to its flattened tip, and Gabriella released it, stumbling backwards into the mud.

The brute had barely moved. He turned his head aside, peering awkwardly down at the wooden shape that protruded from the base of his shoulder. Slowly, he reached for it, tried to grip its blunt end with his fingers, and could not. He looked back at her again and then took a step towards her. His leg buckled, unhinged, and he dropped heavily to his knees in the mud.

"Ahhhh," he breathed, and his eyes bulged grotesquely. His hands rose, hooking into talons, and he reached for her. There was no strength in the gesture however. A moment later, his arms dropped to his sides. Then, perhaps most horribly of all, his eyes seemed to clear. He blinked, and something approaching humanity looked out at Gabriella, meeting her gaze.

"Thank you," he whispered weakly. "Thank you… Princess…"

And he fell forwards onto his face with a heavy thump, twice dead.

Gabriella took Brom's sword. It was larger than her own, and weighted differently. She hefted it, spun and swept it experimentally, and determined that she would be able to use it when the time came. Just as she was about to set off towards the citadel, however, a subtle noise fluttered overhead. She glanced up and was surprised to see Featherbolt swooping gently out of the dark. He was carrying something in his talons, and its weight seemed to be nearly too much for him to bear. He landed awkwardly atop the object as it struck the ground.

"My pack," Gabriella whispered, kneeling before it. "Featherbolt, you amaze me. Thank you."

She had nearly forgotten about her pack. In truth, there was virtually nothing in it any more, save for one or two things. She opened the knot and reached inside, felt the dense weight of Darrick's wrapped candle, and nodded.

"You are a better friend than you know, Featherbolt," she whispered softly, slinging the pack over her shoulder. "You do not need to accompany me from here. Fly, my friend. Return to your home with the magical folk. I cannot vouch for your safety any longer."

The falcon cocked his head, turning one bright eye on her. He hopped forwards nimbly and let out a faint, unlikely twitter.

"Go," Gabriella insisted quietly. "You have done more already than I could have hoped. If it is possible, tell your masters what has transpired. Do not let our tale go untold. Do you understand?"

Featherbolt shook himself, clicked his beak, and ruffled his feathers. Whatever he was trying to say, however, it was lost on her. Hopefully, his magical friends spoke falcon better than she did. A moment later, the bird clapped his wings and launched into the air. The buffet of his passage ruffled Gabriella's hair as she watched him loft overhead. Within a few seconds, he was merely a dark shape against the night sky.

After that, he was gone completely.

Gabriella sighed, and the sigh turned into a shudder. She had not realised how much she had missed Featherbolt's company until he had returned to her. In truth, she would have liked for him to stay with her for the remainder, but she could not abuse the falcon's loyalty that way. It was one thing to risk herself by invading Merodach's lair. She would not make that choice for anyone or anything else.

She gripped her new sword, drew a deep breath, and dodged into the nearby shadows. Quietly and carefully, she began to make her way towards the citadel.

She expected to be accosted at nearly every turn, but the camp was eerily quiet and almost totally dark. She passed the glowing guts of several cook fires, their embers strewn messily and popping with grease, but there were no lanterns or torches. Voices muttered in some tents, grating snores emanated from others, but she saw no sentries. Whatever the truth about the viciousness of Merodach's armies in battle, this one, at least, did not seem to be concerned with being attacked in its own camp.

As Gabriella darted along a main pathway, she wondered how many of the tents were occupied by creatures such as Brom—dead but somehow alive, consuming putrescence to maintain their own putrid flesh. Perhaps most were still human, but not all. How was such a thing even possible? What sort of black enchantments was Merodach dabbling in that he could employ such horrors?

Perhaps she would find out. Or perhaps not. All that mattered was that she face the monster and that he taste her sword. She was terrified to do it, now more than ever, but she refused to give in to her terror. There had been enough of that already. Perhaps (she hoped) she was like David in the scriptures, who had faced the giant Goliath when all the others had refused. The difference, she realised with a sense of sinking dismay, was that David had placed his trust in God for victory. Gabriella had had enough of trusting in God. For good or ill, victory or defeat, she was taking matters, finally and firmly, into her own hand.

The citadel loomed over the tents, a hulking black tower, its top serrated with crenulations. Unlike the rest of the camp, lights burnt within the citadel. The arrow slits glowed and flickered against the inky darkness. Gabriella stole through the shadows, aiming for the left side of the tower. There, a large, dark door stood, flanked by two guards. She skirted this, keeping to the shadows and eventually sidling up against the citadel wall some twenty paces away from the guards. She dropped to an alert crouch in the weeds, considering her options.

The guards were very tall, wearing rusty but heavy amour and carrying nine-foot battle-axes. Even from her vantage point, Gabriella whiffed the stench of the men. They were like Brom, dead yet walking, haunted by the unspeakable.

Could she kill them both? It seemed a ridiculous fantasy. Blades neither killed nor slowed down such monsters. Granted, she had managed to kill Brom with a stake, but that had been a stroke of enormous luck. She had bypassed his armour by attacking from above, driving the point straight down into his heart. It was highly unlikely that she would be able to duplicate such an act, especially on two of the hulking creatures at once. Even if she managed to kill one of the guards and succeed in gaining entry, the second guard would give chase and would likely alert reinforcements. If that happened, her chances of confronting Merodach alone would be greatly diminished. It was absolutely essential that she maintain the element of surprise.

She frowned pensively as she watched the guards. Neither moved in the slightest. They looked like nothing more than oversized statues sculpted from human flesh and bone. How could she possibly defeat such huge, beastly things?

In her mind, the memory of Darrick spoke: *You're small, Bree, so you're quick…* She blinked, remembering. It had been the day of the battle practical. He had been giving her advice on how to defeat Goethe. *He'll squash you if he gets a chance, but you can make sure that chance never comes if you're wary.*

… *If you're wary.*

An idea occurred to her. It was, on the surface of it, so preposterous, so utterly unthinkable, that she very nearly rejected it instantly. The reason she did not, however, was because it also seemed teasingly plausible. If indeed she was very quick and *very* wary. She remained crouched in the weeds, her back to the cold stone of the citadel, and glanced aside at the guards.

They did not budge. It was as if they were hibernating on their feet, simply waiting for something to approach, whereupon they would animate and respond accordingly.

Stealthily, quietly, Gabriella pushed herself upright, keeping her back against the wall but being careful not to let her armour scrape against the stone. Keeping flat against the wall and holding her sword carefully before her at the ready, she began to edge towards the door.

The guards stood a pace forwards of the door, battle-axes leant against their shoulder plates. They did not even seem to be breathing. Gabriella could see their faces in profile. They were huge, jowly, their beards forming brambles on their chests. Their eyes shined dully in the night, unblinking. She crept on, trying not to breathe, lifting her feet carefully so as not to disturb any of the loose stones that ranged around the tower. Amazingly, she began to near the door, sidling behind the guards, pressing back into the shadows of the citadel.

She moved into the range of their stench. If she could smell them, she realised, then there was a good chance that they could smell her as well, no matter how quick and quiet she was. She held her breath as she inched around the edge of the door. The nearest guard was barely an arm's length away. His broad back loomed over her in the darkness.

Collecting her sword into her right fist, she reached back and pressed her left hand to the iron handle of the door. It was latched of course. She felt for it and found the thumb bolt. Gently, she began to exert pressure on it. It resisted. And then, with a soft click, it depressed. The door budged slightly open behind her.

"What was that?"

Gabriella froze, her eyes wide, petrified. One of the guards had spoken, his voice a low, grating growl. The other one stirred slightly.

"I smell something," he muttered, and sniffed the night air harshly, like a dog. "Blood. Sweat." He paused, then added, "Fear."

Both guards were silent for a long, awful moment. Finally, the first guard spoke again.

"Perhaps it is a wounded beast. Check the wood."

The second guard nodded. With a jerk and a rattle of armour, he stepped away from the door, hefting his axe. He paced slowly towards a range of trees that ran along the nearest edge of the tower.

Slowly, still holding her breath, Gabriella pushed herself back against the wooden door, silently begging the hinges not to creak. The door began to press open behind her. Warm air wafted out through the crack, lifting the hair from her brow. The guard sniffed again, growing agitated. He began to look around.

Gabriella pushed harder against the door, knowing her time was nearly up. Finally, swiftly, she slipped through the crack into the warmth and light of the citadel's main entry and caught the door as it began to swing back. Gently but quickly, she eased it shut, leaving it unlatched.

With a deep shudder, she exhaled and closed her eyes. She could scarcely believe that her plan had succeeded, and yet she was inside the citadel, standing in the torch-lit corridor of its main entry. A curving staircase dominated the end of the corridor, ascending into darkness, waiting for her. She leant back against the wall next to the door, weak with relief.

The door rammed open in front of her, very nearly striking her. Cold air coursed into the chamber, buffeting the flames in their wall sconces. Gabriella's eyes flew open as the shadow of the door fell over her. Fortunately, she had leant against the wall nearest the door's hinges. Had she been on the other side, she would have been spotted immediately.

She saw the guard's fingers clutch the edge of the door, holding it open. There was a shuffle of feet as he edged inside.

Gabriella gripped her sword and bit her lips, watching, waiting for the guard to enter fully and close the door, revealing her behind it. She would have to take her chances fighting him if that happened. Quickly, she calculated where the best place to strike would be and determined she would have to take the guard's head off. The beastly man might survive even that drastic a blow, but he would at least be debilitated and possibly blinded. She swallowed and tensed her muscles in preparation.

The guard did not fully enter, however. He stood on the other side of the open door, breathing deep, grating breaths, tasting the air. Finally, with a soft grunt, his fingers released the edge of the door. Gabriella heard him step back outside, and the door swung shut with a rattling clunk.

She swayed on her feet, her sword still clutched before her, staring at the heavy wood of the door. With an effort, she forced herself to relax. The sooner she got herself away from the door and into the upper reaches of the citadel proper, the better.

Trembling faintly, nearly sick with adrenaline, Gabriella crept down the corridor, heading for the dark staircase.

CHAPTER 11

The citadel stairs ascended into shadows, following the curve of the outer citadel wall. Gabriella crept up the stone steps slowly, eyes wide, her sword clutched before her. A faint sound echoed down to her, light and trilling, incongruous in the musty dark. It was music. She frowned even through her fear. There was a harpsichord, a fiddle, a flute, all playing in perfect unison, framing a whimsical tune that would have been perfectly appropriate for a royal summer picnic. Here, however, the jaunty tune seemed nearly mocking, like gaudy rouge on the cheeks of a corpse. She followed the sound of it.

A landing opened before her. It was quite long, carpeted with what had once been a rich, red rug. Now the rug was rotted and mouldy, adhering to the floor like a skin. Beyond this, more stairs curved further up the tower, probably leading to archer nooks and, eventually, the war room at the top. That was not her destination however. The music was not wafting down from above, but echoed quite nearby from the citadel's grand hall. A bar of firelight lay across the carpet, emanating from the hall's unseen double doors, which were apparently thrown wide open.

The music played on, teasingly bright and lilting.

Gabriella stopped. Her heart thudded heavily beneath her breast plate. She was less than ten paces away from her final destination.

Normally, she knew, a knight in this situation would take a knee and pray, the hilt of his sword clasped between his hands. She wished to do the same, but could not quite bring herself to do it, despite her great fear. She and the Almighty had never enjoyed a particularly amicable friendship, even in her youth. After all, God was supposedly the ruler of all things, and He had seen fit to take away her mother. Since then, He had allowed the beast Merodach to grow in strength, to threaten everything she loved. God had taken Rhyss. And most importantly, He had allowed Darrick to be cut down, viciously and senselessly.

She could trust Him no longer. Not with the life of the Little Prince, and not with this, her final mission.

But there was someone she *could* trust.

As silently as she could, she leant her sword against the wall, crouched, and unslung her pack. Reaching inside, she quickly found the small weight of the wrapped candle and drew it out. The cloth fell to the ruined rug as she unwrapped it. Slowly, she raised the candle in both of her hands, touched it to her lips, and closed her eyes. She leant against the wall, touching the smooth wax to her forehead.

Sigrid had not told the truth about the candles in the cathedral. Gabriella had sensed it even as the older woman had spoken of it. The candles *were* magical—perhaps the best and greatest magic left in the kingdom of men, left over from the time when Merlinus himself worked his art for the elder King Arthur and his noble Round Table. The candles were not mere symbols any more than the sun was a mere symbol of the day. Sigrid had not extinguished the Queen's candle on the night she was murdered, despite her claims. The candle had gone out on its own, because it did not burn on wax or wick. The candles burnt on the life force of the ones they represented. When that life force ceased, the candles went dark. Sigrid had been lying. It had been a well-meaning lie of course, meant to offer hope and faith, but it had still been a lie.

And sometimes, unfounded hope and faith were the worst lies of all.

Gabriella lowered her hands and looked down at Darrick's candle. It was not mere wax and wick. It, like the other life candles, was far more magical than anyone remembered. The wick was blackened, but the wax had barely even melted. It was nearly perfect.

She reached up, held the candle to the torch that crackled just overhead. The wick caught the flame reluctantly. It crackled faintly, flickered, and finally took light. Gabriella lowered it, suspecting that she had very little time.

"Darrick," she whispered. "I'm so scared. I don't know what to do."

The candle's flame buffeted slightly at her breath. Smoke curled up from it in grey ribbons.

Bree...

It was him, or at least the memory of him, captured in the candle like a reflection. His voice came out of the air like the last toll of a distant echo.

"Darrick," she rasped, her face breaking into a pained, bitter smile. "Darrick, my love!"

She had not truly expected her idea to work. She had meant to ask for her husband's blessing and counsel, just as she had on the day she had faced Goethe on the battle floor. Now, however, hearing his voice again, all of those intentions fled her and were replaced by a much deeper, simpler question.

"Why...," she whispered in a barely audible voice, "why did you do it? Why... did you break your promise to me?"

I am sorry, dear one, his voice replied, seeming to come from the wafting ribbons of smoke. *I was foolish... foolish to make a promise I did not know I could keep. I did not wish it. But I am not sad. How can I be? I have passed into the Meadows of Heaven, where you will someday join me. I am sorry that I am not there for you now. My love remains. And someday, we will be together again. Here, nothing will be able to breach my promise to you. But Bree, you must not make the same mistake I did. You must not make promises you cannot keep...*

"I am not," she breathed, shaking her head slightly. "I am here to avenge you. And Rhyss. And even my mother. I am here to protect Camelot and our son. *Our* son..."

You have not come here only to avenge us, Bree..., Darrick's voice said with quiet emphasis. *You cannot lie to the dead, dear one.*

She shook her head more adamantly now. "Yes I have!" she whispered harshly. "It has been my intention from the day I knew of your death. Everything has led me to this moment."

Yes, Bree. But there is another, deeper reason why you have come here. You have come here, my love, not just to avenge... but to die.

As soon as he said it, Gabriella knew it was the truth. Her eyes widened in the darkness, staring at nothing. Her lips trembled, and a gasp of misery gathered in her chest. She fought it back. He was right. His words revealed to her the deep longing inside her, the aching desire for it all to end. There had been too much taken from her, too many lifelong hopes shattered.

This was why you did not name our son, the haunting voice went on. *To name him was to make him fully yours, and you knew, even then, that you had no intention of returning to him. You left him to Sigrid, as a gift, and an offering.*

"That's not true," Gabriella insisted, refusing to acknowledge the truth of his words. It was no use. The weight of her own hidden motives settled onto her like a stone.

I know the depths of your sadness, Bree, Darrick said, and the loving sympathy in his voice crushed her. *I tasted them myself even as the madman killed me. The greatest pain was not the steel of his blade, but the knowledge that I had failed you, broken my promise to you. In that instant, I felt a lifetime's worth of regret and misery and despair. I know how you feel. But I got off easily, Bree. My sadness lasted only a moment. Your burden is much, much greater...*

"No," Gabriella protested, her voice suddenly low and hoarse. "No, I will not. I cannot. It is too much for me."

It is not, her husband's voice insisted gently. *You are stronger than you know. You can do what is required of you, if you truly intend to.*

Gabriella covered her face with one hand, and a moan of abject desolation escaped her. "What *is* required of me, Darrick?" she begged.

Our son needs you, my love. He has already lost his father. He cannot lose you as well, no matter how great is your longing to be free.

"Sigrid will care for him," Gabriella pleaded weakly, her hand still covering her eyes. "She will name him, hide him, keep him safe."

No. He needs you, his true mother. You must return to him. Find him and raise him. Tell him about me. Make him the man he is meant to be. Only you can do that now.

"No," she wept, shaking her head feebly. "I cannot. It is too much…"

Gabriella, her husband said, his voice beginning to fade. *Gabriella, you must do the hardest thing of all. My love, my wife… you must live.*

"But how?" she rasped, dropping her hand and glaring desperately into the tiny flame. It was shrinking, fluttering. "Coalroot told me I would face Merodach. He told me that I would die!"

Of course you will die, Darrick's voice replied easily, and there was almost a laugh in it. *Everyone dies. He did not tell you when or how. He is a capricious spirit, overflowing with deceptions. He knows far less than he believes. You cannot trust his words.*

"Whom *shall* I trust?" she whispered fiercely, desperately. "God?"

Nothing lasts forever, Bree…, Darrick answered distantly, drifting away. *Camelot must eventually fall. All of us must someday die. No one ever said trust was easy. But it is always better than the alternative. Live your life, Bree. Go to our son. Raise him. The Meadows of Heaven will await. As will I.*

Gabriella was still shaking her head, her eyes squeezed shut. Not in disagreement, but in refusal. It was too much, the burden too great. But even in her denial, she knew that her lost husband was right. Her duty was clear, no matter how difficult it might be. Ever since she had been a child, she had wondered if she would be able to do what was required of her. Sigrid had promised her that when the time came, she would. She would live up to the demands of being a princess. If she chose to.

If she chose to.

She drew a great, shuddering sigh. As she released it, she opened her eyes. Darrick's candle had fallen dark, this time for good. His voice was gone. Tears trembled in the corners of her eyes. She wiped them away with the back of her hand before they could fall.

She stood away from the wall. Carefully, reverently, she crouched and set Darrick's candle on the floor. The magic was finally gone from it. Now, once and for all, it was merely wax and wick.

"Goodbye, my love," she said quietly. "Until we meet again."

She stood once more, collected her sword where it leant against the wall, and strode forwards, approaching the echoing music and the bar of firelight. The citadel's grand hall, and Merodach himself, awaited.

Darrick had been right. Her duty was clear. And yet she could not allow the madman who had killed him to live.

She just had to make sure that when it was all over, she still did.

The doors to the grand hall were indeed thrown wide open. A pair of ornate wrought-iron floor candelabras flanked the entry, each one as tall as she and decked with a dozen extravagantly melted candles. Beyond this, the massive room stretched into lofty dimness, filled with collections of furniture and plotting tables, a massive, roaring fireplace, and, in the rear centre, a huge, very strange object comprised of some black metal. It looked like a clutching skeletal hand, its eight fingers reaching up from the floor and embracing something unseen, lost in thick shadow. Overhead, hanging from a heavy length of chain and only slightly smaller than the strange metal sculpture, was a hulking monstrosity of a chandelier. It was similarly comprised of wrought iron, so covered with curlicues, spiked edges, and fist-sized bolts that its ugliness defied imagination. Hundreds of candles burnt within it, forming a flickering constellation and releasing streams of black smoke towards the high ceiling.

Bats swirled amongst the rafters, chittering busily amongst the smoke.

Gabriella crept into the room, taking it all in, seeking its occupant. On the far left, a sort of stage had been erected, surrounded by mysterious, golden light. This, hauntingly, was the source of the music. The keys of the harpsichord plunked busily, operated by nothing. Next to it, the fiddle and flute floated in the air, dipping breezily with the tempo of the music. The fiddle's bow wove back and forth jauntily on the strings.

On the opposite side of the room, a man stood. His back was to her as he leant on a large table, studying an oval mirror where it hung on the wall, as if his own reflection was the most enthralling thing he had ever seen. A thick book lay open on the table before him, and his hand was pressed to one of the pages, apparently holding it open.

Gabriella opened her mouth to call out to him, but before she could, he spun wildly on the spot, turning to face her. Behind him, the book snapped shut of its own accord. The man's eyes were wide and haunted above his short, black beard.

"Well," he said in a surprisingly pleasant voice, relaxing very slightly, "you are not exactly whom I was expecting." He cocked his head inquiringly to the side. "So, then, who might you be, love?"

Gabriella gripped her sword before her with both hands, her face tensed into a hard scowl.

"Are you Merodach?" she breathed. It was almost a growl. The level of her rage surprised even herself. It vibrated in her veins like the static before a storm.

"Will it improve the situation if I am?" the man answered brightly. "I cannot help but think that you are not here on a mission of goodwill, my dear. Put down your sword and let us talk. I rarely get such pretty visitors."

Gabriella shook her head and began to step forwards. "You killed my husband," she said with low ferocity.

Merodach shrugged and shook his head minutely. "I've killed many husbands. How should I remember which one was yours? It is so very difficult to keep track of these things."

"Then count what I am about to do," Gabriella said, raising her sword, "as payment for all of them."

"Pray do not be so hasty, my dear," the man said, moving suddenly aside and backing away from her. He lifted his hands, palms out. "I am unarmed as you can see. I sense that you are not the sort of woman who would attack a defenceless opponent. Let us discuss. Surely, you know that killing me will not solve anything."

"Still your tongue," Gabriella commanded, moving to follow the man. "And stop moving. Do not approach that... thing."

"What, this?" Merodach clarified, glancing behind him towards the strange, black metal sculpture. It was the largest object in the room and emitted a distinct chill despite the roaring fire nearby. Shadows seemed to swirl within its enormous skeletal grip, forming a light-less cloud.

"Fear not, love," Merodach went on, smiling back at her. "I have no intention of getting close to *that*. *I* wish to live to see another day." He laughed lightly, still inching away. He seemed to be skirting around her towards the massive fireplace.

"What *is* that device?" Gabriella asked, gesturing with her eyes, her sword still angled towards Merodach's chest.

"It is not mine," the man replied lightly, almost defensively. "It belongs to a... er... *benefactor* of mine. No human can approach it. A few have tried, despite my warnings, for they recognised its significance. But the result was... unpleasant."

He nodded back at the strange shape again. Gabriella looked closer. Several shapes lay beneath it, just inside the clutch of the metal claws. Through the strangely shifting darkness, Gabriella saw that the shapes were skeletons, reduced nearly to dust. She examined the huge metal sculpture more closely, peering into the shadowy depths of its embrace. There was something hidden in the centre of that swirling dark. It almost looked like a black candle seated on a tall, thin stand. Even darker than the candle itself, however, was its flame. It was as black as onyx, its inverted glow sucking all light into itself, as if its fire was not a fire at all, but a portal into the deepest abyss.

"It is evil," Gabriella proclaimed, shuddering beneath her armour. Almost involuntarily, she took a step towards it.

"Granted," Merodach agreed, glancing back at the awful shape again. "But it is useful. I am told that so long as its black light burns, my armies of darkness will march, obeying my command with perfect devotion. Apparently, only those of magical blood may approach it and live, but feel free to make the attempt. Extinguish it if you can. I will applaud the attempt regardless of the outcome."

Gabriella almost did. The abomination of that horrid, black flicker was nearly too much for her to abide, especially if it was the source of power for the horrible undead armies. If she could put it out, then perhaps all could still be saved.

"Go ahead," Merodach nodded silkily. "I will not attempt to stop you."

Gabriella narrowed her eyes as she looked back at him. "I may indeed approach your black magic," she admitted. "But not whilst *you* live to witness it. You shall die first. Your plans will fail. You shall never sit on the throne of Camelot."

She began to advance on him, but he dodged backwards, hands still raised defensively before him. "Me?" he protested, giggling a little. "I assure you, I have *no* interest in sitting on any throne. What fun would that be? You do me a disservice, love."

Gabriella blinked at him suspiciously. "How can you say such a thing? Your singular purpose has been to attack the Kingdom, to overthrow the King and take over his throne for yourself."

Merodach nodded quickly, then reversed course and shook his head. "I seek to overthrow, yes, but not for myself. Truly, the thought of ruling bores me positively to tears. I am a man of action, not policy."

"Who then?" Gabriella demanded, rounding on him as he backed towards the fireplace. "Who do you represent? The barbarian emperor of the north? Are you clearing the way for an invasion?"

Merodach tittered. "You do not understand the magnitude of these things, love. The barbarian empire shall fall as well. My benefactor does not wish merely to be King of Camelot. His goal is to rule all. Soon, he shall ascend to power over the entire land, from shore to shore. And in time, even those natural boundaries will not contain him. His reach shall encompass the whole of the earth. The time of reckoning has come, my dear. The new order of true power is at hand."

Gabriella shook her head in dark wonder. "But why would you obey the command of a man such as this? Why would you do his dirty work?"

Merodach shrugged lightly as he inched up against the fireplace. "I happen to *like* dirty work. I admit it. And besides, my benefactor is no mere human. He found me when I was but a young man. I had been arrested for my crimes, such as they were, and sentenced to death. He rescued me and laid waste to my enemies with power like I had never seen. Why? Because he recognised my potential. He needed a right hand, he told me. Someone to stand in for him until he could ascend to power himself. It is by his strength and authority that I have achieved what I have, but it is my ingenuity and wit that has made it all possible. We are of one mind. Tonight, he shall assume his command in full, and I shall become his hand of judgement, wreaking punishment on those who defy him." Here, Merodach sighed deeply, wistfully. "It is what I was made for, after all."

He lifted his foot and rested it on a decorative bit of scrollwork that framed the huge fireplace. Smiling at her, he shoved it forwards with his foot, as if it were a giant lever.

Gabriella recognised instantly that the villain had sprung a trap on her. She leapt aside, not knowing what was about to happen but knowing that it depended on her being in a specific place. There was a loud twang, a screech of metal, and a protracted ratcheting noise. A second later, the enormous chandelier crashed deafeningly to the floor, barely missing her legs as she lunged away. Candles exploded in every direction, spraying wax and trailing black smoke.

Gabriella hit the floor hard and dropped her sword.

"Damn, but you are quick!" Merodach proclaimed loudly, giddily. "All the better, for I can be quick as well!"

Gabriella heard the ring of metal, knew that the villain was snatching up one of the decorative swords that had been hung over the fireplace. She had barely noticed them until it was too late. She scrambled to her knees, reclaimed her own sword, and raised it just as the man pounced upon her. Metal clanged on metal as their swords met, and Gabriella was nearly driven to the floor again by the ferocity of his attack.

"You really *should* learn to be less curious, love," the man said through a fierce grin. "It is a sign of a lack of *intent*."

He spun his sword around, aiming for her neck, but Gabriella parried just in time, catching his blade and sliding hers along it with a screech of steel. She struggled to her feet and shoved him back. Dimly, she was aware that the ache in her forearm had spiked to a throb. She could not fight like this for long, but she could not let him know that. She thrust forwards fiercely, forcing him back. He angled nimbly away from the fallen chandelier. Behind him, the enchanted musical instruments struck up a heroic battle fanfare.

"This is pointless, my dear!" Merodach chided as their swords clashed. "You cannot win, hard as you might try. And even if you could, it would not bring your dead husband back. Run along, and I may let you live. After all, there are other husbands to be had in the world."

"Curse you!" Gabriella cried, raining blows onto the man's sword, forcing him back. "Still, you do not know who I am! My father is King of Camelot! My husband was his field marshal! You tortured him to tell you where my people would retreat, and then, when he complied, you killed him! You killed him, and when he was dead, you had the singular gall to steal from his poor corpse! For that, and for the sake of those who still live, you shall *die*!"

Merodach fought her wildly, almost gleefully. He laughed with recognition. "Ah yes! You are the Princess Gabriella then! In that case, I *do* recall your husband. He amused me. And yes, I acknowledge that I did take a trinket from him. Tasteless, I suppose, but you must admit, he no longer needed it."

"I will *kill* you!" Gabriella vowed furiously, forcing him further back, using every ounce of her strength.

"If you kill me," Merodach declared, deflecting her blows with wild parries and thrusts, "you shall never find your husband's trinket!"

"Fortunately," she seethed, plowing onwards, "I care less about even that than I do your head."

"But this is pointless," Merodach gasped, turning on her and thrashing back in earnest. "Your kingdom is already finished! I have observed it myself in the enchanted face of that very mirror behind you! I can see anywhere within it using my benefactor's book of magic! At this very moment, your castle is in flames! The fortress of hiding is breached, and all within it are dead! Go and look for yourself if you disbelieve me! You are too late! Too late!" He laughed delightedly between grunts of effort.

Gabriella faltered as his words struck her. Her opponent sensed this and fell upon her fiercely. Swords flashed in the firelight, and the clang of their blades mingled with the merry pomp of the music. Gabriella fell back as the pain in her wrist increased, weakening her grip on the sword. Then, with a skillful swoop, Merodach wrenched the sword out of her fists. It spun away, clattering into the shadows. He laughed at her darkly and made to run her through.

She ducked, dodged, and rolled beneath a plotting table. Merodach's blade fell upon it with a rattling thunk even as she scrambled up from the other side. She bolted towards the door, knocking over the iron candelabras as she went. Merodach leapt after her but stumbled over the toppled candelabras. Amazingly, he was still laughing gleefully.

Gabriella slipped on the rotten carpet of the outer landing. Righting herself frantically, she bolted towards the ascending stairs.

"Do not go yet, Princess," Merodach cackled, leaping after her into the corridor and knocking wildly against the opposite wall. "The night is still young! Much mirth is afoot!"

Gabriella hit the stairs at a full run and took them two at a time. Darkness met her as she followed the curving steps upwards towards a second landing. Here, nooks lined the hallway, each illuminated with a band of moonlight from an arrow slit. Another of the iron floor candelabras stood by the furthest one, empty of candles. Merodach's footsteps clattered behind her, approaching quickly. Gabriella pelted along the landing and ducked into the furthest nook, nearly tripping over the dark candelabra. She threw herself up against the nook's shallow stone wall, gasping for breath

Behind her, unseen, Merodach's footsteps knocked onto the landing, where he seemed to stop.

"This is good sport, Princess," he panted, and giggled lightly. "But I am afraid it cannot end well for you. Come out and give yourself up. It is the best you can hope for."

He began to pace slowly forwards. She heard him, knew that he had his sword raised, ready to cut her down the moment he discovered her. She pressed back against the wall of the arrow nook, trying not to breathe.

"Do you know?" the villain mused thoughtfully as he approached. "It just occurs to me. With your father dead, you are no longer a mere princess. Do you feel special, my dear? It is official. You are the last Queen of Camelot. Congratulations," he said mockingly, "Your Highness."

With a dark shock, Gabriella realised that Merodach was right. If Herrengard had indeed been breached—and she had no doubt that it had—then her father was dead. She was the last of the line. Whatever remained of the Kingdom, it was hers. The realisation did not hearten her.

"Perhaps this is why you still fight," Merodach said ponderously, stalking still closer. "Perhaps you fight as Queen, to protect the remnant of your kingdom. But no!" he said suddenly, interrupting himself. "*Not* for the Kingdom! I see it now! You do not fight for your kingdom, but for your child! Surely, Queen, you know that even that is a hopeless cause. Tell me you are not such a simpleton."

Gabriella remained pressed against the wall but spoke up.

"Darrick lied to you," she announced firmly, her words echoing in the arrow nooks behind her. "I knew he would never betray us, but my father would not listen. You may have killed the King and all those with him at Herrengard, but my son was not amongst them. I sent him elsewhere. He is safe from you."

"How very crafty of you, Queen," Merodach replied, unperturbed. "Did you perchance... send him to Amaranth?"

The blood chilled in her veins as the question hung in the air. She did not reply.

"Do you think I am an utter fool, Your Highness?" Merodach asked, and all the mirth had suddenly gone out of his voice. "Do you truly think I would trust your man's word? I had already learnt about both of the King's primary eastern retreats, Amaranth and Herrengard. I simply did not know which would be his first choice. But I did know this: I knew your husband would die before revealing to me the truth."

Gabriella's eyes grew wider as the madman spoke. Hopelessness began to fill her like lead. She dreaded what Merodach was about to say next, and yet she knew she had to hear his proclamation, had to know for certain what he had done.

He was much closer now, creeping slowly along the aisle of arrow nooks. "Your husband was very brave," he assured her coldly. "He told me the King would choose to retreat to Herrengard. He lied to me, just as you knew he would. And thus, I knew that *Amaranth* was in fact the true destination. To be sure, I sent forces to *both* locations. But I sent my most vicious regiment to Amaranth. My soldiers were there in mere days. And their orders were very simple: wait as long as necessary, and then, when the time came... kill *everything*."

Gabriella's knees grew weak beneath her. Her hands dropped helplessly to her sides.

"Your child is dead," Merodach breathed, relishing the words. "Those that were meant to protect him are destroyed. Everything that you fight for, Queen, all of it... is in ruins. Why continue to resist? There is nothing left for you. Come out. You are the last ruler of Camelot, and as such, you must die. But I can make it quick. Soon, you can join those whom you have failed. Come out and face me. Die like a queen, and I will not even turn your body over to the appetites of my troops. It is only fitting. And admit it. You *desire* this..."

Gabriella's eyes were glassy in the dimness. Her enemy was nearly upon her now. She nodded to herself once. Slowly but resolutely, she stepped forwards, turned past the iron candelabra, and faced her nemesis.

"There," he said, and smiled sympathetically. "That is better, is it not?"

He raised his sword, positioned its tip just above her breastplate, inches from her throat, and began to thrust.

Gabriella's arm swept up and forwards, bringing the wrought-iron floor candelabra with it. The heavy metal clanged against the steel of Merodach's sword, smashing it against the wall, where it shattered. Merodach cried out in pain and clutched his hand to his chest, still gripping the hilt of his sword. Gabriella was not finished however. The candelabra whistled through air, unseen in the darkness, and struck her enemy firmly on the temple. He jerked aside and stumbled, barely keeping his feet.

"Wait," he choked dizzily. Blood began to course down his temple, matting his black hair. "Wait. So be it, Queen. It does not have to end this way..."

Gabriella followed him as he clambered backwards, clinging to the narrow walls of the arrow nooks for support. She hefted the heavy length of the candelabra and swung it again. It made a low whoosh as it arced down, connecting with the villain's left shoulder. He crumpled but still managed not to collapse fully. He supported himself on one knee, still scuttling backwards, waving his broken sword before him. Six inches of its blade still protruded from his fist, ending with a hard, glinting angle.

"Stop," he demanded, and laughed wetly, deliriously. "You cannot! It is not possible!"

Gabriella did not so much as blink. Her shadow fell over him as he scrambled backwards. With a jerk, she caught the candelabra in both hands, hefted it over her right shoulder, and brought it down on him like a spear.

Merodach shrieked as the empty candle holders punctured his abdomen, driving deep into his flesh and sticking there. Blood welled in the wounds immediately. Still, flattened against the stone floor, he scrabbled backwards.

"You cannot stop what has begun!" he babbled, his voice cracking with terror. "It is too late! You have failed! You will die like all the rest!" With that, his face hardened. He mustered his strength, ripped the candelabra from his guts with a grunt of pain, and lunged upwards, aiming to plant the remainder of his sword into Gabriella's belly. She caught his wrist in mid-stab, however, using her good right hand. A moment later, she wrested the broken sword from his grip, spun it around in her fist, and dropped onto him, pinning him with her knee.

"What *are* you?" he spat up at her, terror and rage mingling on his bloody face, contorting it. A look of dreadful suspicion widened his eyes. "Are you a witch?"

"No," Gabriella seethed down at him through gritted teeth, raising the broken sword. "I am just a *very* determined human."

And she drove the shattered blade deep into his chest, burying it there.

Merodach convulsed beneath her, only once but massively. He coughed a mouthful of blood, fell back, and then met her gaze. For a second, the rage was still there, radiating from his eyes like heat from a furnace. And then, with no perceptible change at all, they simply went blank.

Merodach was dead.

CHAPTER 12

When it was over, she could not bear to be near the villain's body. The realisation of what she had done overwhelmed her. She struggled to her feet, began to walk away from the body, then broke into a shambling run, lunging for the stairs.

It simply could not be. Her son could not be dead. Everything else paled in comparison to that sudden, unbearable truth. She no longer cared that her castle home had been attacked and was in flames, or that Camelot, her kingdom, was under siege and effectively overthrown. She did not even care that Merodach, the architect of it all, was dead by her own hand. The moment the life had flickered from his eyes, he had ceased to matter.

All that mattered was the fate of her child.

She refused to believe that he could be no more. It was too huge a tragedy for her to comprehend. Her beautiful son, her only remaining hope...

She made her way to the lower landing and the entrance to the citadel's grand hall. Near the descending stairs, Darrick's dark candle sat. Gabriella stopped, dazed, and stared at it.

You must return to him, her dead husband's voice had said. *Make him the man he is meant to be. Only you can do that now...*

How could he not have known? Was that even possible? Then she recalled something else he had told her, something characteristically teasing but with a ring of truth to it: *No one ever said trust was easy. But it is always better than the alternative...*

Perhaps Merodach had been wrong. Or even lying. Perhaps there was a chance...

A tiny flicker of hope alit inside her chest. It was not much, but it was enough to keep her moving, to keep her from simply falling to the rotten, red carpet, bereft and hopeless. She walked into the bar of light that led into the grand hall and peered inside.

The enchanted musical instruments had stopped playing. The fiddle and flute lay on the little stage as if dropped. Fire still roared in the hearth, flickering over the ruins of the enormous chandelier. Beyond all of it stood the horrible, dark sculpture, the eight-fingered skeletal claw embracing its cursed prize. Eerily lithe shadows surrounded the black candle, protecting and hiding it. The flame burnt like an eye of midnight.

She had to put it out. But how? If others had died simply by moving into its black glow, cursed to ashy bones, then how could she?

"No human can touch it," she mused aloud, frowning. "Only those of magical blood may approach it and live..."

Magical blood. That meant witches and wizards. Those like Helena and Goodrik...

Gabriella's eyes suddenly widened. Her mouth opened in amazement. How could she have forgotten? Quickly, she turned back towards the outer landing, darted to where Darrick's candle still sat on the floor near the stairs. Her pack lay there as well, flat and empty. And yet, as she had suddenly remembered, it was not *completely* empty. She snatched it up, buried her arm inside its depths, and found a long, narrow object in the bottom. Her heart leapt. Slowly, she withdrew the object and peered at it. It looked no different than the first time she had seen it. It was merely a length of wooden stick, slightly tapered to a dull point.

Goodrik had not known how she could use it, but he had said that it might be of use at some point. It might, he suggested, focus the magic of her falcon sigil, make it more potent and useful if the need arose.

The need, Gabriella felt quite sure, had finally arisen.

She dropped her pack and stood slowly, fingering the wand. It was probably an insane errand. Likely, she would die in the attempt. But she had to try. Resolutely, she turned back towards the entrance of the grand hall and paced into its flickering light.

The giant claw awaited her, its cloud of shadows shifting and swirling. Within this, the black candle burnt.

As Gabriella neared it, she sensed the cold of it. It chilled the metal of her armour, even blew her hair back slightly. She stopped outside the cage of the metal fingers, studying it. Then, crouching and setting her wand on the stone of the floor, she began to undo the clasps of her armour. She no longer needed it, and the cold of it was uncomfortable. Her breastplate clanked as she set it aside, followed by her wrist gauntlets, shoulder plates, and shin guards. Her once glorious armour, she realised, was now dull with scratches, dents, even patters of dried blood. It had served its purpose.

Finally, clad only in her trousers and tunic, she collected the wand again. She had hoped she would feel its power somehow, as assurance that her plan would work, but the wood felt perfectly prosaic in her fingers. The sigil at her throat was still warm, however, just as always. She felt it there and sighed. Still on one knee, she raised her eyes.

The bishop had taught her to close her eyes when she prayed, but she was not quite ready for that step yet. Instead, she stared up into the high rafters. Bats still skirled there, chattering faintly.

"Well," she whispered, shaking her head slightly, somewhat at a loss for words, "so here I am. I have blood on my hands, and my heart is filled with doubt. I have exercised vengeance rather than leaving it to You as the scriptures teach. And I cannot even tell You that I repent of those actions. Perhaps I will do so in time, if I am granted it. As yet, I do not regret what I have done. But now..."

She stopped and drew a deep breath. She felt foolish, not because she doubted God was there, but because she feared He would not deign to hear her. She determined to go on anyway.

"Now... I am embarking on a task that I do not believe I can accomplish on my own. I need Your help and Your blessing. Not because I deserve it, but because this evil must be stopped. I am willing to die in the attempt. Just please... if that is how it must be, do not let my death count for nothing."

She gripped the wand in both of her hands and looked down at it. "Amen," she finished, frowning.

She did not feel any different. Perhaps no one ever did. Perhaps the prayer was not about gaining courage, but simply assurance—the assurance that everything that should be done, had been. She pushed herself to her feet, took the wand firmly into her right hand, and held it out.

Very slowly, she began to creep into the shadow of the gigantic claw.

She knew no incantations, could not even remember the words to draw the smoke shapes that she had practised in Professor Toph's classes. She could only hope that the strength of the wand, focusing the power of her sigil, would be enough to protect her, and ultimately to extinguish that dreaded, black flame.

As she pressed between two of the skeletal fingers, the sense of cold increased to a nearly physical presence, almost a barrier. She felt its boundary creep over her outstretched hand up her arm. Faintly, however, the wand in her fist began to glow as it preceded her. Dim, blue light streamed back from it like smoke. It flowed over her hand and arm and formed a sort of corona, spreading to encompass her against the cloud of shadows. Gabriella's heart lightened inside her and began to pound. She pressed on, slowly but insistently, moving fully into the cage of the monstrous claw.

Before her, the candle became even darker and more solid. Its black flame was as tall and straight as an obelisk but perfectly void. Its depths seemed to suck at her as she neared it, and suddenly, she began to understand what had happened to the unfortunate skeletons at her feet. This one candle was the unholy twin of all the magical candles she had known throughout her life. But rather than mirroring life, reflecting it, this black flame fed on it. It sucked life force into itself and converted it into hideous energy. It was this abominable force that fueled the undead armies and gave them breath. Worst of all, Gabriella sensed that there was no limit to the candle's power. It would simply keep feeding, sucking the life energy of those that the armies murdered and thereby empowering more and more of the hellish soldiers.

Her father's life force was inside that flame. Not his soul, but that which had bound him to this world and given his body breath. Darrick's life force was there as well. And perhaps, most horrid of all, even that of the Little Prince.

Gabriella neared it, her wand outstretched. The pressure of the cold, shadowy shield fought back at her, trying to thwart away from its prize, but she did not falter. Her fist trembled, forcing the tip of the wand closer and closer to the black flame. Blue magic streamed back over her, as if blown in a soundless, magical gale. Her hair fluttered back, and even her clothing rippled faintly, blown by the silent force.

The shadows swirled faster, condensing on the candle as if to protect it. The pressure grew nearly too strong for her to overcome, and yet she pressed on, her fist shaking against the force, pushing the wand inexorably towards the candle's flame. The wand's tip began to flare brightly, and Gabriella felt the sigil at her throat thrumming in response, going from merely warm to ember hot.

The black flame began to flicker, to retreat from the advancing flare of the wand. The light and the dark began to war. Neither could abide the other; one had to overcome, and the other be annihilated. The candle shuddered as its flame began to tatter, to shred against the light.

Something swooped out of the swirling shadows. Gabriella barely saw it before it was upon her, battening onto her outstretched fist with a flurry of leathery wings. It was a bat, its tiny teeth gnashing, its claws dragging deep slashes into the flesh of her hand. Gabriella screamed in shock and pain. Her hand spasmed involuntarily, and the wand flashed backwards from her fingers, trailing blue sparks. The protective corona collapsed around her, and she felt herself launched away from the black candle, tossed like a rag doll in a wind storm.

She tumbled to the stone floor and rolled, her hand leaving bloody smears behind her. Her broken forearm blared with pain as she landed upon it. Struggling dazedly to her knees, she turned to look back at the swirling dark.

The black candle still burnt within it. And then a shape fluttered out of the shifting shadows. The bat bobbed out of the cage of the skeletal claw and swooped towards her. As it came, however, it began to change. It bulged, warped in mid-air, became horribly misshapen. It landed before her and grew much larger, taller, taking on the unmistakable form of a sinewy human figure. For an instant, the features were still tainted with those of the bat, and then, finally, they receded. A man stood before her in a black robe. His head was bald, and his face was sharp, full of humourless angles and cold confidence. He regarded her where she knelt on the floor, her hand dripping rivulets of blood.

"I do apologize, Queen," the man said coolly, "but there is nothing more abhorrent to me than the sight of a wand in the hand of a mere human. And a woman at that."

Gabriella was too stunned to speak. She cradled her hand to her chest, clutching it there with her broken left forearm.

"I was pleased to observe your actions thus far," the man said, turning aside and moving towards the fire, "but I am afraid I could not allow you to threaten my greatest triumph. I have worked too long and hard on it, using means that you would not even begin to comprehend. It has cost me much, both in time and effort, but all you can think to do with it is to destroy. This is but one reason why I detest your kind so very much."

Gabriella inched back from the man as he passed near her. "I seek to destroy it," she countered, "because it is evil. As are you, I am quite certain."

"The word 'evil' is a convenient word used by deluded creatures to condemn that which they do not understand," the man said, moving before the hearth and turning his back to it, as if to warm himself. Lazily, he produced a black wand from his robes, pointed it before him, and gave it a flick.

A gasp escaped Gabriella's throat as the ruined chandelier behind her leapt up into the air, dragging its chains noisily and trailing its freight of candles. It lofted back into the upper reaches, its candles reseating themselves into their bases and then, with a series of hissing pops, flaring back alight.

"Do you see?" the man said, as if she were his student and he her instructor. "I do not come to destroy, as you do, but to restore… to create."

"Lie to yourself if you wish," Gabriella said, climbing to her feet. "But I have seen your methods first-hand. Your armies are an abomination of death. You create nothing. You only know how to pervert."

The man smiled coldly, still fingering his wand. "I have taken that which was dead, that which was cast off, useful for nothing more than the sustenance of worms, and I have transformed it back into life. I admit, at present, they may be rather rough, Queen, but refinement takes time."

He drew a deep breath and went on. "For years, I have toiled over my creations, practising and testing, preparing them for this day. At present, they are mere shadows, but soon, they shall reach perfection. When that happens, they will not require mounds of dead flesh, but mere blood, which, in moderation, does not even require the death of the host. I have even," he added, tilting his head conspiratorially, "given some of them the ability to transform themselves into bats. In honour of me, their creator."

Finally, his smile fell away, and he raised his chin. "*You* may choose to call that perversion. *I* call it the ultimate expression of creation. After all these years, I have finally… *finally*, found a use for dead humans."

Gabriella chilled before the man's refined hatred. She backed slightly away from him. "Someone will stop you," she whispered. "If not me, then your own kind. For I know what you are. You are a wizard. And not all wizards are like you. Some of them are good. They will fight you."

"Oh, I doubt that very much," the man replied, stepping towards her, his wand still raised. "You see, I am the most powerful of my kind yet alive. I have cultivated allegiances with wizards of similar motivations, wizards who form an unbroken chain of strength. My Circle of Nine, as I call them. Even now, they advance across the furthest reaches of the land, leading their own dark armies at my behest, conquering all in their path. Nothing shall stand against me, neither human nor my own wizarding kin, should they foolishly choose to oppose. The reign of men shall finally be scoured from the earth. A wizard shall take his rightful place as lord of all things. And I have you partly to thank for that, Queen."

Gabriella narrowed her eyes at him as he approached her slowly. "What do you mean by that?" she breathed, anger welling up even within her fear.

"You still do not know who I really am then, do you?" he said quietly, a small smile curling his lip. "I am somewhat surprised. I had come to believe that you were rather intelligent, for a human."

Gabriella shook her head. "If I had met a beast like you, I would remember it."

"Alas," the man hissed, drawing close to her, "we did not meet. But our paths have indeed crossed, and very importantly. Why, I daresay, if it were not for me, Queen... you would not be alive to stand here with me this night."

Gabriella's eyes widened slowly. She raised her bloody hand, touching her fingers to the sigil at her throat.

"Yes," the man went on, circling behind her. "It was I. My fellows were with me that night when you were but a small child, but it was I who entered your winter cottage. It was by my art that the invading werewolf was chased away. And it was by my choice that I left my marker for your people to find. I did not know then how very useful that marker would be, but I had an inkling. You do not know me, Queen, but I once saved your young life. And since then, I have watched you. Faintly, yes, divined through the vaguest of hazes, broadcast through the magic of my own distant marker, but watch you I have. And with the greatest of interest."

"But why?" Gabriella rasped, wonder and horror mingling inside her.

"Because I choose my tools well," the man declared proudly, moving around her, fingering his wand. "I chose Merodach when he was a young man because I recognised his usefulness. But I also knew that his time of usefulness would someday come to an end. When his purpose had been served, he would need to be destroyed. I could have done so myself, of course, but this way—using you—was so much more... *elegant.*"

Gabriella's knees grew weak as realisation flooded her. The monstrous wizard had planned it all. She, Gabriella, had reviled Merodach for doing this beast's dirty work, and yet she herself had done the same. She had killed on his behalf without even knowing it. He had used her, ultimately, like a puppet.

"Do not be too hard on yourself, Queen," the horrible wizard said, moving alongside her again. "It was only natural that you would seek to kill he who had destroyed your love. But had it not been for my own magic, you never would have succeeded. I expect that you believed the magic of the sigil was your own, but surely, you see now how foolish that was. You may have borrowed it for a time, and it may even have come to reflect you, but let me assure you... the magic never forgot me, its *true* master."

He looked down at her, eyes narrowed, and she refused to meet his gaze. "And now, here you stand," he mused darkly, "the last queen of the last true human kingdom..." He fingered his black wand, and she watched it hopelessly.

"Fear not," he said soothingly, lifting his wand, "I have wasted enough magic on such as yourself."

He tucked the wand back into his robes. When he withdrew his hand, a long, curved dagger protruded from his fist. He stabbed her with it.

Gabriella felt the blade bury itself up to the hilt into her side and was at first too stunned to respond. Her eyes flew open, staring blankly into the darkness of the black candle. It did not so much hurt as simply sap her strength. Hot liquid poured down her side, wetting her tunic and pattering to the floor at her feet. The man studied her face grimly, his nose barely six inches from hers. Then, with a jerk, he pulled the dagger from between her ribs.

Gabriella sank to her knees as weakness overtook her. She watched, dumbfounded, as the dark figure stood over her, the blade dripping her blood from his right hand.

"The time has come," he declared in a low, merciless voice. "With your death, I shall ascend to the throne, unchallenged and unstoppable."

Gabriella struggled to draw a breath. It hurt monumentally, and she crumpled to her side on the cold stone. The enemy stood over her. Then he bent down slightly. His hand reached for her, touched her neck. She tried to bat him away but could not muster the energy. He gripped the falcon sigil in his fingers, then, almost lovingly, he withdrew it from around her neck. He stepped back from her, watching with interest as she bled to death before him. He began to raise the falcon sigil, to lower it around his own neck. As he did so, Gabriella saw its mate, the dragon with its glinting green eye, already hanging there, Darrick's half of their royal wedding gift. Merodach had given it to him of course, having stolen it from the body of her dead husband.

"And now," the enemy breathed, draping the falcon sigil next to its matching half, "as a sign of my triumph, the magic that accompanied you returns to me, its ultimate master. What you believed to be a symbol of your love is rejoined now upon my neck, reverting to its ultimate form. Die knowing this, Queen... and despair."

Beneath the wizard's pointed chin, the falcon and dragon sigils touched. There was a flash of green light, and the halves joined together, snapping into place like two magnets. The emerald eyes glowed.

Gabriella fell back, her hand clutched uselessly to her bleeding side. She heard the wizard turn his back on her. He began to walk away.

Suddenly, unexpectedly, he let out a tiny hiss. His footsteps ceased.

Gabriella slitted her eyes open. The dark figure's back was turned to her, framed against the fire. He brushed something off of his robes, then shook his hand. Gabriella's gaze drifted towards the floor at the wizard's feet. A small spider scuttled on the floor where it had fallen. The wizard lifted a foot patiently and stepped on it.

Another spider skittered out of the shadows, casting a long shadow in the firelight. It disappeared under the wizard's robes. A moment later, he jerked and hissed in pain. More tiny shapes began to dart from the shadows, converging silently on the robed figure.

"Back to your hovels, creeping things," the wizard rasped. He drew his wand, but the spiders took no notice. There was a tiny flash as the wizard flicked a spell. Several spiders tumbled away, their legs convulsing. Then a larger shape darted along the line of the fireplace. Gabriella saw it and shuddered even in spite of her pain. It was a fat, bedraggled rat. It skirted the wizard, then scampered forwards into his shadow.

"Argh!" the wizard exclaimed, leaping backwards. His toe was bleeding. He spun, fired a bolt of green at the rat, but it dodged away. It circled around a chair, then darted forwards again.

More shapes began to trickle forth. Spiders dripped from the ceiling on threads of web, descending on the wizard as he turned and flailed, batting at them. Rats and mice poured from the dim corners, circling the man's feet and then battening onto his robes, climbing him, squeaking audibly.

"What is this?" the wizard demanded angrily, stamping and flailing as the creatures collapsed upon him. "How dare you...?!" Jets of green light sprayed all around as the wizard attempted to quell the creeping rebellion. It was no use, however, since the number of his attackers seemed to grow every moment. He backed away from them, shaking them violently from his robes.

Suddenly, Gabriella heard a muffled bellow from below. There was a thump, a clatter of breaking wood. Then, seconds later, a furious scratching noise welled up the outer stairs.

A river of creatures poured into the room. In the lead, gnashing its teeth viciously, was a fat, grey hedgehog. It spied the writhing wizard, snarled, and leapt forwards. The wizard saw it coming and spun towards it, raising his wand. There was a green flash, and the hedgehog flew backwards, dead in mid-air. A dozen more creatures darted forwards in its place, however, eyes flashing in the firelight, jaws parted and lips pulled back. There were squirrels and opossums, badgers and foxes, beavers and wild dogs. Snakes dripped through the room's arrow slits, dropping to the floor in alert coils and slithering swiftly towards their prey. A huge timber wolf leapt through the double doors and onto one of the plotting tables. It spied the wizard and bared its yellow fangs, snarling furiously. With a scratch of its claws and a blur of grey fur, it launched towards him and landed on his back, driving him to his knees.

More flashes of green lit the room, and the wizard's exclamations grew to screams of fury. He fought back against the creatures, kicking and flailing, hexing everything in sight.

And then, at the height of the fracas, a shuddering boom shook the entire hall. Dust and grit showered from the ceiling. Tools clattered from tables. Gabriella watched, strangely calm, as the wizard fought to his feet, his eyes hectic, his face covered in scratches. He looked around wildly.

Another boom ripped through the hall, and finally, the smaller creatures began to scatter. They darted away in every direction, making way for the newest arrival. The wizard spun on the spot, waving his wand.

A shuddering explosion ripped through the citadel wall behind him, destroying the fireplace. Bricks and stone flew across the room, smashing furniture and burying the small stage and its enchanted musical instruments. Dust filled the air. As it began to clear, a pair of enormous, orange eyes opened in the darkness.

The wizard saw this and began to back away, raising his wand.

A huge, scaly head pushed in through the broken wall. A long, snake-like neck followed it, and then a massive, clawed foot. Lengths of shredded net still clung to the creature. The beast seemed to grow even larger as it shouldered its way into the hall, casting the entire room into its shadow. It kicked the stony debris away effortlessly. Deeply, lividly, the dragon began to growl.

The wizard fired at it with his wand, but the green spells merely exploded against it with no effect. The dragon stalked forwards, its nostrils smoking, its jaw creaking open viciously. Its eyes never left the wizard. It began to coil, to lower itself in preparation to pounce.

The wizard transformed. Gabriella watched from where she lay in her own blood, dying and too weak to move. The awful man dropped away, growing small and sprouting wings. Beyond him, the dragon pounced. It hurtled through the darkness, bashing the chandelier aside and crashing heavily to the floor. Its great tail swept a gout of debris into the air, but the wizard was no longer there. Instead, a small, winged shape fluttered up, screeching angrily and darting into the cloud of bats that still scattered throughout the room's upper reaches. The dragon saw this and lunged after it, snapping its jaws, but to no avail. There were too many of the bats. It was impossible to know which one was the villain in disguise.

But then, silently, one more shape swooped in through the broken remains of the wall. Gabriella saw it and smiled wanly.

"Featherbolt," she breathed.

The falcon arced into the air, circled the dragon's lunging neck, and homed in on one of the swirling bats. In an instant, the two became fluttering streaks, swooping wildly around the room, screeching and squeaking furiously. Finally, Featherbolt dipped his talons, thrust forwards, and caught the bat.

The awful creature began to transform again in mid-air. Featherbolt seemed to sense this. He carried the struggling bat-thing higher, dragging it up into the rafters even as it bulged and writhed in his talons. Reaching the apex, Featherbolt turned, clapped his wings, and gave his talons a mighty, decisive *twist*. The bat-thing was ripped in two. Black guts exploded from between the halves and rained wetly towards the floor far below. With a flap of his wings, Featherbolt released the torn body parts. They fell, still writhing and transforming, and as they did, the dragon lunged upwards once more.

Gabriella squinted as the entire room was filled with a torrent of blue light. The roar of the dragon was deafening in the enclosed space, and the heat of its breath raised the temperature to an almost unbearable level. A long moment later, darkness fell once more, along with a sudden, unexpected silence.

When Gabriella looked up, there was nothing left of the wizard but a caul of black smoke and sifting ash. The dragon watched this, its orange eyes narrowed. Featherbolt perched on one of the rafters and peered down, blinking his gold-ringed eyes.

There was a heavy clink as something fell to the stone floor in front of Gabriella. She saw what it was but was too weak even to reach for it.

The falcon and dragon sigils glinted by the light of the diminished fire. Their emerald eyes no longer glowed, but the magic was not yet gone from them. She could sense it.

The dragon inched towards her carefully. Its great head bent over her and nuzzled her, as if to help her up. As always, its scaly skin was hot to the touch.

"No," Gabriella whispered. "No more riding. It is over."

Featherbolt landed on her other side. He hopped closer and ruffled his wings.

"Thank you, my friends, but it is finished. There is nothing... nothing..."

She stopped. Quietly, peacefully, she blinked. There was, in fact, one more thing. Mustering all of her remaining strength, she pushed herself up onto her elbows. Blackness pulsed in her eyes as the blood drained from her, but she willed herself to stay for just a little longer. She looked through the ruined hall, and her gaze rested upon the ugly metal statue. It was untouched, despite the violence that had overtaken the place. The eight skeletal fingers still clutched the cloud of shifting shadows and the haunted, black candle.

"No human can approach it... and live," Gabriella whispered faintly. "But neither of you... are human."

Both the dragon and Featherbolt followed her gaze. The dragon's neck creaked ominously as it turned, facing the hideous sculpture head on. Featherbolt ruffled his feathers and flapped his wings anxiously.

Gabriella felt her strength ebbing away. Darkness thumped over her with every slowing heartbeat.

The dragon moved first. It stalked away from her, approaching the sculpture, then turned aside of it. Its great, sinewy tail swung back, sweeping out over the room. Then, with a snarl of effort, the dragon heaved back, slamming its tail against the metal claw. Two of the skeletal fingers crashed inwards at the first blow. Blood ran from the dragon's tail where the metal had slashed it, and yet it did not pause. It adjusted its footing, swung its tail back again, and slammed once more against the black shape. Two more of the fingers crashed away, and the swirling shadows within began to leak out, to diffuse into the air of the room. Deprived of its protective cage, the force shield was weakening.

Again the dragon smashed at the shape. This time, all of the claw's fingers were crushed out of true. Blood poured from the dragon's torn tail, but its work was done. It took a massive pace backwards, watching as the swirling shadows broke apart, diffusing and spreading, losing their focus.

Then Featherbolt took off. He soared up into the lofty darkness and circled towards the remains of the black candle's shield. Fluttering his wings gently, he began to lower through the top of the shadowy cloud. It spun around him frantically, quickening, but it was too diminished. It could not fully hold the falcon back. Featherbolt fought steadfastly against its force, lowering into the midst of the writhing shadows. Beneath him, the black candle buffeted, fighting the wash of his wings. The falcon dipped, struggling to keep his balance on the shifting air, and his talons clutched beneath him, reaching… reaching.

The shadowy shield contracted over Featherbolt and the candle, spinning into a raging blur, and still, the bird dipped. The black flame tattered and streamed wildly, resisting the undeniable rush of Featherbolt's wings. A whine of power filled the air, growing in pitch and volume. The talons clawed at the candle. The flame intensified, grew to a seething, black furnace.

And then everything vanished into a silent, icy blast. The hall shook and rumbled. The remains of the hearth fire flared green for one bright moment and then snuffed dark. A chorus of screams rushed through the space, as if a thousand tortured souls had been withdrawn from their hosts, banished back to their abyss of origin.

And then, finally, silence fell.

Gabriella watched all of this and felt nothing but relief. Weakly, she looked around the darkened hall. Nothing moved. Neither the dragon not Featherbolt seemed to be there any longer. The horrible skeletal claw was destroyed, bereft of its writhing shadows. Its candle stand stood empty, bent and dark.

The wizard was no more. His forces were destroyed.

Feebly, pathetically, Gabriella shifted onto her side, feeling the stickiness of her own blood pooling beneath her. Her arm seemed to weigh as much as a millstone as she lifted it, reaching for the twin sigils. She could not do it. Her hand fell short of the sigils, grasping instead onto another loose object. It was the cast-off wand, her gift from the wizard Goodrik. She clutched it weakly and moaned, too exhausted to move again.

And then, blissfully and finally, darkness collected her. She gave herself over to it.

The Queen's eyes closed, and she knew no more.

CHAPTER 13

It was near sunset when Yazim and Thomas crested the hill and saw the tiny hamlet below them. The village was hemmed in on one side by dense forest. The other side was marked by sheer granite cliffs, broken with crags and cut by a ribbon of falling water. The waterfall was so tall that it was reduced to mist by the time it dropped beyond the roofs of the village.

The travelers stopped on the crest of the narrow road, overlooking the sight.

"You knew this was here," Thomas said, somewhat accusingly.

"I did not, I swear it," Yazim replied calmly. "But I had long wondered."

Thomas frowned aside at his friend. "Why?"

Yazim shrugged vaguely. Together, they spurred their horses onwards again, descending into the shadow of the trees and approaching the village. It was still some distance off, its roofs burning bright with the glare of the setting sun. In the centre of these, a small stone church stood, its flat bell tower rising above the other structures.

Thomas sighed. "I thought you said that you did not know the ending of the Princess's story."

Yazim nodded. "I did say that. It is true."

"Forgive me," Thomas commented, shaking his head, "but that sounded like the ending to me."

"That, my friend, is because you lack imagination. You resemble your namesake in that sense. You doubt the bigger plan."

Thomas accepted this as if it were a compliment. "I see things for what they are, if that is what you mean. We live in a much different age than did the Princess Gabriella. We cannot all simply bow a knee and pray to overcome obvious evils. In our time, there is far less black and white. Only thousands of shades of grey."

"It is popular to believe that, yes," Yazim acknowledged.

"So what is the great mystery then? What part of the Princess's tale am I missing?"

Yazim was silent for a long moment. The declining sun made amber beams through the trees, throwing dapples onto the road before them. Finally, he said, "There is the question of the vampire armies for one."

Thomas smiled and shook his head. "Fanciful embellishment. Come, Yazim. Even if you believe the rest of the tale, you do not believe that detail, do you?"

Yazim responded with a smile of his own. "Perhaps," he sighed. "It is said that there were indeed many rogue armies in that day, not just the one that conquered and destroyed Camelot. The legends say that none of those other armies succeeded in their marches however. All of them, for reasons no one knows, simply halted in their tracks. Some tales even go on to suggest that great numbers of the evil soldiers simply fell over as dead. There, they were left, lying in their ranks and divisions, to rot on the nameless hills and fields."

Thomas still smiled crookedly. "Such things do make excellent stories, Yazim. I shall admit that."

"You are correct," Yazim nodded. "Many tell such tales even today. They say that remnants of the villain's undead remain still. Some of the vampires, they claim, were not beholden to the black candle. These were the wizard's earliest dark creations, and they live still today, haunting the shadows and hunting by night, infecting their prey with their own horrible curse." Yazim laughed lightly. "Such things do indeed make for good midnight tales," he finished, turning to his friend, "do they not?"

Thomas blinked at him and then shook his head and rolled his eyes.

Yazim went on. "Then, of course, there is the question of the Little Prince."

"But the Prince was killed," Thomas reminded him reluctantly. "Merodach sent his forces to both hiding places. Whether the woman Sigrid had believed the Princess's warning or not, she would have been confronted by the villain's assassins in either event. Surely, you do not suggest that she might have fended the brutes off?"

Yazim shook his head. "Some say yes, actually. Some say that Sigrid was a fighter herself in her youth and canny as a snake. And she had the guard Treynor with her. Perhaps, some have suggested, they were able to protect the boy together."

"But you do not believe that," Thomas suggested in a low voice, cocking his head.

Yazim sighed. "No, I admit I do not. But there are other guesses, other possibilities. It is far simpler to assume the worst of course, and yet some of us still refuse to abandon all hope in the good. Like the Princess's husband said, trust is never easy."

"But it is always better than the alternative," Thomas finished wryly. "You are correct. Many would disagree with that, you know. I might be one of them."

They rode on in silence, descending into the valley gorge. As the road leveled, the trees thinned on the left. Thomas looked aside through the belt of bushes and weeds and saw the glitter of a small woodland lake. The sun shined on it like molten gold, nearly blinding him. He squinted. Something stood on the far side of the lake, facing him through the distance. It was a tiny stone cottage, barely visible through the glare. The structure was overgrown, buried in wild grass and ivy, but not completely hidden. An ancient, broken vane jutted from its peak.

The scene reminded Thomas of something. He frowned, thinking, and then remembered. It had been part of Yazim's tale, the bit where Professor Toph had been telling the story of the Queen's death and Gabriella's midnight escape. When it was over, the King had looked for his daughter to no avail. Then Toph had told Gabriella:

"After twelve days, your father remembered a small lakefront hunting cottage that his own father, King William Xavier the Second, had sometimes taken him to as a child..."

It was there that the young Princess and her grandmother had hidden. It was there, in fact, that they had been stalked by the rogue werewolf and saved by the clandestine intervention of the magical folk: Merlinus, Goodrik, Helena, and their two fellows, one of whom had turned villain barely a decade later... and had probably been a villain even then, albeit in secret.

"Yazim," Thomas said, still peering through the bushes at the glittering lake and the distant forgotten cottage. "Do you see...?"

But just then, the trees thickened again, cutting off the view.

"What?" Yazim asked, following his friend's gaze.

Thomas squinted through the trees but could see only a flicker of glittering water. He shook his head faintly. "Nothing... I suppose."

He thought to himself. Yazim had said that the lady-in-waiting, Sigrid, had herself been a fighter in her youth. She had had a canny mind and perhaps even a remnant of witchiness in her blood. If she had indeed believed the Princess's warnings, she would not have merely escaped to the alternate fortress. She would have known that *all* of the King's fortresses were potential traps. She would have taken the baby someplace completely different, someplace no one else would ever know or suspect.

No one, that was, except perhaps the Princess herself.

"... a small lakefront hunting cottage... remote, virtually forgotten by all..."

Thomas smiled to himself. Perhaps it was a foolish, ridiculous thing to consider—this tempting possibility that Sigrid and the guard Treynor had bypassed the King's fortresses and instead escaped, along with the young Prince, to the secret hunting cottage—but it was too tantalising an idea to dismiss. Yazim was right. The flicker of hope, of trust in the good, once it was sparked, was very difficult to abandon.

Thomas considered telling Yazim his suspicion. Eventually, of course, he would. For now, however, he enjoyed the silence and the teasing hope of his secret suspicion.

Soon enough, the village opened up before them. A few peasants moved amicably through the streets, gazing up at the two riders as they ambled into the town proper. Thomas smiled at them, nodding. By the time they reached the stone church, the sun was a brilliant orange furnace between the forest and the mountain cliff. Its light glowed fiercely on the bell tower and glittered from the copper bells inside.

The two men clunked the knocker on the double doors, but no one answered.

"Perhaps it is their dinner," Yazim suggested, turning back towards the steps. "Let us check the rear entrance if there is one."

Thomas followed his friend down a narrow path that led between the church wall and an overgrown garden. The rear churchyard was quite small, already half-full of the shadows of the nearby mountain cliff. A tiny cemetery dominated the yard, enclosed in a leaning iron fence. Yazim passed beyond this, approaching a small outbuilding, presumably the parsonage. He knocked on the wooden door.

Thomas stood near the gate of the cemetery. From here, the noise of the mountain waterfall was a dull roar. He saw it in the near distance over the roofs, raining its heavy mist onto some unseen pool. Rainbows danced on the falling water, and each drop glittered like a diamond in the copper sunset. Thomas wandered idly into the cemetery, seeking a better look.

Yazim reached to knock again on the parsonage door, but before he could, it swung open before him. A thin man with a short, white beard met him, smiling vaguely. Yazim could tell by his clothing and demeanour that the man was the church vicar.

"Greetings, my son," the old man said in a tiny voice. "How may I assist you?"

"My friend and I are traveling on the business of the Kingdom of Aachen, of which your village, it appears, is a part. May we come in?"

"Certainly, my son," the vicar agreed easily. "I have heard of this kingdom of yours, of course. I trust you will inform me exactly how it might benefit us. And of course, I suppose, how we must benefit *it*."

Yazim nodded wearily and then turned back to call over his shoulder.

"Thomas, shall you be joining us?"

The red-haired man stood in the middle of the tiny cemetery, unmoving, his head bowed slightly. He did not respond.

"Thomas?" Yazim called again.

Thomas finally glanced back. Yazim saw that his friend's face was unusually pale, his eyes wide.

"You...," Thomas said querulously, "you... might wish to see this."

Yazim frowned. Together, he and the vicar descended the short stoop and angled into the centre of the cemetery, joining Thomas where he stood. Yazim followed his gaze.

The tombstone was quite large but flat against the ground, so that its face always caught the light of the sky. Faint words were still legible on it, cast in harsh relief by the lowering sun.

Yazim read them. His own eyes widened slowly...

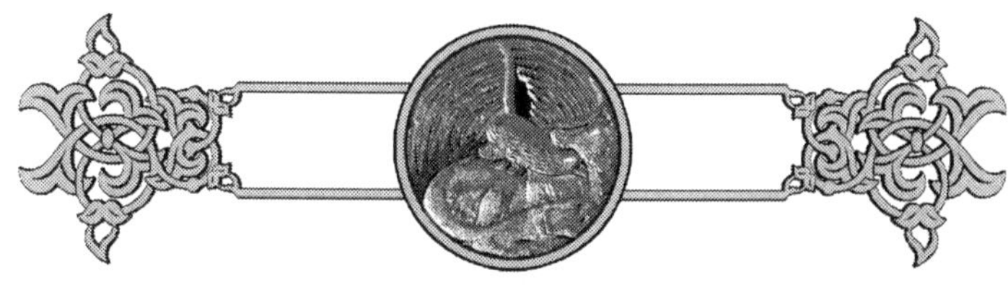

Sigrid sat in the shadow of the lake cottage's back door, snapping green beans in a large bowl and watching the Little Prince with one eye. He was already walking, albeit haltingly and with many false starts and sudden sits. He moved through the tall grass of the yard studiously, chasing butterflies and blinking owlishly up at the clouds.

She, Sigrid, had always wanted a child; the Princess had been right about that. The truth was, however, that the Little Prince would never truly be hers, even if she raised him his whole life. She loved him just as if he were her own son, but he was not, and eventually, he would have to know the truth. She hoped that the knowledge of it would not crush him. She hoped that he would still grow into the noble, strong-hearted man that she sensed even now within him, buried in those sombre, blue eyes.

They were Darrick's eyes of course. Even the Princess, his mother, had seen that. But the rest of his features, from his high forehead to his bow lips, were all Gabriella. He began to amble back towards the dooryard, taking great, careful steps through the grass. Crickets leapt into the air before him, and he smiled at them in wonder.

A figure moved into the open back door.

"He grows faster than those weeds," the man said, running a sleeve across his brow.

"The Little Prince gets fed well," Sigrid replied archly, peering into her bowl. "Venison and rabbit three times a week will do that to a child."

The man smiled and rolled his eyes. "Only you, Sigrid, could turn my skill with a bow into a backhanded compliment."

Sigrid sighed and tossed a handful of green bean stems into the bushes. "All those years you spent as a castle guard, Treynor, when your true calling was as a woodland huntsman."

Treynor stepped out onto the stoop, sat down on its ledge, and stripped off his gloves. "You still call him the Little Prince sometimes," he commented quietly, "do you know that?"

Sigrid did know it. It slipped out regularly even though the boy did have a name now. She was reluctant to forget his true heritage, despite the dangers.

Treynor went on. "His name is noble, even if no one will ever realise his royal blood. Darrick's family was a solid one, even if their vocation was a common one."

"None are truly common," Sigrid smiled faintly. "Not even blacksmiths."

Treynor nodded. "How right you are, my dear." He lifted his chin and called out, "James! Come here, boy. I've a rabbit for us to skin. Would you like to help?"

The boy smiled broadly, tried to run, then dropped to his hands and knees on the grass. He jumped up again, unperturbed, and aimed towards the door.

"Nothing will ever stop that boy," Treynor grinned affectionately. "Not if he does not wish it to."

Sigrid nodded thoughtfully. Together, they watched the young Prince approach. As he got close, Treynor arose to his feet, stepped forwards, and scooped the boy into his arms. James giggled happily and clung to the man's broad neck. They turned towards the cottage.

"Treynor," Sigrid said suddenly, and the tone of her voice made him stop. He glanced aside at her, saw the curious frown on her face as she stared out over the yard.

"What is it?" he asked, suddenly wary.

She replied evenly, "Something is out there."

Treynor turned around again, still holding the boy in his arms. The yard swelled towards a low hill fringed with trees and thick brush. Treynor studied the view.

"I see nothing—" he began, but then stopped. There was movement in the trees, a rustle of grass and leaves. A shadow approached, took on the shape of a figure, and then stepped out into the sunlight.

No one spoke.

Slowly, Sigrid stood. Her eyes were tense with disbelief. Across from her, the figure, a young woman, began to walk forwards again.

The sun caught in her hair. Her eyes sparkled as her steps quickened. A slow, helpless smile began to dawn on her dirty face. She started to run.

"Princess…," Sigrid whispered, dropping the bowl of green beans.

Gabriella ran forwards, and the others dashed into the yard to greet her. She threw off her armour as she came, leaving a trail of it in the high grass. Tears coursed down her cheeks as she laughed with delight and disbelief. She favoured her left side as she ran. Her right hand was streaked with scars. In it, held tightly, was a length of tapered wood: Goodrik's gift wand, its power finally spent.

The four met. They embraced. There were tears, laughter, shouts of joy, but very few words.

And in the centre of it all, the Little Prince reached for his mother. He threw his arms about her neck and went to her happily, as if he had always known this day would come and was not surprised at all that it finally had.

In his little fist, surrounded by rejoicing and the babble of voices, his cheeks smothered with his mother's tearful kisses, he clutched the twin shapes that hung about her neck—two sigils, one in the shape of a dragon, the other a falcon. One represented his lost father, the other, his found mother.

They were still warm.

Yazim smiled slowly as he read the gravestone's inscription.

Thomas spoke first, his voice thin in the evening air.

"Does... does the family indicated on this stone still live here in the village?"

The vicar smiled and shook his head. "No, I daresay that they have long since moved on. The days of their hiding are thankfully over. Their line is scattered to the wind, as are so many others."

"But you understand the significance of this...!" Thomas insisted, glancing back at the vicar. "This tiny village and this...!"

The vicar nodded and shrugged. "Well," he answered, his eyes twinkling enigmatically, "she had to be buried somewhere, did she not?"

The three stood there for another minute. Finally, Yazim turned to his friend, still smiling crookedly.

"Come, Thomas. We have a task to attend to."

Thomas shook his head, frowning, and then laughed lightly.

Without another word, the three men turned back towards the parsonage. They approached it, stepped into the shadow of its open doorway, and then, with a clunk, the door shut behind them.

Beyond the parsonage, the waterfall roared and glimmered. The sun dipped over the horizon, now lighting only the highest ledge of the mountain cliffs.

In the cemetery, shadows deepened peacefully, full of radiant summer warmth and the chirr of evening crickets. In the cemetery's centre, one gravestone seemed to stare up at the darkening sky. Its etchings were still clear in the twilight. The top was engraved with the image of a noble falcon, its beak raised, its wings partly unfurled. Beneath this, in large, simple letters, were the lines of a short inscription:

Here Lieth

GABRIELLA GWYNEVERE XAVIER

Mother of

JAMES

and the

LAST QUEEN OF CAMELOT

Sitting at the base of the gravestone, forming a tiny splash of summer colour in the descending dark, was a discreet pile of berries.

And one acorn.

The end.

ABOUT THE AUTHOR

George Norman Lippert made a name for himself by writing fan fiction. His first book, "James Potter and the Hall of Elders' Crossing", was written in a bout of Post-Potter Depression after the release of the final Harry Potter book. Released online, JPHEC garnered a surprisingly large worldwide readership and attracted the attention of both Warner Bros. and J. K. Rowling (this when both parties were asked by the media if they were secretly responsible for it.) The following sequels, "Gatekeepers Curse" and "Vault of Destinies", were well-received and well-reviewed enough, earning well over a million total readers worldwide, that the author decided to try his hand at writing something entirely original.

"The Riverhouse," a historical ghost story, reached number two on the amazon best-sellers list. "Ruins of Camelot" is the hopeful beginning of a new fantasy series, which will soon continue with the adventures of Gabriella's progeny as they face the scattered remnants of the vampyre army that haunt their world. For now, however, Lippert has promised a new James Potter sequel, tentatively titled "James Potter and the Morrigan Web".

If you liked the story, the author encourages you to spread the word. The more copies of his published works sold, the sooner he can fund the release of a new, free James Potter story.

George Norman Lippert currently lives in St. Louis, Missouri with his wife and two children.

THANKS

To all my friends and readers on Goodreads.com, the James Potter Facebook page, and the ever-longsuffering faithful at the Grotto Keep Forum.

Extra special thanks to: my beta readers (you know who you are); Jane Kalmes and Julianna So, both of whom performed invaluable editorial services for this story; Dawn Bradley, who tirelessly created the eBook versions of virtually everything I have written; Tom Grey and all the others who have slaved over translations of my works—yours is truly a labor of thankless devotion; my toughest critic (who also happens to be my wife) Jael.

And finally, to you, the reader who takes a chance on an unproven author and sticks it out to the bitter end. You deserve a cookie. Or, at least, another story.

More to come.

30516647R00175

Made in the USA
San Bernardino, CA
15 February 2016